THE LADY'S TUTOR

THE LADY'S TUTOR

Robin Schone

Zebra Books
Kensington Publishing Corp.

http://www.zebrabooks.com

ZEBRA BOOKS are published by

Kensington Publishing Corp.
850 Third Avenue
New York, NY 10022

ISBN 0-7394-0428-8
Zebra, the Z logo and Splendor Reg. U.S. Pat. & TM Off.

Printed in the United States of America

To my mother,
Glenna Johnson,
who taught me to never give up . . .

To my husband,
Don,
who never gave up on me . . .

To an incredible photographer,
Carol Robinson,
who had the foresight to give me a copy of
The Perfumed Garden
one Christmas . . .

To the reference librarians
at the Roselle Library,
who tirelessly aid me in my research . . .

THIS BOOK IS FOR YOU!
Thank you for making it possible.

And thank you,
KATE DUFFY,
for letting me write what I love best.

Chapter One

Ramiel would not be blackmailed by *any* woman—no matter how great was her need for sexual gratification.

He leaned against the library door and watched through narrowed eyes the woman who stood in front of the half-circle bay of floor-to-ceiling windows. Wispy tendrils of fog bridged her and the opened drapes, the first a monolith of black wool, the latter sentry columns of yellow silk.

Elizabeth Petre.

He did not recognize her, covered head to foot in a bonnet and shapeless black cloak with her back toward him. But then, he would not recognize her were she naked and facing him with her arms and legs spread wide in lewd invitation.

He was the Bastard Sheikh, the illegitimate son of an English countess and an Arab sheikh. She was the wife of the Chancellor of the Exchequer; her father was the prime minister of England.

The likes of her did not socialize with the likes of him save behind closed doors and between silken sheets.

Ramiel thought of the black-haired woman whose bed he had vacated only an hour earlier. The Marchioness of Clairdon had waylaid him at the *ballum rancum,* a whore's ball, dancing naked as had the other whores. She had used him to fuel her need for sexual titillation, and for a few hours he had become the animal that she thought he was, thrusting and grinding and pounding into her body to find that moment of perfect release where there was no past, no future, no Arabia and no England— just blinding oblivion.

Perhaps he would take this woman, too, if she had not willfully forced her way into his home through intimidation and blackmail.

Muscles coiled in silent aggression, he stealthily pushed away from the cold press of mahogany and padded across the Persian carpet that covered the library floor. "What do you want, Mrs. Elizabeth Petre, that you invade my home and threaten my citizenship?"

His voice, a raspy purr of English refinement masking Arab savagery, ricocheted off the three sash windows and chased the curved brass curtain pole rimming the twelve-foot-high bay ceiling.

He could feel the woman's start of fear, could almost smell it over the damp pervasiveness of the fog.

Ramiel wanted her to be afraid.

He wanted her to realize how vulnerable she was, alone in the Bastard Sheikh's den with neither her husband nor her father to protect her.

He wanted her to know in the most basic and elemental way possible that his body was his to bestow and he *would not be blackmailed into having sex.*

Ramiel paused underneath the blazing chandelier and waited for her to turn and face the consequences of her actions.

Burning gas hissed and popped in the frozen silence.

"Come now, Mrs. Petre, you were not so reticent with my servant," he gently taunted, knowing what she wanted, daring her to utter the words, forbidden words, familiar words, *I want to diddle an Arab; I want to rut with a bastard.* "What could a woman like you possibly want from a man like me?"

Slowly, slowly, the woman turned, a dark swirl of wool framed between shimmering yellow columns of silk drapes.

The black veil covering her face did not hide her shock at the sight of him.

A derisive smile curled Ramiel's lips.

He knew what she was thinking. What every Englishwoman thought when she first saw him.

A man who is half Arab does not have hair the color of sun-kissed wheat.

A man who is half Arab does not dress in tailored clothing like an English gentleman.

A man who is half Arab—

"I want you to teach me how to give a man pleasure."

The woman's voice was muffled by the veil, but her words were unmistakable.

They were not the words he had expected.

For one timeless second Ramiel's heart stopped beating inside his chest. Erotic images flashed before his eyes . . . of a woman . . . naked . . . *taking him* . . . *every way* a woman can take a man . . . for *his* pleasure . . . as well as her own.

Searing heat shot through his groin. Against his will he could feel his flesh swelling, hardening, hearkening to the images that would never be, exiled as he was in this cold, passionless country where women used him for their own needs—or reviled him for his.

Raw rage flicked along his nerves.

At Elizabeth Petre, for invading his home for her own selfish satisfaction under the guise of learning how to please a man.

At himself, who at the age of thirty-eight still ached for what she offered, knowing it for the lie that it was: Englishwomen were not interested in learning what pleased a bastard sheikh.

Deliberately, relentlessly, Ramiel closed the distance between himself and the woman who hid behind a cloak of respectability.

To her credit, she did not back away from his fury.

To his credit, he contented himself with merely flinging back her veil.

Up close and without the sheer black material marring her

vision, she could clearly see his Arabian heritage. His skin was
dark, sun-baked to the hair that was sun-kissed.

Now she would realize that his English-gentleman facade
was just that—a facade. He had learned to be a man in a country
where the worth of a female is half that of a male—a woman
could be sold, raped, or killed for daring far less than what this
woman dared now.

Elizabeth Petre *should* be afraid.

"Now, tell me again what you want," he murmured silkily.

She did not flinch at the smell of brandy and perfume and
sweat and sex that he reeked of.

"I want you to teach me how to give a man pleasure," she
repeated calmly, tilting her head back that she might meet his
gaze.

She did not stand more than five feet three inches tall—she
had a long way to look up.

Mrs. Elizabeth Petre had very white skin, the prized white
that on an Arabian auction block represented a woman's bondage. She was not young. Ramiel judged her to be in her early
thirties. Faint lines radiated outward from the corners of pale
hazel eyes. The face lifted up to his was more round than oval,
the nose more pug than aquiline, and her lips were too thin.
Her pupils were dilated, but otherwise her face was devoid of
the fear that she surely must be feeling.

Ela'na. Damn. Why didn't she show it?

A muscle ticked in his jaw. "And what makes you think I
am capable of teaching you such a feat, Mrs. Elizabeth Petre?"

"Because you are the—" She briefly faltered over his nick-
name, the Bastard Sheikh, bold enough to blackmail him for
sex but not bold enough to call him a bastard to his face.

"Because you are the only man who—" Nor could she
finish that sentence, that he was the only man in England reputed
to have been given a harem on his thirteenth birthday.

She notched her chin up higher. "Because I overheard a . . .
a woman say that if husbands had only half of your skill, there
would not be an unfaithful wife in all of England."

Ramiel's savagery erupted into biting sarcasm. "Then send

me your husband, madam, and I will instruct him on how to keep *you* faithful.''

Elizabeth Petre's lips tightened in a spasm of emotion— fear, anger, it was impossible to tell by looking at her; the woman had a face like a sphinx. ''I see that you will leave me no pride. Very well. I love my husband. It is not he who needs instruction on how to prevent me from straying, but, rather, the opposite. I do not desire to bed *you,* sir. I only want you to teach me how to give my husband pleasure so that *he* will bed *me.*''

All the heat in Ramiel's body dissipated.

''You do not care to be dirtied by the hands of an Arab, Mrs. Petre?'' he asked softly, dangerously.

''I do not care to be unfaithful to my husband,'' she replied evenly.

Ramiel's nostrils flared with reluctant admiration. Elizabeth Petre did not lack courage.

There *were* rumors that the Chancellor of the Exchequer had a mistress.

Edward Petre was a commoner. Were he of the peer, society would not be interested in his extramarital affairs, but his voters were the middle class and the middle class expected their political representatives to be as sternly moral as was their queen.

No doubt Elizabeth Petre was more concerned over the potential loss of her husband's career than she was of losing his services in the bedroom.

''Women who love their husbands do not ask strangers to teach them how to please a man,'' he said caustically.

''No, *cowards* who love their husbands do not ask strangers to teach them how to please a man. *Cowards* sleep alone, night after night. *Cowards* accept the fact that their husbands take their pleasure with another woman. *Cowards* do nothing, not women.''

Cowards echoed in the sudden silence.

Short, quick spurts of gray mist warmed Ramiel's face— her breath. Long, even spurts of gray mist mingled with hers in the winter-chilled air—his breath.

Elizabeth Petre blinked rapidly.

For one timeless moment Ramiel thought she batted her lashes in a gauche parody of flirtation; then he saw the sheen of tears filming her eyes.

"I refuse to be a coward." She squared her shoulders. The motion elicited a creak of whalebones—a corset too tightly laced. "Therefore once again I ask you to teach me how to give a man pleasure."

Blood thrummed through Ramiel's temples.

In many ways Arab and English women did not differ.

An Arab woman wore a veil. An English woman wore a corset.

An Arab wife accepted her husband's concubines with resignation. An English wife accepted her husband's mistresses by ignoring them.

A woman in either culture did not baldly arrange sexual instruction from another man that she might secure her husband's interest.

An acrid aroma stung Ramiel's nostrils—it came from her cloak. She had freshly cleaned the wool.

Women came to him drenched in their musk—no woman had ever come to him smelling of benzene.

Ramiel wondered what color her hair was . . . and what she would do if he reached out and plucked off her head the ugly black bonnet that hid it from his view.

He abruptly stepped back. "And just how do you propose that I teach you to please your husband if I do not bed you myself, Mrs. Petre?" he bit out.

Her eyes remained steady, oblivious of the sexual curiosity that hummed through Ramiel's body. "The women who live in harems—do they learn how to please one man by going to bed with another?"

For a second, Ramiel was back in Arabia, twelve years old again. A blond-haired concubine, the bored favorite of a vizier, had been curious to try the sheikh's uncircumcised infidel son. Ramiel, trapped between sleep and opium-scented breasts, had thought she was a *houri,* a Muslim angel sent to give him a taste of paradise.

The concubine had been stoned the following day.

"An Arab woman would be put to death if she did so," Ramiel said flatly.

"But you have been with these women—"

"I have been with many women—"

She ignored his curtness. "Therefore if it is possible for an Arab woman to learn how to please a man without benefit of personal experience, I see no reason why you, a man who has benefited from that training, cannot in turn instruct an Englishwoman."

Many Englishwomen had asked Ramiel to demonstrate the sexual techniques Arab men use to pleasure a woman; no woman had ever asked him to teach her the sexual techniques that Arab women use to pleasure a man.

It was the remnants of hard liquor and a night of even harder sex that prompted Ramiel's next question. Or perhaps it was Elizabeth Petre herself. And the stabbing realization that no woman, either Eastern or Western, would risk for him what this woman now risked for her husband. She imperiled her reputation and her marriage to learn how to please a man sexually so that he would turn to her instead of to a mistress.

What would it take for a woman like her, a respectable woman, to want a man like him, a man born in England who had adopted Arabia and now belonged to neither?

What would it be like to have a woman willing to do anything to gain his *love?*

"If I should undertake your tutoring, Mrs. Petre, what would you expect to learn?"

"Everything that you have to teach me."

Everything vibrated in the chill morning air.

Ramiel's gaze slammed into hers. "Yet you said that you have no desire to bed me," he said harshly.

Her face remained composed, the face of a woman who is not interested in a man's passion—or her own. "I am assured that you possess enough knowledge for the both of us."

"No doubt. But my knowledge is of women." Suddenly, he was repelled by her innocence. "I am not in the habit of seducing men."

"But women . . . they flirt with you, do they not?" she stubbornly persisted.

The duchess's naked body had gleamed with perspiration as she danced her need. She possessed no subtleties . . . either out of bed or in it.

"Debutantes flirt. The women I bed are not virgins." He insolently perused Elizabeth Petre's voluminous black cloak that revealed neither a thrust of breasts nor a curve of hips to entice a man. "They are experienced women who know what they want."

"And what is that, pray tell?"

"Pleasure, Mrs. Petre." He was deliberately crude and rude. "They want a woman's pleasure."

"And you think, because I am older than these women, and my body is not perfect like theirs . . . do you think that I do not also want a woman's pleasure, Lord Safyre?"

Ramiel's gaze snapped back to hers.

An electrical current of pure, unadulterated need shot through his body.

It came from Elizabeth Petre.

Sensual longings, sexual desires . . .

And still her face was that blank, expressionless mask.

A virtuous woman did not seek out a man to teach her how to please her husband.

A virtuous woman did not admit to wanting physical gratification in her marriage.

Who was Elizabeth Petre that she dared what other women did not?

"A man is more than a series of pulleys and levers that need only be cranked in order for him to receive gratification," Ramiel exhorted sharply, keenly aware of the cool perfection of her pale skin and the hot blood that pulsed in his groin. "His satisfaction is dependent upon a woman's ability to receive pleasure. If you want the latter, he will receive the first."

She stiffened her spine with another telltale creak of her corset. Anger flickered in her eyes—or perhaps it was a flare of light from the overhead chandelier.

"I have two children, sir. I am fully aware that a man does not consist of pulleys and levers. Furthermore, if my husband's satisfaction depended upon a woman's desire, then he would not have left my bed. For the last time, Lord Safyre, will you or will you not teach me how to give a man pleasure?"

Ramiel's body tightened.

Elizabeth Petre offered him a man's ultimate fantasy. A woman whom he could teach every sex act he had ever wanted a woman to do . . . with him . . . *to* him.

"I will pay you," she offered stiffly.

Hc studied her through the shield of his lashes, trying to see behind the emotionless mask that was her face. "How will you pay me, Mrs. Petre?"

There was no mistaking his coarse suggestiveness.

"With English currency."

Nor was there any mistaking her deliberate obtuseness.

He cast a telling glance about the library, at the ceiling-to-floor shelves filled with leather-bound books, at the priceless silk-screen panels that dotted the remaining three walls, at the credenza inlaid with mother-of-pearl, at the carved mahogany fireplace that was a masterpiece of English craftsmanship.

"That is one of the benefits of having a sheikh for a father. I have no need of your money," he replied with feigned disinterest, all the while wondering just how far she would go in her quest for sexual knowledge—and how far he would go in his quest for oblivion. "Or that of anybody else, for that matter."

Her gaze did not waver from his.

She would blackmail . . . but she would not beg.

"Do you know what you are asking, Mrs. Petre?" he asked softly.

"Yes."

Ignorance shone in her clear hazel eyes.

Elizabeth Petre thought that a woman like herself, a woman who is older and whose body is not "perfect," a woman who is respectably married with two children, could hold no appeal to a man like himself. She did not understand the driving power a man's curiosity could become or the powerful attraction a woman's desire could ignite.

Ramiel knew these things only too well. Just as he realized that mutual need could bind a man and a woman together more surely than vows spoken in a church or a mosque.

A dull sulfuric glow penetrated the bay windows. Somewhere above the yellow fog that heralded another London morning shone sunlight and the beginning of a new day.

Pivoting sharply, he crossed the Oriental carpet and reached to pluck from the ceiling-high wall of books a small leather-bound volume.

The Perfumed Garden of the Sheikh Nefzaoui.

In Arabic it was titled *Al Raud al atir wa nuzhat al Khatir—The Scented Garden for the Soul's Delectation.* More popularly it was translated as *The Perfumed Garden for the Soul's Recreation.*

Ramiel had memorized it as assiduously as boys in England memorize Greek and Latin primers. But whereas the primers prepared English boys to read Greek and Latin scholars, *The Perfumed Garden* had prepared Ramiel to satisfy a woman.

It also gave excellent advice for a woman who wished to learn how to satisfy a man.

Without giving himself time to reconsider his action, he returned to the bay window and offered her the book. "Tomorrow morning, Mrs. Petre. Here. In my library." Muhamed had said she had arrived at— "Five sharp."

A small, slender hand gloved in black kid sprang out of the heavy concealing folds of her wool cloak. The book, some five by eight inches in measurement, was grasped snugly between thumb and fingers. "I do not understand."

"You want me to tutor you, madam; therefore, I shall tutor you. Lessons begin tomorrow morning. There is your textbook. Read the introduction and the first chapter."

She lowered her head; the upturned veil blocked the overhead light so that her expression was hidden in shadow. *"The Per-*

fumed Garden of the . . ." She did not attempt to pronounce the rest of the title, *Sheikh Nefzaoui.* "I take it this is not a book on how to cultivate flowers."

His lips twitched with sudden amusement. "No, Mrs. Petre, it is not."

"Surely there is no need to start lessons so soon. I will need time to assimilate what I read—"

Ramiel did not want to give her time to assimilate.

He wanted to shock her.

He wanted to titillate her.

He wanted to peel away the drab black wool and her cold English reserve and find the woman underneath.

"You asked me to tutor you, Mrs. Petre. If I am to do so, you will follow my instructions. Excluding the preface and introduction, there are twenty-one chapters in *The Perfumed Garden;* tomorrow we will review the introduction and the first chapter. The morning after we will discuss the second, et cetera, until we finish your schooling. If you prefer more time to ponder your lessons, you will have to find another tutor."

The distant slam of an attic door echoed through the walls; as if on cue, the dull clang of metal followed, an iron skillet sharply contacting an iron stove as below stairs the cook started breakfast for the rising servants.

The book and her gloved hand disappeared inside the black wool of her cloak. Her corset audibly protested the abrupt motion. "Five o'clock is too late; we will have to start at four-thirty."

He cared little what time they conducted the lessons; his only interest was how much a woman like her would learn from a man like him. "As you will."

Her neck was slender, as had been her hand. The shoes peeking out from underneath the concealing cloak were narrow.

What did she seek to restrain so tightly within the confines of the creaking whalebone—flesh . . . or desire?

"Every school has rules, Mrs. Petre. Rule number one is this: You will not wear a corset while you are in my house."

Her fine white skin turned ruby red.

He wondered if she turned that same fiery color when she was sexually excited.

He wondered if her husband had ever sexually excited her.

Her head jerked back. "What I wear or do not wear, Lord Safyre, is none of your concern—"

"On the contrary, Mrs. Petre. You sought me out to teach you what pleases a man. Therefore what you wear *is* my concern if it is detrimental in accomplishing that goal. I assure you, a creaking corset does not please a man."

"Perhaps not a man of *your* nature—"

Ramiel's mouth involuntarily tightened.

Infidel. Bastard. There was nothing he had not been called, either in Arabic or English.

He was strangely disappointed that she should be afflicted with the same prejudices as were other people.

"You will find, Mrs. Petre, that when it comes to sexual pleasure, *all* men are of a certain nature."

She tilted her chin in a gesture that was becoming increasingly familiar. "I will not tolerate any physical contact with you."

Ramiel smiled cynically. There were things that affected a person far more deeply than mere touch.

Words.

Death.

Dabid . . .

"So be it." He briefly inclined his head and shoulders in a half-bow. "I give you my word as a man of the East and the West that I will not touch your body."

Impossibly, her spine stiffened even more; it was accompanied by the creak of her corset. "I am sure you understand that our lessons must be kept in the strictest of confidence. . . ."

Ramiel was struck by the irony of English etiquette. *She* blackmailed him yet expected *him* to be a gentleman and remain discreet about her indiscretion.

"The Arab people have a word for a man who speaks of what goes on in privacy between himself and a woman. It is called *siba,* and it is forbidden. I assure you that under no circumstances will *I* compromise *you.*"

Her mouth tightened into what the English so aptly termed a stiff upper lip. Clearly, she did not trust the concept of Arab honor. "Good day, Lord Safyre.

He bowed his head. *"Ma'a e-salemma,* Mrs. Petre. I am sure you know your way out."

Elizabeth Petre's retreat was marked by a harsh swish of wool and a sharp click of the library door opening then closing. Ramiel stared at the swirling yellow fog outside the bay windows and wondered how she had traveled to his house. Hack? Her own carriage?

Hack, he would guess. She fully realized the danger should their liaison be discovered.

"El Ibn."

Ramiel's stomach clenched.

The son.

He was the Bastard Sheikh. He was Lord Safyre. And he was *El Ibn.* The son . . . who had failed. Never again would he bear the title of Ramiel *ibn* Sheikh Safyre—Ramiel, son of Sheikh Safyre.

He turned, body tensed as it had not been the past thirty minutes.

Muhamed wore a turban, a man's baggy trousers and *thobs,* a loose, ankle-length shirt. He had been with Ramiel for twenty-six years. A gift from Ramiel's father, a eunuch to protect the bastard son of a sheikh who at the age of twelve had failed to protect himself. And had done no better at the age of twenty-nine.

He reached inside his dress coat and retrieved the card tucked away there. An address was printed in the lower right-hand corner in ornate script.

"Follow Elizabeth Petre, Muhamed, to make sure that she doesn't get into any more trouble than she already has."

Ramiel's expression hardened.

A man like the Chancellor of the Exchequer married moral women to bear his children—he would not relish his wife performing those sexual acts he sought from his mistress. Ramiel had been exiled from his father's country; he had no desire to be exiled from the country of his mother. If trouble accrued from this tutelage, he would have to be prepared.

"When she is safely inside, surveil the house. Follow her husband. I want to know who his mistress is, where he meets her, when he meets her, and how long their association has been going on."

Chapter Two

The heavy morning air pressed around the sour-smelling hack as if it were a living entity, heart beating in time to Elizabeth's heart, breathing when she breathed. Her reticule, heavy with the book she had stuffed into it outside the Bastard Sheikh's door, pressed into the jointure of her thighs. Outside the grimy window of the hack, dim shapes shifted in the lifting fog. Vendors shouted their wares and servants haggled over their prices as if she had not spent the longest thirty minutes of her life convincing the most notorious womanizer in England to teach her how to give a man sexual pleasure.

The Bastard Sheikh's voice mocked her still, a rasping purr of English civility. *Do you know what you are asking, Mrs. Petre?*

Yes.

Liar, liar, liar, liar, the carriage wheels grated. A woman like her could not possibly know the price a man like him would exact for carnal knowledge.

Anger poured over Elizabeth in scalding waves.

How dare he tell her that a man's satisfaction lay in a wom-

an's ability to receive pleasure, as if it were her fault that her
husband kept a mistress!

The smell of his perfume—his *woman's* perfume—clung to
her nostrils.

It was as if he had wallowed in it.

No, it was as if he had wallowed in the woman who had
worn it.

He had smelled as if he had rubbed every inch of his flesh
against every inch of her flesh.

Elizabeth shut her eyes against the unbidden image of darkly
tanned skin pressing down, around, and inside a woman's pale
body.

Blue and green lights flashed behind her eyelids.

No, the lights were neither blue nor green. They were turquoise. The same color as were the Bastard Sheikh's eyes.

His hair was English and his skin was Arabic, but his eyes
belonged to neither the East nor the West.

They spoke of places Elizabeth had never been to, of pleasures she had only imagined.

They had judged her as a woman and found her wanting.

The rear wheel of the hack fell into a rut, startling open her
eyes. Bracing herself, she stared at the worn leather facing her.

Women like her, older women, imperfect women, they would
not be chosen by men like the Bastard Sheikh, but they deserved
pleasure, too, and she *was not* going to back down because he
made her feel every second of her age, every imperfection of
her body.

She had spent seventeen years being an obedient daughter,
bending her will to that of her parents. She had spent an addi-
tional sixteen years being a dutiful wife, suppressing her desires
that she not repel her husband.

The Bastard Sheikh had said there were twenty-one chapters
in the book he planned to school her with.

She could endure those mocking, knowing turquoise eyes
for three weeks.

She could endure *anything* to get the knowledge that she
needed.

The hack came to a tooth-jarring halt.

It took Elizabeth several seconds to realize it had reached her destination as opposed to being jammed in traffic again. It took her several more seconds to locate the door handle and wrench it open.

The street corners looked alien through the black veil, as if they had changed in some obscure but overt manner in the past two hours. A change that could not be accounted for by the mere passage of dark dawn into day.

"That'll be one shilling and twopence, ma'am."

She stared up at the cabbie.

He was a shell of a man, worn thin by lack of nutrition and fourteen-hour-long workdays. A halo of light surrounded his head—the morning sun peering through the overlying clouds of smoke and fog that surrounded London in November, December, and January but had this year extended into the month of February.

Elizabeth was healthy and wealthy with a prominent husband and two sons. *Why could she not be content with what she had?*

Digging into her reticule, she grabbed a florin and tossed it up to him. "Keep the change."

He caught it deftly and doffed his hat. "Thank'ee, ma'am. Will ye be needin' a hack agin?"

It was not too late, the old Elizabeth whispered. She could pay the driver now to deliver the book back to the Bastard Sheikh and she need have no more contact with him.

But she was not the same woman she had been last week. Nor would she ever be again.

Her husband had openly flaunted his mistress in public. While he took his satisfaction elsewhere, she had suppressed her physical needs in the belief that conjugal bliss lay in family, not flesh.

Her marriage had been based on lies.

"Not today, thank you. I will, however, need one tomorrow morning. Four o'clock."

A grin momentarily wiped away the lines of exhaustion

etched into the cabbie's face and revealed the youth that was his in years if not in experience. He clicked to the horse. "I'll be 'ere, ma'am."

Elizabeth stared after the hack. It was quickly swallowed up in the morning stream of horses and carriages and yellow ribbons of fog.

She had not expected to have to wait an hour for the Bastard Sheikh to return home from his nocturnal carousing. Now she would have to think of some excuse as to why she was returning home at a time when normally she would still be abed.

A sudden shiver of awareness prickled her skin.

Someone was watching her.

Stomach churning, she pivoted.

There was no one on the sidewalk.

"'Erring a ha'penny! Fresh 'erring! Git yer 'erring fer breakfast! 'Erring a ha'penny!"

Across the street on the opposite sidewalk a young boy pushed a wheelbarrow, shouting his wares. Leaning against a brick building nearby stood a dark figure—

A team of horses obliterated her view. Steam rose from their bodies. They pulled a wagon piled high with barrels. When it passed, Elizabeth saw that the fish vendor had paused. The back of a dark cloak curved over his wheelbarrow.

A woman, no doubt a servant, buying fresh herring for breakfast.

Fear mingled with relief. No one knew that she had met with the Bastard Sheikh.

This time.

After walking the three blocks to her town home, she was bathed in sickly sweat.

And still she could smell the perfume.

Stealthily unlocking the front door and pushing it open, Elizabeth surprised her butler in the act of struggling into his jacket.

Her heart skipped a beat.

When the Arab butler had denied her entrance, she had given him her card to intimidate him with her family's political clout.

The servant, surely, had passed the card on to his master.

Where it no doubt still remained. *With the corner turned down to indicate she had called in person.*

The Bastard Sheikh had said every school has rules. His first rule was that she could not wear a corset in his house.

She had used blackmail to gain audience with him. Why would he not use blackmail to humiliate her?

" 'Ere now, what d'ye think ye're doin'—"

Elizabeth jerked back her veil just as a pair of large, freckled hands reached to bodily evict her.

The butler froze, black jacket askew. "Mrs. Petre!"

"Good morning, Beadles." She had never seen her butler without gloves on. The image of his freckled hands lingered in her mind even as a hurried explanation spilled out of her mouth. "It's a beautiful day. I thought an early morning walk would sharpen my appetite. Has Mr. Petre had breakfast yet?"

Beadles hastily straightened his jacket, expression instantly changing from one of malevolence to deference. "Indeed not, madam." Suddenly realizing his gloveless state, he jerked his hands behind his back. "You should have rung for a footman. It's not safe for a woman to be out alone in the early hours of morning."

Elizabeth was vaguely amused at how quickly he assumed a gentleman's flawless accent when only seconds earlier he had spoken pure cockney.

"There was no need, Beadles. I did not walk far." Underneath the voluminous wool cloak she strangled her reticule while she calmly continued as if it were commonplace for the mistress of the house to go off on a walk before her servants arose from their beds. "Please ring for Emma. I need to change for—" What? Bed? "Breakfast."

Beadles was far too dignified to comment on his mistress's odd behavior. The top of his balding head gleamed in the weak beam of sunlight that had trailed her steps.

Elizabeth bit her lip to contain a hysterical laugh.

It was all so anticlimactic . . . so *normal.*

Who would ever suspect that Mrs. Elizabeth Ann Petre, daughter of the prime minister and wife to the Chancellor of the

Exchequer, had blackmailed her way into the Bastard Sheikh's house that she might convince him to tutor her on how to give a man pleasure?

Perhaps she would awaken to find that this was all a dream and that her husband was exactly as she had always thought him to be, a man who was more comfortable with politics than he was with women.

Perhaps she would awaken and find that the nasty, hurtful rumors that he had a mistress were false.

Suddenly, her plan to be tutored by the Bastard Sheikh—a plan that had previously seemed bold and daring—now seemed merely tawdry.

She had discussed her marriage with another man. A man who had said things that no gentleman ever said in front of a lady. Crude words like "bedding" a woman.

She had spoken of matters and used words that no lady uttered—ever .

Elizabeth forced herself to walk and not run up the stairs.

She needed to see her husband.

She needed him to reassure her that she was still a virtuous, respectable woman.

Her bedroom adjoined his. She would just peek in to see if he was awake. Then they would have the talk that but for her lack of courage they would have had years before.

Heart pounding, she gently eased open Edward's door.

His room was empty. The starched linen sheets and forest-green-velvet spread were neatly turned down.

Clearly he had not slept in his bed.

Moisture burned the backs of her eyelids.

Softly closing the door—afraid she would jar free the tears that seemed never far from the surface this last week—she turned around . . . and almost died of heart failure.

A plain, round-faced woman enigmatically smiled across Elizabeth's unmade bed. "You are up early this morning, Mrs. Petre. I brought you a pot of hot chocolate. Though the worst of winter is over, it is still quite cold outside."

Elizabeth took a deep breath to fight down the scream that

clamored for release . "Thank you, Emma. That was thoughtful of you."

"The dean rang up on the telephone. Young Master Phillip has been at it again."

A smile lit Elizabeth's eyes at mention of her younger son, now in his second term at Eton. Eleven years old, Phillip was bold and bright and she missed him dearly.

It did not matter that he had not inherited the scholarly abilities of his father and grandfather. He had the gift of laughter. And that, combined with his boyish love of mischief, had afforded Elizabeth ample opportunity these last few months to further her acquaintance with the dean.

Emma set the silver tray onto the nightstand and arranged its contents to her satisfaction. "The dean talked to Mr. Petre's secretary."

Elizabeth casually crossed the dark blue wool carpet—so very English in comparison to the bright Oriental carpet covering the Bastard Sheikh's library floor—to her desk. "I see. I suppose Mr. Petre had already left for an appointment."

The muted sound of pouring liquid was followed by the overwhelmingly sweet odor of chocolate. "I wouldn't know, madam."

So many lies, Elizabeth grimly thought as she slid the reticule with the forbidden book inside it underneath the rolltop lid of her desk.

Emma was fully aware that Mr. Petre had not slept in his bed. As, no doubt, were all the other servants.

How long had they shielded her from the fact that her husband preferred another woman's bed?

She peeled off her cloak and bonnet and tossed them onto the ladderback chair in front of her desk. The black gloves followed.

Silently, she accepted the delicate rose-patterned china cup and matching saucer that Emma offered her. Unable to face the abigail's knowing eyes, she shied away to stare out the window.

Pale yellow sunshine shone on a gnarled, lifeless rose garden.

Dried-out hay covered the barren ground to protect hidden roots, unattractive but effective.

The Bastard Sheikh's voice danced and shimmered inside her head.

You will find, Mrs. Petre, that when it comes to sexual pleasure, all men are of a certain nature.

How many times, when she had thought that her husband had merely risen early to attend parliamentary duties, had he in actuality not come home at all?

She leaned her forehead against the cold glass. Hot steam spiraled up from her cup and fogged the window.

Today was Monday. Elizabeth was scheduled to tour a hospital at ten and hostess a charity luncheon at twelve. She needed to plan her wardrobe and a short speech, but all she could think about was the empty room adjoining hers.

What if it weren't her lack of sexual knowledge that repelled Edward? What if it were . . . *she?* Her body, her personality, the utter lack of political charisma she had failed to inherit from either her mother or her father?

A sparrow darted up toward the sky. It carried in its beak a piece of hay to add to its nest.

Suddenly, Elizabeth knew what she needed.

She needed to surround herself with a child's uncomplicated love.

Or perhaps she needed to make sure that her clandestine meeting with the Bastard Sheikh had not somehow tarnished her relationship with her two sons.

Elizabeth turned her back onto the lifeless rose garden. "Tell Mr. Petre's secretary to send a note to The Good Women's Charity Organization. Tell him to write that I cannot attend the hospital tour or speak at the luncheon because of an unexpected emergency."

"Very good, madam."

Renewed life flowed through Elizabeth's veins. Being a desirable wife might be beyond her capabilities, but being a good mother was not.

She flashed Emma a rare smile. "Have Cook prepare a picnic

for two ravenous boys. Then order a carriage to drive me to the train station. I am going to spend the day with my sons.''

A soft, elusive scent teased her nostrils.

The perfume.

''But first I would like you to draw me a bath, please.''

''Would you care for refreshment, Mrs. Petre?''

The dean pointedly stared at his ornate gold pocket watch. His neatly trimmed whiskers, silver with age, twitched with annoyance.

He did not like conducting business with a mere woman, even if that woman was the mother of two of his students. Especially when she had barged in without an appointment.

Elizabeth smiled, refusing to be intimidated by the older man's obvious attempts to do just that. Having confronted the Bastard Sheikh, she did not think any man could ever discomfit her again.

''No, thank you, Dean Whitaker. What has my son done now?''

''Master Phillip attacked a student at breakfast this morning.'' The dean slipped his watch back into his pocket and pinned her with a glare from beneath bushy white brows. ''He had to be physically restrained.''

''And what did this other student do to provoke him?'' she asked sharply, her maternal instincts bristling.

''Master Phillip claims Master Bernard is a Whig, madam, and as such is an outrage to his social conscience.''

Elizabeth was torn between amusement and shock.

On the one hand, Phillip had never shown any interest in politics. On the other hand, he had never before engaged in fisticuffs.

That he would simultaneously develop the two tendencies rang a warning bell inside her head.

''And what does Master Bernard have to say?'' she asked mildly.

"He does not say, madam. Your son's shocking display of violence has reduced him to a quivering mass of nerves."

Elizabeth surveyed the dean's outrage for long seconds. Finally, "What form, pray tell, is Master Bernard in?"

"Master Bernard is in the . . . fifth form."

The dean was reluctant to relay the information.

With good reason.

Phillip was eleven and in the first form. Bernard, in the fifth form, had only one more form to complete before graduation.

Her son was indeed ferocious to reduce a student who was four to six years older than himself into a "quivering mass of nerves."

"Are you suspending Phillip, Dean Whitaker? Because if you are, I must inform you that I have been considering removing Phillip for quite some time. Harrow, I believe, offers a higher standard of education than does Eton. And, of course, if I remove Phillip, then I will also take Richard. I know he has only six more months before he takes his exams, but still . . ."

"There is no need to jump to conclusions, Mrs. Petre." The dean was loath to lose not only money but prestige—the two boys had a very influential grandfather and father, both of whom had attended Eton. "I am sure that with the appropriate monetary funds—after all, damages were minimal, and boys *will* be boys—"

Elizabeth stood up. "Please contact Mr. Kinder, my husband's secretary. He will make arrangements to pay you for damages. I would like to see my two sons now."

"Master Phillip is in detention and Master Richard is in class. Perhaps another time . . ."

"I think not, Dean Whitaker," she said briskly. "Harrow is looking more and more desirable."

"Very well, Mrs. Petre." He picked up a small brass bell and rang it. Immediately, his clerk, a middle-aged man with stooped shoulders who was as timid as the dean was aggressive, entered the room.

"Bring Petre major and Petre minor to the visitor's salon, Mr. Hayden. Mrs. Petre, if you will follow me."

Two pairs of shoes echoed hollowly along the wooden hall-way, the dean's soft and unassuming, hers sharp and intrusive.

Eton was a depressing place, Elizabeth thought, all gleaming wood without one single finger smear to account for the hundreds of boys who occupied its hallowed halls.

The dean threw open a door and stepped back for her to enter. "Pray, make yourself comfortable, Mrs. Petre. Master Phillip and Master Richard will be here directly."

The visitor's salon was not a room that invited comfort. It contained two leather wing chairs that confronted a rigid walnut sofa with a three-medallion back and eight legs. A small, mean coal fire burned in the dark granite fireplace beside the sofa.

Taking off her cloak, bonnet, and gloves, Elizabeth perched on the edge of the sofa and stared at the glowering coals.

She wished she could keep her two sons home with her, warm and safe from harm.

She wished it were enough being a mother.

She wished—

"Hullo, Mother."

Elizabeth swiveled around on the edge of the sofa.

Phillip stood in the doorway, auburn hair ruthlessly combed back from his face. He nervously shuffled from one foot to the other.

His left eye was swollen shut. His right one was bright with unshed tears.

She wanted to run to him and smother him with hugs and kisses.

She wanted to sweep him away from Eton and all of its dangers.

She wanted to give him the dignity he was so valiantly struggling to hold on to.

"Hello, Phillip."

"You talked to the dean."

Elizabeth did not bother responding to what was plainly obvious.

"Am I going to be expelled?"

"Do you want to be?"

"No."

"Do you want to tell me why you picked a fight with a boy in the fifth form? Those are pretty vicious odds."

Phillip balled his fists. "Bernard's a Whig—"

"Please do not insult my intelligence by repeating that nonsense. Besides, we do not call them Whigs anymore—they are Liberals."

His shoulders drooped. "I'm not a boy anymore, Mother."

"I know you are not, Phillip." She offered him a wry smile. "You have the black eye to prove it."

He stood a little taller at her words . . . and seemed to grow even younger than his eleven years. "Please don't ask me why I started the fight. I don't want to lie to you."

"Obviously, I must ask you, and because you have never lied to me before, I do not believe you will now."

Phillip stared down at his shoes; finally, he mumbled, "He said something."

"About you?"

"No."

"About Richard?"

He lifted his chin and stared over her head. "I don't want to tell you, Mother."

Elizabeth was suddenly filled with foreboding.

Children, regardless of their age, repeated the same gossip as did their parents. If she had overheard rumors concerning Edward's extramarital relationship, it was quite probable that her children had too.

"Did Master Bernard say something about your father, Phillip?"

He blinked, gaze still fixed over her head.

Obviously, the blink meant yes.

Why had she been such a complaisant wife? None of this need have happened, not to her husband, not to her, and not to her children.

"Phillip."

Her son gazed at her in mute appeal, well acquainted with that particular tone of voice.

Elizabeth's heart ached for him.

Save for the color of his hair, Phillip looked so like his father, the same dark brown eyes and patrician nose . . . yet there was nothing at all of Edward inside him.

Elizabeth could not imagine Edward with a black eye. Not even at Phillip's age.

She patted the sofa beside her. "I brought you something."

His dark brown eye regarded her warily. "What?"

"A box of Cadbury chocolates."

Bribery achieved what all the mother's love in the world could not have accomplished. Phillip darted toward the basket sitting by her feet.

"You shouldn't reward violent behavior, Mother."

The reproving voice belonged to neither a boy nor a man, but someone in between the two stages of life.

Elizabeth turned to her elder son with unfeigned pleasure. "And you should not allow your little brother to pick on boys that are twice his—"

Her mouth dropped open in shock. "Richard!"

He was pale and gaunt and nearly unrecognizable as the boy who had daily hounded her between terms for a new safety bicycle. Even his hair, midnight black like his father's, was dull and lifeless.

She stood up and reached for his forehead. "Richard, are you ill?"

He suffered her touch. "I'm fine now."

"Why didn't the dean contact me?"

"It was nothing, Mother, just the sniffles."

"Are you eating properly?"

"*Mother.*"

"Would you like to come home for a rest?"

He recoiled from her hand. "No."

"Would you like a box of toffees?" she asked tartly.

A reluctant smile tugged at his lips. "I wouldn't object to it, no."

"Then come join us and we'll feast. I had Cook prepare a picnic basket."

Phillip had already invaded the basket and discovered inside the hidden treasures. Solemnly, he handed the box of toffees to Richard.

It was as if the two boys were sealing a pact.

In between gulps of apple cider and bites of sliced roast beef, rich Stilton cheese, pickled vegetables, and crumpets smothered with strawberry jam, Richard bragged about his studies while Phillip bragged about his tricks to escape studying. All too soon their time together was over.

Elizabeth packed away the last of the plates and utensils into the basket—the remaining food she folded into two napkins. "Richard, eat. Phillip, no more fights. And now I do not care whose dignity I offend, I am claiming a hug from each of you."

Phillip, as if all along he had been waiting for permission, barreled into her and pressed his face into her midriff. "I love you, Mum."

Elizabeth was overcome by a fierce surge of protectiveness. 'Mum' had been Phillip's special name for her ever since he had overheard a maid call the queen "Queen Mum."

Richard towered over Elizabeth by five inches. He surprised her by wrapping his arms about her and burying his face into her neck the way he had when he was a toddler. Warm, moist breath tickled her skin. "Same for me, Mum."

Elizabeth breathed deeply of his skin; it smelled of soap and perspiration and his own unique scent. Manhood was stealing Richard from her, but he still smelled like her little boy.

She blinked back prickly hot tears. "Your father and I love you too."

Silence greeted her declaration. As if by unspoken agreement, Richard and Phillip stepped back out of her arms.

Elizabeth vowed then and there that she would do anything to unite her family.

The train ride back to London was agonizingly long and slow. The monotonous swaying should have lulled her to sleep; it didn't.

She thought of Edward and his empty bed. She thought of her sons and their silent withdrawal at mention of their father.

She thought of the Bastard Sheikh and the perfume he had been drenched in.

And no matter how she tried to envision it, she could not imagine Edward ever taking the pleasure in his mistress that the Bastard Sheikh had obviously taken in his.

The coachman was waiting for her at the station. Her husband was not waiting for her at home.

Politely but firmly refusing first the butler's and then her abigail's insistence that she take a light supper, Elizabeth prepared for bed. The moment Emma closed the door to her bedchamber, Elizabeth retrieved the book from her desk.

It smelled of leather and fresh ink, as if it had but recently been printed. Carefully, she flipped over to the title page and read the stark black print on rich white vellum paper.

THE PERFUMED GARDEN OF THE SHEIKH NEF-ZAOUI; *A manual of Arabian Erotology (XVI Century): Revised and Corrected Translation. Cosmopoli: MDCCCLXXXVI: for the Kama Shastra Society of London and Benares, and for Private circulation only.* (Pagination: xvi + 256).

Erotology.

Elizabeth had never encountered such a word.

The printing date was 1886—the book *was* fresh off the press.

Impatiently, she rifled past the table of contents, stopped when she flipped to the Introduction. Her gaze seemed to leap by its own accord to the opening paragraphs.

Praise be given to God, who has placed man's greatest pleasure in the natural parts of woman, and has destined the natural parts of man to afford the greatest enjoyment to woman.

He has not endowed the parts of woman with any pleasurable or satisfactory feeling until the same have

been penetrated by the instrument of the male; and like-
wise the sexual organs of man know neither rest nor
quietness until they have entered those of the female.

A sharp stab of longing shot up between her thighs. It was
followed by the memory of the Bastard Sheikh's mocking
turquoise eyes.

And she had no doubt whatsoever that he had agreed to tutor
her so that he might humiliate her.

A man like him would never forgive a woman for forcing
her way into his home by threat of blackmail.

A man like him would never understand that a woman whose
hair showed the first silvery strands of age and whose body
showed the effects of two children ached with the same needs
as did young, beautiful women unburdened by virtue.

Grimly, she sat down at the desk and retrieved pen and paper
from the top drawer.

He need never know the extent of her yearning for the woman's pleasure that he had taunted her with. All the Bastard
Sheikh ever need know was that she wanted sexual instruction
to keep her husband satisfied.

Chapter Three

The outdoor gas lamp shone like a beacon. A tinny whicker penetrated the morning fog—the horse hitched to the hack that waited for her across the street.

Fingers trembling, Elizabeth reached for the brass knocker. It was cold and wet and hard, unadorned reality dangling between the jaws of a lion.

Every nerve inside her body screamed for her to stop.

A respectable woman did not appear in public without wearing a corset.

A respectable woman did not read sixteenth-century erotology.

A respectable woman did not seek sexual instruction but *she did* and she knew that *nothing* was going to stop her now.

The muffled rap of brass impacting brass ripped through the fog. Immediately, the door swung open.

Elizabeth braced herself, but it was not the hostile Arab butler in his flowing white robe who greeted her. A demure-faced girl in traditional English-servant garb of white pinafore and cap curtsied, as if a woman visiting the Bastard Sheikh without a chaperone at four-thirty in the morning was an everyday occurrence.

And perhaps it was, Elizabeth thought grimly, stepping inside.

"Good morning, ma'am. Beastly outside, it is. M'lord, he said to take you to him directly. If I may have your cloak, please?"

Elizabeth clutched her reticule underneath the heavy black wool. Her breasts without support of a corset felt heavy and full, her nipples stiff and abraded. "That won't be necessary."

For a second the maid looked as if she were on the verge of protesting; curtsying again, she murmured, "Very good, ma'am. Follow me, please."

The mahogany walls of the hall were inlaid with mother-of-pearl. The bright overhead light created a latticework of wood and shell, shadow and light. Man-sized porcelain vases guarded the bottom of a circular staircase. A bright yellow and red Oriental carpet marched up the steps and disappeared into darkness.

No doubt the Bastard Sheikh had ordered the hall lights turned high so that she could see the folly of her desperate attempt to bribe him twenty-four hours earlier.

It worked.

What a fool she had been, to think that she could sway the Bastard Sheikh with money. Obviously, the wealth of his sexual expertise was surpassed only by his material possessions.

If—as she suspected—this morning meeting arose out of his desire to humiliate her, it would be her one and only lesson. Whatever knowledge she gained would come only through sheer determination and an absolute disregard of English sensibility.

The introduction and the first chapter in *The Perfumed Garden of the Sheikh Nefzaoui* had contained much that she did not understand. She was determined to learn at least that much.

The maid softly scratched on the library door before swinging it open.

The scene that awaited Elizabeth was not the one she had

anticipated. She had expected the library to be blazing with cold, sterile light as it had the morning before.

It was not.

The Bastard Shiekh sat in a tweed morning coat behind a massive mahogany desk, head bent over a book, golden hair gleaming in the gas lamplight. Yellow and orange flames danced in the beautifully crafted mahogany fireplace immediately to his left. Hot steam rose from a demitasse cup by his right elbow—coffee, the rich aroma filled the air. A silver tray with a matching silver pot perched on the edge of the desk.

His very Englishness sent off a fresh peal of alarm inside her head.

Sex was mysterious and exotic and foreign. If he dressed in Arab garb—as his servant yesterday had worn—she could sit across from him and study with equanimity the art of erotic love. Discussing it with a man who could easily preside over her dinner table took sexual gratification out of the philosophical realm and became the forbidden fruit that she had been denied for sixteen years.

The maid softly cleared her throat. "Excuse me, m'lord. I've brought the lady to you. Shall I get you anything else?"

Either the Bastard Sheikh did not hear the maid—or he ignored her.

Or perhaps he ignored Elizabeth, to demonstrate how unimportant she was to a man like him.

She suddenly felt like her English rose garden, old and out of season. As he no doubt planned that she should feel.

She drew her shoulders back . . . and wondered if her plants felt as naked and vulnerable without their leaves as she did without her corset.

Long, interminable heartbeats passed before he closed the book with a snap and raised his head. "Thank you, Lucy. Please take Mrs. Petre's cloak and bring another cup and saucer."

Elizabeth felt the blood drain out of her face. Dimly, she was aware of the maid dropping a curtsy, then the heavy cloak slipped off her shoulders and the library door clicked loudly in the silence.

The Bastard Sheikh—and yes, Elizabeth thought as shock gave way to fury, he *was* a bastard—stood up and waved a hand toward a burgundy leather chair drawn up in front of his desk. "Please take a seat, Mrs. Petre."

Elizabeth had never felt so angry—or so betrayed. She had expected him to try to humiliate her. *She had not expected him to lie.*

"*Siba,* Lord Safyre." She compressed her lips to stop their trembling. "You assured me that an Arab man does not compromise a woman."

He raised his eyebrows in mock surprise, a slash of golden brown several shades darker than the leonine gold of his hair. "And you think I have?"

"If I wished to be identified, I would not wear a veil. There was no need to address me by name. Servants talk."

"And English gentlemen do not, I take it?" The light mockery remained in his eyes, tinged with something darker. "If you did not wish English servants to know you, Mrs. Petre, you should not have left your card with one."

"Your butler is Arab," she said tightly.

"Is he? What am I, do you think? Arab or English?"

It took all of her self-control not to tell him *exactly* what he was.

"Your nipples are hard, Mrs. Petre. Does anger stimulate you?"

Elizabeth's breath caught in her throat.

Suddenly, he smiled, flashing even, white teeth.

It was an inviting smile, full of warmth and mischief.

She was irrepressibly reminded of Phillip, her younger son. He smiled just so when he did something totally outrageous and wished to avoid punishment.

"Please, Mrs. Petre, sit down. My servants are too well trained to repeat the names of my guests. In Arabia, disrespectful servants are whipped or sold."

"In England, it is illegal to whip one's servants," she retorted icily. "Nor do we condone slavery."

"But it is not illegal to buy a servant a one-way passage

onto an Eastern freight steamer. Ah, here is Lucy. Place the cup and saucer on the tray . . . there. Thank you. We will not need you again.''

Elizabeth fought her body to keep it from independently following the maid out of the library. Even if the Bastard Sheikh had not betrayed her, he had used the word *nipples.*

Common sense, however, told her she had sought him out to tutor her in the ways to please a man. If she could not survive a member of a woman's anatomy passing through his lips, how would she react when he discussed a *gentleman's* anatomy?

As if unaware of her inner struggles, he poured a surprisingly black brew into the extra demitasse cup, then added what looked to be a splash of water. He offered her the coffee, formally presenting it by holding the edge of the saucer. ''Come, Mrs. Petre. Sit down. Unless you've changed your mind, that is.''

He had neatly tossed the gauntlet into her lap. If this lesson failed, it would be her fault and her fault alone, that tauntingly correct gesture implied.

It was a challenge she could not refuse.

Elizabeth stiffened her spine; it thrust her breasts forward, increasing the friction to her nipples. Slowly, she crossed the wide expanse of Oriental carpet that separated them and perched on the edge of the burgundy leather chair.

Proper etiquette decreed that a woman remove her gloves if she intended to visit for more than fifteen minutes. Just as it decreed that she not hide her face behind a veil.

Coolly, methodically, she peeled off her gloves, then tucked the veil over her bonnet. Balancing the gloves and her reticule on her lap, she reached for the blue-veined porcelain saucer. ''Thank you.''

The coffee was thick and sweet and so strong it nearly crossed her eyes. It was also boiling hot.

Gasping, she hurriedly set the saucer and cup onto the desk. ''What *is* that?''

''Turkish coffee. It is best when freshly boiled. You should blow on it, then quickly drink it down. Did you read the designated chapters?''

She brought her hand up to her throat—it felt as if the inner skin had been scalded. "I did."

He leaned back in his chair, his face a study of light and shadow. "And what did you learn?"

The turquoise eyes were no longer mocking. They were the eyes of a painfully attractive man summing up a painfully plain woman.

The pain in Elizabeth's throat was immediately forgotten. Composing her features into the bland expression that society demanded a respectable woman wear in public lest she betray common, vulgar emotion, she rummaged inside her reticule and produced his book and a sheath of papers. The first she laid on the desk beside the demitasse cup and saucer; feeling as if she were a young girl back in the schoolroom, she consulted the latter.

"*The Perfumed Garden of the Sheikh Nefzaoui* is estimated to have been written in the beginning of the sixteenth century. The author is presumed to have been born in Nefzaoua, a town situated on the shore of the lake Sebkha Melrir in the south of Tunis, hence his name, Sheikh Nefzaoui, as many Arabs take their name from their birthplace. While *The Perfumed Garden of the Sheikh Nefzaoui* is not exactly a compilation of authors, it is likely that several parts may have been borrowed from certain Arabian and Indian writers—"

"Mrs. Petre."

Elizabeth ground her teeth.

The Bastard Sheikh pronounced her name as if she were indeed a schoolgirl—a rather stupid one at that.

She glanced up. The turquoise eyes were shadowed by thick dark lashes.

"Yes, Lord Safyre?"

"Mrs. Petre, I did not tell you to read the Notes of the Translator, did I?"

Her fingers clenched, crimping her notes. "No."

"Then let us dispense with the history of the book and the author and proceed to the section otherwise known as 'General Remarks About Coition.' "

He smiled, daring her to continue.

Elizabeth thought of her husband with another woman.

She thought of her two sons, estranged from their father.

She took a deep breath to still the pounding of her heart. "Very well," she said calmly, returning to her notes. "The sheikh claims that man's greatest pleasure lies in the natural parts of woman and that he knows neither rest nor quietness until he"—raising her head, her gaze locked with his—"enters her."

She refused to look away from those turquoise eyes. Just as she refused to acknowledge the tightening in her breasts.

Suddenly, Elizabeth wanted to humiliate him as he planned to humiliate her. *She* wanted to be the one who embarrassed and shocked *him.*

"So, Lord Safyre, it appears your remark yesterday morning that all men are of the same nature holds true. I am confused, however, about the sheikh's reference that a 'man is at work as with a pestle, while the woman seconds him by lascivious movements . . .' "

The hiss of the gas lamp on the table was loud over the roar of her heart. The burning logs in the fireplace snapped and sizzled.

Finally, softly, "In what way are you confused, Mrs. Petre?"

The time had come. There could be no more pretense of modesty.

Sex was not a modest subject.

Elizabeth wondered if he could hear the drumming of her heart.

"Before I became wed, my mother instructed me to lie still when my husband visited me. I do not understand how a woman can move without hindering the actions of the man."

The Bastard Sheikh sat as if turned to stone. Even the steam drifting up from his coffee seemed to freeze.

She had succeeded in shocking him.

She had succeeded in shocking herself.

It was one thing telling a stranger about her husband's infidelity. It was another thing entirely telling him about her marriage bed.

The heat in the library was suddenly unendurable. Blindly, she groped for her gloves and her reticule. "I'm sorry—"

A sharp creak of wood snapped her head upright.

The Bastard Sheikh leaned forward in his chair. His turquoise eyes blazed in the light of the lamp.

"In Arabic the word *dok* means to pound, to concuss. It is a combination of the thrusting motion that a man uses to bring himself to climax inside a woman and the grinding of his pelvis against hers to heighten her sensation, hence the 'pestle' simile. *Hez* is a swinging motion. A woman may thrust, or swing her hips upward, to meet the downward thrust of a man, or she may swing her hips side to side to complement his grinding motions. There will come a point when the motions of the man are too rapid or too powerful for the woman to move without dislodging him. At that time she may best please both him and herself if she wraps her legs around his waist and simply holds on while he brings them both to climax."

Electric sensation jolted Elizabeth's body.

The Bastard Sheikh's words suddenly became visual images, as if she watched mechanical slides in a magic lantern show. The pictures, however, flashed behind her eyes instead of onto the wall before her. They were not the innocent hand-painted slides she showed to her sons to amuse and educate them. They were erotic pictures, explicit pictures illuminated by a light far hotter than was the limelight inside a magic lantern.

There was the man, naked, images advancing in rapid succession so that he alternately thrust and rubbed his dusky brown body between pale, outstretched legs that hitched higher, higher over lean, muscular hips. For the first time in her life, the auburn-haired woman underneath him was completely open and vulnerable. There was no stopping the man, he pounded and ground himself into her softness and there was *nothing* she could do to hold back her pleasure—

Reality returned with the distant echo of a door slamming shut.

Elizabeth blinked.

The palms of her hands were wet. As were other, unthinkable parts of her body.

And they were not even halfway through the first lesson.

She squared her shoulders. "Excuse me, may I borrow pen and ink? I would like to make notations."

The breathtaking hypnotism of his eyes frosted over. "Do you plan on consulting your notes when your husband comes to your bed, Mrs. Petre?" he asked acidly.

"If need be, Lord Safyre," she returned imperturbably.

He pushed a brass inkwell across his desk in reply. Opening a drawer in his desk, he produced a pen.

A heavy gold pen.

It warmed between her fingers as if it were made of flesh instead of metal.

Determinedly dipping the nib into the inkwell, she poised the gold pen above her notes. "Would you repeat what you said, please?"

The forbidden images were blessedly absent in his colder, more terse explanation.

"Thank you, Lord Safyre." She finished writing with a small flourish and again consulted her notes. "The Introduction ends by giving the full title of the sheikh's work, *The Perfumed Garden for the Soul's Recreation.* Shall we go on to Chapter One?"

The Bastard Sheikh smiled, a male smile, planning his revenge. "By all means."

"The sheikh claims that men are excited by the use of perfumes—"

"You are ahead of yourself, Mrs. Petre. Not only have you skipped the beginning of the chapter, you have omitted two subchapters, 'Qualities Which Women Are Looking for in Men' and 'Various Lengths of the Virile Member.' "

Virile member echoed inside her ears.

Elizabeth gripped the thick pen to calm her quickening breathing. This was the moment she had dreaded, but now that it was there, she felt strangely exhilarated.

"I found little that was noteworthy, Lord Safyre," she lied.

"A pity, Mrs. Petre. You will remember that the Introduction ended with the sheikh's friend and adviser urging him to add to his work a supplement to include such things as how to remove spells and methods to increase the size of the virile member. Chapter One is named 'Concerning Praiseworthy Men.' The sheikh places great emphasis on a man's genitals. If your husband suffers from sexual despondency, you must be able to judge whether it arises from the size of his member, in which case you must know the correct length to, ah, stretch it."

The turquoise eyes glinted. He was enjoying his efforts to embarrass her.

"According to the sheikh, a 'meritorious' man must have a member which is 'at most a length of the breadth of twelve fingers, or three handbreadths, and at least six fingers, or a hand and a half breadth.' "

Elizabeth struggled to keep the heat that traveled through her chest from spreading to her face. "Is that three handbreadths of a woman's hand or that of the sheikh's hand?"

He laid his hands one above the other on top of the desk, the first a rich dark wood, the latter dusky warm skin. "You be the judge, Mrs. Petre."

She had never seen her husband; she had only the size of her two sons when they were small children to compare a man to.

Curiosity outweighed prudence.

Clutching pen and paper in one hand and gloves and reticule in the other, she leaned forward.

His hands were big and tan and measured far wider than did the breadth of her own two hands.

"Two handbreadths . . ." The Bastard Sheikh's hand closest to her moved five inches forward. "Three handbreadths."

Elizabeth's eyes widened.

Impossible. No woman could accommodate fifteen inches.

"Well, Mrs. Petre?"

She sat back. "Either Arab men have extremely large members or they have very small hands, Lord Safyre. Until we reach the chapter containing recipes for increasing a man's 'meritoriousness,' I suggest we go on to the benefits of perfume.''

Reaching forward, she dipped the pen into the inkwell and prepared to write. "What perfumes are used in a harem?"

Rich, masculine laughter filled the library.

Elizabeth had never before seen or heard an adult give way to uninhibited laughter. Ladies tittered, gentlemen guffawed. Real laughter, she discovered, was infectious.

The Bastard Sheikh possessed a perfect set of molars.

She bit her lips to keep from succumbing to a sense of the ridiculous. For one unguarded moment her eyes locked with his, sharing with him the absurdity of their circumstances.

"Touché, taalibba." His turquoise eyes continued to sparkle even after the laughter died. "I bow to your superior wit . . . this morning. Amber, musk, rose, orange flowers, jasmine—all those scents are popular among Arab women. What perfumes do you use?''

His voice was husky, intimate. It was not the voice of a man intent upon humiliating a woman.

Elizabeth's head jerked back. "I regret to say that I am allergic to perfume. What is it that you called me . . . *taalibba?*''

The light in his eyes dulled, turning the color of polished turquoise to raw, uncut stone. *"Taalibba* is the Arabic word for student, Mrs. Petre.''

Absurdly, Elizabeth was filled with disappointment. Edward had never called her by an endearment, not once in their three-month-long courtship and sixteen years of marriage.

She made a pretense of jotting the Arabic word down on her notes. "Is it necessary that a woman wear scent in order to . . . attract a man?''

"What if I said that it was?''

A large blob of black ink spread across the paper. "Then I will consult with the chemist to see if there is something that will stay my allergies for the duration of time it takes to please my husband.''

"There is no need to sacrifice your health." The warmth as well as the laughter was gone from his voice. "A great sheikh, when giving his favorite daughter up in marriage, counseled her that water makes the best of perfumes. Are you allergic to flowers?"

"No."

"Then crush flower petals against your skin—underneath your breasts and in the triangle of hair between your thighs. The combined scent of the flower and the wet heat of your body will be far more effective that anything you buy in a bottle."

Perspiration beaded underneath Elizabeth's breasts. She busily scribbled *crush flowers underneath* ... The steel nib scratching across the surface of the paper momentarily drowned out the popping of burning wood and the hiss of flaming gas.

He had inferred that a man enjoyed the scent of a woman's body.

She discreetly sniffed.

All she could smell was the benzene of her clean wool gown, the thick aroma of coffee, and the smoke of burning wood.

"Do you know what a climax is, Mrs. Petre?"

Her determined scribbling stopped abruptly. Embarrassment turned to shame, which in turn flared to bright red anger.

She would not let him humiliate her.

Elizabeth raised her head.

The turquoise eyes were waiting for hers.

"Yes, Lord Safyre, I know what a climax is."

Eyes narrowed, he studied her as if she were an animal or an insect that he had never before encountered. "What is it?"

What is it?

She was momentarily speechless with shock.

Patently, he did not believe she possessed such knowledge.

That he should ask her to describe such an intensely personal experience was outrageous, but that he should think her a liar could not be endured.

Her lips tightened. "It is a ... a peak of pleasure."

"Have you experienced this peak of pleasure?"

She tilted her chin, and would have answered a resounding, defiant *yes* but for the sudden blaze of heat in his eyes.

"I hardly think that is any concern of yours."

"You say you wish only to learn how to please your husband, Mrs. Petre," he said harshly. "Do you not also want to learn how to enhance your own pleasure?"

Elizabeth was suddenly, fiercely glad that she had studied so diligently. While she could not match his sexual knowledge, she could certainly hold her own when it came to matching wits.

A small, triumphant smile stretched her lips. "Surely, Lord Safyre, you cannot have forgotten the words of the sheikh. The parts of a woman are not endowed 'with any pleasurable or satisfactory feeling until the same has been penetrated by the instrument of the male.' Therefore by pleasing her husband a woman must please herself."

And Edward, she thought bleakly, was most pleased when she made no demands on him at all.

He had not even bothered to crack open her bedroom door to check on her when he had come home earlier that morning.

But she did not want to think about her past failure as a woman. Satisfaction must exist in the marriage bed. All she had to do was . . . learn how to obtain it.

"Do you become aroused by kisses, Lord Safyre?" she asked impulsively.

"Does your husband?"

A coldness settled inside Elizabeth.

Edward had never kissed her.

No, that was not strictly true. After the minister had pronounced them husband and wife, Edward had briefly pressed his lips against hers.

Elizabeth glanced down at the little silver watch pinned to the bodice of her dress. It was ten minutes after five.

Leaning over, she laid the heavy gold pen onto his desk. "I will not discuss my husband with you or anyone else, Lord Safyre." With more haste than grace, she rolled up the sheath of notes and thrust them into her reticule. "I believe our lesson is over."

And she had survived with her pride if not her modesty intact.

She should feel relieved. She did not.

"Very well, Mrs. Petre." The Bastard Sheikh stood up, eyes once again mocking. "I will see you at four-thirty tomorrow morning."

The breath caught in Elizabeth's throat.

Striving to hide the sudden burst of gladness that there would be another lesson, she slowly rose to her feet. "Four-thirty tomorrow morning."

He picked up the small leather book from the desk and offered it to her. "Chapter Two, Mrs. Petre."

Nodding her head, she accepted the book and turned without comment toward the door.

"Rule number two. Tomorrow morning and every morning thereafter you will leave your bonnet at the front door—as you will leave your cloak."

Anger rushed up her spine. She had obeyed the men in her life for thirty-three years—she was not going to obey this stranger.

"And what if I do not?"

"Then our agreement is over."

Her heart skipped a beat, kicked into a chest-thudding rhythm. Which agreement was he referring to? The lessons . . . or his word as a gentleman of both the East and the West that he would not discuss them with anyone?

"I take it you do not care for bonnets any more than you do corsets," she said frigidly.

The laughter was back in his voice. "You take it correctly."

"What *do* you care for, Lord Safyre?"

"A woman, Mrs. Petre. A warm, wet, wanton woman who is not afraid of her sexuality or ashamed of satisfying her needs."

* * *

The smell of benzene lingered in the library.

Ramiel picked up the pen Elizabeth Petre had used to take her notes. "Which of the two are you, Mrs. Petre?" he murmured, lightly stroking the soft, body-warmed metal. "A woman who is afraid of her sexuality . . . or a woman who is ashamed of satisfying her needs?"

She had small hands. Clutched between her slender fingers, the thick, heavy pen had looked like a primitive gold phallus. The wife of the Chancellor of the Exchequer would need both hands to fully encompass a man of Ramiel's size.

Memory jolted his entire body.

I do not understand how a woman can move without hindering the actions of the man.

After her stark comments yesterday morning, he should have been prepared for her honesty. He had not been. She had succeeded in surprising him yet again.

How could such a naive woman generate so much sexual tension?

"El Ibn."

Ramiel's fingers convulsively clenched around the gold pen. Body instinctively preparing for defense, he raised his head.

Muhamed stood behind the burgundy leather chair that Elizabeth Petre had only moments earlier vacated. A black, hooded cloak covered the butler's turban and white cotton *thobs*.

Turquoise eyes locked with eyes so dark, they appeared to be black.

Cornish eyes.

A cynical smile curled Ramiel's lips.

Muhamed looked Arab but in fact was not. Ramiel looked English but in fact was not.

Elizabeth Petre, like so many of her people, saw only what she was prepared to see.

"What is it, Muhamed?"

"The husband did not leave the house yesterday morning.

Only the woman—Mrs. Petre. She drove away in a carriage before ten. I do not know where. Later that evening, while she was gone, the husband came home for dinner. He left—''

''You said he did not leave the house,'' Ramiel interrupted sharply. ''Yet you say he came home for dinner.''

Muhamed's face, still strong and muscular at the age of fifty-three, remained impassive. ''I do not know the reason for this.''

Ramiel did.

Edward Petre had spent the night with his mistress. As no doubt Elizabeth Petre had known he did.

Where had she gone yesterday morning, to leave her house before the fashionable hour?

Shopping?

Visiting?

Running?

No, Elizabeth Petre would not run. Either from her husband's infidelity or from an agreement with a bastard sheikh.

''Where did the husband go after dinner?''

''The Parliament building. He stayed there until two in the morning. Then he returned home. He is there now.''

As Elizabeth would shortly be.

Did she and her husband keep separate bedrooms . . . or did they share the same bed?

Immediately, Ramiel repulsed the idea of Elizabeth sharing a bed with another man. She would not be able to sneak out of the house if she did.

But that did not mean she could not join her husband in his bed.

Anger fisted inside his gut.

Elizabeth Petre knew what a climax was.

Had she learned that from her husband? Did he penetrate her cold English reserve underneath the covers of respectability and give her a ''peak'' of pleasure?

''You did not discover the identity of Edward Petre's mistress,'' Ramiel said flatly.

Muhamed's black eyes glittered. ''No.''

"Yet you have left his house unattended. I instructed you to follow him until you discovered who the mistress is."

"I thought it wise to return, *El Ibn.*"

Ramiel was not fooled by Muhamed's stoicism. Disapproval radiated from his dark Cornish eyes.

"Explain."

"Mrs. Petre is trouble."

She had not looked like trouble, perched on the edge of the burgundy chair awkwardly balancing her reticule, her gloves, and her notes. Her pale face framed by the ugly black bonnet had been the picture of propriety. Until he had explained that a man pounds and grinds his body into that of a woman as if he were a "pestle." Then her clear hazel eyes had blazed with fire. Her full breasts had swelled inside the wool of her dress, sensitive, so sensitive.

To words.

To the soft abrasion of clothing rubbing unfettered flesh.

With each breath she had drawn, her nipples had grown harder and harder.

It was not her body that she attempted to restrain in whalebone. It was her desires.

What kind of a man was Edward Petre, that he would forsake honest passion for paid pleasure?

Ramiel steepled his hands underneath his chin, his thoughts and a sudden rampant hunger hidden behind hard implacability. "Perhaps. But she is my trouble."

"Have you forgotten, *El Ibn?*"

Every time Muhamed called him *El Ibn*, Ramiel remembered.

Sometimes he forgot . . . when he had sex. Elizabeth Petre made him forget by words alone.

How long had it been since Ramiel lusted for a woman . . . and not for forgetfulness?

How long had it been since he had laughed?

"I have not forgotten, eunuch," Ramiel countered coldly, deliberately.

Muhamed's head snapped backward.

Ramiel instantly regretted his words. Muhamed had not asked
for his burden any more than Ramiel had asked for his.

He wondered how the servant survived, unable to escape his
past, however briefly, inside a woman's body. Ramiel, at least,
had that luxury. Entire minutes where nothing mattered but the
sound of wet, pounding flesh and the silky heat of a woman's
flesh gripping him, milking him until she took the pain and
left only the memories.

*Praise Allah and please God, let him find a woman who
could accept what he could not.*

"Go," Ramiel commanded softly, reigning in the ever-
prevalent anger and self-disgust. "Hire whomever you need. I
don't care how much it costs. I want to know everything that
Edward Petre does. Every place that he visits. Every person he
talks to. Every woman he's ever fucked. If he pisses, I want
to know about it. And I do not expect you to fail me again."

Body as taut as the scimitar that he carried underneath the
loose folds of the cloak and his *thobs,* Muhamed bowed out
of the library.

Ramiel glanced down at the empty cup by his elbow, then
at the full cup of black brew that Elizabeth Petre had hastily
set down after sipping the scalding Turkish coffee.

Muhamed was right. A woman like Elizabeth Petre could
cause a man like him a great deal of trouble.

Here, in England, he would be prepared.

"Muhamed."

The Cornishman froze at the sound of Ramiel's voice, hand
reaching to close the library door.

"I do not repeat the mistakes I have made in the past."

Chapter Four

The jarring clang of silver hitting silver jerked Elizabeth out from underneath the Bastard Sheikh's naked body. A thick, cloying aroma invaded the air.

What do *you care for, Lord Safyre?*

A woman, Mrs. Petre. A warm, wet, wanton woman who is not afraid of her sexuality or ashamed of satisfying her needs.

Elizabeth's eyes snapped open.

Emma's round, pleasant face was wreathed in steam; she bent over the nightstand by the bed, stirring a silver spoon around and around in a porcelain cup. A small silver pot sat beside the cup and saucer on a silver tray.

The cloying aroma filling the air was not the sugary smell of Turkish coffee, Elizabeth vaguely realized. It was the sweet smell of chocolate.

"If you are ill, Elizabeth, you should have sent a note around to my house."

Elizabeth blinked.

Her mother's face stepped into view. It was framed by a black silk bonnet. Emerald-green eyes berated Elizabeth as they had when she was a child and failed to meet her parents' expectations.

Elizabeth came fully awake, heart pounding.

She knows about the Bastard Sheikh was her first thought. It was immediately followed by *How could she?*

The previous morning had been awkward, but this morning Elizabeth had arrived back home at five thirty-five, a quarter of an hour before the servants arose. No one could possibly know about her two visits with the Bastard Sheikh.

But why else would her mother be here unless—

You should have sent a note around to my house pierced the fog of sleep and the mind-numbing start of fear.

Elizabeth's gaze flew to the window.

Today was Tuesday.

Her mother and she always went shopping on Tuesday mornings. Then they took lunch.

Judging by the gray winter light streaming through the curtains, it was fast approaching noon.

Hot blood flooded Elizabeth's cheeks.

Emma and her mother had stood over her and watched her while she dreamed that the Bastard Sheikh worked her body as if his virile member were indeed a pestle and she was a stubborn herb that needed to be thoroughly pounded and ground into submission.

Hez, taalibba, he had whispered, alternately thrusting hard and deep then side to side. *Swing your hips for me . . .*

She squeezed her eyelids together, acutely aware of the harsh flavor of the Turkish coffee that lingered in her mouth and the frustrated desire that continued to pulse deep inside her. *If only Emma had delayed pouring the hot chocolate.*

A surge of resentment flared up inside Elizabeth. Her mother did not belong in her bedroom any more than the Bastard Sheikh belonged in her dreams.

Opening her eyes, she rolled over onto her back and summoned a smile. "Good morning, Mother. I am afraid I have overslept. If you will wait in the sitting room, I will dress and

join you. Emma, please escort my mother downstairs and ring
for tea.''

"Very good, ma'am.''

Her abigail stepped backward; her mother stepped forward.

"Your cheeks are flushed, daughter. If you are ill, there is
no need to get up. I apologize if I intrude on your rest, but I
was worried. Monday you canceled all of your appointments,
and now this. You know that your father is grooming Edward
to stand for prime minister when he retires. You have to seed
the ground for him, just as I do for your father.''

The smile froze on Elizabeth's face. Rebecca Walters was
worried . . . because Elizabeth had failed to fulfill her obliga-
tions.

The only memories that stood out in Elizabeth's childhood
were of her mother ''seeding'' the ground for her father. Every
spare moment, every spark of energy, every deed of charity,
had been dedicated to a political cause.

"Do you never get tired, Mother?''

The emerald-green eyes snapped with impatience. "Of
course I do. So does your father. And so does your husband,
I might add. Is that what this is about''—she gestured toward
Elizabeth in bed—''you lying abed . . . because you are tired?''

Yes, that was exactly what it was about, Elizabeth thought
with a spark of anger. She *was* tired . . . tired of coming fourth
place with her husband. Edward had his politics, his mistress,
his children, and then there was his wife. Just for once in her
life she would like to come first.

Just for once in her life she would like to lie abed, free of
social and political commitments, with a man who loved her.

Her face blanched. Not with ''a'' man, she harshly corrected
herself. She wanted to lie abed with her husband.

"No, Mother, I am not tired. I had the migraine last night
and took laudanum to ease the pain,'' Elizabeth lied, acutely
aware of Emma, who hovered by the door and who must know
that she lied. "Perhaps I overdid the dosage.''

"And Monday?''

Elizabeth forced a smile. And added another lie. "The dean rang up. He wanted to see me immediately, so—"

"What has Phillip done now?"

It should have been amusing, her mother repeating the words Elizabeth herself had asked the dean. It was not. Whereas Elizabeth viewed her younger son's antics with tolerant amusement, her mother vociferously disapproved of Phillip's innocent pranks.

"It was nothing," Elizabeth said hurriedly. "He was involved in a dispute with another schoolboy. If I do not get dressed soon, Mother, we shall be too late to take lunch. Emma . . ."

Elizabeth was mildly amazed at the way Emma gently but firmly propelled Rebecca Walters out of her bedroom. The abigail had not blinked an eye at Elizabeth's lies.

Perhaps Edward had "seeded" the household for deceit, she thought cynically.

Flipping back the covers, she dragged her legs over the edge of the bed.

They were pale legs with neat if not dainty ankles. The rub of her thighs as she scooted across the mattress created warm, moist friction.

Do you know what a climax is, Mrs. Petre?

"Shall I run a bath for you, ma'am?"

Elizabeth gripped the sheet in both hands to anchor herself to the bed.

Emma stood in the doorway, blandly watching Elizabeth and the nightgown that had ridden over her knees.

She jerked down the hem of the shapeless white cotton gown and slid off the bed, heart thumping. "Yes, please. That was rather quick. I thought you were going to escort my mother downstairs."

"Mrs. Walters did not want my escort, ma'am. She said that you more urgently needed my assistance to dress."

Elizabeth bit her bottom lip to keep from snapping that Emma was *her* abigail and that *here,* in this house, the wife of the Chancellor of the Exchequer outranked the wife of the prime minister. Instead, she said, "Then I had better hurry. You should not have let me sleep so late."

"My apologies. I thought you might need the rest."

Elizabeth's heart seemed to do a somersault inside her chest. *Did the servants know? . . .*

Her lips were cold and stiff. "Why did you think that, Emma?"

"You have a very demanding schedule, ma'am. I sometimes think that you work harder than Mr. Petre does."

The abigail's words were too enigmatic to be reassuring.

Did she mean that Elizabeth worked hard at "seeding" the political grounds for her husband? Or did she mean that Elizabeth had a very demanding schedule now with early-morning rendezvous?

The hot bath did not thaw Elizabeth's unease.

She should stop the lessons now, before suspicion became fact. If rumors spread that she was meeting the Bastard Sheikh, her marriage would be over. As would her husband's career.

But even as she contemplated giving up the dangerous tutelage, thoughts of *The Perfumed Garden* crowded aside reason. What had the sheikh written in the second chapter?

She rubbed a bar of soap underneath her breasts. And wondered if the Bastard Sheikh had ever rubbed flower petals against a woman's flesh where she now rubbed the soap.

Emma waited in Elizabeth's bedchamber with a pile of clothing. Stepping behind a white enameled dressing screen, Elizabeth donned cotton drawers, wool stockings, and a linen chemise before rejoining Emma so that the maid could help her with her corset—

Elizabeth sucked in her breath to accommodate Emma's ministrations. She had worn a corset for twenty-three years. It should not feel like a whaleboned prison. Nor had it until now.

The corset was rapidly followed by two petticoats. Elizabeth took a tentative breath, inhaled the scent of starch and laundry soap.

What did Edward's mistress smell like? she wondered.

Did Edward move like a pestle while his mistress swung her

hips side to side in lascivious accompaniment? Or were certain sexual motions peculiar to Arabs?

Emma twitched a heavy navy wool dress over Elizabeth's bustle. "If you'll step up to the dressing table, I'll repair your hair, Mrs. Petre."

The blood drained from Elizabeth's face.

Emma had brushed out her hair the night before and braided it, as she did every night before Elizabeth retired to bed. When Elizabeth had later dressed for her lesson she had twisted the braid up into a bun.

After so cleverly changing back into her nightgown and hanging up her clothes that no one would know she had been outside the house, *she had forgotten to take down her hair.*

"Thank you, Emma," she said through stiff lips.

Elizabeth's face in the dressing table mirror was chalk white—the same color as was the reflection of Emma's apron. The abigail's square, competent hands moved deftly through the dark auburn strands, unpinning, unbraiding, brushing, twisting, repinning.

Emma stepped back—a square chin and an attractively plump neck appeared in the mirror above the white apron. "Would you like your jewelry box, ma'am?"

"That won't be necessary."

"Very good, ma'am."

Elizabeth realized that Emma was as much of an enigma now as she had been sixteen years earlier.

"Have you ever been married, Emma?"

"No, ma'am. Employers do not encourage servants to marry."

"I would not object."

Emma turned, presenting a rather broad black backside to the mirror, and then that, too, was gone and Elizabeth had no alternative but to stand and face the abigail. She patiently held out a black cloak.

Elizabeth slipped first one arm and then another into the sleeves. The wool was still damp from Elizabeth's earlier outing.

"Your gloves, ma'am."

Elizabeth stared into Emma's gray eyes and could see . . . nothing. No curiosity, no disapproval, no awareness that anything was amiss.

"Thank you, Emma."

"Don't forget your reticule, ma'am."

Elizabeth sighed with relief. At least she had possessed the forethought to put the Bastard Sheikh's book and her notes into her desk.

"Mr. Petre." She slowly fitted her left hand into a black leather glove. "Is he lunching at home today?"

"Yes, ma'am."

Elizabeth concentrated on drawing the remaining glove onto her right hand. "Did he inquire as to why I overslept?"

"No, ma'am."

Elizabeth blindly examined the contents inside her reticule.

It was bad enough that she had to question a servant about the whereabouts of her husband. Worse yet, she had to ask a servant if he was interested in his wife's comings and goings. But far, far worse was to be informed by a servant that her husband was not interested in her welfare.

A dozen excuses raced through her head. She leapt upon the most plausible.

No doubt Edward, due to the late hour that he had come home, had slept late himself and had not realized she was home. It *was* Tuesday.

The horsehair-lined bustle weighting her down suddenly felt pounds lighter.

Downstairs, a brown-haired footman dressed in a short black coat and black bow tie stood at attention by the sitting room doors.

Elizabeth frowned. She did not recognize him.

"Hello," she said cordially, advancing forward. Up close, he was older than what she had first thought, probably in his late thirties or early forties. "I am afraid I do not recall seeing you before."

He bowed briefly, then as if he were not quite certain what

to do with his hands, he clasped them behind his back and stared over her shoulder. ''I be Johnny, Freddie Watson's cousin. There be an emergency with his mam, came up sudden this morning. Yer butler didn' think there'd be no trouble if I worked Freddie's position until he came back.''

Freddie, a young man in his early twenties, had been employed in the Petre household for a year. Because he needed to help take care of his mother and younger brother, who both had tuberculosis, he lived at home.

''I am so sorry,'' Elizabeth said in all sincerity. ''Of course it is all right. Please let me know if Freddie or his mother need any assistance. I would be happy to advance him a month or so of wages.''

He nodded his need. ''Thank ye, ma'am. I'll tell 'im.''

Elizabeth patiently waited. Starting, as if suddenly realizing the duties of a footman, he leaned down and jerked open the door.

Whatever ''Cousin Johnny'' did in the normal course of events, she thought with a flicker of amusement, it was not being a house servant.

Elizabeth smiled. ''Thank you, Johnny.''

Inside the drawing room, Edward and Rebecca leaned close together on the stuffed, floral upholstered divan. Their heads, he with his midnight-black hair rigidly controlled with an application of macassar oil and hers capped in black silk, nearly touched. They stopped talking at the sight of Elizabeth.

Edward stood, as a matter of courtesy rather than welcome. ''Hello, Elizabeth. I was just telling Rebecca that the House is going to repeal the Contagious Disease Acts.''

Elizabeth searched her husband's face, the dark, olive-shaped brown eyes, the neatly trimmed side whiskers and mustache, the generous lips that always curved in a smile.

He had not come home Sunday night. He had come home at two-thirty in the morning last night—she had heard the grandfather clock chime the time—*and all he had to tell her was that the Contagious Disease Acts were being repealed?*

''Mrs. Butler must be pleased,'' she said neutrally.

Mrs. Josephine Butler, the wife of a clergyman and the secretary of the Ladies National Association, had devoted sixteen years of her life persuading Parliament to repeal the Contagious Disease Acts.

"It is a victory for all women," Rebecca pointed out, smoothing out a wrinkle in her dove-gray wool gown.

Both Elizabeth and Rebecca visited charity hospital wards as part of their "political" duties. Perhaps she could forget the women who came there diseased and starving, but Elizabeth could not.

"Not all, Mother."

Rebecca turned frosty green eyes onto Elizabeth. "Whatever are you talking about?"

Edward silently watched Elizabeth, brown eyes oddly calculating. For once that supercilious smile did not curve his lips.

It suddenly dawned on her that Rebecca attended the same routs and rallies and dinners as did Elizabeth. She, too, must have heard that Edward kept a mistress.

Why had she not said anything?

Why did she stand beside her son-in-law, defending his politics, while he made a mockery of his marriage vows?

"The women on the streets will receive no medical care now," Elizabeth explained woodenly. "They will die of disease, they and their children, and they will pass it on so that others will die."

"The Acts demean these women, Elizabeth," Rebecca sharply admonished. "Prostitutes must endure routine medical examinations. A woman's modesty cannot survive the indignity of a vaginal inspection."

Elizabeth stared at her mother in shocked disbelief.

Shocked, because she had never heard Rebecca use anything other than the most euphemistic terms for the human body, "limbs" for "legs," "bosom" for "breasts," "privates" for "genitals." Disbelieving, because a prostitute daily endured more than one vaginal inspection—and not by a physician.

Incongruously, she thought of *The Perfumed Garden*.

The sheikh reverently described a woman's vulva as a thing

of wonder and beauty. Her mother spoke of a woman's "vagina" with her mouth primped, as if the female body were a thing of shame. And her husband—

She scrutinized his familiar face.

Edward's brown eyes revealed neither disgust at Rebecca's vulgarity nor dismay at her priggishness. He looked, Elizabeth thought, as it he had no interest . . . in *any* woman.

She suddenly felt if she did not engage his attention that very moment, it would be too late and his mistress would have won before Elizabeth even attempted to seduce him.

"Mother and I can stay home and lunch with you, Edward," she compulsively offered.

Edward's lips curved in his politician's smile, a smile of impersonal warmth and uncommitted caring. "I know how you look forward to spending time with your mother, Elizabeth. There is no need to forgo your lunch on my account."

"I want to, Edward," she quietly, desperately, insisted.

"I have papers to go over, Elizabeth."

And no doubt a mistress to go over after the House meeting tonight.

Her lips tightened at the polite rebuff. "Of course. Please do not let us keep you from your work. Mother. Are you ready?"

Rebecca critically eyed Elizabeth before standing. "I have been ready this last hour."

The sky outside the town house was even more gray than the light inside; coal smoke hung over London in heavy black clouds. Elizabeth was overcome by such an acute yearning for fresh, sun-warmed air that it was painful.

Parliament would break for Easter. Perhaps she and Edward could take a holiday.

It suddenly dawned on her that she had never holidayed with her husband. Always it had been her and the two boys driving down to Brighton or Bath or wherever the latest fashionable resort happened to be.

"You really should hire better trained footmen, Elizabeth. I

swear your latest has no notion of the responsibilities his position entails.''

For once Elizabeth was impervious to her mother's criticism.
Staring at the soot-stained horses and carriages crowding the
street, she tried to imagine her mother and father locked in a
passionate embrace . . . and failed utterly.

Her breath misted the coach window. ''When is the last time
you saw Father?''

''Your father is a busy man, as is your husband, Elizabeth.
It is not your position to question their politics. You were not
raised to do such. A woman's duty is to support her husband.
Love is not a play that demands an audience. It is sacrifice.''

Elizabeth turned her head and met Rebecca's disapproving
gaze. ''When did you last see Father, Mother?'' she repeated.

Rebecca was not used to being questioned by her daughter.
Perhaps that was why she answered, albeit reluctantly,
''Sunday.''

Sunday.

''You will not aide your father and husband if you go on in
this fashion. Tomorrow night we attend Baroness Whitfield's
ball—the baron opposes your father and husband on a new
Act, and it is very important that we win their favor. Thursday
you speak for the Women's Auxiliary. Andrew and I cannot
attend the Hanson dinner party, so you and Edward will have
to go in our stead. Saturday is the charity ball. I trust you will
not take to your bed because you do not receive the attention
that you feel is your due.''

Elizabeth bit back a sharp retort; *There are more important
things than politics.*

But there had never been anything more important than politics to her mother and her father. And now Elizabeth was
married to a man who showed every sign of following in their
footsteps. Except, of course, Edward had a mistress.

The carriage jarred to a stop.

Rebecca had not seen Andrew for three nights and two days.
Did Elizabeth's father have a mistress too?

Is that why Rebecca dedicated her life to politics . . . because of her husband's neglect?

The coach door opened.

If Elizabeth did not change the course of her marriage, would she one day be like her mother, with nothing but her husband's career to occupy her time and conversation?

Chapter Five

"You have beautiful hair, Mrs. Petre."

The door closed behind Elizabeth, sealing her inside the warm intimacy of the library with the seductive echo of the Bastard Sheikh's compliment ringing in her ears.

No one had ever complimented her hair.

She self-consciously raised her hand to her bare head—caught herself. If she had beautiful hair, then her husband would not now be out with another woman.

Damn him. Edward had not come home *again*.

"I have unfashionable hair, Lord Safyre," she corrected him icily.

The flickering gas lamp on the massive mahogany desk alternately cast the Bastard Sheikh's saturnine face in shadow and light, hair shining first gold then dark wheat. "Beauty is in the eyes of the beholder."

"As is a man's 'meritoriousness.' "

A smile hitched up the corner of his mouth. He gestured toward the burgundy leather chair. "Please. Sit down. I hope you slept well."

Holding her spine straight and her head high, Elizabeth

crossed the Oriental carpet. The abrasive rub of her linen shift and heavy wool dress against the tips of her nipples was an acute irritation. It reminded her that she had needs no respectable woman should have, *but she had them* and they had led her to this, being mocked by a man who could have any woman he wanted while her husband stayed overnight with the woman whom *he* wanted.

She perched on the edge of the chair, anger simmering inside her, searching for an outlet. "Thank you. It was not difficult after reading Chapter Two."

He cocked his head. "You did not enjoy the sheikh's writings on 'Concerning Women Who Deserve to be Praised.' "

It was not a question.

"Indeed." She forcefully peeled off her gloves. "The moral of the chapter is, after all, what every woman yearns to read."

Especially a woman who showed every sign of losing her husband to his mistress.

The Bastard Sheikh poured coffee into a blue-veined demitasse cup. Steam rose like a curtain between them. He added a splash of water to the cup. "And that is?"

She reached into her reticule for her notes . . . and realized that she was looking forward to this, to channeling the anger that she had nurtured the day before and that now blossomed in the new day.

She deserved more from her husband than a casual remark about the repeal of the Contagious Disease Acts.

After sifting through several pages of notes, Elizabeth found what she was looking for. " '. . . A man who falls in love with a woman imperils himself, and exposes himself to the greatest troubles.' "

"You do not agree with the sheikh, Mrs. Petre?"

"Do *you*, Lord Safyre?"

He offered her the cup and saucer, so very correct in this most incorrect schooling. "I believe nothing that is worth having comes easily."

That was not the answer she wanted to hear. She snatched the saucer out of his hand and raised the cup to her lips.

"Blow on it, Mrs. Petre."

Elizabeth blew on the brew. Once.

Hardly registering the scalding liquid, she took two sips.

"What did you think about the sheikh's advice on the qualities that make a woman praiseworthy?"

Impervious to the dictates of polite manners, Elizabeth set the saucer onto the desk so hard that black coffee slopped over the rim of the cup. The rustle of paper filled the room as she flipped through her notes.

" 'In order that a woman may be relished by men, she must have a perfect waist, and must be plump and lusty. Her hair will be black, her forehead wide, she will have eyebrows of Ethiopian blackness, large black eyes, with the whites in them very limpid. With cheek of perfect oval, she will have an elegant nose and a graceful mouth; lips and tongue vermilion; her breath will be of pleasant odour, her throat long, her neck strong, her bust and her belly large . . .' "

She lowered her notes. "I think, Lord Safyre, that Arab men desire different attributes in their women than do English men."

The turquoise eyes glittered with laughter. "We have already agreed that beauty is in the eyes of the beholder, Mrs. Petre. However, it was not the sheikh's description of a woman's physical attributes that I was referring to."

The hot anger coiled more tightly in the pit of Elizabeth's stomach.

Her mother was scornful. Her husband was indifferent. She was not going to endure ridicule from her tutor.

"I take it, then, that you are referring to the sheikh's edicts that a praiseworthy woman rarely speaks or laughs. She has no friends, 'gives her confidence to nobody,' and relies solely on her husband. 'She takes nothing from anyone' except her husband and her parents. She 'has no faults to hide . . .' She does not try to gain attention. She does what her husband wishes *when* he wishes and always with a smile. She assists him in his political and social affairs. She soothes his troubles that she might make his life more content even if it requires sacrificing her own contentment. She never expresses *any* emotion for fear he will be repulsed by her *base, childish needs.*''

Elizabeth lifted her chin, refusing to let the stinging tears that welled in her eyes fall. ''Is that what you were referring to, Lord Safyre?''

The Bastard Sheikh cradled his cup in the palms of his hands and rocked back in his chair. ''You do not think that such a woman is praiseworthy?''

Her lips tightened mutinously. ''I *think* that I would rather be a 'meritorious' man.''

He stared at her for long seconds before replying. ''That is because you have not yet read one of the prescriptions for increasing a man's 'meritoriousness.' ''

Elizabeth could not imagine anything worse than the life she had just described. *She had spent sixteen years being a* praiseworthy *wife,* holding her emotions in abeyance, always deferring to her husband. It might make a man's life more pleasant, but it certainly did nothing to enhance the life of a woman.

''And that is?''

''Imagine washing a man's genitals in warm water until he becomes pleasurably erect . . .''

He paused, studying her face.

Elizabeth returned his stare. Not for the life of her would she admit that she had never imagined washing a man's genitals, either in warm or cold water. Furthermore, it was hard to imagine a man growing pleasurably erect when one had no idea of what a man looked like . . . *erect.*

''Now imagine taking a piece of soft leather that is spread with hot pitch and slapping it onto the man's unsuspecting member.''

Shock raced across Elizabeth's face; it was chased by incredulity.

Hot pitch was hot pitch. And while she had never seen a man's erect member, she was quite certain that it was as sensitive as was a woman's genitals.

''According to the prescription, the man's member rears its

head, trembling with passion. When the pitch cools and the man is again in a state of repose, the operation must be repeated several times in order to increase his 'meritoriousness.' ''

... *The man's member rears its head, trembling with passion* shimmered in the air between them.

A flash of heat rippled through Elizabeth's body.

"Does a man tremble with passion, Lord Safyre?"

"Not wrapped in hot pitch, he doesn't," the Bastard Sheikh murmured dryly.

Edward had looked so distant yesterday, so above the dictates of the flesh, so unlike a man who would tremble, whether it be in passion or the result of any other emotion.

Was it a facade? Did men project the qualities they thought women wanted to see in them?

"Does a man tremble with passion?" she repeated, enunciating the words slowly, carefully, needing to know, *needing to hope.*

He leaned forward in his chair, a sharp crack of protesting wood. His hair and eyes blazed in the lamplight. "When sexually excited . . . yes, Mrs. Petre, a man trembles with passion."

She instinctively glanced down at his hands, still cradling his cup. They were large and muscular and rock steady.

"Just as a woman trembles in her passion." His voice was a dark rasp.

Elizabeth recoiled. Absolutely, that was not the voice of a tutor to his student.

His dusky brown fingers tightened, knuckles whitening. Suddenly, he brought the demitasse cup to his lips and neatly downed its contents. The dull impact of china on wood echoed in the stillness.

"Tobacco is enjoyed by both men and women in Arabia," he said abruptly. "Would you care for a smoke, Mrs. Petre?"

A smoke?

Only women of ill repute smoked.

"Perhaps another time, Lord Safyre," she said repressively.

The skin over his cheekbones stretched taut. "Men are excited by words. If you want to learn how to please your husband, perhaps you should memorize, or at least take note, of some of the Arabic love poems in *The Perfumed Garden*.''

It was a direct challenge.

Elizabeth's hazel eyes shifted, stared at a point over his golden head. '' 'Full of vigor and life,' '' she quoted softly, '' 'it bores into my vagina, And it works about there in action constant and splendid. First from the front to the back, and then from the right to the left; Now it is crammed hard in by vigorous pressure, Now it rubs its head on the orifice of my vagina. And he strokes my back, my stomach, my sides, Kisses my cheeks, and anon begins to suck at my lips.' ''

She shifted her focus back onto Ramiel. ''Like that, Lord Safyre?''

His gaze snared hers. ''Exactly like that.''

Liquid heat spread through her stomach. She was suddenly, breathtakingly conscious of the rhythmical rise and fall of her uncorseted breasts and the stiff caress of her linen chemise and lined wool bodice.

''In the poem . . . earlier on,'' she said daringly. ''What does it mean, that a man's member has a head like a brazier?''

The turquoise eyes narrowed. ''It means that it is red with desire and hot for a woman.''

Elizabeth felt as if the air had been sucked out of her lungs. ''Does a man . . . enjoy it when a woman . . . puts him inside of her?''

'' 'When he sees me in heat he quickly comes to me,' '' he recited huskily. '' 'Then he opens my thighs and kisses my belly, And puts his tool in my hand to make it knock at my door.'

''When a woman wraps her fingers around a man's member, she holds his very life in her hand. She can hurt him . . . or she can give him indescribable ecstasy. When she guides him to her vagina and pushes the head of him against her, there is a moment of resistance, the threat of rejection, then her body opens up and swallows him in hot welcome and *yes*, Mrs. Petre, it is enjoyable. More, it is a moment of bonding. By taking control, a woman demonstrates to her man that she accepts him for who and what he is. By relinquishing control, the man tells his woman that he trusts her implicitly.''

A moment of bonding.

Edward had come to Elizabeth in a darkened room. Underneath stifling bedcovers and tangled nightclothes a fumbling caress had preceded a slight prick of discomfort and their moment had been over. There had been no acceptance or loss of control. Only silence broken by the creak of the bedsprings.

She jerked her head down, away from those hypnotizing eyes, and rummaged through her notes.

A woman did not memorize erotic poetry unless it stimulated her. *Sexually.* As the Bastard Sheikh must know.

As he no doubt knew that words affected a woman as strongly as they did a man.

My God, what he must think of her!

She squirmed with embarrassment and something far more shameful, creasing the paper in her search, *where was that passage—*

''Or would you have me memorize this poem?'' She stridently read, '' 'Oh, men! listen to what I say on the subject of woman . . . her malice is boundless . . . As long as she is with you in bed, you have her love, But a woman's love is not enduring, believe me.' ''

Elizabeth cringed at the jarring note of cynicism in her voice.

''How long can a woman comfortably go without coition, Mrs. Petre?''

The sheath of papers crackled between her clenched fingers.

Twelve years, five months, one week, and three days.

That was how long it had been since Edward had visited her bed. But not one day of it had been comfortable.

''A woman is not like a man. She does not need . . . that particular kind of comfort.''

A piece of wood dropped in the fireplace, underscoring her lie. Sparks snapped, fire flamed.

''How long, Mrs. Petre?'' he repeated relentlessly, *as if he knew exactly how long it had been since Edward had visited her bed.*

Squaring her shoulders, she raised her head. *"The Perfumed Garden* claims that a wellborn woman can comfortably remain celibate for six months."

She could see the next question shaping his lips: *How long have* you *been celibate, Mrs. Petre?* Masking haste with haughtiness, she intercepted. "How long can *a man* comfortably remain celibate, Lord Safyre?"

The ruthless intensity in the Bastard Sheikh's eyes eased. He leaned back in his chair. "Celibacy is never comfortable for a man, Mrs. Petre."

She did not have to ask *him* when *he* had last been with a woman. *Any more than she had to ask her husband where he spent his nights.*

"And why is that?" she lashed out. "Why cannot a man suffer celibacy in comfort, as a woman is expected to?"

"Perhaps, Mrs. Petre, because women endure their suffering in silence and men do not," he responded quietly.

The air was suddenly too thick, the conversation too intense. "Do you recommend a diet of white bread and egg yolks 'fried in fat and swimming in honey' to give a man stamina?" she abruptly asked.

Warm, rich, masculine peals of laughter suddenly cocooned her.

Elizabeth blinked.

The hard, chiseled face of the Bastard Sheikh had transformed into one of an uninhibited little boy. A very jolly little boy.

Her lips quivered. She wanted to share his laughter even though she knew it was directed at her.

Finally, "No, Mrs. Petre, I do not."

"Do you speak from experience, Lord Safyre?"

All signs of laughter disappeared and once again his face was dark and hard and cynical. "There is very little I have not tried."

No man should look so bleak . . . or alone.

Not even a Bastard Sheikh.

Elizabeth wanted to incite more laughter.

"I take it, then, that you tried the poultice of hot pitch," she said tartly.

Ramiel winced. "Then you take it wrongly. There is a difference between adolescent ego and infantile lunacy."

"Then what, pray tell, was the sheikh's purpose in including such a recipe if it is injurious?"

"*The Perfumed Garden* is over three hundred years old. Times change, people change, but the need for sexual satisfaction does not."

"For men," she said firmly.

"And for women," he adjured. "I will share with you some information that is not contained in the English translation here. In Arabia, there are three things that men are petitioned not to take lightly: the training of a horse, shooting with a bow and arrow, and, lastly, making love to one's wife."

"In that order?" she asked stiffly, reality a sharp slap in the face.

Fourth place, *third place*, it mattered little: A woman still did not come first. Either in Arabia or England.

"You think a wife merits greater importance in the scheme of a man's life?" he asked lightly.

"Yes," she retorted defiantly.

"So do I, Mrs. Petre."

Elizabeth's anger dissipated. A sudden image of a man's member rearing red and hot while he trembled with passion flashed before her eyes.

"Do you have the entire book memorized, Lord Safyre?"

"Yes."

She stared, surprised. "Why?"

A wry smile twisted his lips. "My father. He would not give me a woman until I learned how to please her."

"Your father wanted you to learn how to please a woman . . . by learning not to trust one?"

He glanced down, reached out a long, brown finger to lightly caress the blue-veined porcelain cup. "My father wanted me to learn that a woman is capable of the same kind of sexual satisfaction as is a man. He also wanted me to learn that there

are good women and that there are untrustworthy women—''
expression hardening, he looked up—''just as there are good
men and there are bad men.''

She tried to picture him as a golden-haired boy, poring over
a manual of erotology, then practicing what he had learned on
a beautiful blond-haired concubine.

''But you were only thirteen years old,'' she blurted out.

''Would you keep your two sons boys forever, Mrs. Petre?''

Elizabeth froze. ''I will not discuss my sons with you, Lord
Safyre.''

The mockery was back in his face. ''And you will not discuss
your husband with me.''

''That is correct.''

''Then what *will* you discuss with me, Mrs. Petre?''

Sex.

Love.

A bonding of flesh that is more than sacrifice or duty.

''Do you agree that the Contagious Disease Acts should be
repealed?''

Dear Lord, that was not what she had intended upon asking
him.

''No.''

Nor did his answer surprise her.

''Because you frequent that type of woman.''

''I do not pick up women off the streets, Mrs. Petre.'' His
voice was raw instead of raspy, angry instead of seductive. ''I
am a man of means if not one of respectability. The women I
bed will not be affected by a parliamentary act.''

She bit her lip, wanting to apologize but not even certain
what it was that she should apologize for.

''Why did you agree to tutor me? You must know that I
would not have gone to my husband.''

Dark lashes veiled his eyes. He resumed the idle caressing
of the cup, his fingertips lazily stroking and soothing. ''Why
did you chose me to tutor you?''

''Because I needed your knowledge.''

He lifted his lashes. "Perhaps you have something that I need too."

Elizabeth's heart fluttered inside her chest. She gathered together her notes and stuffed them into her reticule. It was not necessary to consult the silver watch pinned to her bodice to know that it was time to leave. "I think this lesson is over."

"I think you are correct," he agreed, his expression inscrutable. "Some of the chapters in *The Perfumed Garden* consist of a few pages only. Therefore, tomorrow we will discuss chapters three, four, and five. I advise you to pay particular attention to Chapter Four. It is entitled 'Relating to the Act of Generation.' "

Clutching her gloves and reticule, Elizabeth stood.

Polite manners decreed that he also stand.

He did not.

She looked down at his head, golden in the light. Then she stared at his fingers, dusky brown against the blue-veined porcelain.

Elizabeth remembered the span of his two hands. And wondered at *his* size.

She pivoted, almost fell over the chair.

"Mrs. Petre."

Back stiffening, she waited for rule number three. No doubt it would be totally objectionable and humiliating.

"Ma'a e-salemma, taalibba."

Her throat tightened. He claimed that the word was not an endearment, so why did it touch a place deep inside of her that desperately ached to be touched?

"Ma'a e-salemma, Lord Safyre."

Chapter Six

Ramiel studied the four-year-old newspaper. It contained a grim photograph of Edward Petre, recently appointed Chancellor of the Exchequer, and wife, Elizabeth, with two sons, Richard, age eleven, and Phillip, age seven.

A current newspaper contained a lone picture of Edward. He had short, dark hair worn with a side part. As was the fashion, he possessed a thick, droopy mustache. Women would consider him handsome, Ramiel thought dispassionately, while men would be impressed with his self-confidence.

A month-old newspaper contained a picture of Elizabeth standing behind a podium, only her head and shoulders visible. A dark hat with curled feathers concealed all but a glimpse of her hair, dark gray instead of auburn red. Women would consider her a modern woman who actively supported their good works and her husband's politics; men would think her a useful but uninspiring wife.

A six-month-old newspaper contained a picture of Edward and Elizabeth together, seemingly the perfect couple, he smiling benignly, she blandly staring. And then there was the twenty-two-year-old newspaper that featured an artist's sketch of

Andrew Walters, elected prime minister, and wife, Rebecca, with eleven-year-old daughter, Elizabeth.

Andrew Walters had been very fortunate in politics. His first term of office as prime minister had lasted six years. After losing the support of his cabinet he had fought his way back. His second term, already four years in the running, showed no signs of dissolution.

Ramiel compared the two family portraits.

Elizabeth bore a striking resemblance to her father. Whereas Elizabeth's children . . . bore a striking resemblance to *their* father.

Ela'na! Damn! It would be so much more simple if they resembled Elizabeth.

He scooped up a copy of *The Times* dated January 21, 1870. A photograph of Elizabeth accompanied a notice announcing her engagement to promising politician Edward Petre.

She looked so young. And naive. The photographer, either by accident or design, had captured the dreamy expectation of an untried girl poised on the threshold of womanhood.

Elizabeth had married at the age of seventeen; that made her thirty-three. And now her face bore no expression at all, not in life as she sat across from Ramiel discussing sexual intimacy, not in the various photographs taken after her husband's appointment in her father's cabinet.

The papers were full of her activities. She campaigned extensively for her husband, attending parties, organizing charity balls, kissing orphaned babies, and doling out baskets to the poor and the infirm.

By all accounts, Elizabeth was the perfect daughter, wife and mother. *A woman who deserved to be praised.*

He threw the newspaper onto his desk.

Disgust warred with anger, desire with compassion. They were chased by fear.

Fear that Elizabeth Petre did indeed know about her husband. Fear that she had deliberately sought Ramiel because of that knowledge.

She had to know about her husband!

But then again . . . there was no way that she *could* know . . . about Ramiel.

The age-yellowed newspaper fluttered; a soft rush of air filled the library.

"El Ibn."

To the untutored ear Muhamed's voice was politely expressionless. It was not. Muhamed silently asked that Ramiel repudiate Elizabeth Petre, as he already had in his heart.

Perhaps Muhamed was right.

Elizabeth had blackmailed the eunuch. She sought sexual instruction from Ramiel.

Neither act demonstrated innocence.

"Could this detective that you hired—" Ramiel paused, hating himself for asking but unable to stop the question. "Could he be mistaken?"

Black eyes locked with turquoise ones. "There is no mistake, *El Ibn.*"

Ramiel remembered the blaze of red in Elizabeth's dark auburn hair . . . and how self-conscious she had been when he complimented her. Her actions had been those of a woman who rarely receives praise.

Raw rage, cold and hard, worked its way up into his chest. *She deserved better than Edward Petre.*

"What is Petre doing tonight?"

"He is attending a ball."

"Who is giving it?"

"Baroness Whitfield."

"The woman the Chancellor of the Exchequer was allegedly seen with . . . who is she, Muhamed?"

Muhamed's dark face remained stoic. "I do not know, *El Ibn.*"

Ramiel regarded him with narrow-eyed intensity. "But you have an idea."

"Yes."

"Then get me the necessary proof."

Night swirled outside the bay windows.

Was Elizabeth dancing in her husband's arms at the Whitfield ball? *Did she know?*

That morning she had taken two sips of Turkish coffee even though she obviously disliked it. Or did she?

Given the opportunity, what would Elizabeth choose: respectability or passion?

He suddenly envisioned her reclining naked on a stack of silk cushions, smoking a hookah.

The image should be ridiculous—she wore creaking corsets and heavy wool dresses perfumed by benzene. It wasn't. He could all too vividly imagine her dark auburn hair spilling down her back and across her full breasts while she sucked on the bit.

"Have a carriage drawn around," Ramiel abruptly ordered. "Tonight I will follow Petre."

The ball was everything and worse than Elizabeth had expected. She chatted with young debutantes who had not quite taken and to men who were too shy to approach the opposite sex. Or she attended those men and women who were too elderly or too infirm to dance. And all the while she listened to the practiced scales of feminine titters and masculine guffaws as the gilded *ton* swirled and twirled on the dance floor, absorbed in their pursuit of pleasure.

The Bastard Sheikh had complimented her hair. How long had it been since Edward had given her a compliment . . . on anything?

How long can a wellborn woman comfortably go without coition?

"Mrs. Petre . . ."

It took a second for Elizabeth to realize that she was being addressed. Her companion, Lord Inchcape, an eighty-year-old peer whose distinct body odor necessitated that one keep one's head turned upwind, did not need her conversation, only an ear.

"Mrs. Petre, I have someone here who begs an introduction."

Elizabeth gratefully turned to Baroness Whitfield, her hostess.

The welcoming smile on her face froze.

The Bastard Sheikh, dressed in black evening clothes and white tie, towered over the baroness's short, plump figure. On his other side, a tall woman claimed his arm—the top of her head reached well past his chin. She was slender, elegant in a turquoise gown that matched his eyes. Her face was a perfect oval. Golden blond hair was caught in a chignon; it was the same color as was the Bastard Sheikh's.

Recognition was instantaneous: *She must be the woman whom he had wallowed in until her perfume had become his scent.*

A fleeting pain stabbed through her chest: Jealousy, *envy.* The woman was everything that Elizabeth would never be, exactly the kind of woman she would choose for a man like him.

Baroness Whitfield's plump cheeks were flushed with champagne and the heat radiating from over a hundred bodies and three chandeliers. "Catherine, may I present to you Mrs. Elizabeth Petre, the illustrious wife of our Chancellor of the Exchequer. Mrs. Petre, Countess Devington."

Elizabeth's first stunned thought was *She's not the Bastard Sheikh's mistress, she's his mother,* and then, incongruously, *She's not old enough to be his mother, surely.*

Smiling warmly, the countess extended a white-gloved hand. "How do you do, Mrs. Petre? I've heard so much about you."

A cold frisson of fear raced down Elizabeth's spine. Ignoring the friendly overture, she stiffly executed a curtsy. "How do you do, Countess Devington?"

"Catherine, you are acquainted with Lord Inchcape."

"Indeed I am. How do you do, Lord Inchcape?"

Lord Inchcape nodded his liver-spotted head. "Not still galavantin' off to those foreign countries and gettin' yourself kidnapped, eh, what?"

The countess's smile subtly altered. "Alack, not recently."

Amusement lit up the baroness's small, plump face. "Behave yourself, Catherine. Mrs. Petre, may I present to you Countess Devington's son, Lord Safyre. Lord Safyre . . . Mrs. Petre."

Turquoise eyes clashed with Elizabeth's hazel ones. Everything she had read and discussed the last two mornings was in his gaze.

What does it mean, that a man's member has a head like a brazier?

It means that it is red with desire and hot for a woman.

Dear God, what was he doing here?

Had he told the countess about their lessons?

Elizabeth nodded stiffly. "Lord Safyre."

Before she could divine his intentions, the Bastard Sheikh reached down and grasped Elizabeth's hand. His dusky brown skin was covered by a white glove. The press of his fingers through the dual layers of his silk glove and hers was scorching. *"Ahlan wa sahlan,* Mrs. Petre."

Elizabeth watched in horrified fascination as his golden head bowed over her hand. His lips, when he kissed it, were even hotter than his fingers.

The blood that had receded from her head upon first seeing him flooded her face in a tide of scalding crimson. She snatched her hand back.

The baroness, as if nothing were amiss, smiled at Elizabeth's companion. "Lord Inchcape . . . Lord Safyre."

Lord Inchcape drew himself up as tall as his stooped shoulders would allow. "In my day we did not present our bastards."

Elizabeth's breath caught in her throat at the crude cut. She was vaguely aware of the baroness's stifled exclamation of, "Oh, dear . . ."

The countess's eyes shot gray pellets of ice. "In your day, Lord Inchcape, you had no title, therefore you would not be presented to anyone, whether they be a bastard or a grocer."

Lord Inchcape's sallow face turned a mottled puce.

"Ummee." The Bastard Sheikh's husky murmur filled the explosive silence. "Mrs. Petre will think us uncivilized."

The countess's frigid gaze did not waver. "I doubt very much if it is we who Mrs. Petre will think uncivilized."

Elizabeth bit back a shock of laughter.

Lord Inchcape turned and stalked into the milling crowd of promenading men and women. The countess glared at his retreating back.

"The bad man is gone now, *Ummee,*" the Bastard Sheikh said dryly. "You can relax, your chick is safe."

Lightning-quick dismay shone in the countess's gray eyes. It was followed by rueful laughter. "I beg your pardon, Mrs. Petre, but the provocation was great. Being a mother, I am sure you understand my upset."

Countess Devington had been a whore to an Arab sheikh. She had given birth to a bastard son. A bastard she had sent to Arabia when he was twelve years old that she might escape the inconvenience of schooling an adolescent boy.

Elizabeth doubted if she had a maternal instinct in her entire body.

"Yes, of course," she said coldly.

The Bastard Sheikh's eyes flashed with angry turquoise fire.

The countess gripped his arm; her smile remained warm and friendly. "We came to fetch you for the next dance, Mrs. Petre. My son desires to waltz. Please don't say no; if you do, I may never be able to convince him to attend another ball."

Elizabeth cast a furtive glance at the teeming, seething mass of jewel-colored silks and white ties that encircled them, desperately searching for her husband, her mother, a reason to reject the offer. *A respectable woman did not dance with a man of his reputation.*

"My husband and I do not waltz—"

"Your husband is in the card room, Mrs. Petre," the Bastard Sheikh smoothly interrupted. "I feel certain he would not mind my standing in his stead. Especially, as you say, if he does not waltz."

The Bastard Sheikh was not discussing a waltz. He was

discussing sex. Edward did not dance with her in public, he was telling her, any more than he slept with her in private.

Elizabeth could feel the curious stare of the baroness, the strangely sympathetic one of his mother. And heard herself say, "I would be pleased to waltz with Lord Safyre."

Before she could retract her words, Elizabeth was propelled through the sea of brightly colored silk dresses and stark black evening coats. Hard, hot fingers curled around her elbow just where her glove ended and her bare skin began.

Elizabeth sidestepped, only to be catapulted into the Bastard Sheikh at the tuning shrill of a violin.

His body was as hot and hard as were his fingers. She could smell the heat of him underneath the silk of his clothes. It was not marred by the scent of a woman.

Blindly, she stepped back, but to no avail. She was penned in by the suffocating press of perfumed silk and the brush of solid flesh as women and men positioned themselves to dance.

The Bastard Sheikh captured her right hand and brought it up and away from her body so that her breasts lifted inside her corset and jutted forward. It was exciting; it was dangerous. *It was not what they had agreed upon.*

"You said you would not touch me."

"As your tutor, Mrs. Petre. Not as your dance partner."

"Why are you here?"

"Because I knew that you would be here."

"I would not have come if I had known you would be here."

A hard hand gripped her waist. "Now, why is that, I wonder?"

He was too close—Elizabeth couldn't catch her breath. She skittered away from the intense heat that radiated from his body. Her bustle squarely impacted another bustle, springing her back into place.

"You will create more gossip if you do not touch me than you will if you do, Mrs. Petre."

He was right.

Gritting her teeth, she reluctantly reached up, up, up—and

rested the fingers of her left hand on his shoulder. Her left breast almost lifted free of the corset.

The music started, a cry of violins and the crashing chords of a piano. Warm air tunneled around Elizabeth, and suddenly, she was a part of the gilded *ton,* of the soft swish of brightly colored silk and banners of black coattails, men stepping, women swirling.

She concentrated on the stark white of her glove, the shiny black satin that comprised his lapels, anything but the uncomfortable pounding of her heart and the painful hardening of her nipples underneath the slick friction of silk on silk.

She desperately searched for a safe topic of conversation. *She was not supposed to respond to a man who was not her husband.* ''I did not know that you danced.''

''You mean that you did not know I was accepted in polite society.''

The was no sense in lying. ''Yes.''

''There is a lot about me that you do not know, Mrs. Petre.''

''Do you sleep with the baroness?''

Elizabeth missed a step at the words that came unbidden from her mouth. His fingers dug into her waist; a whalebone jabbed into her rib.

''You seem to be current on the prevailing gossip. Why don't you tell me?''

She stared hard at a diamond stud in his shirt. It winked in the bright light from the overhead chandelier.

''How else could you know that my husband and I had accepted an invite to the ball?''

''My mother,'' he said lightly, twirling her. ''She and the baroness are bridge partners.''

''Does your mother know about our . . . lessons?'' she asked breathlessly.

''*Siba,* Mrs. Petre. I have told you I will not speak of what goes on between me and a lady behind closed doors.

''You do not need to wear a corset.'' His leg stepped between hers as he twirled her again; solid heat pressed into the jointure of her thighs. "You are suffering from lung collapse for nothing."

Elizabeth's fingers dug into his shoulder—no padding there, just hard muscle. "We are not in your home, Lord Safyre. Whether I wear a corset or do not wear a corset is of interest only to me and my abigail."

"What about your husband, Mrs. Petre? Doesn't he have anything to say about what underclothes you wear?"

The sharp retort did not make it past her lips.

Her husband had never seen her underclothes, let alone expressed an interest in them. Whereas she had no doubt that the Bastard Sheikh had seen a lot of women's underclothing.

"How do you come to dance so well if you do not often attend social events?"

"How do you come to waltz so well when your husband does not?"

"I did not say that he does not waltz," she retorted stiffly.

Edward waltzed; he merely did not waltz with her. He saved the social amenities for his constituents.

"Tell me about your two sons."

"I told you I do not discuss my children."

"But I am not your tutor now. I am a man who is making small talk to pass the time while we dance."

Elizabeth's head jerked back, her mouth opening to tell him that if dancing with her was such a boring chore, he need not bother.

It was a mistake.

The only thing that separated their faces was ten inches. *The span of his two hands.*

"My sons are both at Eton," she blurted out.

"Richard and Phillip, those are their names, aren't they?"

"Yes. But how—"

"I do open an occasional newspaper. What do they like—politics?"

A smile rimmed Elizabeth's mouth, remembering Phillip's

fight because Master Bernard, a "Whig," was supposedly an outrage to his "Tory" beliefs.

"No, my sons are not interested in politics. Richard is studying to be an engineer—he says technology is the way of the world and will help people far more than government. Phillip wants to be a sailor"—her smile widened—"preferably a pirate."

An answering smile softened the Bastard Sheikh's face. "Richard sounds like a clever boy."

Elizabeth searched his eyes for mockery but found none. A rush of maternal pride overcame her caution.

"He is. He takes his exams for Oxford next fall. It will be hard on Phillip when Richard leaves Eton though. They have always been very close—despite their age difference and perhaps because their personalities are so opposite. Richard is more quiet and studious; Phillip is a rascal. It would not surprise me if they raided the school kitchen for midnight snacks—they always do when they're home."

"You love your sons."

They were all that she had.

Elizabeth evaded his too-knowing gaze. *"Ahlan wa sahlan.* What does it mean?"

"Roughly translated, it means that it is nice to meet you. Do you love your husband?"

She stepped on his instep—hard. "If I did not, I would not have come to you."

"Does your husband love you?"

"That is none of your business."

"I intend upon making it my business."

Surely he could not mean—

"I think perhaps it would be best if we cancel our lessons, Lord Safyre. I will have your book returned to you."

"It's too late, *taalibba.*"

Alarm feathered Elizabeth's skin. "What do you mean?"

"We have an agreement."

Dawning comprehension flared in her eyes. "I blackmailed you, so you are going to blackmail me."

"If need be."

It was what she had feared that first morning; therefore, she should not feel so . . . *hurt.*

"Why?"

"You want to learn how to give a man pleasure . . . and I want to teach you."

Elizabeth felt incandescent with anger. "You want to humiliate me."

His lashes created hollow shadows underneath his eyes. "As I said before, you know very little about me. Do you remember the story of Dorérame in Chapter Two of *The Perfumed Garden?*"

"He was killed," she retorted grimly. Quite gruesomely, she recalled.

"The king who killed him freed a woman from his clutches."

"A married woman."

"Then the king took the woman and freed her from her husband."

"This is absurd." She did not want to think about a married woman being "freed" from her husband. "I do not see the purpose of this conversation."

"Simply this: A woman in Arabia has certain rights over her husband. Among them is her right to sexual union. She has the right to seek divorce if her husband will not satisfy her."

Mortification exploded inside Elizabeth's chest. Only women of loose morals were not satisfied in marriage.

How dare he—

"For your information, my husband *does* satisfy me," she hissed.

"There will be no more lies between us, *taalibba.* You had the courage to ask me to tutor you; now have the courage to face the truth."

"And just what do you think the truth is, Lord Safyre?"

"Look to your husband. When you see what he is and not what you want him to be, you will have your truth." Suddenly, he dropped her hand and released her waist. "The dance is over, Mrs. Petre. Let us promenade."

Elizabeth jerked her left hand down, away from his shoulder. "I will not be blackmailed."

"I think you will. You love your children but you know nothing about your husband . . . or yourself. I will expect to see you tomorrow morning."

She nodded at an acquaintance, her mind busily digesting and analyzing his words. "You know who my husband's mistress is."

"No."

"Then, why are you doing this?"

"Because I think you are a meritorious woman."

"I do not have a male member, Lord Safyre," she retorted frigidly.

The harsh line of his mouth eased. Mischief danced in his eyes. *He looked like the impish schoolboy he must have been when he was twelve, spurned by his mother.* "We will see."

"I will not be there tomorrow morning."

"You will be. Just as I will be waiting for you."

For the first time in her life, Elizabeth understood why Phillip used to stomp his foot in anger. She stared across the ballroom . . . directly into the eyes of her husband.

A man joined him—a fellow Cabinet member. Edward turned to the older man and walked toward the card room.

Edward had seen Elizabeth, she realized numbly, and dismissed her.

She met the Bastard Sheikh's turquoise stare. He had seen Edward's dismissal too.

The smell of gas from the chandeliers, of women's perfumes and men's macassar, rushed to her head. Elizabeth firmed her lips and straightened her spine. "I will not lie to you if you will not malign my husband."

"Very well."

"And if you insist upon the truth, you must be prepared to give it."

His thick, dark lashes created jagged shadows on his cheeks. "I am here to tutor you, *taalibba,* not the other way around."

"Perhaps we will both learn."

"Perhaps." He offered her his arm.

She tentatively rested her fingers on his sleeve. Underneath the silk, his muscles were whipcord taut.

Heat washed over her chest—it came from his gaze, staring at her breasts. She drew her shoulders back, corset creaking, too late realizing the motion pushed her breasts up and out.

He lifted his lashes; laughter shimmered in the depths of his eyes. "Rule number three. Starting tomorrow morning, you will not wear one single article of wool in my house. You may wear silk, muslin, velvet, brocade, whatever you wish so long as it is not wool."

"And you, Lord Safyre," she asked rashly, brashly, "what will you wear?"

"As little or as much as you wish me to wear."

Elizabeth's mouth went dry, imagining warm brown skin capped by red-hot desire.

She abruptly remembered who he was and who she was not.

A man like him did not lust after a woman whose hair was touched by silver and whose body had thickened from the birth of two children.

"We are engaged in a tutelage, Lord Safyre, not a burlesque."

Heads turned to see who dared laugh with such unadulterated enjoyment.

Elizabeth bit her lips to keep from joining in with his mirth.

It was pure nervousness, of course. There was nothing even remotely humorous about society witnessing the Bastard Sheikh's uninhibited laughter, especially when she held his arm and also came underneath their scrutiny. But no matter how hard she tried, she could not keep her lips in a straight line.

Emerald-green eyes caught Elizabeth's.

Her mother's eyes.

They were not amused.

Elizabeth jerked her hand away from the Bastard Sheikh's arm.

His laughter abruptly died.

Elizabeth turned, giving him the cut direct.

And felt as if something inside her died too.

Chapter Seven

Elizabeth Petre wore a heavy brown velvet gown and cold English civility. Last night she had smiled at him . . . and then she had cut him directly as if he were a gutter dog.

"*Sabah el kheer,* Mrs. Petre."

"Good morning, Lord Safyre."

A reluctant smile crooked his lips as she methodically removed her black leather gloves. He poured steaming coffee into a blue-veined porcelain demitasse cup, then added a splash of cold water before handing it to her.

Clearly, she was reluctant to accept it. It was equally clear that her rigid English manners decreed she not offend her host by *not* accepting it.

Ramiel studied her through the veil of his lashes, willing her to take the coffee.

The exultation that surged through him when she accepted the Turkish beverage was a throwback to his Mogul heritage.

He wanted her.

He wanted her to acknowledge her physical needs.

He wanted her to want *him,* the Bastard Sheikh, a man born in the West who had become a man in the East and *El Ibn,* a man who had tasted the bitter dregs of human sexuality and still yearned for more.

Turkish coffee was a good place to start.

Hot mist enveloped Elizabeth's face; she blew into the cup before taking one sip, two, three. . . . Sliding the cup and saucer onto the edge of his desk, she pulled a sheath of papers out of her reticule.

"Your choice of textbook is confusing, Lord Safyre." She raised her head and caught his gaze. Sexual awareness briefly glimmered in her clear hazel eyes, was quickly buried. "The sheikh gives very little instruction on how to give a man pleasure."

Ramiel refreshed his own cup of coffee, inhaling the thick, sweet aroma, a bittersweet reminder of what he had once taken for granted. " 'O you men,' " he murmured, " 'prepare her for enjoyment, and neglect nothing to attain that end. Explore her with the greater assiduity, and, entirely occupied with her, let nothing else engage your thoughts. . . . Then go to work, but, remember, not till your kisses and toying have taken effect.' "

He deliberately raised his cup to his lips and drank. The thick brew was hot and wet, exactly the way she would feel when he was lodged deep inside of her.

She watched him, outwardly calm and sedate. Her nipples stabbed at the soft velvet bodice.

Last night they had stabbed his chest when they danced.

Ramiel returned his cup to his saucer. "You do not think that men need preparation, Mrs. Petre?"

Indecision warred with propriety in her clear hazel eyes. The need to know won.

"Are you saying that men and women are excited by the same types of caresses?"

"We both have breasts, lips, thighs. . . ." He lightly rimmed the warm porcelain cup with his finger. "Yes, that is exactly what I am saying."

"Then you believe that a man becomes aroused when a woman kisses his cheeks . . ." A pulse beat erratically at the base of her throat. They had irrevocably crossed the boundaries of tutor and student—he knew it, she knew it. He had planted doubt in her mind about her husband—and himself. ". . . and nibbles at his nipples?''

Ramiel's groin tightened. "I *know* that a man becomes aroused by kisses and nibbles, Mrs. Petre.''

She evaded the heat in his gaze. "I can understand that it might be pleasant for a man when a woman titillates his lower body, but I do not see why a man would enjoy having his navel and his . . . his thighs kissed.''

Ramiel knew exactly how much pleasure a man derived from a woman kissing his navel and thighs. Erotic sensation pulsed in his groin, the memory of harem pleasures, a woman's tender explorations, legs spread, manhood glistening with need as he wound silky-soft hair around his hands and gave himself up to the primal ecstasy of a hot, wet mouth.

He wanted that—he wanted to experience again the innocent joy of sex . . . with Elizabeth Petre.

She must acknowledge her needs.

"Do you not enjoy having your navel and thighs kissed?'' he asked in a low, sultry voice.

"I—'' Ramiel's eyes dared Elizabeth to tell the truth. She did not let him down. "I don't know. I have never been kissed there.''

"Does it excite you, thinking of being kissed there?''

An ember exploded in the fireplace.

She tilted her chin, daring him to mock her. "Yes, it does. Does it excite *you,* thinking of being kissed there?''

Ramiel's breath rasped in his throat. "Yes, it excites me.''

"And does a man like a woman to bite his arms?''

The sizzling sexuality building between them abruptly dissipated.

"Bite *at* his arms, Mrs. Petre,'' he said dryly. "The sheikh is not suggesting that a man or a woman engage in cannibalism.''

"I beg your pardon. Does a man like a woman to bite *at* his arms?''

A cynical smile curled Ramiel's lips, other memories surfacing, more recent memories, *Western* memories. "Pain has its moments."

"When?"

"When is pain pleasurable for a man . . . or when is it pleasurable for a woman?"

Her English reserve firmly fell into place. "For a man."

"When a man brings a woman to her peak—"

"Excuse me. I would like to take notes. May I borrow your pen again, please?"

Elizabeth was running.

From him. From herself.

She knew how to be a mother, but she was terrified of being a woman.

Edward Petre's neglect of his wife at the ball the previous night, coupled with his dismissal, had told Ramiel everything he needed to know about the sixteen-year marriage. The look on Elizabeth's face had told its own story.

Edward did not care—Elizabeth did.

He wondered how long she had lain awake when she went home, alone, waiting for her husband.

He wondered what her reaction would be when she discovered her husband's secret.

Ela'na. Damn. Her entire household knew about Edward Petre's sexual predilections. How could she be so naive?

Ramiel retrieved his pen from inside the top drawer. She stared at the gold instrument.

Or perhaps she stared at his fingers, remembering the span of his hands and wondering how he would fit inside her.

Would she accept him easily or would he stretch her to the point of pain? Would he give her an orgasm or would he leave her aching with frustration as Edward Petre had no doubt left her?

Squaring her shoulders, Elizabeth plucked the pen out from between his fingers. "Thank you."

How long had it been since she had taken a man inside her?

Ramiel scooted the brass inkwell across his desk.

Elizabeth dipped the steel nib into ink and poised the pen

over her paper, eyes trained on the white vellum. "You were saying?"

"Have you ever had a climax, Mrs. Petre?"

Her head snapped up.

"No lies, no evasions," Ramiel warned gravely. "That was our agreement."

Her expression of shocked outrage turned to frigid disdain. "Yes, Lord Safyre, I have experienced a climax."

Jealousy coiled inside his stomach like a cobra preparing to strike.

"Then you are aware that just before climax the ability to distinguish between pleasure and pain diminishes. When a woman reaches her peak, she sometimes scratches or bites her lover. The pain can be the impetus he needs to reach his own climax."

The steel nib busily scratched its way across her paper.

He watched the play of light and shadow on her hair, dark wine-red and golden fire. And pictured her head solemnly bent to take her husband into her mouth.

Ramiel did not know what disturbed him the most, the fact that at the end of their lessons she would use his knowledge to please another man or the fact that using it to please her husband would destroy her.

"Now I will tell you what a woman sometimes needs to reach her peak."

The scribbling stopped.

"I have known women who like their nipples to be bitten or pinched." His description was bluntly sexual. "Other women enjoy it when I throw their legs over my shoulders and ram them so hard and deep that I can feel their womb contract around me."

She gripped the pen in a stranglehold and stared at what she had written down. "What do you prefer?"

He ached for her ignorance . . . and for her needs that she so valiantly tried to hide.

"Whatever the woman prefers."

Whatever you prefer, Elizabeth Petre.

But it was so painfully clear that she did not know what she wanted, just that she wanted.

Her voice was low. "Do you really like a woman to nibble on your nipples?"

A bolt of heat shot through Ramiel's testicles. "Yes, Mrs. Petre."

Body tensed, he waited for her next question.

Her breasts underneath the brown velvet dress rose and fell in time to her breathing. She raised her head. The pupils in her eyes were dilated with arousal.

"Do you . . . do *you* derive pleasure from nibbling on a woman's nipples?"

"Kissing. Licking. Suckling. Nibbling," he said harshly. "Yes, I take pleasure in a woman's breasts."

"What about your . . . member? Yesterday you said that when a woman wraps her fingers around a man she holds his life in her hand. How do you like to be . . . held?"

A hiss of breath whistled in the air. Ramiel vaguely identified it as his.

"I like a woman to pump and squeeze my manhood until the crown is no longer capped by the foreskin."

Elizabeth did not move, not even a flicker of an eyelash.

Ramiel could sense the blood rushing through her veins underneath her alabaster skin, a statue waiting to be sexually awakened.

"Muslim men are circumcised."

Silently, viciously, he cursed himself. Why had he said that? "The Arab women must have found you fascinating."

Her appreciative response was not what he expected.

Warmth brushed Ramiel's cheekbones, his first blush in twenty-five years. "Yes."

The women had found him fascinating but foreign. A concubine would not mate with a man like him, an infidel, when their tenure in the harem ended, not even at the price of freedom.

"Have you ever encountered a woman who was not pleased by you, Lord Safyre?"

Arab. Bastard. Animal. In bed, out of bed, the names did not stop.

"If you are asking if I have ever failed to give a woman an orgasm," he said roughly, "the answer is no."

Paper crackled—the crumpling of her notes. *"Never?"*

He raised an eyebrow. "I do not claim to be a martyr, Mrs. Petre. There have been times when I climaxed before a woman. But there are other ways of providing release. Fingers. Hands. Lips. Toes. Almost any part of a man's body can be used to satisfy a woman."

He had shocked her. Again. *"Toes?"*

"Toes."

Disbelief flitted across her face. It was followed by intrigue, then that, too, was hidden away.

She glanced down at her lap and smoothed out the paper that she had crinkled, the gold pen thick and shiny between her fingers. "Perhaps you carouse with women of ill repute who respond differently than do respectable women."

Elizabeth so obviously repeated what she had been raised to believe as opposed to what she herself knew to be true that he wanted to shake her.

"Do you honestly believe that respectable women and women of ill repute are anatomically different?"

She wanted to lie; he could feel it. Just as he could feel the passion in her that she so desperately strove to hide, bubbling and chuckling like an oasis in arid desert land.

Several seconds passed before she had smoothed the sheath of papers to her satisfaction. "No, of course not."

"Then why do you think that respectable women are incapable of sexual pleasure?"

"Perhaps it is the wanting, or the acknowledgment of her baser nature, that makes a woman not respectable. She may outwardly appear to be virtuous, but if she craves sexual pleasure, surely that makes her no better than a . . . a woman of the streets."

Ramiel leaned forward in his chair, wood creaking, suddenly

wanting to stop the words that he knew were coming. "Mrs. Petre—"

"Lord Safyre . . . *you*, as a man . . ." She raised her head, hazel eyes filled with self-loathing. "Are you not disgusted with a woman who wishes to rut like the beasts in the field?"

He had wanted to see what was underneath her sedate exterior. Now he wanted to give her back her composure.

He could do it too.

He could lie. He could tell her *yes*, a woman's base sexual needs revolted a man like him.

He could tell her that respectable Arab women were trained to give a man pleasure, not seek their own, and that passion, while praised in a concubine, was condemned in a wife.

He could send her home and spare her the decision that he would ultimately force her to make and hope that she never learn the truth about her husband.

Too late . . .

"No, Mrs. Petre, I am not disgusted by a woman's sexual needs."

"But you are part Arab."

There was no reason for the surge of raw rage that coursed through Ramiel's veins. It had not bothered him when Inchcape called him a bastard. Elizabeth's inference that he was half Arab and therefore not capable of the same sentiments as an Englishman burned like acid.

"I am a man, Mrs. Petre. Whether I am called a bastard by an Englishman or an infidel by an Arab, I am still *a man*."

Ramiel was not prepared for the dawning comprehension in her eyes.

"If I thought differently, Lord Safyre, I would not have sought you out for instruction," she declared firmly. "I offer you my sincere apologies if I offended you. I assure you it was not my intention."

His nostrils flared.

He was not used to apologies, nor would he tolerate pity. "Then what did you mean, Mrs. Petre?"

"I merely meant that the English people do not accept a

woman's sexual nature. You do not find such needs repulsive because of your Arabic upbringing, whereas if you did not have your unique background, perhaps you would feel different. But perhaps it is only Englishwomen who are raised with these notions. My husband has a mistress, so obviously he is not repulsed by feminine sexuality. *I do not know,* Lord Safyre. I do not know what anything means anymore.''

The honesty in Elizabeth's eyes was too stark. Ramiel stared at the proud tilt of her chin, at the blazing highlights in her auburn hair.

Red.

Arabs used the color to represent many things. Rage. Desire. Blood.

Here, in this room, it was simply the color of an Englishwoman's hair. A woman who felt rage and desire. And perhaps, in the end, who would see blood.

''If a man is repulsed by a woman's sexuality, *taalibba,* then he is not a man.''

''Perhaps not when she is young—''

''Mrs. Petre, you are a woman in her prime.''

''I have two children, Lord Safyre. I assure you my days of prime are long gone.''

She returned his perusal as if unaware that he had openly gazed down her dress last night and savored every glimpse of her smooth, round white skin. As if she could not imagine a man ever trembling with passion for her.

''You have a womanly figure, not the flat breasts and shapeless hips of a young girl.''

Elizabeth visibly bristled, her vanity pricked. ''We are not here to discuss my person, Lord Safyre.''

''Mrs. Petre, there are certain things that a man can do with a full-breasted woman that he cannot do with a less generously endowed one,'' Ramiel explained softly, gaze dropping to her chest in seductive speculation. ''Be proud of your body.''

''And just what sort of things can a man do with a womanly figure, Lord Safyre?'' she asked caustically. ''Use her breasts as twin buoys?''

Ramiel laughed.

Elizabeth Petre would never cease to surprise him.

He had associated sex with pain; he had associated it with death. He had never associated it with laughter.

"If you are quite finished, perhaps we can continue with our lesson. How does a woman entice a man?" she inquired frigidly. "And please do not say by baring her breasts. I find it hard to believe that half the ladies who comprise society flash their bodies to you."

Ramiel bit back another chuckle. "You surprise me, Mrs. Petre. I was not aware that you knew such language."

"You would be surprised at some of the words that I know, Lord Safyre. A lady may not say them, but it is difficult not to hear them when she works with the poor."

"Here, in my home, you may say what you will—I guarantee you I have heard it before—and from a very, very grand lady."

The countess, Ramiel's mother, would laugh to hear him describe her as such. Elizabeth Petre was not convinced either.

Ramiel relented. "A woman who enjoys her body is enticing, Mrs. Petre. The way she dresses, the way she walks, the way she talks—all of these things tell a man what he needs to know."

"And that is?"

His voice deepened. "That she wants him."

Her expression froze. "I am not flirting with you, Lord Safyre."

The urge to laugh died a quick, irrevocable death. "I know."

"You are my tutor."

"In this room, yes."

"Before you agreed to tutor me, did you know that my husband had a mistress?"

Ramiel stiffened. She could not know . . . *could she?* "I do not run in the same circles as does your husband."

"But you *had* heard rumors?"

"There are always rumors," he rejoined cryptically. "Else you would not be here."

Elizabeth glanced down at the small silver watch pinned to her dress.

"Thank you for being so candid." She laid the gold pen on top of his desk beside her unfinished coffee. "It has been an education."

An education that had only started.

"Chapter Six, Mrs. Petre. You will find it of particular interest."

Elizabeth had her curiosity fully in check. She stuffed her notes inside her reticule.

"Rule number four."

She did not raise her head. "There are only so many articles of clothing I can shed, Lord Safyre. It is February. Furthermore, gowns are designed for bustles."

He studied her intently. "How do you know what I was going to say?"

Clutching her gloves, she stood up. "You do seem to be obsessed with a woman's clothing, or lack of, I should say."

One day—hopefully soon—they would conduct their lessons without clothes.

"Very well. When you retire for bed, lay on your stomach and practice rotating your pelvis against the mattress."

Her breath audibly caught in her throat.

"Love is hard work." He stared at the velvet draping her gently rounded stomach, imagining her fleece, red like her hair, imagining his manhood tunneling deep inside her. "You must condition your body."

She turned without comment. And barely sidestepped the chair.

"Mrs. Petre."

Elizabeth paused, hand reaching for the knob on the library door. Seconds passed, she silently struggling, he patiently waiting.

How far would the Bastard Sheikh go? her stiffened spine shouted. How far could a respectable woman let him go and still remain respectable?

The squaring of her shoulders told him her answer.

Further than this, they said.

"Ma'a e-salemma, Lord Safyre."

Hot blood filled Ramiel's manhood. *"Ma'a e-salemma, taa-libba."*

Chapter Eight

Kissing. Licking. Suckling. Nibbling.

The winding hallway, dimly lit and in need of a coat of paint, echoed with the sharp click of Elizabeth's heels.

. . . There are other ways of providing release. Fingers. Hands. Lips. Toes. Almost any part of a man's body can be used to satisfy a woman.

She skidded around a sharp turn in the hallway, instinctively slapped her hand against the wall to retain her balance.

I am a man, Mrs. Petre. Whether I am called a bastard by an Englishman or an infidel by an Arab, I am still a man.

Elizabeth leaned into the peeling paint, riding a wave of remembered pain.

His pain.

The pain of a bastard sheikh.

A cockroach scurried across the back of her gray kid glove. Biting back a scream, she snatched her hand away from the wall and jerked it back and forth, back and forth, even though the cockroach was long gone.

It suddenly dawned on her that this was not the way back to the meeting room.

A door stood ajar at the end of the corridor.

Elizabeth froze.

Something watched her . . . and it wasn't an insect.

"Hello!" The hollow echo of her voice ricocheted off the dingy gray walls. "Are you there?"

There. There. There raced up and down the hallway.

Determinedly, she stepped forward.

The door slammed back against the wall.

There was no stopping the scream that escaped Elizabeth's mouth.

"What ye be doin' here, missy?" A tall, balding man with a bulbous red nose and matching eyes stood in the doorway. "Ain't no fancy men in this buildin'."

Irritation rippled through her fear. First the Arab butler had mistaken her for a woman of the night, and now this man.

She drew her shoulders back. "I am Mrs. Elizabeth Petre. The Women's Auxiliary meet here; I gave a speech and then I needed to . . ." The man did not need to know that she had left the meeting to use the water closet, and having used it, had gotten lost in the massive building on her return trip because she could not stop thinking about a man she had no business thinking about. "I seem to have taken a wrong turn. Would you be so good as to direct me to the meeting room?"

"Meetin's all done. Ain't no one here 'cept you an' me."

"But—"

"An' I knows what ye be after. What th' likes o' all o' ye hussies be after."

Elizabeth realized that the man was stark, raving drunk.

"There are people waiting for me, sir. If you would be so good as to direct me—"

Staggering, the tall, reed-thin man stepped forward. "I be th' custodian o' this place. Ain't no one waitin' fer ye. Tol' ye there be no one here save fer ye an' me. If ye're lookin' fer a place t' bring yer mutton mongers think agin, missy, cause I got a shotgun an' I ain't afraid o' killin' th' likes o' ye."

Elizabeth's heart skipped a beat, galloped to catch up. She wound the strings of her reticule around her fingers.

It contained paper, a pencil, a handkerchief, a coin purse, a comb, her house key and a small mirror—nothing that would aid in her defense.

Panic was not a solution either. She took a deep breath to still the pounding of her heart.

"I see." Her hands inside the leather gloves were cold and clammy. "Thank you for your trouble. I will find my own way back. Please accept my apologies if I have inconvenienced you. Good evening."

Slowly, slowly, she backed up, expecting at any moment for him to reach behind him for his shotgun.

He swayed back and forth, watching her retreat, glaring bloodshot daggers.

When Elizabeth rounded the bend in the corridor, she swirled around and did not look back. Her heart hammered in time to her footsteps as she ran what seemed like miles through the winding hallways in search of the meeting room.

She was not alone.

Common sense told her that this was a respectable building filled with business offices rented by businessmen who had no doubt long gone home for their supper.

Logic failed.

She could sense hidden eyes, hostile eyes, and knew that behind one of those doors lining the meandering hallway or around that bend, *somewhere,* someone was watching her.

Someone, perhaps, who *did* have a shotgun. *Or a knife.*

The building directly adjoined the Thames. It would be a simple matter to kill her, rob her, and drop her body into the icy, murky waters.

She would be dead and she would never know how a man's toes could be used to satisfy a woman.

Elizabeth gasped in relief when she spied the easel holding the sign posting the designated room and hours of the Women's Auxiliary meeting.

The double doors were closed . . . and locked.

Because she took so long to first find the lavatory and then to find her way back, the women must have thought that Elizabeth had gone home . . . and so they, too, had gone home.

As the custodian had known they had.

She twirled around, cloak billowing behind her; underneath it her horsehair-stuffed bustle swung back and forth like a pendulum. The entrance was just around the corner—

She wrenched open the water-stained front door. And gasped.

The fog was a wall of swirling yellow.

Elizabeth took a disbelieving step forward—and tottered on the edge of a cobbled step.

"Will!" Please, God, let her coachman be nearby. "Will, can you hear me?"

It was like shouting into a wet blanket.

Cautiously, she maneuvered the three steps that comprised the stoop. "Will! Answer me!"

She turned her head to the left, to the right, jerked it back to the left. Was that a horse whickering?

Slowly, she slid her feet along the sidewalk. "Will! Is that you?"

"Aye, Mrs. Petre, it be me."

The coachman's voice was so close, it could have come from directly in front of her. Yet it was so muffled by the fog, it could also have come from across the street.

"Where are you?"

A hand reached out and latched on to her right arm. "Here, ma'am."

Elizabeth's heart leapt into her throat.

Full comprehension of just how vulnerable she had been in that building, with Will incapacitated by the fog, coursed through her. She had not felt this degree of fear walking the streets before dawn and blackmailing her way into the Bastard Sheikh's home.

"Will." She blindly grabbed the coachman's gnarled hand; it was reassuringly warm and solid through her kid gloves. "You should have come for me when the fog started getting heavy."

"It came all of a sudden like. One minute it just be fog—the next it be like this. Can't see my hand in front of my face."

Yes, London fog happened like that sometimes. More often, the peculiar phenomenon occurred in November, sometimes in December or January. Elizabeth had never seen a night like this in February.

She peered in front of her, where she knew the coachman stood. He remained hidden from her view.

Yellow fog had swallowed London and everything in it.

Elizabeth struggled to control her fear. "Have Tommie walk the horses."

"Can't do that, ma'am. Tommie, he came down sick all sudden like while ye was in the meetin'. Sent him home."

The sensible thing would be to have Will secure the horses and the two of them wait out the fog in relative comfort inside the building where the Women's Auxiliary meeting had been held.

It was suicide to travel with no groom to act as guide for the fog-blinded coachman and horses. Men and women had been known to lose their way on nights like this and drop into the Thames. Yet she could not go back inside that building. Even on the off chance that she could find it.

The dense yellow mist stank of river water and the garbage that spewed into it. Elizabeth's stomach roiled with apprehension. She could not drive a coach; therefore, "I will walk the horses."

Will's snort clearly penetrated the fog. "You, ma'am!"

"Would you rather I drove the carriage?" she rejoined sharply.

"Mayhaps we can go back into that building where the meetin' was."

Elizabeth shivered, remembering the feel of those eyes. "There is only the custodian there, and he threatened to shoot me if I did not leave."

" 'Ere now! Just let me get my gun and we'll see who'll be shootin' who!"

Her fingers tightened around his hand. "I will take my chances with the river, Will."

"Aye, but if ye take a dip, the horses an' carriage will too."

A choked laugh escaped Elizabeth's throat. "You're not concerned about your own life, Will?" *Or hers?* she wanted to ask.

"I swim like a fish. Good enough to save the both of us; couldn't do nothin' 'bout the horses though."

Elizabeth refrained from pointing out that the coachman could not save her from drowning if he could not find her. Aside from that, a woman's clothing was not designed for water sports—she would sink straight down. Nor could he save himself if he could not see the riverbank.

She imagined icy water and foul sewage clogging her nose, filling her lungs. She remembered the cockroach and the custodian and the watching, waiting eyes.

"I am not going back into that building."

"Aye."

Warm fingers patted the backs of hers. Elizabeth reluctantly let go of Will. Immediately, he guided her right hand to the horse's head.

It started at her touch, as if it was as unused to humans as Elizabeth was to animals. Will curved her fingers around hard leather.

"Stand to the side of old Bess here, ma'am, else she'll walk over you. Keep close to the walkway—when it ends, it means a thoroughfare; we can count the number of streets and figure out wheres to make our turns."

The comforting heat of Will's body slipped away into total obscurity. "Keep yer left hand out, ma'am—it'll keep ye from knockin' face into a lamp pole and fallin' on yer fanny."

Elizabeth should rebuke the coachman for his impertinence. Perhaps a week earlier she would have.

She squeezed her eyes shut. *A week earlier she would not have asked a man if he was disgusted with a woman who wished to rut like the beasts in a field.*

The impact of wood and metal shuddered into life as Will

climbed up the side of the coach. The horse beside her whick-
ered softly, stepped to the side. A hoof plopped down dangerously close to Elizabeth's foot.

Her eyes snapped open. "Remember your place, old Bess,
and I will endeavor to do the same," she whispered to the
nervous horse.

Her arm was jerked up into the air. The harness jingled
wildly while Elizabeth fought to bring the horse's head down.

"Ready, Mrs. Petre?"

She inhaled sulfuric coal smoke, the sustenance of yellow
London fog; it burned all the way down. "Ready, Will."

A clicking sound shot over her head; the horse instantly
sprang to life, dragging Elizabeth with it.

It was like walking inside a foul-smelling, bitter-tasting
cloud. Her only link with reality was the bite of a leather
harness, the animal heat of the horse's body, the cold, damp
fog that swirled about her like a living entity, and her own
voice, calling out what she hoped were intersecting streets and
not dead-end alleys.

Elizabeth was too busy protecting her feet and her head to
savor the full complement of terror the situation warranted.
After being stepped on twice and running headfirst into a lamppost, she realized that the farther away they got from the river,
the less dense the fog became.

"Who—aa!"

She came to an abrupt halt, as if she and the horse were one.
A yellow ball of fire glowed on the side of the coach—the
lantern, now visible. Another yellow ball hovered over her
head—a gas lamppost.

"Ye can git in the coach, Mrs. Petre. Me an' old Bess an'
Gertrude here can make it on our own now."

Exhilaration anesthetized the sharp throb radiating from her
instep and the bump on her forehead. *She had done it, she who
had never done anything more hazardous than give speeches
and take tea and issue sympathy; she had led them safely out
of danger.* "Thank you, Will."

Once inside the coach, the aftermath of terror washed over

her. She clamped her mouth shut to hold back a tide of nausea. And experienced a totally ludicrous desire to tell the coachman to take her to the Bastard Sheikh and a home where she could say whatever she wished.

The coach had no sooner pulled up in front of the Petre town house than the carriage door flew open. Beadles beamed up into Elizabeth's startled face. "Welcome home, madam! Welcome home!"

Elizabeth was taken aback. The butler seemed genuinely glad to see her. She allowed him to assist her down. "Thank you, Beadles."

"Take care of that head, Mrs. Petre." The gruff voice drifting down from the coach was sympathetic. "It be a nasty bump you got there, I'm thinkin'. Could hear the crack of yer skull agin that pole all the way up here in the box."

Hot color flooded Elizabeth's face. She had not thought the coachman had noticed her encounter with the lamppost. "Thank you, Will. I'm sure it is nothing."

Beadles followed her up the steps. "Mr. Petre is in the drawing room, madam. He rang up the constable. He was afraid something had befallen you."

Elizabeth reached beneath her bonnet and gently probed the skin under her hair—there was indeed a bump there. It was the size of a pigeon's egg. "Who was afraid that something had befallen me, Beadles—my husband or the constable?"

Beadles pulled his shoulders back. "Mr. Petre, madam. Shall I ring up the doctor?"

Elizabeth surprised herself with her response. "What do you think, Beadles?"

The butler's stiff shoulders relaxed into a semblance of normalcy. "I should go with an ice pack, madam."

"Then I will do so."

"Elizabeth, you're late." Edward stood inside the drawing room doorway; his hair gleamed like black oil against the pallor of his skin. "You should have been home hours ago. You have caused me a great deal of worry."

She felt a rush of gratitude at his concern. It was followed by a vague sense of guilt.

He had come home to eat with her during the dinner break at Parliament . . . and she had not been there.

"I am sorry, Edward. The meeting ran over and then we got trapped in the fog."

Edward glanced at Beadles, who stood politely at attention beside Elizabeth. "Beadles, tell Emma to prepare a bath for Mrs. Petre. She will be up directly."

Elizabeth stared at Edward in astonishment. He had not been this solicitous of her welfare since . . . she could not remember when.

"Thank you, Edward, but there is no need to send Beadles." She stank of fog, and her head and foot throbbed. "I am going upstairs now."

"Take Mrs. Petre's things, Beadles, then run along and do as you are told."

The butler bowed and silently did as bid. Elizabeth reluctantly gave up her reticule, then peeled off her gloves and laid them in his waiting hand, freckles genteelly covered with white gloves. Sighing, she removed her bonnet; that, too, was taken from her. Bowing again, Beadles pivoted toward the stairs.

Edward offered Elizabeth his arm. "The constable is here. Let us put his mind to rest that you are unharmed."

She wanted a hot bath, a cold compress, and ten hours of sleep. She did not want to play hostess. Furthermore, Edward's gallantry after his recent inattentiveness was—disconcerting. By accepting it, she felt slightly traitorous, as if she wronged her husband . . . or the Bastard Sheikh.

"Why did you telephone the constable, Edward?"

"I told you. You were late. I was worried."

"There was no need to bother the constable."

"You are not the type of woman who incommodes her husband because of a little fog, Elizabeth. Naturally, I assumed the worst. Come inside now and have a cup of tea while Emma runs your bath."

Incommode her husband? Because of a "little" fog?

The fog could hardly be called "little," and why would she incommode Edward's dinner, especially since she had not known he was going to take it with her?

Elizabeth placed her fingertips on the sleeve of his black dinner jacket. The muscles underneath it were firm as opposed to corded, relaxed rather than taut.

A big man with gray muttonchops rose from the floral-patterned divan in the drawing room. "Mrs. Petre. I'm so glad to see you safe and sound."

Elizabeth ignored the pain in her head and plastered a smile onto her face. She held out her hand. It trembled ever so slightly. "Constable Stone. As I was telling my husband, there was no need for anyone to worry. Everyone is late on a night like this."

The constable's palm was hot and sweaty; she pulled her fingers back as quickly as good manners allowed. "Please, sit down."

He kept standing until she sat down across from him. "Your husband says you have an important engagement tonight, so I will not take up your time. His concern is understandable."

The Hansons' dinner party.

Edward had been concerned . . . because she had been late for a dinner party. He had not ordered her bath out of courtesy but out of expeditiousness.

The building custodian had mistaken her for a prostitute and threatened to shoot her. She could have been raped, robbed, or killed, but her husband telephoned the constable *because she had upset his plans.*

"I apologize for the inconvenience you have been put to, Constable Stone." Her voice was disembodied, as if it did not belong to her. "The fog descended while I was in the Women's Auxiliary meeting. When the meeting ended, Will, our coachman, and I made it home as quickly as possible. No doubt my inexperience delayed us further."

"How so?"

The hair on the back of her neck prickled. Constable Stone

acted as if she were guilty of a crime far worse than missing a dinner.

"I walked the horses so that we would not find our way into the Thames."

The constable was surprised.

Edward frowned. "That is why we have a groom."

"Tommie was not there. He took ill while waiting for me, so Will sent him home."

"Where was this meeting, Mrs. Petre?"

Elizabeth told the burly constable.

He stared at her in disapproval. "Are you telling me you were in that district with only a coachman in attendance?"

"I have repeatedly told Elizabeth to hire herself a secretary. Then she would have a companion so that she need not attend these events on her own." Edward picked up his cup of tea and smiled deprecatingly at the constable. "But you know how women are. They never think about their safety until it is too late."

Elizabeth felt a coldness seeping into her body that had nothing whatsoever to do with the winter fog she had trudged through.

Edward had had no reason to summon the constable unless he possessed foreknowledge of the drunken custodian. A person who would perhaps do damage to her knowing full well that she was not a prostitute . . .

She abruptly stood up. "If you will excuse me, Constable Stone, Edward, I would like to retire now. It has been an exhausting evening."

Edward and the constable simultaneously stood up. It was the constable who spoke. "Of course, Mrs. Petre. I will see myself out."

The closure of the drawing room door was a soft click. Edward and Elizabeth stared at each other over the tea cart.

She mentally braced herself. "It is too late to go to the dinner party, Edward."

"Andrew expects us to be there in his stead, Elizabeth. We will go."

"No, Edward, I will not go." Dull pain radiated from her temple. It throbbed in time to her heartbeat. "Not tonight."

"Very well," he surprised her by saying. "The important thing is that you are safe. You must have endured quite an ordeal."

"Yes." Why could she not bring herself to tell him about the custodian and his threat to kill her? "I hit my head on a lamppost."

"Shall I ring up the doctor?"

"No, thank you, Edward; you have done quite enough."

"Good night, Elizabeth. Take care of your head."

Elizabeth bit her lip. She was cold, she hurt, she was still frightened, *and she did not know why.* The incident with the custodian had been pure mischance. She was safe in the Petre household. "Are you leaving?"

"I am expected at the Hansons."

And she had let him down.

"Will you be back"—no, she could not ask that, if he would spend the night with his mistress after the parliamentary meeting ended or if he was coming back home—"in time for the House session?"

"It will not matter if I am a few minutes late. You had best hurry. Your bath will get cold."

Perversely, Elizabeth wanted to go with Edward.

He turned and walked to the twin doors. Bowing, he held one open for her. "Good night, Elizabeth."

Elizabeth tried to remember the feel of his body on top of her, inside her. Had he been as cold and controlled then as he was now?

Had Edward changed . . . or had she?

"Good night, Edward."

Emma, in her calm, methodical fashion, quickly saw to it that Elizabeth had her bath and was tucked into bed with an ice pack on her head. Elizabeth was too exhausted to think. Besides, her thoughts were utter nonsense, the product of cold, pain, and fatigue.

But the thoughts refused to stop.

I have repeatedly told Elizabeth to hire herself a secretary. Then she would have a companion so that she need not attend these events on her own.

A woman in Arabia has certain rights over her husband. Among them is her right to sexual union.

You are not the type of woman who incommodes her husband because of a little fog, Elizabeth.

Look to your husband. When you see what he is and not what you want him to be, you will have your truth.

What truth did the Bastard Sheikh refer to?

Had he lied? Did he know who Edward's mistress was and thought that Elizabeth did not stand a chance of winning the attentions of her husband, regardless of her erotic tutelage?

Mrs. Petre, there are certain things that a man can do with a full-breasted woman that he cannot do with a less generously endowed one.

Elizabeth cupped her breasts through her cotton nightgown. They spilled over her fingers—full, yes, but still firm.

What type of figure did Edward's mistress have?

You love your children but you know nothing about your husband . . . or yourself.

Her nipples tightened underneath her fingers. She jerked her hands away.

No doubt Edward's mistress was flat-chested with slender hips. Everything that Elizabeth was not.

The ice pack had slipped and succeeded in numbing her ear while her head steadily throbbed. Rolling over, she turned up the flame in the gas lamp beside her bed.

Chapter Six.

She had yet to read her lesson in *The Perfumed Garden.*

The book was where she had hid it, buried in her desk drawer. Pulling out paper and pen, she proceeded to take notes as she read "Concerning Everything That Is Favorable to the Act of Coition."

The ache in her head and the residual trembling of her hands traveled lower and settled between her thighs until she stopped writing altogether and merely read.

*The ways of doing it to women are numerous and variable.
And now is the time to make known to you the different positions
which are usual.*

Dear Lord, *she had never dreamed . . .* that there could be
such variety in an act that all of her life had been referred to
as "a woman's duty to her husband."

It listed everything, every possible position that a man and
a woman could engage coitus in. *Lebeuss el djoureb,* a man
sitting between a woman's outstretched legs and rubbing his
member against her vulva until she grew moist from the alter-
nate friction and shallow probes; *el kebachi,* a woman kneeling
on her hands and knees like the beasts in the fields; *dok el arz,*
belly pressed to belly, mouth glued to mouth.

Lying on the back, the stomach, the sides, sitting, *standing,*
it was all there in detailed format, like a child's workbook.
Positions, the mutual movements of a man and a woman once
penetration was engaged . . .

*He who seeks the pleasure a woman can give must satisfy
her amorous desire for hot caresses, as described. He will see
her swooning with lust, her vulva will get moist, her womb will
stretch forward, and the two sperms will come together.*

Feeling as if she were drugged, Elizabeth dragged her gaze
up from the closing paragraph and stared at the pen clutched
between her fingers, unwittingly comparing it to the sheikh's
description of a man's member, *"big as a virgin's arm . . .
with a round head . . . Measuring in length a span and a half."*

The practical brass pen wasn't nearly as thick as was the
Bastard Sheikh's precious gold pen. For a heart-stopping
moment she thought of how it might be used to ease moist
need and empty flesh.

Revolted, she tossed the brass pen away from her. It slammed
into the back of the secretary and bounced onto the blue carpet.

Sleep.

She had been through an ordeal. Sleep would regain her
some much-needed control.

She turned off the gas lamp and burrowed underneath the

bedcovers against the ice pack. But the ice had melted and the rhythmical throbbing inside her body persisted.

Rolling onto her stomach, she experimentally rotated her hips.

The dull pulsations between her legs sharpened, deepened.

She could have died tonight . . .

Why had not Edward stayed home with her, comforted her? Why did he go to his mistress when she ached for him to be with her?

If a man is repulsed by a woman's sexuality, taalibba, *then he is not a man.*

Her hips independently pushed and rubbed against the mattress.

Hez, taalibba.

The mattress became a man who counteracted the swaying of her hips by grinding up inside her body until her vulva dripped with moisture and her womb stretched forward.

Love is hard work.

Elizabeth rubbed faster, harder, wanting, needing . . . her nipples to be suckled and bitten. A man to throw her legs over his shoulders, thrusting inside her so deeply that her womb contracted around his manhood.

The soft internal explosion brought tears to her eyes. She buried her face into her pillow.

How would she be able to face the Bastard Sheikh, knowing what she now knew?

Chapter Nine

Elizabeth stared at the dark gleam of mahogany wood, at the hot steam that rose from the demitasse cup with its delicate blue veining, at anything but those knowing turquoise eyes.

"You practiced rubbing your pelvis against the mattress."

It was not a question.

She turned up her cup and gulped bittersweet Turkish coffee. The scalding liquid traveling down her throat did nothing to counteract the scorching heat infusing her face. She placed the empty cup on the saucer and with careful precision set it on top of the massive desk. Resolutely, she raised her head and met his gaze. "I did."

The Bastard Sheikh's eyes glinted in the gas lamp. "The pleasure is far greater when a woman is with a man."

She refused to give in to her shame. "How do you know that, Lord Safyre?"

"Because the pleasure is greater when a man is with a woman."

"Do men practice rotating their hips on a mattress, then?" she asked politely.

"No, *taalibba*. Men practice with their hands."

The breath caught in her throat. Surely he could not mean what she thought he meant. Surely a man like him would have no need to—

"Do *you?*"

The question popped out before she could stop it.

He did not pretend to misunderstand her. "Yes."

"*Why?*"

"Loneliness. Need. We all want to be touched, even if it is by our own hand."

"But you can have any woman you want, anytime you want her. You do not have to rely upon—" Her jaws snapped together.

"Remember what I said, *taalibba,*" he murmured softly. "Here, in my home, you may say what you will."

Elizabeth had said quite enough. Yet . . . Instead of squirming with embarrassment, she felt strangely unburdened. This man knew more about her than any other person . . . and he did not condemn her for her needs. Perhaps, even, he shared her needs, wanting to touch, to be touched. . . .

Impossible. A woman like her had nothing in common with a man like him. She wanted, she studied. He wanted, he took.

Elizabeth jumped onto the most innocuous subject matter contained in the sixth chapter. "The sheikh places a great deal of importance on kissing."

"*Ferame.*"

"I beg your pardon?"

"The sheikh places a great deal of importance on a specific kind of kiss, Mrs. Petre. The kiss that is intended to arouse a man or a woman is called *ferame.*"

The kiss that involved the use of tongue and teeth.

"I find it hard to believe that a man would nibble on a woman's tongue, Lord Safyre," she said repressively.

But she could imagine it. . . .

Jagged shadows spiked his cheeks. "A woman's tongue is like a nipple, to be nibbled and suckled. Her mouth is like a vulva, to be licked and probed. Have you ever had a man's tongue in your mouth?"

Lightning sensation jolted up between Elizabeth's thighs. She pictured his dark face bending to hers, kissing and licking and probing her mouth with his tongue. Immediately, the image was replaced with his dark face poised between her legs, kissing and licking and probing her vulva with his tongue.

The vision was riveting. Shocking. It caused her breath to quicken and her heart to race.

Edward was a fastidious man. Not even with a young and beautiful mistress would he engage in such an act.

"Have you ever had a woman's tongue in *your* mouth?"

"Evading the question, Mrs. Petre?" he asked silkily.

"Yes." She took a deep breath. "No, I have never had a man's tongue in my mouth." *Or anywhere else.* "Are you evading my question?"

"You already know the answer."

Yes, she knew the answer. He had probably had more tongues in his mouth than Cook had prepared for dinner.

She studied the light and shadow molding his high cheekbones and his slightly hooked nose instead of his eyes and the erotic draw of his lips. "If a man were fastidious . . . and he were hesitant to try this kind of kissing, how would you recommend that a woman . . . broach the matter?"

"By doing this." The Bastard Sheikh brought up a long, practiced finger and touched the corner of his mouth.

Elizabeth's lips quivered in response. She sucked them in. "You mean touch his mouth? But where?"

"Touch yourself, Mrs. Petre."

"I would prefer it if you demonstrate where your lips are most sensitive, Lord Safyre."

"This is an experiment, Mrs. Petre. There is a reason for my suggestion."

"Then, if this is an experiment, perhaps I should explore your lips."

The gas lamp flickered, flared high.

She could not have said what she heard still ringing in her ears.

His eyes narrowed, as if he, too, did not believe what she had said.

A sharp creak of wood sounded in the silence, and then Elizabeth was staring at an ivory button instead of his turquoise eyes. He silently padded around the desk while she continued staring where but for her outburst he would still be sitting.

He stepped into her line of vision, blocking the light from the lamp. She could feel the brush of his brown leather trousers against the dark gray velvet gown covering her knees.

The leather over his crotch bulged, as if stretched across something very large and very hard.

Elizabeth threw her head back. The light shining behind the Bastard Sheikh outlined his hair so that it looked as if he wore a bright gold halo. Lucifer before the fall.

"I am at your disposal, *taalibba*."

Warning bells crashed and clanged inside her head.

She had never seen a man and she *wanted to*.

She had never kissed a man and she wanted that too.

"You promised you would not touch me." She hardly recognized her voice.

"In this room, yes." His voice was all too recognizable.

Elizabeth remembered the fear she had felt only hours earlier, confronted with a man who threatened to shoot her with a shotgun. She remembered the fear she had felt plowing through London streets and into the occasional lamp pole. She remembered the fear she had felt defying her husband after he had telephoned the constable *because she had inconvenienced him*.

She did not want to die without once touching someone other than herself.

Pushing back the leather chair, she stood up.

Her head came to the top of his shoulder. He was too close. She could feel the heat of his body, could almost hear the beat of his heart.

"You—you're too tall."

He promptly perched on the edge of the desk, eyes nearly level with hers, gaze never wavering. His knees spread out on either side of her so that she could step between them . . . if she dared.

She dared.

Heat radiated from the V of his legs. Elizabeth studied his mouth, glad of an excuse to escape the intensity of his eyes.

She had never before scrutinized a man's lips. Had never realized what a masterpiece of sculpture they were, as if chiseled out of human flesh, the top lip sharp, concise, the bottom one fuller, softer. Slowly, tentatively, she reached out a finger and brushed that sensuously rounded bottom lip.

Electricity shot through her body.

He jerked his head back. She simultaneously snatched away her hand. "I'm sorry. I am so sorry. I did not—"

"You did not hurt me, *taalibba.*" His breath smelled of coffee and sugar, familiar smells, hot, exotic, like the man himself. A lock of wheat-blond hair fell across his forehead. "The lips of a man are as sensitive as those of a woman."

"But if they are that sensitive"—she tried to regulate her breathing, but failed—"how can two people bear to kiss?"

A stillness settled over his dark face. The golden halo that edged his hair alternately blazed and waned. "Your husband has never kissed you," he said flatly.

She bit her bottom lip, struggling to keep her relationship with her husband anonymous.

What would the Bastard Sheikh think, learning that her husband lacked even the simple desire to kiss her?

No waltzing, no sex, no kisses. *No bonding.*

"The truth, Mrs. Petre."

She did not know what the truth was anymore.

She tilted her chin. "Once. He kissed me when the minister pronounced us husband and wife."

The derision she expected did not come.

"Lick your lips."

"What?"

"The purpose of a kiss is the same as that of coition—to incite moisture so that the lips move freely without irritation, just as a man's toying excites wetness in a woman's vulva so that his member will more easily thrust back and forth inside her body.''

She had been dry when Edward had come to her bed.

The Bastard Sheikh's long, dark lashes were clustered in thick spikes. She concentrated on that instead of on the wet heat that was building between her thighs. ''Is it painful for a man if a woman is not . . . moist?''

''Yes, although probably not as painful for the man as it is for the woman. A vagina is easily bruised, like a ripe piece of fruit. Care must be taken in plucking it, fingering it. . . .''

Elizabeth instinctively licked her lips, her saliva hot and slick.

Satisfaction glimmered in his eyes. ''Now touch your lips . . . glide your finger over them . . . gently.''

Her lips were moist and slick; the delicate tissues inside her mouth throbbed in time to the pounding pulse in the pad of her fingertip. She stared into his eyes, blue, green; the longer she looked into them, the more she could discern tiny individual flecks of color.

''Lick your finger.''

She obeyed him unhesitatingly.

''Now touch my lips.''

Slowly, slowly, she again reached out. The sensation was less shocking this time, more sensuous, like touching wet silk. Heat rose to the surface, stoked by the slick glide of her finger.

''Your top lip is not as sensitive as your bottom one.'' Her voice was hushed. ''Is it the same with every man?''

''Perhaps.'' The word was hot, moist; it seared the entire length of her finger.

She raised her left hand and touched her own top lip while she touched his, gliding, stroking, the corners, the chiseled peaks. His lip twitched, her lip twitched, so sensitive. *She had never known lips were so sensitive.*

Curiously, breath bated, she explored the seam of his mouth. She had never felt anything so soft or smooth. At the same time, she explored the seam sealing her mouth, lost in sensation, the texture of their skin, the prickly heat that trailed her lips and the pad of her—

Wet heat leapt up from between her legs and flicked the tip of her finger—his tongue.

She jerked her hand back. *My God,* what was she doing?

"Do men and women kiss in the same manner?" she abruptly asked, bringing her clenched hands safely to her sides. He had agreed not to touch her; perhaps he should have demanded the same of Elizabeth. "That is . . . are there things that a man is required to do that a woman does not, or vice versa?"

"That is the beauty of sex, Mrs. Petre. A man and a woman are free to do anything that gives the other pleasure."

His lips glistened with her saliva; they looked swollen, as if she had bruised them, Eve manhandling the forbidden fruit.

She stepped back, bumped into the leather chair. It skidded out from behind her.

Mortified, she snatched up her gloves and reticule that had decanted onto the Oriental carpet. "Please forgive me. I seem to be unusually clumsy this morning. Perhaps I should go home—"

The Bastard Sheikh loomed over her, behind her. Something nudged the backs of her legs—the chair.

"Sit down, Mrs. Petre."

Elizabeth sat down, a graceless *whoosh* of bustle and leather.

As if nothing untoward had taken place, he resumed his position behind the mahogany desk. "The sheikh describes forty positions that are favorable to the act of coition."

"Yes." She could feel her heartbeat—in her lips, between her legs, her nipples.

"Did you take notes?"

"No." *She had been too busy reading and wanting.*

He opened his top desk drawer and produced the gold pen. She had no option but to take it from him . . . and remember how she had compared her own pen to his. And how she had wanted even that small comfort.

A stack of thick white paper was pushed across the mirror-polished desk, along with the brass inkwell.

"Take notes, Mrs. Petre."

Another time she would take umbrage at the order; now she was just grateful to concentrate on something other than the pulsating ache her entire body had become.

"Unless one is inclined for acrobatics, there are only six positions that a man and a woman may use. A woman may lie on her back with her legs either raised to various levels or not; she may lie on her side; she may lie on her stomach or kneel with her buttocks raised—"

Buttocks raised . . . like the beasts in the fields.

"She may stand; she may sit, and if she sits, the man may either be lying on his back or sitting also."

Belly to belly, mouth glued to mouth.

She clenched the thick gold pen between her fingers and stared down at the black ink scribbled across the white paper. "Which position is most enjoyable for a man?"

"If a man is tired, he will prefer to lie on his back and let the woman straddle his hips."

Rekeud el aïr, "the race of the member," as if a man were a stallion.

She tried to imagine Edward lying back with her straddling his hips . . . and could not.

"Have you engaged a woman in all positions, Lord Safyre?"

"All forty, Mrs. Petre."

All forty vibrated deep inside of her body. As if it had a life of its own, the steel nib scratched a dark line of words across the paper.

"What is your favorite position?"

A harsh intake of breath sounded over the pounding of Elizabeth's heartbeat. She did not know if it came from him . . . or her.

"I am fond of several." The Bastard Sheikh's voice deepened. "My favorite positions are those where I am free to touch a woman's breasts and her vulva."

Kissing. Licking. Suckling. Touching. *Plucking.*

"And your least favorite, Lord Safyre?"

"The position which does not please the woman."

Her head snapped up. "Why would a woman not be pleased by you?"

The Bastard Sheikh threw his head back and stared at the ceiling, as if he could not bear to look at her. *Why would a woman not be pleased by you* reverberated inside her head.

She stiffened her spine, no corset to help her out. *What a silly, wanton woman he must think her.*

"I may enter her too deeply." The harsh words were addressed to the ceiling. "Or I may not thrust deeply enough. A woman who is new to sexual play or has been abstinent for a while would find it painful if I put her legs over my shoulders."

Elizabeth forgot to take notes. She forgot that he was a bastard and she was the wife of the Chancellor of the Exchequer. She forgot everything but the fact that he was a man sharing with her his most intimate reflections.

He lowered his head, his stark face a study of light and shadow. "On the other hand, a woman who has borne two children will need the deeper penetration to achieve her climax. She will like it when I press and grind against her womb, knocking for entrance. She will not mind that I am an Arab bastard. She will only know true satisfaction at my touch."

Elizabeth had borne two children.

The wood smoke and the gas fumes had obviously gone to her head. *A man like him would have no interest in a woman like her.*

"Why did you leave Arabia, Lord Safyre?"

The sharp lines of his face hardened. "Because I was a coward, Mrs. Petre."

Elizabeth had heard many rumors about the Bastard Sheikh; cowardliness was not one of them. "I do not believe that."

He ignored her shocked denial. "You, on the other hand, are not a coward. You did not run from the pain of betrayal. You took control of your life. I did not."

A bastard sheikh was not supposed to have so much pain.

"You had the courage to leave Arabia and start a new life."

"I did not leave Arabia; my father exiled me."

Elizabeth had never seen such bleakness in a man's eyes.
"Surely you misunderstood him."

"I assure you, Mrs. Petre, there was no misunderstanding."

"How do you know? Have you ever been back—"

"I will never go back."

But he wanted to. She could see it in his eyes, feel it resonating from his body.

"You are not a coward," she repeated firmly.

A smile lit his face, erasing the shadow, filling it with light.
"Perhaps not, Mrs. Petre. Not now, at any rate."

"Are harem women beautiful?"

"I used to think so."

"What do harem women enjoy?"

"Whatever the man enjoys."

That could not be. "They have no personal preferences?"

"Like you, Mrs. Petre, their main interest is in pleasing—
a man."

He sounded as if the idea were distasteful. If a man like the
Bastard Sheikh could not be seduced by his own lust, how
would she ever tempt her husband?

"Is that not what a man wants . . . for a woman to put his
own desires above hers?"

"Some men. Sometimes."

"Is that not what *you* want?"

"I will tell you what I want, *taalibba*," he rasped.

She had gone too far.

"You have already told me what you want, Lord Safyre. A
woman, you said."

*A warm, wet, wanton woman who is not afraid of her sexuality
or ashamed of satisfying her needs.*

Leaning forward, she placed the gold pen onto the cool wood
of his desk—only to have it plucked from her fingers. The
Bastard Sheikh leaned forward in his chair, the pen stretched
between his two dusky brown hands, five inches of solid gold.

Elizabeth recoiled, too late; his eyes snared hers.

"The sheikh writes of six movements a man and a woman
practice during coition. The sixth movement is called *tâchik el*

heub, 'the boxing up of love.' The sheikh claims it is the best
of all movements for a woman . . . but it is difficult to achieve.
A man must thrust his verge so deeply inside her body that
their pubic hair meshes. He cannot withdraw, not even an inch,
not even when the woman grips him more tightly than a fist
and his testicles ache for release. The only member that he can
thrust is his tongue, in and out of her mouth while he grinds
his pelvis against hers, *dok,* grinding and grinding against her
clitoris until she climaxes over and over."

As she had ground her pelvis against the mattress.

Hot moisture pooled between her thighs. She watched, riv-
eted, as he made a fist of his left hand and slid the pen inside
the sheath of his fingers until only a blunt golden tip protruded
from his dark skin.

He watched her watching him; she knew that he watched
her and still she could not look away.

"By giving the woman release"—he rotated the gold pen
around and around inside his fist—"she will give me release."

"Have you ever engaged in this"—she sounded as if she
had raced up a flight of stairs—"sixth movement?"

The thick gold shaft slid out of the sheath of his fingers,
slowly, inch by inch, as if a woman's vagina worked to pull
it back inside. She clenched her thighs together, feeling the
draw deep inside her own flesh.

"Have you ever seen a man, Mrs. Petre?"

Elizabeth wrenched her gaze away from the lure of the gold
pen; his eyes were waiting for hers, hot, bright, knowing *exactly*
what he was making her feel.

"No."

"Would you like to?"

There was not enough oxygen in the room to fill her lungs.

What exactly was his question?

Would she like to see a man? *Or would she like to see him?*

She licked her lips; he watched that too. "Yes, Lord Safyre,
I would like to see a man."

He stood up.

Her gaze rested on the apex of his thighs. The brown leather trousers were domed, as if a circus tent had been erected inside.

She leaned closer—

"It is time for you to leave, Mrs. Petre."

Elizabeth remembered the cut she had delivered him at the Whitfield ball—and wondered if he had felt the same sharp pain of rejection then as she felt now.

Hot shame engulfed her. He had shared his knowledge and she had turned her back on him.

She squared her shoulders and stood up, clutching paper, her reticule, and her gloves. "I apologize for my actions at the ball, Lord Safyre."

His expression did not invite an apology. "Which actions are those, Mrs. Petre?"

"I did not mean—" Yes, she had meant to cut him. She had seen her mother's disapproval and had instinctively acted to avoid it. "I walked away from you."

"Would you dance with me again?"

Dance with a bastard. Her breasts pressed against his chest, thighs to thighs, swirling and whirling, impervious to propriety and ugly, hateful truths. *He was a man who belonged to neither the East nor the West; she was the wife of a man who preferred his mistress's bed to hers.*

"I would be honored."

A smile twisted his mouth. "I wonder, Mrs. Petre. Where is your husband?"

Her spine stiffened. "At home," she lied. Or perhaps she did not. "In his bed."

Where she should be.

"Is he, Mrs. Petre?"

"You lied, Lord Safyre," she riposted. "You know who his mistress is."

"I did not lie, *taalibba.* I do not know. I merely wondered if you knew."

"You do not think that I will be able to seduce my husband, do you?"

There. It was out.

"I do not know."

She lifted her chin. *I do not know* was better than *no.*

"Perhaps you underestimate your abilities as a tutor."

"Perhaps you underestimate your husband."

All the pent-up desire burst into frustrated anger. "This is not a game, Lord Safyre. You told me that whether you were called a bastard or an infidel *you are still a man.* Well, I am a woman and my choices are few. I must make my marriage work because that is all I will ever have."

Tears filled her eyes.

She hated tears. For thirty-three years they were the only protest she had voiced, muffling her loneliness in a pillow.

"Go home, Mrs. Petre." His turquoise eyes were unreadable. "You have dark circles underneath your eyes. Get some sleep. Tomorrow we will discuss Chapters Seven and Eight."

"Very well."

The paper was not hers. She blindly placed it on the desk and turned around, careful of the chair, careful of the emotions that sat like fragile eggs on her shoulders.

"Mrs. Petre."

For a second Elizabeth thought about opening the door and walking away and becoming the safe, blameless person she had been a week before. She wasn't courageous, *she was desperate.*

"What?"

"Rule number five. Touch yourself and find the places on your body that are most sensitive. Lie down on your back, bend your knees and practice the same motions you practiced on your mattress."

"Will this teach me how to please my husband, Lord Safyre?" she asked stiffly.

"It will teach you how to please a man, Mrs. Petre."

Why did he make the two sound separate, as if Edward were not a man?

Or as if he did not believe that Elizabeth would be able to satisfy her husband . . . ever.

"Very well."

"Ma'a e-salemma, taalibba."

"Ma'a e-salemma, Lord Safyre."

Elizabeth opened the door and stood face-to-face with the Arab butler.

Chapter Ten

Muhamed's head loomed over Elizabeth's auburn hair. A black hood cast his face into shadow.

Every muscle in Ramiel's body coiled in preparation—to drag Elizabeth back and finish what they had started—to protect her from the man she thought was an Arab.

His engorged manhood throbbed a painful tattoo inside his leather pants.

She had wanted to see him.

He had wanted to show her.

He *still wanted to show her* . . . what he looked like, how to please him, how to swallow his flesh for their maximum enjoyment.

Staring over her head at Ramiel, Muhamed inclined his shoulders in a half-bow. *"Sabah el kheer."*

"Sabah el kheer, Muhamed," Elizabeth responded, the wrong response, but her pronunciation was flawless.

Muhamed was surprised out of his stoicism. He stepped aside to allow her passage.

"Thank you." Elizabeth nodded her head, dark red lights

gleaming in the tight, braided bun in which her hair. *"Ma'a e-salemma."*

Fierce pride swelled inside Ramiel. Elizabeth was indeed a meritorious woman.

Ramiel watched Muhamed watch Elizabeth's retreating back. He knew the exact moment she exited his home; the Cornishman turned in a swirl of black wool and the white *thobs* he wore underneath the cloak.

"El Ibn."

Ramiel was not fooled by Muhamed's bow. He waited for the Cornishman to step forward and close the library door.

"Eavesdropping, Muhamed?"

"I do not have to eavesdrop, *El Ibn.* I could smell your lust through the door."

Ramiel bit back the lightning-quick retort, *I did not know that a eunuch had such a keen sense of smell.* He said instead, "I will not tolerate your interference."

"The sheikh commands me to watch after you."

"You are no longer his slave." *How angry Elizabeth had been when he had addressed her by name in front of the little housemaid.* "I have it on the best authority that the English do not condone slavery."

"A young girl died, *El Ibn,* because you did not resist the *haraam,* that which is forbidden."

The concubine who had taken Ramiel's virginity when he was twelve.

Hot desire turned to icy anger, English civility to Arab savagery.

Muhamed must be made to understand, once and for all, how important Elizabeth Petre was to Ramiel. He could think of only one way to drive home his point.

"You have been with me for twenty-six years, Muhamed. I value your loyalty and your friendship. But I will kill you if you ever harm Mrs. Petre. The Arabic way, very, very slowly, an inch at a time."

"I would not harm a woman," Muhamed said woodenly.

His gaze glanced off Ramiel and focused on the wall behind him.

Ramiel relaxed. "Good."

"It is not I who will harm her."

Fear coursed through Ramiel's blood.

Edward Petre.

Did he beat her? *Did he know of the lessons?*

"Explain."

"The husband went to the Hundred Guineas Club."

Ramiel's nostrils flared in surprise.

The Hundred Guineas Club was a notorious club that obliged its homosexual members to assume a female persona.

"Is he still there?"

Aversion radiated from Muhamed's shadowed face. "No. He left the club with a man dressed as a woman."

The woman he had allegedly been seen with. Only she was not a woman.

"You followed them."

"To an empty shop on Oxford Street."

"Who was the man?"

"I cannot say."

Not *I do not know.*

"You did not recognize him?" Ramiel asked sharply.

"You demanded proof, *El Ibn.* I have no proof but my own eyes."

"You have not lied to me before, Muhamed. Your word is proof enough."

"No, *El Ibn,* it is not. Not in this; you will not listen to reason. I will take you to the shop and you will see for yourself."

Ramiel sensed impending danger, senses fine-tuned as they had not been nine years ago. *Who was Petre's lover, that the Cornishman feared he would not be believed?*

Nothing would shock Ramiel, not sex, not death. Unless—

"Elizabeth was here, with me."

Ela'na, damn, he sounded defensive. Elizabeth was not responsible for her husband's actions. Nor was she knowledge-

able about the kinds of sex games that were played in a hellhole
like the Hundred Guineas Club.

Muhamed continued staring at the wall, face stoic.

Ramiel glanced down at his desk, at the gold pen he had
earlier inserted between his fingers as if it were his manhood
and the sheath of his hand Elizabeth's vagina.

White paper balanced precariously on the edge of the mahogany wood. Black ink marched across it.

Leaning over, he scooped up the paper.

El kebachi—buttocks raised—like beasts in fields, he read.
*Dok el arz—belly to belly—mouth to mouth. Rekeud el aïr—
riding a stallion.*

It was Elizabeth's notes, the words she had written while he
recited the six main positions for coitus. They were not the
words he had used, nor even the basic positions he had cited.
She had listed alternative positions . . . and listed them by their
Arabic names.

Either she had memorized Chapter Six in its entirety . . . or
these were the positions that most excited her. To be taken
from behind while she knelt on her hands and knees; to sit in
a man's lap, her legs around his waist; to straddle a man's
groin while he lay on his back with his legs raised.

Ramiel's testicles tightened. He imagined taking Elizabeth
while she knelt; letting her take him while he laid back; *dok
el arz,* both taking, both giving as they sat facing each other,
belly to belly, mouth to mouth.

He would lay odds that her only experience was the first
position, one that she had not bothered recording, that of a
woman passively lying on her back in an act of duty.

The last scrawled sentence grabbed his thoughts. Ramiel
stared, transfixed. The pulse in his fingertips hammered against
the paper.

*Forty ways to love—lebeuss el djoureb—please, God, let
me love just once.*

Jagged pain ripped through his chest. He had fucked in all
forty positions, and not once had a woman called it an act of
love.

He licked his lips, tasting her, Elizabeth Petre, a thirty-three-year-old woman who had borne two children yet had never been kissed in passion.

She had touched him. She had licked her finger and explored his lips with the innocent wonder of a woman bent on sexual discovery.

Lebeuss el djoureb.

He could give her that. He could spread her legs and tease her vulva and her clitoris until each glide, each slight notching of his penis inside her, produced so much moisture that she would open up and take it all, his tongue and his verge, his past, her ecstasy, English pride and Arabic sexuality.

Reaching down, Ramiel opened the top drawer in his desk and carefully laid the paper inside, anchored it with the gold pen.

She had not understood when he had twirled her on the dance floor and recalled the story of Dorérame and the king. He had told her that he would free her from her husband. Now it was time to act.

"Yalla nimshee," he said harshly to Muhamed. Let's go.

A gig waited outside in the gray dawn; hot steam rose from the horse, a pale, silvery mist. The small, lightweight carriage groaned, once when Ramiel climbed up, a second time when Muhamed followed, gracefully maneuvering in his flowing black cloak and Arab garb.

Without comment Ramiel allowed Muhamed to take the reins. The Cornishman whistled once, a low, shrill command for the horse to go. Ramiel braced himself against the resulting jolt of the carriage.

Cold, damp air moistened his face. The rhythmical clip-clop of the horse's hooves and the grind of the carriage wheels filled the street. Above the tall rooftops, pink light tinted the sky.

He did not question Muhamed further. There was no need to. Ramiel would soon see who had inadvertently sent Elizabeth to him.

There had been dark circles underneath her eyes.

What had kept her awake? Her social life? Her marriage? *The Perfumed Garden?*

Whom had she thought of as she rubbed her pelvis against the mattress—Edward Petre . . . or him?

The carriage swayed, turned a corner.

Oxford Street this far from Regent Street was no longer reputable. Both the narrow streets and the buildings were falling into disrepair. Ramiel glimpsed the dark shadow of a man tupping a whore in a doorway—down the street a vendor's cart ambled along, making its way to a richer neighborhood.

"El Ibn. We are approaching the shop."

Ramiel pulled his hat down low over his ears and wound a dark wool scarf around his neck.

Muhamed softly clicked and pulled the horse to a halt. He pointed. "There."

Upon first glimpse the building looked like the rest of the small brick shops. Gradually, he could see that the front was darker than those surrounding it—the windows had been boarded over. Above the shop shone a pale sliver of light— there was a room above the store. And someone was in it.

Ramiel lightly jumped down from the gig onto the cobblestone street; wood creaked, the horse nervously stepped backward. Ramiel absently soothed it, then continued on his mission, steps echoing in the early dawn light.

The door to the shop was boarded up, the wood pasted over with bills—no entrance there. Another door off to the side no doubt led up to the room. It was locked.

Frustrated, he stared up at that pale sliver of light only fourteen feet away. He would have to wait until Petre and his lover came down.

He looked around for a spot to hide and stepped into the recessed doorway. He pulled the wool scarf over his nose to filter out the odors of urine, gin, and rotted refuse.

The rhythmic clip-clop of a lone horse and the grind of wheels heralded the arrival of a light carriage. A hack pulled to a stop in front of the boarded-over shop, a mere twenty feet from where Ramiel stood. A side lantern on the carriage shed a yellow circle of light, revealing the drooping withers of a black and white nag. The cabbie, perched on his seat at the rear of the hack with a bowler hat pulled low over his eyes, looked neither left nor right.

The locked door leading to the room over the shop swung open. A man stepped out, profile unrecognizable, a typical gentleman dressed in a conservative overcoat and top hat. His breath misted the cold gray air.

Unaware that he was being watched, the man leisurely turned and closed the door. Ramiel ducked back into the doorway, body tense, waiting, waiting, *ela'na,* damn, he could not have gotten this close and be unable to identify anyone—was he Edward Petre or the man Muhamed had refused to name?

A man and a boy, both bundled against the cold, hurried past Ramiel, heads bowed to keep out the cold and perhaps to prevent themselves from becoming unwitting witnesses. The muted click of footsteps warned Ramiel that his quarry was walking toward the hack. He leaned forward, peered around the brick.

The lantern on the side of the cab aureoled the man in yellow light. He opened the carriage door, then took off his tall hat before stepping inside.

The color of his hair was vaguely familiar, but it was not black—it must be Petre's lover.

As if sensing that he was being scrutinized, the man turned, a gold-handled cane clenched in his hand. Light from the carriage lamp clearly delineated his features.

Elizabeth's hand hovered over the knob to the door connecting her and Edward's bedrooms.

Was he home?

No. She could feel the emptiness seeping underneath the door, as if loneliness were ether, invisible but no less tangible for its invisibility.

A woman's tongue is like a nipple, to be nibbled and suckled.

Her mouth is like a vulva, to be licked and probed. Have you ever had a man's tongue in your mouth?

Did Edward put his tongue in his mistress's mouth? Was he even now doing so?

Would he put his tongue inside her mouth when she seduced him?

She closed her eyes and sagged against the door, overcome with an inexplicable wave of revulsion. The blackness behind her lids grew brown, bulging leather tightly stretched over masculine flesh.

Dear Lord, she *did not* know herself. What would she have done if the Bastard Sheikh had unfastened the front of his trousers?

And then, contrarily, she wondered if he was bigger than the gold pen. Longer? Thicker?

He had said that a woman who was new to the ways of love or one who had been abstinent for some time would require shallow penetration. Whereas a woman who had borne two children would need the full length of a man inside her to achieve her satisfaction.

The muscles in Elizabeth's stomach clenched at the thought of her pale legs thrown over the Bastard Sheikh's brown, muscular shoulders.

Her eyelids snapped open. Edward was her husband; the Bastard Sheikh was her tutor. She should be imagining her legs thrown over her husband's shoulders.

Straightening, she stared at the dim glow of her bedside lamp.

The Bastard Sheikh had commented on the dark circles under her eyes.

A ridiculous sense of gratitude washed over her. It was followed by disgust. She was indeed desperate for attention if she should be gratified that a man commented on her hollow eyes.

Impulsively, she crossed the thick carpet and turned the flame in the gas lamp as high as it would go. Light and shadow danced across the familiar room, turning the dawn-darkened carpet to blue, a rectangular box into an oak secretary, an oblong frame into a cheval mirror.

Putting away her gloves and emptying her reticule of *The Perfumed Garden* that she religiously carried to the lessons—as if the Bastard Sheikh's library were indeed a school and the book of erotology a textbook—she hung up her cloak and her bonnet, then unpinned the little silver watch and dropped it into a drawer in the bottom of the wardrobe. Unbuttoning the velvet bodice of her dress, she hung that, too, inside the wardrobe. Gratefully, she shed the heavy bustle.

A glimpse of stark white snared her attention—she turned and stared at the woman in the cheval mirror. She was dressed in a plain white chemise and petticoats. Her skin was almost as pale as were the undergarments.

You have a womanly figure . . . Be proud of your body . . .

Staring, Elizabeth untied the first petticoat; it slid down the woman's hips and puddled around her feet. Two more followed. Elizabeth raised her arms; the woman in the mirror raised her arms, too, and then she was obscured by white linen before reappearing again minus the chemise, dressed only in drawers, stockings, and shoes.

Her breasts were pale alabaster globes, heavy and full. The nipples were dark, tight.

Daringly, Elizabeth unlaced her plain white drawers, slid her hands inside the body-warmed cotton. Bending, she snagged the thigh-length stockings and pulled them down with the drawers. Fighting the instinct to cringe and hide, she straightened and assessed the naked body in the mirror.

Her waist had thickened slightly after two pregnancies; her hips had rounded proportionately. The triangle of hair at the apex of her thighs was dark red.

Had it always been so . . . *lush*? Or had maturity . . . *enhanced* her body?

Shadow outlined her collarbones; it dimpled her knees. She raised her arms and reached behind her to release her braid from the pins that held it in a bun. The breasts in the mirror lifted, jutted out from the woman's chest.

Dropping the pins onto the carpet, Elizabeth loosened the braid, used both hands to shake out her hair. Warm silk slithered down her back, over her shoulders, her breasts. At the same time, she watched a waterfall of auburn fire spill over her shoulders and breasts. Sliding both hands around the nape of her neck, then, she raised her arms high, pulling her hair up and back so that it cascaded over her wrists, elbows veed on either side of her head, breasts lifting, swelling, pouting.

Elizabeth stared at the naked woman in the mirror, entranced. She was—voluptuous. A woman who had borne and nursed two children. A woman who was worthy of love.

She licked her lips, a flash of pale pink tongue. They seemed fuller than they normally did. Kissable.

Touch yourself . . .

As if they had a will of their own, her hands slid free of her neck, dropped the warm tresses of auburn silk. Tentatively, she cupped her breasts; the small, feminine hands in the mirror matched Elizabeth's movements.

The skin was soft, heavy, slightly damp on the underside. Elizabeth could feel the hard prod of her nipples in the palms of her hands.

Did a man's nipples grow hard when a woman touched them?

Do you really like a woman to nibble on your nipples?

Yes, Mrs. Petre.

Liquid heat surged through her groin. She trailed her hands down her ribs, cupped the rounded swell of her stomach.

We all want to be touched. . . .

She touched herself openly, watching herself touch herself. Auburn hair curled around the white hand in the mirror; underneath it was soft, wet flesh like saliva moistened lips.

Tâchik el heub.

Elizabeth imagined a man thrusting so deeply inside her body that their pubic hair meshed, dark auburn and bright gold. Soft, firm lips covered hers; a tongue thrust into her mouth, filling it while he filled her body with his manhood. Her tender netherlips swelled underneath her fingertips, like ripe fruit, begging to be plucked, fingered—

The soft click of a door closing sounded over the drumming of Elizabeth's heart and the quickening of her breathing.

Edward. He was home.

She froze, fingers glued to her skin, unable to move.

He must see that her light was on.

He would come into her room and find her, like this, naked, touching herself, *wanting . . .*

Muffled sounds penetrated the closed door separating their bedrooms; a man preparing for bed, a man sliding into bed, a man leaving a woman alone.

The Bastard Sheikh had said that she was not a coward. So why didn't she cross her room and open the door that kept Edward and her apart?

Why didn't she go to her husband, naked, and show him that she could please him as well as his mistress did?

Tears spilled down her cheeks, hated tears, a coward's tears. She snatched her nightgown off the bed and jerked it over her head. Quickly clearing away all signs of her decadence—the pins, the underwear, her shoes—*she had been so eager to touch herself that she had not even taken her shoes off*—she turned the gas lamp off and burrowed underneath the bedcovers.

The Bastard Sheikh's voice followed her into sleep.

A woman who has borne two children . . . will not mind that I am an Arab bastard. She will only know true satisfaction at my touch.

Chapter Eleven

Elizabeth's nipples underneath her soft black velvet bodice were hard. As hard as the male flesh pulsating against Ramiel's right thigh.

He wanted to arouse her. He wanted to bind her to him so inextricably that she would never, *ever* think about pleasing another man. Ramiel had planned this lesson very carefully to accomplish his goal.

"Which is the most sensitive, Mrs. Petre—your lips, your nipples, or your clitoris?"

For one long second she held the cup of Turkish coffee poised near her lips, nose wreathed in curling steam. He saw shock in her hazel eyes; it was followed by arousal. Then he saw nothing but the fan of her lashes and blue-veined porcelain as she tilted the cup and took a leisurely sip. By the time she returned her cup to the saucer balanced on her lap, her face was composed. "I feel quite certain that you know where a woman is most sensitive."

"But my knowledge is not of you, *taalibba*." Yet. "Every woman's body is different. Some women enjoy one touch while another does not."

She tilted her chin. "Perhaps, Lord Safyre, some women would enjoy being touched—anywhere."

Ramiel did not want her to settle for just any touch, anywhere. He wanted her to demand the rights that were her due as a woman—total, utter satisfaction.

"How long has it been since your husband came to your bed?"

The jarring clatter of china on china chased his words. Her lips tightened. "We agreed that we would not discuss my marriage."

How had he thought her stoic?

Her lips gave away *everything,* quivering with sensitivity, compressing to hold back her emotions. Anger, fear, pain. *Passion.*

His eyes narrowed. "I agreed not to malign your husband."

"How long has it been since *you* have been with a woman, Lord Safyre?"

"Six days."

"An excessive amount of time."

Her voice was sarcastic. But the knowledge was there. *He had not been with a woman since she had blackmailed her way into his home.*

"Yes, Mrs. Petre, it is an excessive amount of time," Ramiel said deliberately. "Before now, the longest I had ever gone without a woman is three days. How long has it been since you have had coition?"

"Suffice it to say that it has been longer than six days," she retorted repressively.

Ramiel thought of Edward Petre. He thought of the damage he must have done to her over the course of sixteen years.

"Longer than six months?" he goaded.

She stared into her coffee cup. The shadows underneath her eyes were darker than they had been yesterday.

Another mark against Edward Petre.

Were Elizabeth his wife, he would bring her to orgasm so many times she would fall into exhausted sleep every night.

He hardened his voice. "You agreed not to lie. How long, Mrs. Petre?"

She raised her cup, sipping, hiding, trying to hold the truth at bay: *she was married to a man who would never satisfy her.* Carefully placing the cup on the saucer, she extended them toward Ramiel. "It has been longer than six months, Lord Safyre. It has been longer than six years. May I have more coffee, please?"

Ramiel inhaled sharply.

He expected her answer; he did not expect the riot of emotions it would unleash.

Longer than six years.

Ela'na. Damn. She would be tighter than a virgin.

Taut anger overcame the piercing desire to find out just how tight she was.

Anger at Edward Petre. Anger at Elizabeth.

He had used her. She had allowed it.

Ramiel would not.

Today she would see what a man looked like. Very soon she would experience what a man felt like.

The man would not be Edward Petre.

He lifted the silver coffeepot at his right elbow and poured more coffee into her cup. Hot steam roiled between them. "In Chapter Eight the sheikh lists various names for a man's sex organ."

"Thirty-nine." She waited until he added the prerequisite splash of cold water to settle the coffee grounds before pulling back her hand. As if it were commonplace for a woman to admit that she had not had coition with her husband for more than six years, she balanced the saucer and cup on her lap. "An excessive number, surely."

"You counted them."

"I thought that was the intent."

The intent was for her to become acquainted with the various stages of arousal in a man.

"Which names did you favor?"

She tilted her chin. "That is difficult to say, Lord Safyre. I was rather taken with 'the pigeon'; however, 'the tinkler,' the 'one-eyed,' and 'the expectorant' ran a close second.''

Laughter and lust. Ramiel could feel the two disparate emotions mingling deep inside of his body.

''Do not be too harsh, Mrs. Petre. English translations of Arabic words do neither the culture nor the language justice. When a man ejaculates, his manhood shrinks and nests on his testicles, hence the 'pigeon' simile. When a woman is wet, suction arises when the man thrusts in and out of her body; if he should pull out of her, it will create a 'tinkling' sound. The one-eyed is rather obvious. As for the expectorant, it is called thus because a man secretes moisture when he is excited, just as a woman does.''

She glanced down, as if she could see through the desk and ascertain the truth of his statement herself. ''Does every man . . . secrete moisture . . . before he ejaculates?''

A circle of damp warmth penetrated Ramiel's trousers where the crown of his manhood strained against the black broadcloth. ''Yes.''

Her gaze jumped up from the desk, safely settled on the cup and saucer in front of Ramiel. ''How much?''

''Enough to lubricate a woman's netherlips so that he can glide between them.'' Ramiel dipped a long finger into his coffee and circled the rim of his cup with it. ''Enough to wet his fingers so that he can caress her clitoris and bring her to climax.''

She tore her gaze away from his cup and met his eyes. ''What Arabic terms do you prefer, Lord Safyre?''

Ramiel's manhood thickened. He shifted in his chair, stretching out his legs to find a more comfortable position. *''Keur . . . kamera . . . zeub.''*

''Virile member, penis, and verge,'' she translated softly.

Ramiel lowered his lashes, veiling his eyes. ''You have an extraordinary memory, Mrs. Petre.''

She did not look away from him. ''I took notes.''

But she wasn't looking at her notes.

''Then you remember that *mochefi el relil,* the 'extinguisher of passion,' best satisfies a woman. It is large, strong, and slow to ejaculate. It will not take its leave until it thoroughly excites the woman's womb, 'coming and going, tilting high and low, and rummaging right to left.' Do you want to see a man?''

Dark rose bloomed in her pale cheeks. She gripped the saucer so tightly, he thought it would shatter. ''You asked me that yesterday morning.''

And then I sent you away, fool that I was.

''I am asking you again.''

Defiance glimmered in her eyes. Defiance . . . and desire.

''Yes.'' She abruptly lifted her saucer off her knee and set it down on the edge of the desk. A decisive thud echoed in the library; a black wave of liquid splashed over the rim of the cup. ''Yes, I want to see a man. Are you willing to show me one, sir?''

Ramiel leaned back and opened the top drawer in his desk. He could feel her eyes on him. His manhood pulsed in time to the rise and fall of her breasts underneath her soft velvet bodice.

She was expecting him to display himself.

He wanted to display himself for her. He wanted to satisfy her every curiosity.

Ela'na, damn, let him get through the next few minutes.

He grabbed a rectangular box and pushed it across the desk. ''Take it.''

Clearly, it was not what she expected. She leaned forward and picked up the white box. ''What is it?''

''Open it.''

She opened the box—and promptly dropped the lid. Her intake of breath was loud over the hiss of the gas lamp and the crackling of burning wood. Shocked hazel eyes leapt to meet his turquoise gaze.

''Take it out,'' he said harshly.

A pink tongue flicked her bottom lip.

Ramiel gripped the edge of his desk to keep himself from jumping over it and giving her her first kiss, *ferame,* the kiss between a man and a woman.

More than six years.

He wanted to give her everything Edward Petre had denied her. He wanted to give it to her *now*.

Lowering her gaze, Elizabeth studied the leather object nestled in a bed of red velvet. It was so shaped that not even a woman with her limited experience could mistake what it was fashioned after.

Sexual awareness throbbed in the seductive thrust and retreat of light and shadow. The gas lamp sucked up the oxygen inside the library. Ramiel could not breathe, waiting for her reaction, waiting for her acceptance . . .

If she ran now . . . Allah and God help them both.

She gingerly lifted it out of the box. "It does not have a red head."

"It is tooled leather."

"It is cold."

"Hold it and warm it in your hands."

"You are trying to embarrass me."

"I am trying to educate you."

Elizabeth refused to meet his gaze. "Lord Safyre—"

"You wanted to see a man, Mrs. Petre; that is what a man looks like. You wanted to learn how to please a man. I am going to show you."

She closed her eyes in silent struggle. It was so obvious that she wanted to do as he instructed, to hold it as she would hold a man, *as she would hold him, when the time came.* It was equally obvious that she was still bound by thirty-three years of ingrained prudery. He fought himself not to make the choice for her, to take her hands in his and close them around the leather.

Opening her eyes, she closed her left hand around the leather. Her fingertips brushed her thumb, meeting on the underside of the object. Its circumference was large, but not so large that it would intimidate her.

"What is it called?" He strained to hear her over the blood thrumming in his temples.

"There are many words. Let us call it an artificial phallus."

"It is circumcised."

Unlike Ramiel.

The Arab women must have found you fascinating.

"You have seen your two sons when they were younger." His voice was labored.

"Yes."

"A circumcised man and an uncircumcised man do not greatly differ when they are erect."

She gently ran a fingertip over the leather crown. "Erect men . . . are they plum-shaped . . . like this?"

Ramiel gritted his teeth, feeling the caress all the way down to his testicles. "Some men."

"Are you?"

He leaned forward in his chair, wood squeaking, heart hammering. "Yes."

"Shortly after I married I became pregnant." She stared fixedly at the phallus. "I went to the art museum. There was a statue there, a naked statue of a man. Except that it had a leaf . . ."

Ramiel did not have to ask what part of the statue the leaf covered.

"I was seventeen years old and I was going to have a baby and I wanted to see what had made me that way. But the leaf would not budge."

The muscles inside his chest constricted. At her unexpected confidence. At the young woman she had once been, seeking illumination from an object of art that had purposefully been tempered to preserve a woman's ignorance.

When she had been seventeen he would have been twenty-two years old with ten years of sexual experience behind him. She had known pain and frustration; he had known only pleasure.

Then.

The pain had come later.

For the first time in nine years, Ramiel almost forgave the circumstances that had exiled him to England to live out the rest of his life. While he could not change his past, he could give Elizabeth a future.

"Your curiosity is natural, *taalibba*."

"The guard did not think so."

Ramiel's lips hitched upward. The picture of Elizabeth determinedly trying to lift a marble leaf that would not budge while a British guard struggled to stop her was so vivid that he almost laughed. The thought of her humiliation immediately sobered him.

"Some men are afraid of comparison," he said easily.

"But you are not."

The words were drawn from him unwittingly. "I have my own fears."

Her head shot up. "What does a man like you have to fear?"

That I am not a man. That I will never be a man again.

But some things a man does not confess out of the sheer fear that putting it in words will make it true.

He could not live with himself, knowing that it was true. *He could not live with himself* not knowing *that it was true.*

How could he expect a woman to live with that which he could not?

"What do you fear, Elizabeth Petre?"

Her lips opened—soft pink lips; immediately, she closed her mouth in a thin, firm line and returned her attention to the phallus. "Is this a meritorious member?"

He wondered what she was hiding now. Was she afraid that she would never find satisfaction with her husband? Or was she afraid that she would find it with a Bastard Sheikh?

"You know the formula. Measure it."

He watched with bated breath as she positioned the leather across the palm of her hand.

"One and a half handbreadths . . ." She raised her eyelids; her hazel eyes were lambent. "By my hands. You did not answer my question, Lord Safyre."

His mouth was dry, as if he had eaten desert sand. "It is meritorious enough."

"Is a man this hard when he is erect?"

Ramiel took a deep breath. "A man is more flexible."

"Thursday morning you said that you liked a woman to

pump and squeeze you. How else can a woman pleasure a man?''

"She can take him into her mouth and lick and suckle him," he said baldly.

The words were riveting, for her as well as for him.

"Like a nipple."

He did not miss a heartbeat. "Or a clitoris."

"Women . . ." Her voice was husky. *She would sound like that,* he thought, *when he was buried deep inside of her.* "They take a man into their mouths?''

Ramiel closed his eyes in acute physical pain, imagining Elizabeth's mouth, Elizabeth's hair, Elizabeth's pleasure. "Yes, Mrs. Petre. Women do that."

"*What does it taste like?*''

Ela'na. Damn. *She could not know.*

He opened his eyes, stared at her rapt curiosity. *No, she did not know.* He briefly mourned the innocence that he would be instrumental in destroying. "I am afraid that is something you will have to test for yourself," he said impassively.

"What does a woman taste like?''

What would Elizabeth taste like?

"Sweet. Salty. Like . . . a woman. Soft and hot and wet and passionate."

The gas flame in the lamp pulsed with heat, luring, warning. Passion could burn, badly.

How far would she go before her Western propriety pulled her back? How far could *he* go without losing control?

"What did you think when you saw a woman for the first time?''

What had he thought, at the age of thirteen, when the experienced concubine his father had provided him with had laid down on her back and spread her legs?

"I thought . . . that a woman's vulva was the most fascinating thing I had ever seen. Like a pink iris. When touched, it grew moist. When excited, its petals unfurled to reveal a secret little bud. It was the ultimate toy."

Elizabeth's gaze skidded away from his. She bowed her head.

"It is impossible, surely, for a woman to fully take a man into her mouth."

But she would try. When the time came, she would give him everything and more that he had ever wanted.

"A woman does not have to swallow all of him, just the crown and the first couple of inches. She may squeeze and fondle his shaft while she kisses and suckles him."

Kisses and suckles vibrated in the air between.

Like a nipple.

Like a clitoris.

"Has a woman ever taken you fully into her mouth?"

Ramiel remembered the pleasure of a woman's lips and tongue. The memories were fueled by her manifest interest in performing fellatio. Sexual heat flooded his cheeks. "No."

"Would you like that?"

Only if you can do it without injury to yourself, taalibba, he thought.

"I would rather that a woman take me fully inside of her vagina."

An ember popped inside the fireplace. Ramiel tensed, preparing for her next question. He had given her the reins; would she run with them?

"Have you been with women who could not . . . fully take you inside their vagina?"

"Yes." The word was dragged out of his chest.

"Virgins."

"Yes."

"Women who have long been abstinent."

"Yes."

"But not women who have borne two children."

"No," he agreed softly, emphatically. "A woman who has borne two children will fully accept me."

He would not be able to live if she did not take all of him.

Ramiel stared at her bent head, waiting, watching the dark play of auburn lights in her hair.

"What things can a man do with a full-breasted woman that he cannot do with a less generously endowed one?"

Ramiel sucked in oxygen, not enough; the need for more burned inside of his chest. He stared at her breasts, covered by black velvet, remembered how white and soft and deliciously full they had been, spilling over the modestly cut green silk ball gown when they danced.

"He can position his manhood between her breasts and press them together . . . so that he is buried between them . . . as if they were a vulva."

She instinctively hunched her shoulders, pressing her breasts together as if to protect them from his sight . . . or to facsimile the pressure of his hands.

"What is this?"

Ramiel glanced down at the phallus cradled in her hand.

A shaft of pure heat raced along the length of his manhood, as if she wrapped her fingers around him and not the unfeeling leather. He forced himself to concentrate on her stroking finger and not his own body. "That is called the glans. It and the crown—the plum-shaped head—are the most sensitive parts of a man's body."

Her head snapped up. "More sensitive than a man's lips?"

The memory was clear in her hazel eyes, the lightning jolt of sensation that had coursed through their bodies when she had touched his bottom lip.

He imagined what it would be like, her fingers lightly strumming the crown of his manhood. And did not doubt in the least his answer. "Yes."

"Does it quiver . . . like your lip did?"

It quivered just talking about it.

"Call it by a name, *taalibba,*" he commanded.

"*El lezzaz,*" she responded promptly.

"The unionist." So named because once inside a woman, it pushes and grinds until pubic hair meets pubic hair and still it pushes and grinds as if trying to force even the testicles inside of her.

The sixth movement.

The ache inside his groin traveled up to his chest.

Her wants . . . His wants . . . They were becoming increasingly difficult to keep separate. And over the both of them loomed her husband.

Of all the people to choose as a lover, why would he choose the person Ramiel had seen last night?

"How long will you continue to remain celibate, Mrs. Petre?"

She clenched the artificial phallus so tightly, her knuckles paled.

Ramiel winced.

"How long will *you* continue to remain celibate, Lord Safyre?"

"As long as it takes."

"Likewise."

He studied her intently. "Everyone deserves to be loved just once, Mrs. Petre."

Even a Bastard Sheikh.

Confusion shone in her clear hazel eyes; it was followed by dawning comprehension; that by unmitigated horror.

In her haste to escape him the previous morning, she had forgotten about writing on the paper he had instructed her to take notes on.

Elizabeth remembered now.

She remembered what she had written . . . and she remembered thrusting the paper onto his desk. Where she had left it . . . and he had retrieved it.

Forty ways to love—lebeuss el djoureb—*please, God, let me love just once.*

Without warning she dropped the phallus inside the velvet-lined box and slapped it onto the desk beside her cup. "I have to go now."

"There is no shame in needing love, *taalibba.*"

Clutching her gloves and reticule, she stood up.

Ramiel reached out and plucked the phallus out of the white box. It was still warm from her touch. He cradled it in his palm, a mere handbreadth long, as she had cradled it in her palm.

She stared at his hand and the artificial phallus. At the dried leather and warm, living flesh.

Her thoughts were so plain that he felt as if he violated her privacy by looking at her.

"Objects such as this are harem favorites."

Her spine stiffened. She glanced up, eyes filled with revulsion . . . and so much more. "You mean—women use these—"

"Yes." He suggestively curled his fingers around the leather, making of them a sheath. "There are too many women and only one man."

She stepped back. The burgundy leather chair shot across the carpet.

"I obtained this one in a shop yesterday; they are as much in demand in England as they are in Arabia."

She pivoted, fled for the door.

"A woman always has choices, Mrs. Petre," he called after her, knowing that she would understand that reference too.

Yesterday morning she had said that she was a woman and that her choices were few, that she must make her marriage work because that was all she could ever have.

Elizabeth was wrong.

She had choices . . . if she only had the courage to make them.

Chapter Twelve

Elizabeth's skin felt tight, like overripe fruit. Her heartbeat raced the sour-smelling hack.

She had wanted it. She had held the phallus in her hands and imagined the plum-shaped head nudging her most sensitive flesh, pushing up into her body and filling her like she knew the Bastard Sheikh would fill her.

Mochefi el relil. His member would be like that, large and strong, completely satisfying a woman's amorous wishes.

She squeezed her eyelids together. Why had she told him about the statue? Now he would know that her unnatural desires were not triggered by the shock of discovering that her husband kept a mistress—she had always had them.

Oh, my God. *He had read her notes.* Scribblings listing her most secret sexual desires, to be taken from behind, *to be taken,* period.

What kind of a woman was she? What kind of man could possibly want a woman who was filled with such uncontrollable lust? Like the beasts in the fields . . .

How could she be married to one man and lust after another?

When the hack rumbled to a stop, she stumbled out and

tossed the cabbie she knew not what—a groat, a sixpence, a florin, a half crown, *a crown,* it did not matter as long as she was free to gain the sanctuary of her bedroom. She raced off into the nebulous ribbons of yellow fog, away from the woman she had become.

"But what about tomorrow mornin'? Should I—"

The cabbie's voice was swallowed in the cold twilight. The tiny dots of burgeoning gray light that comprised Elizabeth's vision through the black veil blurred with tears.

A woman always has choices, Mrs. Petre.

She fumbled with the key to the front door of the town house, fingers nerveless—oh, no, she almost dropped the bit of metal, caught it, and jammed it home.

Pulling her cloak about her, she raced up the stairs, a foot landing on a weak board—she knew better than to step there; she used to lie abed and listen to Richard and Phillip creep down the stairs for a midnight snack. A muffled s*hh!* had always accompanied the creak of that board. Only this time it was Elizabeth sneaking up the stairs, and she had raided rather more than a biscuit jar.

Tonight was the night of the charity ball; surely Edward would be home, *please God,* let him be home. She needed to see his face, to replace the image of warm, tanned skin and turquoise eyes with Edward's cool, pale skin and brown eyes.

She needed to see his body instead of the artificial phallus cupped in the Bastard Sheikh's hand.

Edward's drapes were closed, his bedroom dark and silent. Empty again—

No. A sound alerted her of his presence, the rhythmic soughing of his breath.

Nausea churned in her stomach.

There would be no forty positions of love in Edward's bed.

Six days ago the knowledge would not have bothered her. *Six days ago she had not possessed such knowledge.* Now she needed Edward to wipe away that knowledge.

She needed to know that she could obtain satisfaction in her marriage.

Laying her reticule on the dark monolith of a chest, she peeled off her gloves and dropped her cloak onto the floor. She could hear the release of each button as she unfastened her velvet gown, certain Edward would awaken any moment.

And what if he did? she wondered half hysterically. They were man and wife. Why shouldn't he see her naked?

Why shouldn't she see him *naked?*

The air was icy against her arms. It was as cold in Edward's bedroom as it had been in the Bastard Sheikh's library that first morning. There had been no welcoming fires lit for her either then or now.

Her petticoats sloughed off like the skin of a garden snake. Her chemise followed, leaving her breasts bare, exposed, but not nearly as vulnerable as her hips and thighs felt when she stepped out of the protection of cotton drawers.

Her stockings were snug around the tops of her thighs. Briefly, she debated leaving them on. For some reason, though, it seemed more decadent approaching a man wearing only stockings than it did wearing nothing at all.

Removing stockings, however, was not a graceful process. Too late she realized she should have undressed in her room.

Standing stark naked in the darkness, she felt more nervous than she had been on her wedding night. Where she had been warm and wet but an hour earlier, captivated by Ramiel's husky voice and the discovery of a man's body, she was now cold and dry.

The carpet underneath her bare feet was thick and soft; it cushioned her steps. The bedcovers folded back without protest, the comforter a muted whisper of velvet, the quilt and top sheet a coarse sigh.

Edward's nightshirt was even whiter than was the bottom sheet. He lay on his back, still as a corpse, limbs neatly arranged as if he controlled his dreams as easily as he did his waking life.

Hand trembling, heart pounding, Elizabeth reached out and encountered cold cotton and even colder fear.

It should not be like this, her husband lying insensate while she attempted to seduce him. The Bastard Sheikh would not just lie there. *He would welcome a woman's needs.*

Carefully, slowly, she eased up Edward's nightshirt, revealing forbidden male flesh, a knee, a thigh. His legs were darker than the nightshirt, darker than hers. Wiry hair brushed the backs of her knuckles—who would ever have thought that a man was so hairy? Or so warm—

Unyielding fingers grasped her wrist. Elizabeth gasped.

"What are you doing, Elizabeth?"

She fought back a laugh, spoke with calm resolve. "What do you think I am doing, Edward?"

"I think we are both going to catch our death from cold."

His voice was equally calm and so much more reasonable. And not at all amorous.

She did not pull back her hand; he did not release her wrist. "I am trying to seduce you, Edward."

"By sneaking into my room and groping underneath my nightshirt while I lie asleep?"

She flinched, suddenly feeling cheap and tawdry. *It was not supposed to be like this.* During their lessons the Bastard Sheikh had by turns angered and shocked and aroused her but he had *never* made her feel dirty. "Some men might appreciate the attention."

"I am not some man, Elizabeth. I am your husband. What do you want?"

The situation was becoming increasingly farcical. How could he not know what she wanted?

Perhaps he had poor night vision. Perhaps he did not see that she did not wear a nightgown.

"I want . . ." Her heart gave a lurch. How did a respectable woman tell her husband that she wanted to make love? she thought. And then, resentfully, why did she have to explain her intentions when she sat naked on his bed? "I want to be intimate."

"You have two sons. I have done my duty by you."

Elizabeth felt as if she had stepped into the pages of a penny dreadful.

Edward had a mistress, for heaven's sake. Sex was not a duty. *He must know what she wanted.*

"I do not come to you out of duty, Edward."

"Then go back to your room and we will forget about this visit."

Elizabeth's throat ached. She felt silly and awkward and numb with cold, wearing nothing but her lust.

Anger came to her rescue. *If she could ask the Bastard Sheikh to teach her how to give a man pleasure, she could certainly ask her husband to let her give* him *pleasure.*

"Edward, I know you have a mistress. Please let me satisfy your needs."

His fingers tightened about her wrist; she would have a bracelet of bruises there in a few hours. "I do not have a mistress, Elizabeth, and you do satisfy my needs."

He was lying.

She struggled to keep her voice even. "What needs do I satisfy, Edward?"

"You are the perfect wife for a politician."

"Because of my father, you mean."

"Yes."

She knew that; she had always known that Edward married her because of who she was and not what she was. The knowing should make the pain of confirmation less, not worse.

"I want to be more, Edward."

I want to experience that moment of bonding when a woman takes a man into her body.

"I don't need you to be more."

"Our sons need us to be more."

"Your sons, Elizabeth. I gave you children so that you would be satisfied."

Dear God, she did not need to hear this. Regardless of Edward's lack of commitment to the marriage bed, they were the perfect family . . . weren't they?

"What if *I* am not satisfied by this arrangement? You have not been to my bed in over twelve years."

"A respectable woman does not desire physical demands

from her husband. If you want more children, we will discuss it over breakfast.''

Hysteria clawed at her throat.

She wanted to laugh. She wanted to cry.

Never in her wildest dreams had she imagined this response from her husband.

A coldness settled over her that had nothing to do with the chill air. *The Bastard Sheikh had known.*

"I want to discuss this now, Edward.''

"You will not like what I have to say.''

"I do not like it now. I cannot imagine that I will like it any better over tea and crumpets!''

"You are getting hysterical.''

"No.'' *Yes.* Elizabeth took a calming breath. "I am trying to understand our marriage. You say you do not have a mistress; rumors abound that you do. Phillip is fighting to protect your reputation; Richard is sick with unhappiness. If there is anything I can do to please you, I will do it. *Tell me what you want, Edward.''*

He released her wrist. "Very well. Cover yourself.''

She fumbled for the velvet comforter, wrapped it around herself. Edward pulled the sheet and quilt up to his waist, as if afraid she would attack him.

"I do not want your body, Elizabeth. You have great udder breasts and flabby hips. It was a chore bedding you the number of times I did to get you with children. Richard and Phillip are healthy. I will not put myself through the trouble of bedding you again just so that you can lie with a man. Do I make myself clear?''

The pain started low in Elizabeth's chest and worked its way up into her throat. She couldn't breathe past it; she couldn't swallow. She could barely talk.

But oh, she could think. And reason. *And remember.*

"You said the children were for me, but that is not true, is it, Edward? They were for you, so that you could gain popularity with the voters.''

"The middle class prefers a candidate who has a family.''

He had come to her bed *to seed the grounds* for his political career.

"How many children does it take to please your voters?"

He walked into her trap. "One will suffice."

Elizabeth's voice in the dark was unnaturally calm. "The last time you came to my bed was when Richard was ill with diphtheria."

"The doctor said he was dying."

And he had been. Her four-year-old baby had burned with fever. But Elizabeth had refused to let him go. She had bathed him with toilet water and held him and sang to him until she fell into an exhausted stupor.

Edward had carried her downstairs to her bed and joined her there. At the time, she had thought he made love to her to comfort her.

"So you gave me another child to replace Richard. Just in case the doctor proved to be right and you lost favor with your voters."

"But Richard lived and I gave you Phillip, a bonus, if you like." His voice in the darkness was so reasonable, the voice he used when answering a dissenter's questions after a speech. "You have two sons, Elizabeth. No respectable woman could ask for more."

"What do you have, Edward?" Elizabeth asked in a brittle voice.

"I will be prime minister."

While she continued living a life that was no life at all, wanting the love of a man.

Raw rage pushed aside the hurt. "Where do you spend your nights, Edward, when you aren't at home? Who is the woman you have been seen with?"

"I have told you there is no woman. Politics is demanding. Your father has twice been prime minister now. I will do whatever I have to do to succeed him."

Anything but bed her.

Elizabeth stared at the dull blackness of Edward's hair and mustache, all that was visible against the white pillow.

"This whining of yours is neither complimentary to you or pleasant for me. I will turn onto my side now so that you will not further humiliate yourself by displaying your naked body to me when you leave my bedroom. You have a busy day today; I expect you to attend the charity auction this evening and later the ball."

Suiting action to words, Edward rolled onto his side, away from her.

Elizabeth could no longer feel the cold February air pressing around her. "I will not be a pawn, Edward."

"You already are, Elizabeth."

Tears burned the backs of her eyes. Defeat was an ugly emotion. It was far worse than the frustration she had lived with for the past sixteen years.

She clumsily slid off the bed; her ankle twisted, a sharp, welcoming pain. One by one she picked up her discarded clothes, scooped up the reticule from the chest of drawers. The connecting door closed behind her with a final click.

Inside her bedroom the curtains were closed, blocking out a world that rejected a woman's need for sexual satisfaction.

Great udder breasts.

How dare he! How dare any person so humiliate another!

Throwing the bundle of clothes as far and as hard as she could, she turned up the gas lamp by her bed. Standing naked in front of the cheval mirror, she studied herself with eyes unclouded by wishful fantasies or lustful desires. Ruthlessly, she appraised the heavy weight of her full breasts and the faint stretch marks that marred her rounded hips.

A womanly figure, the Bastard Sheikh had said. *Be proud of your body,* he had added.

The Perfumed Garden praised breasts and hips on a woman.

What things can a man do with a full-breasted woman that he cannot do with a less generously endowed one?

He can position his manhood between her breasts and press them together . . . so that he is buried between them . . . as if they were a vulva.

Elizabeth threw her head back, eyes squeezed shut. Even as

she trembled with rage and pain she remembered the feel of the artificial phallus and the mesmerizing pull of turquoise eyes.

She had wanted him.

A man with his experience would know that.

The Bastard Sheikh was probably laughing at her. As was her husband.

Dear God, Edward had turned onto his side away from her lest he get another glimpse of her "womanly" figure.

Springing into action, she twirled around, breasts jiggling, and leapt toward the scattered clothes. She dug her reticule out from underneath the horsehair-stuffed bustle.

The book lied. *The Bastard Sheikh lied.* There was no satisfaction for a thirty-three-year-old woman who showed the first strands of silver in her hair and the effects of two children on her body.

Slamming open the roll-back top of her desk, she grabbed pen, ink, and paper.

Her writing was scrawled as opposed to the neat, precise lines that her governess had forced her to practice all during her childhood. As the notes she had left on the Bastard Sheikh's desk had no doubt been scrawled, *forty ways to love,* damn all of them.

Ramiel reread the note.

Thank you for the loan of your book. While interesting, it has not proved to be practical.

Best regards

The words that Elizabeth had spoken only hours earlier flooded his head, poignant words, pain-filled words. *I was seventeen years old and I was going to have a baby and I wanted to see what had made me that way. But the leaf would not budge.*

Ramiel felt like a fist squeezed his heart.

Dust motes danced in the watery noonday sunlight. He had slept for four hours, dreaming of Elizabeth's mouth, her breasts, her naked need.

He crumpled up the note.

Muhamed waited in the doorway of the bedroom. He was not disturbed at the sight of Ramiel's nudity. "It is for the best, *El Ibn.*"

Ramiel's eyes glittered. "Do you read my correspondence, Muhamed?"

The Cornishman's turbaned head snapped back. "You know I do not."

"Then how the bloody hell do you know what's in it?" he lashed out.

"The book, *El Ibn.* She has returned the book."

Ramiel stared at the plainly wrapped package in Muhamed's hands.

The Perfumed Garden of the Sheikh Nefzaoui. An Arabic celebration of love and folly, sex and humanity, the absurd and the sacred.

"How do you know what book she sent?"

"Because I know, *El Ibn.* You hunger for a woman to take the Arab in you. The paper lying on your desk Friday morning contained information from the sheikh's book. The handwriting was not yours."

Conflicting emotions slashed at Ramiel's gut. Anger, that Muhamed had read words that only Ramiel should have seen. Pain, that Elizabeth thought so little of him that she terminated their lessons with a note rather than face-to-face.

Why had she returned the book?

He uncrumpled the ball of paper he had reduced her note to.

It smelled faintly of her, the natural sweetness of a woman's flesh; overriding it was the fresh scent of ink and vellum. The words ran together, as if she had written with great speed.

Or under great duress.

Ramiel reread the last part of her note: *While interesting, it has not proved to be practical.* And realized what he had inadvertently pushed her into doing.

She had tried to appease the passion he had deliberately aroused in her by seducing her husband.

What had she done to entice Edward Petre? Had she done to him the things that Ramiel wanted her to do to him? Had she taken him into her hands and pumped and squeezed him? *Had she taken him into her mouth?*

Perhaps Edward would have liked that, Ramiel thought on a surge of jealousy. With his eyes closed, Elizabeth's mouth would feel no different from the mouth of a man.

Ela'na. Damn. Elizabeth was inexperienced. Uncertain. Vulnerable. She would not understand that it was her sex and not her body that failed to please her husband.

The fist wrapped around Ramiel's heart convulsively clenched. *She had touched him . . .* With her words, her passion, her curiosity, her honesty, *her saliva-slick finger.* How could she go to another man?

What had Edward Petre done to her that she would so abruptly end their lessons?

Ramiel snared Muhamed's gaze. "Where is Petre now?"

"At the Queen's Hall."

"Why?"

"There is an auction for a charity."

"Where will he be tonight?"

"The auction will be followed by a ball."

And where Edward Petre politicked . . . Elizabeth would follow.

Ramiel may have lost the right to be loved nine years ago, but he would not lose Elizabeth. Women begged him to bed them in the dark of night and spurned him in the light of day and *it had not mattered* until she had shown him that an Englishwoman needed an Arab bastard for more than raw sex.

If she truly desired to terminate their relationship, she would do it to his face. *Tonight.*

And then he would convince her otherwise.

Chapter Thirteen

Blazing chandeliers spotlighted a sea of black tails and jewel-colored gowns. Silk, tulle, and velvet fabrics wafted benzene, heavy perfume, and unwashed musk. Elizabeth swayed, light-headed from lack of oxygen and sleep.

"As you are aware, the benefits of this auction will feed and clothe homeless women and children whose brave, heroic husbands and sons lost their lives in Africa, fighting to advance the freedom of our great Commonwealth."

An enthusiastic round of applause filled the prime minister's strategic pause. Elizabeth concentrated on the man standing on the dais in front of the musicians, who patiently waited with their instruments, instead of the suffocating mass of bodies pressing in and around her.

Andrew Walters's hair was more silver than auburn; his hazel eyes were bright with the charm he never failed to exercise in front of the public. She had only to look at him and see what she herself would look like in twenty-seven years.

With practiced ease he held small, slender hands up for silence. "In reward for your charitable contributions we have arranged a buffet and dancing. But first, let me digress for a moment. As you know, my daughter has presented me with two fine grandsons—future prime ministers.''

Masculine guffaws and feminine titters rippled around Elizabeth.

"Now, now, no laughter. They are young now, but they will grow into their positions. And that, of course, brings me to my son-in-law. Ladies and gentlemen, may I present to you your next prime minister, Edward Petre, Chancellor of the Exchequer!''

The applause was thunderous. Edward lightly jumped up onto the dais beside Andrew and threw both arms up into the air.

Elizabeth had never seen him so handsome. His pale face was flushed; his eyes glowed. It was as if the events of the morning had never happened.

"My father-in-law is precipitate. He will be prime minister for many more years yet. However, it is my greatest ambition to follow in his footsteps. When the time comes, God willing, I only hope I will be worthy of being your prime minister.''

More applause, Edward skillfully leading it, building it, quieting it.

"And now I would like to thank the two women in my life. One gave me my wife and the other gave me two sons, whom I will train to follow in my footsteps as Andrew Walters has trained me to follow in his. Ladies and gentlemen, I give you Mrs. Rebecca Walters, my mother-in-law, and Mrs. Elizabeth Petre, my wife. Without their hard work and devotion, the auction today and the forthcoming dance would not be possible!''

Elizabeth's stomach churned. Edward was a liar and a hypocrite—he cared nothing for his two sons. She could not do it. *He could not expect her to get up there and speak on his behalf after what he had said to her.*

But in the end she had no choice. Well-meaning hands pushed her forward. Rebecca stepped up to Andrew's left; Elizabeth reluctantly stepped up between Andrew and Edward, every word, every move, masterminded to gain political support.

Rebecca delivered her speech, the meaning the same with the words slightly altered for greater spontaneity, that her greatest pleasure was derived from being her husband's helpmate and that she looked forward to many more years of community service. Polite applause obligingly followed.

Elizabeth licked lips suddenly more dry than rice powder and glanced down at the hundred or so pairs of eyes expectantly staring up at her. Every line she had rehearsed faded from her memory. She laughed, a brittle, nervous laugh that could not be mistaken for anything but what it was. "Well . . . my family is a difficult act to follow."

A few guffaws, then a few titters.

"I am not certain that my two sons are aware of their appointed status as future prime ministers, but I will certainly tell them. Perhaps the dean will be more lenient when next they do poorly on an exam, knowing that he is harboring England's future."

More guffaws, even more titters, scattered applause. Elizabeth could feel warning waves of disapproval emanating from her father and her husband. Or perhaps it was heat emanating from the blazing chandeliers.

She should say that she thought Edward will make a wonderful prime minister when the time came and that it was her greatest pleasure being his helpmate. She could not. "Thank you for your support. And thank you for your generous contributions."

Edward's fingers, covered in a white silk glove, closed painfully around Elizabeth's right hand. Her father's fingers, equally cold through his glove, trapped her left hand. Her mother's right hand, she knew from experience rather than from sight, would be clasped in Andrew's left hand, a family united in the eyes of the voting public. Elizabeth and Rebecca curtsied; Edward and Andrew bowed.

She wondered what the voters would say if they knew their trusted Chancellor of the Exchequer had cold-bloodedly begat a family for their benefit. She wondered if her parents had begat her for the same reason. And did not doubt for one second that they had done so.

Straightening, she realized this was the first time she had curtsied to a crowd and not feared she would trip on the hem of her gown. The small sense of satisfaction that the thought gave her froze beneath the steady regard of turquoise eyes.

Panic thudded to life inside her chest. Panic . . . and the memory of a hard leather phallus cupped in strong, tanned fingers.

Elizabeth did what she had always feared she would do, held off balance with either hand clasped: She stumbled. Immediately, the chain of hands snapped; the prime minister stepped down the dais to shake hands with the applauding voters while Edward unobtrusively righted Elizabeth.

Her clumsiness had been so gracefully camouflaged that the whole thing might have been deliberately choreographed. No one knew that she had stumbled save for her father, her husband . . . and the Bastard Sheikh.

"Are you all right, Elizabeth?" Edward's voice was warmly solicitous; his brown eyes were the color of the Thames River frozen mid-current.

Elizabeth stepped away from him. "Fine, thank you, Edward. Please do not let me keep you from your voters."

He smiled. "I won't."

The musicians behind her restlessly shuffled; they were eager to start the music and get the evening over with. So was Elizabeth. Holding the hem of her gown out of danger's way, she stepped off the small wooden platform.

The crowd of middle-class voters surged away from the dais. The Bastard Sheikh was nowhere to be seen.

Had she imagined him?

"I expected better from you, Elizabeth."

The sound of a tuning violin sliced across her bare shoulders. Elizabeth whirled around.

The Bastard Sheikh stood so close, her breasts brushed against the lapels of his black dress jacket.

Heat raced through her blood. "What are you doing here?"

Hot breath fanned her upturned face. The dark face above hers was shuttered, the gold of his hair a shining halo. "I came for you."

Elizabeth's breath caught in her chest. This morning he had said that he had not had a woman in six days.

For a second he sounded as if—

Nonsense. Her *own husband* did not want her.

"I take it you received my package. If I damaged the book in any way, I will be happy to reimburse you."

The turquoise eyes were as hard as the stone they took their color from. "What did you do to your husband?"

A scale of piano keys introduced a popular waltz. A tide of heat surged behind her, men and women taking their positions on the dance floor.

He could not know what had happened between her and Edward. No one knew of her humiliation save for her . . . and her husband.

Her lips were cold and stiff. "Whatever do you mean?"

"You left my home in heat. And you went to your husband to satisfy your desire. How far did you go before he turned you away?"

Udders. *Heat.*

Edward likened her to a cow, and the Bastard Sheikh talked of her passion as if she were a dog.

That morning with her husband had been a tragic farce. This was a nightmare. Not only did the Bastard Sheikh realize how strong had been her passion when she handled the artificial phallus, but he knew that her husband had rejected her because of that passion.

She smiled as if they talked about the auction, the dance, the music, anything but the animal he had compared her to and which Edward had made her feel. "I do not know what you are talking about, Lord Safyre. If you will excuse me, I really must see if the buffet needs to be replenished."

She turned away, still smiling.

He turned with her. "Then I will accompany you. And you

will tell me which of the things I taught you that you tried out on your husband.''

Elizabeth kept walking, smiling at a large contributor there, making certain not to discriminate against the less wealthy couple who could not afford large donations.

"Did you kiss him?"

"Excuse me," she murmured as she pressed through an elderly couple who smelled of mothballs.

"Did you take his tongue inside your mouth?"

She wondered how much longer she could continue smiling.

"Did you pump and squeeze his manhood?"

"Hello, Mr. Bidley, Mrs. Bidley."

The middle-aged couple, no less conservative than the elderly couple who smelled of mothballs, did not hear Elizabeth over the music. Elizabeth wished she could share their deafness.

Moist heat feathered the top of her head. "Did you take his manhood into your mouth?"

As if by their own will, her feet came to an abrupt halt. She closed her eyes against the images and sensations that his words conjured; a man's tongue inside her mouth; the Bastard Sheikh's member, plum-shaped head crying for a kiss.

She had not known that a man grew moist with arousal—just like a woman. Edward had not.

"How do you know that my husband rejected me, Lord Safyre?"

"Your note, Elizabeth."

Edward pronounced her name with distant courtesy.

Rebecca pronounced her name with cold authority.

The Bastard Sheikh pronounced her name as if they had shared physical as well as verbal intimacies.

"I did not give you leave to address me by my given name." Tears pricked the back of her eyelids. "I did not ask to be treated with disrespect."

"I have never treated you with disrespect."

She blinked back the tears and met his turquoise gaze. "What do you call it, Lord Safyre, when you hunt me down to question me about my sexual activities with my husband?"

His hard, relentless gaze did not waver. "Just answer my question."

"No, I did not kiss my husband. I did not pump and squeeze his manhood. I did not take his tongue or anything else into my mouth. He does not want me, so you should be satisfied. My humiliation is complete. Isn't that what you wanted, to humiliate me for blackmailing my way into your home? Well, you have succeeded. I wish you happy, sir."

Pain. For a second it was mirrored in his eyes.

She did not stand around to see if it was an illusion. Her own pain was real enough for the both of them.

The Bastard Sheikh did not follow her this time.

Men and women were milling around the buffet tables, talking over iced shrimp, laughing over caviar, content with rich food and sexless morality. Elizabeth smiled, greeted, talked, but could not remember one single thing that was said.

Her mother conferred with the caterer—they stood together, Rebecca regal in royal blue velvet, the harried caterer in serviceable brown silk. When Rebecca caught sight of Elizabeth, she waved her over. Elizabeth turned and blindly smiled at the person nearest her.

Her smile froze.

"Dance with me."

Refusal sprang to her lips.

He was a bastard. An exotic, dark-skinned, golden-haired peacock surrounded by that most unforgiving breed, the middle class. Their association might be overlooked among the *ton*. It would not at a charity ball.

She could feel icy green eyes watching her, judging her, and did not have to turn around to identify the watcher as her mother.

The Bastard Sheikh's turquoise gaze was guarded; he expected her to reject him. To judge and condemn him like Lord Inchcape had done. Like Rebecca Walters would do.

Would you dance with me again?

"I would be honored, Lord Safyre."

Blue flame flickered in the turquoise eyes. He, too, remembered the lessons, the shared confessions. Silently, he led her onto the dance floor. Just as silently she reached up, up, up and laid her left hand on his shoulder.

The heat of his gloved hand burned through her own glove. He held her far closer than the regulated eighteen inches, and it felt *good.*

Warm breath gusted in her ear. That felt good too. Hot, intimate, all the things she would never experience.

I will not put myself through the trouble of bedding you again just so that you can lie with a man.

Oh, God. How could she live another sixteen years with Edward?

"No matter what happens, I want you to promise me something."

A man's and a woman's stiff elbows gouged into Elizabeth's shoulder. The Bastard Sheikh expertly twirled her aside.

"You are creaking, Mrs. Petre."

"I beg your pardon?"

"Your corset. How can you breathe with it laced that tightly?"

Her lips tightened. Emma, under Elizabeth's instructions, had laced her corset tighter than usual. *To contain her udder breasts and flabby hips.*

"How can you dance so well if you do not attend balls?"

A low laugh rumbled in his chest. "There are balls, *taalibba,* and there are balls."

"Where women dance bare-breasted?" she asked bitingly.

"Some of them," he murmured lazily.

He sounded as if the idea of her dancing with her naked breasts brushing his jacket appealed to him.

Impossible. Edward had made it clear that a full-breasted woman did not appeal to a man.

"What do you want me to promise?" she asked curtly.

"I want you to promise me you will never forget that you have a right to sexual gratification."

Elizabeth stiffened. "This is not Arabia, Lord Safyre."

"I want you to promise me that you will never forget that

a man trembles in his passion . . . just as a woman trembles in her passion.''

She tried to force their bodies into the regulated eighteen-inch dance position that decency demanded but that the crowd of people prohibited.

"I want you to promise me that you will come to me when the pain of being alone becomes too great.''

She quit struggling against him. "I will not commit adultery, Lord Safyre.''

"Marriage is more than words spoken in a church. You cannot commit adultery if you are not truly wed.''

"I have two children.''

"Your two sons will shortly be men. Whom will you have then, *taalibba*?''

Pain twisted inside her chest. "Whom do you have, Lord Safyre?'' she sharply countered.

"No one. That is why I know that sometime soon the pain will become too great for you to bear alone.''

It already was. "You bear it alone well enough.''

"I bear it because I have to.''

"And now I have to.''

"No, you do not.

"So you expect me to come to you like a bitch in heat?''

Elizabeth had not thought she could shock herself anymore. She continually proved herself wrong.

"I did not call you a bitch.''

She stared at the gold studs on his shirt. "You said I was in heat.''

"Sexual heat.''

She threw her head back and defiantly stared at him. "Is there a difference?''

His turquoise eyes were flat. "There is a difference.''

"What? *What is the difference?*''

He pulled her closer, silk on silk, breasts to chest . . . and that felt good too. Proof of her wanton nature.

"A bitch takes without giving.''

His voice was harsh. All she could see of his face was the

sharp outline of his chin, the angular curve of his cheeks, and the slight hook of his nose.

She remembered the bleakness in his eyes that Monday morning when she had asked him to teach her how to give a man pleasure . . . and the clinging aroma of a woman's perfume.

"I take it you are familiar with that type of woman."

"I am familiar with that type of woman," he agreed flatly.

"But a man and a woman . . . there can be a bonding between them. Can't there?"

She waited, hardly breathing, wanting him to tell her she knew not what, *no, yes,* there was nothing more to be had in a marriage *but there must be.* Otherwise she could not bear it.

"I believe so."

"You do not know?"

"I know now. Yes, *taalibba,* a man and a woman can bond, two bodies becoming one."

"You know who his mistress is, don't you?"

It was not a question.

Suddenly, her body was separate from his and they were once again just a man and a woman waltzing together. Elizabeth did not want to see the knowledge that would be there in his face. She squeezed her eyes shut.

The mistress must be very beautiful indeed for the Bastard Sheikh to be so certain that her husband would not bother bedding his wife. A beautiful, beautiful bitch.

He twirled Elizabeth around, a rush of overheated air and billowing silk. Her eyes snapped open.

"*Siba,* Elizabeth."

He knew . . . and he would not tell her.

She could not keep the bitterness out of her voice. "I see no honor in withholding information that might save a marriage."

"Some things are believed only when they are seen," he responded cryptically, swirling her around and around until she was dizzy. "When you are ready for the truth, you will see for yourself who your husband's lover is."

The music died with a crash of piano chords. The gas chande-

lier and Ramiel's dark face continued to spin. She clutched at him for support.

His lips twisted in a smile that did not reach his eyes. "I will be waiting, *taalibba*."

Gently, he disengaged her clutching fingers and stepped back. The throng of dancers swallowed him up.

What did he mean, he would be waiting? Her note had been quite explicit: There would be no more lessons. She had returned the book. *There could be no more lessons.*

Elizabeth stared at the place where the Bastard Sheikh had stood but moments earlier. His voice reverberated inside her head. *When you are ready for the truth, you will see for yourself who your husband's lover is.*

She looked around wildly. Was her husband's mistress someone she knew, someone she trusted?

The crowd parted, surging toward the buffet to replenish the energy dancing had drained. Edward stood with his head bent toward a young woman—Elizabeth estimated her to be eighteen years old, a year older than she had been when he had married her. The girl had blond hair and a wispy figure that managed to look graceful in the cumbersome bustle that continued to grow in both size and popularity.

Did Edward prefer "the flat chest and shapeless hips of a young girl"?

A blond-haired man joined Edward. He bore a marked resemblance to the young woman—no doubt the girl's brother, older perhaps by a couple of years. Edward raised his head and greeted the newcomer.

Elizabeth blinked at the warmth of her husband's smile.

"Mrs. Petre, we want to thank you for helping to organize such a wonderful party. You can be sure that we support your father and husband."

Elizabeth tore her gaze away from her husband and stared into pale, protruding eyes. It took her a second to identify the tall, gaunt woman and the short, squat man beside her.

"Mr. and Mrs. Frederik, thank you so much for joining us."

Elizabeth smiled and took the woman's hand into hers. "Your bid on the porcelain figurine was very generous."

"We don't like to think of women and children going hungry, Mrs. Petre." This from Mr. Frederik. "Not when their menfolk died for our country."

Elizabeth's smile grew stilted. "There are women and children on the streets who do not have husbands and fathers, Mr. Frederik. They need our help too."

Their reproving expressions did not bode well for future donations.

Elizabeth pushed aside thoughts of the Bastard Sheikh and the desperately poor women and diseased children who suffered because of people's ignorance. "Have you tried the shrimp, Mr. Frederik? It is a specialty of the caterer, quite delicious. I believe it is cooked in sherry. Mrs. Frederik, what a lovely gown. You must tell me who your modiste is."

Mr. Frederik was mollified by the food; Mrs. Frederik basked in Elizabeth's attention. It was a relief when Elizabeth was pulled aside by her mother.

"What was Lord Safyre doing here? Who invited him? And why did you dance with him?"

The smile on Elizabeth's face faded. "I have no idea why he was here. Perhaps he is a supporter of the Conservative Party."

"He's a Liberal. And a bastard. We do not associate with the likes of him. Not even for contributions."

That was a first. Elizabeth sometimes thought her mother would consort with the devil himself to further the campaign.

"I am sorry, Mother. I have no idea why he came."

I came for you.

Hot blood flooded Elizabeth's face.

"Why did you dance with him?"

Because I want to know what it is like for two bodies to become one.

"Because he asked me to," she said quietly.

"That is the second time you have danced with him, daughter. Even you must be aware of his reputation."

Elizabeth calmly met her mother's eyes. "Do you think Lord Safyre is trying to seduce me?"

Rebecca's emerald-green eyes glittered. "Don't be ridiculous. Obviously, he is attempting to undermine our cause. He is fully aware that if you are seen dancing with the likes of him, it will reflect badly on your father and your husband. The Liberals do not want a Conservative for prime minister."

Elizabeth ignored the pain of her mother's condescension. "Is it so inconceivable that a man might dance with me because he finds me attractive?"

"Do *you* find *him* attractive?" Her mother's voice was razor sharp.

"Yes, I do. Don't you?"

For the first time in Elizabeth's life she shocked her mother into silence.

The shock quickly wore off, to be replaced by distaste. "Are you flirting with that man, Elizabeth?"

Ineffable weariness washed over Elizabeth as the excitement of the Bastard Sheikh's pursuit and the warmth he had imparted to her while they danced evaporated.

"No. As you said, a man like him would not be interested in a woman like me."

It was farce at its most pure.

The man who should be solicitous of her needs refused to touch her—while a man who could have any woman he wanted would take her out of pity.

Chapter Fourteen

". . . temptation," swelled over the heads of the congregation. The candles lighting the wooden altar flickered; dark shadows danced on the gleaming wood.

Elizabeth sat in the front pew, wearing the black bonnet and veil that she wore every Sunday. Edward, mustache waxed, sat on her right, impeccably attired in his gray wool four-button cutaway suit. Rebecca, wearing a black bonnet and veil, sat on Elizabeth's left; she appeared to be transfixed by the minister's words. Elizabeth did not have to turn her head to know that her father, who sat on Rebecca's left, was equally attentive.

She had married Edward in this church. The minister who proselytized now on the chapter of Matthew had pronounced them man and wife.

A wedding breakfast had followed the ceremony. The bubbles in her allotted glass of champagne had fizzed and fizzed.

How disappointed she had been that she was not to have a honeymoon. How excited she had been at the prospect of having her own home. And how full of expectation she had been on their wedding night.

Blindly, she glanced down at the open Bible lying across her lap.

Rebecca had decorated Edward's town house; Rebecca had hired the servants. The only claim Elizabeth had had on her new life was Edward. And the only time he had spent with her had been those few minutes each night underneath the bedcovers.

All to make her pregnant so that he could gain votes.

A riffling of paper filled the church. Beside Elizabeth, Rebecca flipped to the next page in her Bible.

Elizabeth instinctively followed her mother's lead. She looked at the tiny black print through the tiny holes in her black veil. What was she supposed to be following?

Bowing her head, she squinted at the text. The Beatitudes, the Similitudes, murder, *divorce* . . .

Divorce, according to Matthew, was forbidden unless fornication could be proven.

Edward had a mistress. *Adultery was fornication.*

I will be waiting, taalibba.

Elizabeth's head snapped back. Her heart thudded against the tightly laced corset. The minister's voice, raised so that he might reach the parishioners at the rear of the church, cannonaded inside her head.

What was she thinking? *Respectable women did not sue for divorce.*

She concentrated on the minister, on the gleam of the wooden altar, on the wax running down the candles, on the elaborate embroidery decorating the minister's vestments. Respectable things that respectable women thought about.

"Elizabeth."

Elizabeth dumbly looked up at her mother. The hollow echo of shuffling feet reverberated inside the church.

The first pew was emptying out. Others waited impatiently for their turn to exit—including her husband and her parents.

Flushing, she stood up. A loud thump sounded over the retreating footsteps.

Her Bible.

Edward quickly bent, retrieved it for her. An enigmatic expression flitted across his face.

Elizabeth snatched the book from his hand. "Thank you."

Sunshine spilled in the aisle, turned the crimson runner to blood red. Elizabeth nodded and smiled at familiar faces as she passed the long rows of pews. Outside, she took a deep breath of air.

"Elizabeth. Edward and your father are going to the club; we'll take luncheon together, shall we?"

Every Sunday after church, Edward and her father went to their club; every Sunday Rebecca extended the same invitation. And every Sunday Elizabeth accepted.

They had much to talk about on Sundays. The upcoming week of social and political events, synchronizing their schedules . . .

"No, thank you, Mother. I have correspondence that must be taken care of," she lied.

Rebecca's emerald-green eyes glittered through the black veil. Elizabeth tried to remember if those eyes had ever lit up with laughter or love. She could not.

"There are certain changes in our schedules—"

"We will lunch on Tuesday, Mother. We can go over the changes then."

"Very well. I, too, have things to take care of this afternoon. Your father speaks on Wednesday."

"I remember."

"I will drop you off at your town house. Andrew and Edward are taking the other carriage."

Elizabeth nodded. "Thank you."

Andrew and Edward always took the Petre carriage.

A spattering of laughter came from the church steps. She did not have to see or hear Andrew and Edward to know that they were charming the congregation. That, too, occurred every Sunday.

Knowing her role by rote, Elizabeth turned and mingled with the lingering church members. Andrew and Edward would not leave their public until there was no public to leave.

Later, in the carriage, Rebecca surprised Elizabeth by keeping up a light stream of gossip. And then, "Are you seeing a doctor, Elizabeth?"

Elizabeth turned her face to the window and watched the passing buildings. "No. Why should I?"

"You have not been yourself lately. Perhaps you need a tonic."

Perhaps she just needed to be loved.

"Why did you never have more children, Mother?" she asked impulsively.

Silence greeted her question. Elizabeth turned away from the window.

Rebecca gripped her Bible. "I could not have any more children."

Elizabeth felt a pang of remorse. "I'm sorry."

"My mother, your grandmother, had one child too. Myself. You are very fortunate in your two sons."

Elizabeth had never known her grandmother; she had died years before Elizabeth was born.

It was on the tip of her tongue to ask Rebecca if she thought Elizabeth was fortunate because she had two children as opposed to one, or if she was fortunate because her children were sons as opposed to daughters. Then it occurred to her that perhaps Rebecca's mother might have preferred a son to a daughter. Unloved herself, perhaps Rebecca could not love her own daughter.

"Yes, I am," Elizabeth said quietly.

The carriage jerked to a stop.

"I will see you on Tuesday, daughter. I expect you to be punctual."

Elizabeth tamped down a spark of anger. "I expect I will be."

A footman—the new footman, Elizabeth noted—wrenched open the coach door.

"Good day, Elizabeth."

"Good day, Mother."

Standing, back stooped, she held out her hand for the footman to help her down.

He stood rigidly at attention beside the coach, as if Elizabeth were a gunnery sergeant and he a foot soldier. She half expected him to salute.

A smile tugging at her lips, she stuck a foot out, down, found the step. No sooner had she attained the sidewalk than the carriage door closed smartly behind her.

"Thank you, Johnny."

"My pleasure, ma'am."

"Johnny . . ."

He continued staring straight ahead. "Ma'am?"

She had thought to instruct him on the proper behavior of a footman. She thought better of it. It was a kind thing he was doing, working in his cousin's stead while Freddie took care of his mother.

"You have never before been a footman?"

"No, ma'am."

"You are doing a fine job."

"Thank you, ma'am."

Elizabeth turned and walked up the two steps to the door of the town house. Sighing, she reached out to open the door herself.

Instantly, a white-gloved hand was there before hers. The heat of Johnny's body caged her shoulder.

"You did a brave thing, ma'am, walking the horses in the fog." Leaning forward, he pushed the front door open.

Suddenly, the sun was a little brighter. "Thank you, Johnny."

Beadles waited in the foyer; he wrung his hands. "Mrs. Petre! Are you not well? Shall I ring up the doctor?"

The smile faded from her face. So much concern . . . from everyone but her husband.

"No, Beadles. I am not lunching with my mother because of correspondence I need to take care of. Please send up Emma."

But once Elizabeth had changed clothing—there was nothing to do. She wrote letters to her sons. She thumbed through a book of poetry—English poetry. There was not a vulva or a meritorious member to be found.

Kisses, yes, but no tongues; sighs, but no climaxes; love, but no coition. Flower petals fell off in symbolical death, but nary a one of them unfurled to disclose a hidden bud.

A woman in Arabia . . . has the right to seek divorce if her husband will not satisfy her.

She threw the book at the wall.

A soft knock followed the explosive *whop*.

"Mrs. Petre." The knock was repeated more insistently. "Mrs. Petre."

Smoothing her hair, Elizabeth opened her bedroom door. "Yes, Beadles?"

"You have a caller, madam." Bowing, Beadles extended a small silver tray.

A card lay on it. The right-hand corner was bent, signifying whoever it was waited to be received.

Curious, Elizabeth picked it up. *Countess Devington* was printed in dark, ornate scroll.

The Bastard Sheikh's mother.

Her head jerked up. "I am not receiving callers, Beadles."

"Very well, madam."

Elizabeth closed the door and leaned against the wood. How dare she call uninvited. She had abandoned her son at an age when he most needed a mother's love.

The wood between her shoulders vibrated.

Elizabeth's heart skipped a beat. Surely the countess would not be so brazen as to—

"Mrs. Petre."

Beadles.

She cautiously opened the door.

Beadles bowed again; his dignified demeanor was marred by the labored sound of his breathing from climbing the stairs twice in such rapid succession. A folded piece of paper lay on the silver tray. "The countess bade me give this note to you, madam."

The countess's handwriting was bold, the message plain.

You may have the pleasure of my company now or the pleasure of my son's company later.

Elizabeth's lips sealed in a tight line. *She knew.* So much for *siba.* Elizabeth should be incapable of feeling any more pain from a man's betrayal: She wasn't.

"Please show the countess to the drawing room, Beadles. Have Cook prepare a tray."

Countess Devington stood in front of the white marble fireplace in the drawing room, warming herself. She wore an elegant dark crimson day dress and a smart black velvet hat jauntily perched on her golden blond head.

Gray eyes snagged Elizabeth's in the mirror above the mantel. "I see by your expression that you realize I am aware of your liaison with my son."

Elizabeth felt all the blood drain from her head. The countess was as blunt as was the Bastard Sheikh. "Yes."

The countess turned in a graceful swirl. Her gray eyes warmed with understanding. "Please do not be angry with Ramiel. It was Muhamed who told me, not my son."

"There was no need for this visit, Countess Devington. My so-called liaison with your son is over," Elizabeth said frigidly.

The countess tilted her head to one side so that her hat sat perfectly straight. "You do not understand why I sent Ramiel to Arabia to be with his father."

A tide of hot mortification flooded Elizabeth's face. "That is none of my concern, surely."

The countess peeled off slender tan gloves. "Elizabeth—I may call you by your first name, may I not?—my parents sent me to a finishing school in Italy when I was sixteen. I was abducted one day when I wandered away from a class tour. My abductor put me aboard a ship that was filled with other blond women—blond women are highly sought after in Arabia, you see. In Turkey we were put on a slave block and stripped naked so that men could see us and even examine us, as a horse is examined before purchase. One by one we were sold. The Turk who bought me raped me brutally. But I was fortunate.

Because the Turk got tired of raping me and sold me to a Syrian trader.''

Elizabeth stared, speechless.

''The Syrian taught me how to survive in a country where women are worth less than a good horse. Eventually, he sold me to a young sheikh. I learned to love that sheikh with all my heart, and I took from him the thing that an Arab values most—I took his son. When Ramiel turned twelve, I could no longer deprive either him or his father of each other's company. It was not out of convenience that I sent my son away, but out of love.''

''But—his father gave him a harem when he was thirteen!'' Elizabeth blurted out.

''It is certainly not an English tradition, but I assure you, in the court of Safyre it is what fathers do for their sons.''

''And yet you sent him there, knowing the type of education he would receive.''

''As you deliberately sought out my son, knowing the type of education he *had* received.''

Elizabeth's chin shot up. Her mouth opened to object; instead, she acknowledged the truth. ''Yes.''

''I cannot cast stones, Elizabeth, because I would not trade one single moment I spent with my sheikh for a lifetime of English virtue. I am very glad that Ramiel was spared the hypocrisy of becoming a man in a country that denigrates one of the true pleasures of life. Now that we have that out in the open, may I sit down, please?''

Elizabeth should be shocked. She should be outraged. Instead, she wondered what it would be like to be loved as the countess had so obviously loved. Openly. Wholly.

She wondered what it would be like to be able to accept one's sexuality without guilt.

''I am sorry for your misfortunes, Countess Devington,'' Elizabeth said quietly. ''Please sit down.''

A blinding smile lit the countess's face.

Elizabeth blinked.

The countess was a beautiful woman, but it was a mature

beauty. That smile made her look as if she were sixteen again, young and innocent. It did not belong to a woman who had been brutally raped and sold into slavery any more than it belonged to a woman who by her own admission had given herself to a man outside wedlock and borne his illegitimate son.

She sat across from Elizabeth with a sigh of silk and a whiff of tantalizing perfume—Elizabeth had never smelled anything like it. It smelled as if an orange had drowned in a bowl of vanilla.

The countess confided with ease, "Ramiel would not be happy if he knew that I was here."

"Then I am afraid I do not understand," Elizabeth said carefully, not wanting to like this woman but finding that she did. "You said that if I did not see you today, your son would call later."

"You threatened to revoke Ramiel's citizenship if Muhamed did not let you into his house."

"I have told your son I never intended such an action," Elizabeth disclaimed stiffly.

"Nor did I intend to threaten you with my son."

Hazel and gray eyes locked unflinchingly. "I made a mistake, Countess Devington. I am sorry for it. I never intended to cause your son harm. I do not know what Muhamed told you, but I can assure you that our association is over."

The gray eyes darkened. "Perhaps you will best understand Muhamed's position when I tell you that he, too, had been sold to the Syrian trader. He was a very handsome boy who had been abused by his former owner. I am not at liberty to disclose exactly what had been done to him, but suffice it to say that perhaps Muhamed has his reasons for disliking women. If the Syrian trader and I had not nursed him back to health, he would have died like so many European boys sold into slavery do. Upon gaining my freedom, I returned to England; Muhamed chose to stay. When I sent Ramiel to his father, Muhamed watched out for him. Try to remember that Ramiel is the son that Muhamed never had and perhaps you will better understand his position.''

Muhamed—European! The Bastard Sheikh had deliberately allowed Elizabeth to assume differently.

"It is not up to me to understand your son's servants, Countess Devington.''

"You think I am interfering.''

The countess was full of surprises. "Yes.''

"You have not yet been to my son's bed.''

Elizabeth was mortified. "Of course not.''

"But you would like to.''

"Countess Devington, I am a married woman—''

"It is rumored among certain circles that your husband takes a mistress because you are a cold, frigid wife who cares more about advancing his career than about warming his bed.''

The blatant unfairness of such a statement took Elizabeth's breath away. She could only stare and hope that the pain that ripped through her body did not show on her face.

"What exactly is the purpose of this visit, Countess Devington?''

The countess smiled sympathetically. "Rumors are cruel.''

Pain gave way to fury. "That rumor is totally unjustified! I went to your son to learn how to give my husband pleasure—''

Her teeth snapped together.

An emotion that Elizabeth could not define sparkled in the countess's gray eyes. "You went to my son to get him to teach you how to give a man pleasure?''

She had not backed down in front of the Bastard Sheikh; she would not back down in front of his mother. "Yes.''

"And did he . . . teach you this art?''

Bleakness rolled over Elizabeth in cold gray waves. "Perhaps some women are not meant to give a man pleasure,'' she said evenly. "Perhaps they are meant to be companions and mothers instead of lovers.''

Warm understanding filled the countess's gray eyes, as if she knew that her son's tutelage had failed to elicit the desired results. Elizabeth wondered if everyone in London knew that Edward had rejected her.

Common sense immediately asserted itself.

According to the countess, everyone in London thought that she was a frigid bitch who would rather campaign until her throat was hoarse and her eyes burned from lack of sleep than offer her body in a loving embrace.

A short knock interrupted Elizabeth's bleak thoughts; the drawing room door swung open. Beadles wheeled in the tea cart.

"Thank you, Beadles. That will be all."

"Very good, madam."

Elizabeth resolutely poured tea. "Cream, Countess Devington?"

"Lemon will be fine, thank you."

"Biscuits?"

"Please."

Elizabeth dutifully passed the platter. Long white fingers made a healthy selection.

The countess must be one of those women who could eat biscuits all day long and not gain a pound, Elizabeth thought resentfully. "You still did not tell me why you are here."

"Because I wanted to learn more about the woman who blackmailed my son."

Elizabeth's chin jutted up in denial.

"And who then had the kindness to dance with him."

She cringed, remembering Lord Inchcape's rudeness. "It was not a kindness, Countess Devington. It was an honor."

"Many disagree with you."

"That is their opinion."

Little finger crooked, the countess brought the rose-patterned china cup to her lips and delicately sipped. She lowered the cup to the saucer. "I think you underestimate Ramiel's teaching abilities as well as your own natural talents. But that is between you and my son. Now, tell me about yourself. I have read so much about you in the newspapers."

Elizabeth felt like Alice, a character in one of Phillip's favorite storybooks. Only it was not the Mad Hatter who took tea with her, it was the Bastard Sheikh's mother.

Ramiel's name was not mentioned again. Elizabeth did not know if she was relieved or disappointed. By the time they drank three cups of tea and devoured the platter of biscuits, Elizabeth felt as if she had known the countess all her life. When the countess pulled on her gloves, Elizabeth was genuinely sorry to see her leave.

Impulsively she offered, "Come visit again, please. I have enjoyed our time together so much."

The countess smiled, that lovely warm smile of hers that embraced the good and the bad, the innocent and the forbidden. "I will. But in return you must promise to come take tea with me."

Reality was a harsh intrusion. "I cannot do that."

"Life is a trial of decisions, Elizabeth. You cannot be ruled by the opinions of others."

"I am quite capable of making my own decisions," Elizabeth stiffly protested. "I simply do not think it would be wise to chance meeting your son."

The countess sighed, as if she were disappointed by Elizabeth's answer. "You are so young, Elizabeth."

"I am thirty-three years old, madam." *A woman in her prime.* "I assure you I am not young."

"I am fifty-seven years old; I assure you, to me you are young. How old were you when you married?"

"Seventeen."

"So you know nothing of men."

"I will remind you, Countess, that my husband, in addition to being the Chancellor of the Exchequer, is a man."

The countess nodded. "So Muhamed is wrong," she murmured.

"About what?"

The countess's smile was kind. "If you ever need anyone, Elizabeth, even if it is just to talk, my door will always be open to you."

* * *

"I had tea with Elizabeth Petre, Ramiel.

Ramiel abruptly focused on his mother. "Did Mrs. Petre invite you, *Ummee?*"

"No."

"Then you invited yourself." Ramiel's voice was flat; it did not tolerate interference. "Why?"

The countess was not deterred by his abruptness. "You asked me to take you to Isabelle's ball and gain an introduction for you to the wife of the Chancellor of the Exchequer. Of course I was curious about her. Rightfully so, as it happens. Elizabeth told me that she came to you and asked you to teach her how to give her husband pleasure."

"*Ela'na!*" Ramiel swore.

The tips of his ears burned. He did not know what embarrassed him the more, that his mother had knowledge of his position as Elizabeth's tutor or that he was still capable of being embarrassed—twice now in nearly as many days.

The countess raised her eyebrows; her gray eyes sparkled with mischievous laughter. "It is nice to know that I can still surprise you, Ramiel."

"Then you were in good company; Elizabeth, too, is full of surprises," he said dryly.

"She does not know."

Ramiel did not pretend to misunderstand. "No."

"And you cannot tell her."

"No."

"She will be hurt."

Yes, Elizabeth would be hurt. By so many things.

"She tried to seduce her husband."

"*Allah akbar,* Mother!" Ramiel fought to contain his jealousy, that Elizabeth would confide in his mother but not him. "Did she tell you everything over a cup of English tea?"

"She did not have to. I asked her if you had been successful as a teacher. She said that perhaps some women were meant to be companions and mothers as opposed to lovers."

Ramiel grimly stared at the red and yellow silk pillows piled high on the built-in seat underneath the drawing room windows. Dusky night streaked the gray sky.

He remembered the feel of Elizabeth's waist beneath his hand at the charity ball, her flesh cruelly constrained by a corset. He remembered her nipples stabbing her gray velvet dress as she held the artificial phallus in her hand.

He remembered her words, *He does not want me so you should be satisfied.*

"She's wrong," he murmured, not even aware that he spoke out loud.

"I agree that Elizabeth Petre is not meant to be merely a companion and a mother. I am still not certain about some women."

"I will not let him hurt her."

"Spoken like the son of a sheikh."

Ramiel's head snapped back. "You mean spoken like the Bastard Sheikh."

"You are a good man, *ibnee.*"

The countess's gray eyes were too penetrating. Ramiel sometimes thought that he fought a useless battle, protecting her from the truth. At times like this he felt she already knew.

"How was Elizabeth?" He leapt up from the plush velvet divan. Restlessly, he strode toward the fireplace, leaned against the mantel, and stared at the fire instead of the encroaching darkness. "Did she ask about me?"

"She is terrified of you."

He pivoted, facing the countess. The fire behind him roared with heat. "I would never hurt her."

The countess scrutinized his face in the flickering firelight. Satisfaction shone in her eyes. "No, you would not. I told her my door would always be open for her."

The significance of the countess's offer was not lost on Ramiel. "You are offering her your friendship?"

"I already have."

"Do you accept her as a daughter?"

An expertly darkened eyebrow arched. "Did you offer her marriage?"

"Even in Arabia a woman is allowed only one husband at a time," Ramiel returned wryly.

"Her mother is the daughter of a bishop, you know." The countess relayed the information as if it bore some significance.

"No, I did not know."

"That is initially how Andrew Walters was elected to Parliament, because of her father's connections."

"How do you know so much about Elizabeth's family?"

A shadow dimmed the countess's gray eyes. "Rebecca Walters took it as a personal affront that I had survived being kidnapped and sold to a sheikh. And having survived it, that I had the temerity to come back to England."

With a bastard son in tow.

Ramiel sometimes forgot what his mother must have endured. In England he had been the darling of the nursery while she fought dragons.

"I learned a lot about that young lady," the countess added ruefully.

"But she could not best you," Ramiel said gently.

The countess smiled a smile filled with cynicism, irony, and a certain ruthless satisfaction. "No, she could not. I was not respectable, but because of my title and my money, I was fashionable. The more viciously Rebecca slandered me, the more fashionable I became. Whereas the opposite is true of Rebecca. People who live in glass houses should not throw stones. I heard certain rumors . . . so I in turn passed them on. Your mother is a very wicked woman."

Ramiel couldn't help but laugh. The sound echoed in the drawing room.

Women like the marchioness, who waylaid him so that she could rut with a bastard Arab, were wicked. His mother was the kindest, most intelligent person he had ever met. To hear her compare herself with women who had never had an unselfish thought in their small, greedy lives was absurd.

His turquoise eyes glittered. "Let us hope that Elizabeth soon finds her own wickedness, *Ummee*."

The shadow disappeared from the countess's eyes. "I think she already has, *ibnee*. And I am going to help you."

A sharp well of emotion rose inside Ramiel.

When he had first returned to England nine years earlier she had hugged him, fixed him a cup of hot chocolate, and sent him off to bed, just as she had done when he was twelve years old. Not once in the intervening years had she asked him why he had left Arabia.

"Why?" he asked now, the heat that had previously pricked the tips of his ears burning his eyes.

"Because I am your mother and because I love you. Elizabeth is like you in some respects. She runs from her passion and you run from your past. Perhaps together the two of you can stop running."

Chapter Fifteen

Elizabeth distractedly stared at a middle-aged man with bristly muttonchops. Unaware of her regard, he pulled back a chair so that his lady friend could rise from the table directly in front of the one Elizabeth and Rebecca occupied. His black Prince Albert coat swung at the backs of his knees.

One week.

It had been exactly one week this Tuesday since Elizabeth and Ramiel had had their first lesson. It seemed like a year, like a hundred years ago. And no matter how she pretended otherwise, she knew that she could not go back and be the woman she had been before.

"Elizabeth, you are not listening to a thing I am saying. I was telling you that you will be attending the marchioness's ball. While she is rather unsavory, she does have royal connections."

"I'm sorry, Mother." The apology came automatically. Focusing on Rebecca, Elizabeth lifted her cup to her lips and sipped cold, weak tea. The sudden desire for hot Turkish coffee was almost overwhelming.

"You and Edward are having dinner with the Hammonds tonight."

I will not put myself through the trouble of bedding you again just so that you can lie with a man.

Nausea rose in Elizabeth's throat at the memory of Edward's words that, no matter how hard she tried, she could not forget. Carefully, she set her cup back inside the saucer. "Mother, I want a divorce."

Glass exploded—Rebecca's teacup. The saucer lay on the dark red carpet where it had fallen. It overflowed with tea and fragments of delicately painted porcelain.

A great hush fell over the restaurant as men and women turned in their seats to see what had happened. At the same time, a footman rushed forward to clean up the mishap. Elizabeth was acutely aware of the staring eyes. She was even more acutely aware of Rebecca's frozen face.

Suddenly the baldheaded maître d' was bending over Rebecca and placing another cup and saucer in front of her. "Clumsy footman," he said, as if the man kneeling on the floor were responsible for the broken cup. "Please forgive us, madam. It will not happen again. May I get you a little something extra, at no charge, of course . . ."

"My daughter and I do not need anything more, thank you." Rebecca did not once glance at the maître d'. Her emerald eyes were fixed on Elizabeth. "You may leave us."

"Very good, madam."

The maître d' bowed several times; splinters of light reflected off his shiny pate. The footman quickly collected the broken porcelain and wiped up the spilled tea. The staring eyes, finding nothing of major import to sustain their interest, turned away, leaving Elizabeth and Rebecca alone once more.

Rebecca calmly reached for the porcelain teapot and filled her cup. "We will forget what you said, Elizabeth."

Elizabeth worked to swallow past the knot in her throat. "I am a woman, Mother, not a child. I will not be ignored."

Rebecca pursed her lips and daintily blew on her tea before taking a small sip. "Does Edward beat you, Elizabeth?"

Elizabeth's fingers tightened spasmodically around her cup. "No, of course not."

"Then I see no reason for a divorce."

She took a deep breath, agonizing over her next words, but then there was no need to because try as she might, she could not hold them back. "He has not been to my bed in over twelve years."

Rebecca returned her cup to the saucer with a sharp click. The sound was repeated a dozen times in the restaurant, from behind Elizabeth, to her side, in front of her. "Decent wives would thank God every morning and evening for your good fortune."

Elizabeth winced at the implication she was not "decent." She resolutely raised her chin. "Nevertheless, I want a divorce."

"You will ruin what your father and husband have worked so hard to achieve."

Anger warred with the guilt her mother's words incurred. "What about me, Mother? Do I not deserve anything? He refuses to come to my bed, yet he keeps a mistress. I . . . he is hardly ever at home."

"Men will do what men will do. You have two sons—what more could you possibly want?"

A man!

A man who loved her.

A man who would share her bed and be a father to her children before they were too old to need one or care if they had one.

"Edward came to my bed when he thought Richard was dying." Elizabeth tried to keep the horror and disgust out of her voice, and failed. "He did not give me a child, Mother, or you a grandchild—he gave his voters a family."

Rebecca raised her napkin, blotted her mouth. "It matters little why your husband gave you children, Elizabeth. The fact is that you have two healthy sons who are well provided for. How do you think your decision will affect them? They will suffer. The society they have taken for granted will outcast them. Their lives will be ruined.''

Elizabeth remembered Phillip's black eye; Richard's gauntness; the countess's words: *I did not send my son to Arabia out of convenience, but out of love.*

"They already suffer.''

"We make the best of what we have, Elizabeth. That is all a woman can do.''

No, that was not all a woman could do. A woman did not deserve to have her body and her desires ridiculed.

A woman owed it to herself to demand fidelity.

"Perhaps some women. Will Father help me? Or should I get a lawyer?''

"I will discuss it with Andrew when he has the time.''

As if Elizabeth's needs were inconsequential to the needs of the country.

All of her life she had taken second place! Just once—

Elizabeth took a deep breath. "Thank you, Mother. That is all I can ask.''

"We really must swing by the milliner's.'' Rebecca dropped her napkin onto the table beside her cup and saucer and scooted her chair back slightly. "I want a new hat for your father's speech this Wednesday.''

Instantly, the maître d' was there to pull back Rebecca's chair. She tugged her gloves on while Elizabeth awkwardly rose, impeded rather than aided by the maître d'.

Elizabeth watched Rebecca calmly smooth the wrinkles out of her gloves as if it were the most important thing in the world. More important than a daughter. More important than a divorce.

"Would you change anything in your life, Mother?''

Did Father ever give you one single moment of ecstasy that you would not trade for all the days of your life?

But Elizabeth already knew the answer. The same answer she herself would give if asked.

Rebecca paused infinitesimally in her grooming. "The past cannot be changed.'' She lifted her hands, deftly readjusted the tilt of her hat. "When you accept that, you will be content.''

"Then perhaps, Mother, it is best that women not be content." Elizabeth's voice was unaccustomedly brittle. "Otherwise, we would not have the likes of Mrs. Butler, who is even now changing English law."

Rebecca walked out of the restaurant. Elizabeth followed, pulling on her gloves as she went.

Divorce was not mentioned again. Not in between short rides to various shops. Not during the longer ride to Rebecca's house.

The coach turned a corner. Elizabeth grabbed the carriage handle.

Rebecca's face in the darkening gloom was ghostly white. "Shall you come in for tea, Elizabeth?"

"No, thank you, Mother. I need to get home so I can dress for dinner."

"Ted Hammond is an ambitious young man. He will be very beneficial to Edward."

"Yes."

"Elizabeth."

Elizabeth's fingers tightened about the carriage handle. "Yes?"

"Your decision does not have anything to do with Lord Safyre, does it?"

Did it?

Was she asking for a divorce because of the Bastard Sheikh . . . or because of Edward? Because she had learned that a woman was not sexually depraved for wanting fulfillment . . . or because she lusted after her tutor?

She could feel her mother's eyes in the darkness . . . and remembered how they had glared when she danced with the Bastard Sheikh. "You said that a man such as he would not be interested in a woman like me, Mother."

"You also said that you found him attractive."

"And so I do. Edward is a very attractive man too."

And if her handsome husband would not sleep with her, why would the Bastard Sheikh?

Elizabeth winced. Especially if he saw her naked.

"I will not have a man like him jeopardizing the careers of your father and husband."

The coach pulled to a halt. "Lord Safyre has nothing to do with Edward's or Father's careers."

That, at least, was true.

The carriage door opened. Cold air and gathering mist flooded the interior.

"I have packages in the boot, Wilson."

The butler, an old family retainer, briefly bowed before offering up his hand to assist Rebecca. "Very good, madam."

"Good night, Mother."

"Elizabeth." Rebecca paused in the doorway of the coach.

Elizabeth tensed. "Yes?"

"Men are selfish. They will not place the needs of a child before their own. That is a woman's duty. A man like Lord Safyre would not want sons—especially sons that did not spring from his own loins—to interfere with his pleasures."

Rebecca stepped out of the coach with a harsh swish of wool; the door slammed behind her, leaving Elizabeth with the echo of her mother's words ringing in her ears. Bracing herself against the jolt of the carriage, she lay back against the leather seat and watched the passing streets. Lamp boys scrambled to light the streetlamps for the coming night, leaving a trail of golden orbs in their wake.

Had she known that it would come to this, she wondered, when she sought the Bastard Sheikh's tutelage? Would she have had the courage to seek him out if she had known that her simple desire to learn how to give her husband pleasure would culminate in divorce?

If she went through with it, she would truly be alone, without even the facade of a happy family. Was she strong enough to stand alone?

I want you to promise me that you will come to me when the pain of being alone becomes too great.

Was she endangering Richard and Phillip's future because she lusted after a man who was not her husband? A man who, according to Rebecca, would not tolerate her two sons?

As soon as the coach pulled up in front of the Petre town house, Elizabeth wrenched open the carriage door and jumped out. Beadles stood on the bottom step, mouth gaping open at her impropriety.

"Please send Emma up to my room, Beadles."

"Very good, ma'am."

Elizabeth lifted her skirts and raced up the steps, panting. The corset was too tight—*she would pass out from lack of oxygen.* Which was a far more comfortable sensation than the feel of lead that weighted down her stomach

The burgundy runner chasing the stairs seemed brighter. More inhospitable. It had lasted sixteen years and would probably see another sixteen.

She dreaded the coming night, sitting at dinner, smiling and pretending. Or perhaps it was spending the evening with Edward that she dreaded.

He had told her she had great udder breasts when she asked him to be intimate. What would he say when she asked him for a divorce?

It's not too late, the pounding of her heart drummed out. All she need do was run back downstairs and telephone her mother and say that of course she did not want a divorce, that the whole idea stemmed from the roast beef she had toyed with at lunch. No doubt, she could say, it had been spoiled and her request had stemmed from indigestion.

Upstairs in her room, dark pink roses marched up the walls. She glanced at the heavy cherry bed in which she had spent her wedding night.

The drapes had been drawn; there had been no warming fire in the fireplace. The chest drawers had contained her underwear and nightgowns and the wardrobe had been filled with her clothes, but it had seemed as if they were someone else's clothes, someone else's body that waited between cold, damp sheets.

She had given birth to her two sons in that bed. How could she abandon it?

A soft knock echoed inside the room. Elizabeth's heart jumped into her throat.

"Mrs. Petre. May I come in?"

She swallowed; her heart settled back into her chest where it belonged. Emma. Of course. She had asked Beadles to send her up.

Why would she think that her husband would come to her after so adamantly rejecting her advances? No doubt he was still at Parliament and would not be home for another hour or so.

"Come in, Emma."

Emma's round face was pleasantly familiar. "Shall I run a bath for you, ma'am?"

"Yes, please."

Hot steam writhed above the tub. Elizabeth gratefully slipped into the hot water.

What would the boys think about her decision?

How would a divorce affect their lives at school?

She leaned her head back against the copper tub. And wondered what kind of bathroom the Bastard Sheikh had. Immediately, a picture of the artificial phallus flashed behind her eyes.

It had not been nearly as long as his two handbreadths had been.

Elizabeth stood up in the tub in a cascade of water. She overrode her thoughts by brutally rubbing herself dry, replacing mental pain with physical pain. After Elizabeth donned her stockings, drawers, and chemise in lonely solitude, Emma silently dressed her, as if she sensed Elizabeth's need for silence.

Edward was waiting downstairs for her, dressed for dinner. He surveyed her thoroughly, as if she were a horse for sale. *Or a slave on an auction block.*

Taking her cloak, he draped it about her shoulders while Beadles solemnly watched. Inside the coach she and Edward were enclosed in darkness and a distance that had nothing to do with the leather seat that separated their bodies and everything to do with the needs that divided their lives.

"I talked to my mother today, Edward."

There. Relief mingled with dread.

"Of course. It's Tuesday."

The sudden acceleration of Elizabeth's heartbeat drowned out the clip-clop of the horses' hooves and the bump and grind of the carriage wheels.

"I told her that I wanted a divorce."

"And you expect your mother to influence your father on your behalf."

He did not sound surprised. His voice was calm, reasonable, slightly sympathetic. The same voice that had spoken to her in his darkened bedroom, telling her things she would rather not hear.

She strove to restrain a surge of desperation. "You have a mistress, Edward."

"I have told you that I do not."

"I do not think the courts will believe you."

"Elizabeth, you are incredibly naive. If you were to have a lover, then most certainly I could sue you for a divorce The most you, a woman, could ever hope to obtain if you proved that I kept a mistress is to sue for separation.

Elizabeth was stunned. "I don't believe you."

The Bible had clearly stated that adultery was grounds for divorce . . . *if the woman was adulterous.* It had said nothing about a man's infidelity.

"If you could prove that I beat you outside the realms of 'ordinary chastisement,' then perhaps the courts would feel different. But I don't beat you, Elizabeth. You have everything a woman could possibly want. A home, children, a substantial allowance. If you stand up in front of a court and claim that you want a divorce because I do not frequent your bed, I will not be able to protect you."

"What do you mean?"

"The court would see you as a nymphomaniac, a disturbed woman who needs the help of a doctor. There are many asylums that specialize in the treatment of mentally deranged women. They could recommend that you be committed to one."

Elizabeth's lips were suddenly dryer than tinder. "And you would let them."

"You would leave me no choice."

"Then I will sue for separation."

"I would rather see you in an asylum. It would garner more public sympathy."

It was becoming increasingly harder to remain calm. "Edward, you do not love me."

"No, I do not."

"Why continue with this farce of a marriage?"

"Because my voters do not think it is a farce."

Fog pressed against the window; a dim light proved to be a streetlamp. Hours earlier it had been a golden orb; now it was a dingy circle of light.

A rustle of clothes sounded in the heavy darkness, followed by a creak of springs. Elizabeth's clenched hands were suddenly clasped.

Gasping, she turned toward Edward. A week ago she would have taken this unexpected contact as a promising sign. Now she uselessly jerked her hands to free them.

Edward was surprisingly strong. "Elizabeth, I do not understand what has happened to you. A week ago you were content. There are things far more important than sharing a man's bed. We have two sons; you have been an invaluable asset to my career. It is demanding, but there are rewards. You are one of the most respected women in England. I know you love Richard and Phillip. You must know that a woman who sues for divorce or separation does not receive custody of her children. A father is a child's lawful guardian; a father has the right to protect that child until he is eighteen. If the father deems that the mother threatens his child's welfare, he has the right to remove the child from the mother's influence. Do you know what that means?"

She ceased struggling.

Oh, yes, she knew what that meant.

Not only would she lose her children if she was granted a

divorce or separation, she would lose them now if she did not continue as they had carried on for the past sixteen years.

"I understand, Edward." Her voice was hollow.

He released her hands and patted her cheek. "I thought you would." Another rustle of cloth and a squeak of springs signaled he returned to the other side of the carriage. "I have been meaning to tell you. You are looking decidedly dowdy. While your gowns must be tasteful, of course, there is no need to look like a frump. Hammond's wife, now, is quite charming. Perhaps you should ask for the name of her modiste.

"By the bye, Elizabeth. You will not admit Countess Devington into my home ever again."

Chapter Sixteen

Elizabeth stared at the groom's gloved hand, then at the ornate knocker that was clearly engraved with COUNTESS DEVINGTON. The brittle staccato sound of brass banging brass cut through the sickly pale sunshine.

The town house was Edward's home; she would abide by his dictates inside the house, but she *would not* bow down to his will like a child. She would visit whom she liked . . . and today she would visit with the countess.

It had nothing whatsoever to do with the countess's offer that if she ever needed to talk, her door would be open. Elizabeth could not talk with her own mother. She certainly would not burden the Bastard Sheikh's mother.

The white door swung open. A butler stared impassively first at the groom and then at Elizabeth.

She gave him her card, the corner folded down. "I would like to see Countess Devington, please."

The butler bowed, revealing a full head of short, curly black hair. "I will see if her ladyship is at home."

Elizabeth nodded her head at the groom in dismissal. "Tommie, you may wait by the carriage."

Tommie, the young boy of nineteen who had gotten sick before the fog unexpectedly descended five nights ago, doffed his wool knit hat. "Very good, ma'am."

She watched weak rays of sunshine play on the brass knocker. Dark, angry, *frightened* thoughts clouded her mind.

Edward had threatened to take her sons. Then he had threatened to commit her to an asylum.

She could not live like this.

Scarce minutes passed before the butler returned. He bowed again. "If you will follow me, Mrs. Petre."

She followed behind him, heels muffled on the Oriental runner that lined the floor of the oak-paneled hallway. Light filtered through skylight windows, danced across gleaming wood. At the end of the corridor the butler opened a door, revealing a stairwell. It, too, was lighted by a skylight.

He silently walked down the steps in front of her, back ramrod straight—Beadles would be envious of his posture. Abruptly stopping, bowing, he opened the door at the end of the staircase and stepped back.

Hot, heavy, moist steam billowed out into the stairwell. Elizabeth curiously stepped through the doorway.

She had heard of steam rooms, but she had never seen one. Nor, she realized with shock as her eyes adjusted to the dim lighting, was she seeing one now.

The countess leisurely swam toward Elizabeth in a bath the size of a pond. *And she was not wearing a bathing suit.* The pale lines of her naked body reflected beneath the steam and the water.

Elizabeth had never seen a naked woman other than herself.

"Countess Devington," she stammered. "I beg your pardon, I did not mean to intrude. The butler—I will call another time, when it is more convenient."

Soft laughter drifted up from the water. It was as uninhibited as was the Bastard Sheikh's. "Elizabeth, my dear, don't be silly."

"But you—you're—" She sucked in thick, heavy steam.

"Bathing." The countess possessed none of Elizabeth's

modesty. "I thought you might be curious to find out about life in Arabia. Bathing is very important to the Arab people, both to the men and to the women. I grew quite fond of the Turkish bath, so I installed one here when I returned to England."

She lifted slender arms out of the water and clapped her hands. It afforded Elizabeth a perfect view of her breasts. They were round and firm, not at all what one would expect in a fifty-seven-year-old woman.

Elizabeth quickly averted her eyes.

This was absurd. She had handled an artificial phallus; surely she could overcome her embarrassment at seeing another woman's naked body. But no matter how hard she tried, she could not gaze at the countess.

"Joseffa, take Mrs. Petre behind the screen and help her disrobe. She is not yet used to our ways."

A tiny, wrinkled woman wearing a gown that could only be described as a roll of silk wrapped about her body, purposefully stepped toward Elizabeth.

Elizabeth stiffened with alarm. She was English, not Arabic, and she was not about to expose her *udder* breasts and *flabby* hips. "I really do not think—"

"In Arabia, the women in the harem bathe together. It is a time to laugh and talk and relax without the interference of men." The countess's voice was wistful. "I am sorry if this embarrasses you. I thought perhaps you might enjoy one of the more pleasurable Arab customs, but I see that I was wrong. . . ."

Elizabeth unaccountably felt stuffy . . . and childish. She uttered the first excuse that came to mind. "I do not know how to swim."

"The floor of the bath is graduated; the one end starts at three feet deep and goes to five feet at the farthest end. It is far more safe bathing here than in the ocean. But if you truly do not wish to join me, please don't think I will be offended. It is not a European custom; many English people find it repugnant to bathe daily, let alone to bathe communally."

Elizabeth was not certain if she had been insulted or not. She bathed . . . daily.

"It is not that I find it repugnant, Countess Devington, it is just . . ." She took a deep breath, almost choked on the thick steam. "I have never before been in a complete state of undress in front of anyone"—*save for her husband, but that memory was better left alone*—"Even the doctor did not see me when I gave birth to my two sons. . . ."

"Then you are fortunate the doctor delivered a bouncing baby boy and not a pair of tonsils."

The countess's cynical remark surprised a laugh out of Elizabeth. Caught off guard, she was ill prepared to fend off the surprinsingly strong hand that grabbed her arm and commenced dragging her toward the rear of the room.

Elizabeth's mouth dropped open in astonishment, closed, opened. The little old lady—an Arab lady, Elizabeth surmised by her dark skin, but then again, perhaps not. Muhamed was European and she had thought *him* an Arab—was like an ant relentlessly pulling twice its weight behind it.

Muffled laughter swirled the steam—it came from the countess.

Lips compressed, Elizabeth tried to pull free, then realized struggling was more undignified than being dragged. A large lacquered screen loomed out of the hot mist. Before Elizabeth could gather her bearing, the little old lady shoved her behind the screen and proceeded to snatch at her reticule, her cloak, her hat, her gloves. *Hands were everywhere.*

This was too humiliating for words. Elizabeth had never been manhandled. As a child, a word of criticism had been enough to command obedience. She simply had no reference to compare this incident to.

Suddenly, she was pivoted so that her back faced the old Arab woman. Elizabeth tripped, fell forward with hands outstretched. Only to slam into a moist enameled wall. Small, adept hands attacked the buttons lining the back of her dress.

Elizabeth tried to turn around. "Please do not do that. I do not want—*stop*, please—" But despite her protests, the buttons were freed and the heavy wool dress was being peeled down over her shoulders.

She forgot dignity; she forgot that English ladies do not raise their voices. "Countess Devington!"

"Joseffa does not understand English when she does not want to," the countess shouted back, her voice strangely choked. "It is not your time of month, is it?"

Mortification singed Elizabeth's skin. There were some things one did not mention, *ever*. Not even woman to woman.

She twirled free of the marauding hands, clutched the bodice of her dress. "I said *stop that!*"

Snorting, the little old woman stepped back with her hands on her hips. She let loose with a string of totally incomprehensible words.

Arabic, Elizabeth presumed. But it certainly sounded nothing like what the Bastard Sheikh spoke. He sounded erotic, sensuous. This woman sounded . . . *venomous*.

"That is quite enough, Joseffa!" The countess's command pierced the steam.

The old Arab woman glowered at Elizabeth in silence.

Elizabeth pulled the dress more tightly against her chest. "What . . . what did she say?"

"There is no need to translate." The countess's voice was closer—she had swum to the deeper end of the pool beside the screen.

"Please." Elizabeth defiantly tilted her chin at the old woman. "I would like to know."

"She said that you English ladies are all the same. That you despise her country and you insult her mistress."

"That is not so!" Elizabeth yelped indignantly. "I have a great respect for the Arabic culture! Why, I know some Arabic phrases! And if I meant to insult her mistress—you—I would not visit your home to do so!"

More rude words escaped the Arab woman's mouth. Uncannily bright eyes glittered at Elizabeth.

"What did she say now?" Elizabeth called out more belligerently.

"She said she does not believe that you know any Arabic. That Englishwomen lie because they do not know how to tell the truth."

Elizabeth stiffened her spine, unable to pass up the challenge. "*Ma'e e-salemma,*" she said clearly, loud enough for the countess to hear. *Taalibba—no, that was between her and the Bastard Sheikh.* "*Sabah el kheer.*" And then, just for the Arab woman's ears, "*El besiss mostahi,*" the impudent, shamefaced one. Or at least she hoped that the rather insulting phrases were not used in a purely sexual connotation.

The old Arab woman stabbed a finger at Elizabeth and uttered a volley of vituperative Arabic.

The countess did not wait to be asked to translate. "Joseffa said you speak her tongue with the finesse of a camel and that you still mock her culture and insult her mistress by not sharing the bath. But she forgives you, because you are English and Englishwomen are puny cowards."

The thick, suffocating steam rose directly to Elizabeth's head. She jerked the heavy wool bodice over her arms and down her hips. "I am not a coward," she said through gritted teeth, untying the horsehair-padded bustle from around her waist. A dull thud, the impacting fall, was absorbed by the steam.

Elizabeth stared at the old woman, needing to further prove herself, doing so by untying the tape of the first petticoat.

She had asked the Bastard Sheikh to teach her how to please a man.

Elizabeth untied the tape of her second petticoat. It dropped in a heap of dampening cotton.

She had asked her husband for a divorce and been threatened with the loss of her two sons.

"I . . . am not . . . a coward," she repeated, standing in her corset, chemise, and drawers, daring her to repeat the offending remark.

Joseffa made a circling motion with her right hand for Elizabeth to turn around while her bright eyes dared her to do so.

Elizabeth thought of her husband's brutal appraisal . . . and

knew that true or not, the old Arab woman would respect her
more for courage than beauty. She turned around.

Moisture collected between her breasts, itched a path down
her abdomen. Shedding the corset was a luxury. But that was
as far as she was going to go . . . now.

Folding her arms over her breasts, Elizabeth faced the old
woman and nodded toward the screen . . . then breathed a sigh
of relief when she left. Muted murmurs drifted through the
steam. Elizabeth decided she did not want to know what comments Joseffa might be relaying about her body.

Without the direct challenge the old woman represented,
Elizabeth felt her courage dwindling. It simply was not done;
she could *not* bathe naked with the countess. . . .

Yes, she could.

Elizabeth had no sooner removed her shoes and peeled down
her drawers and stockings than the old woman stepped back
around the screen.

She stifled a gasp, too startled to cover anything. But not
for long. The old woman held out a large, thick towel; Elizabeth
gratefully accepted it. Folding it around her body, she padded
out from behind the screen, the old woman at her heels. Elizabeth did a little dance; the wooden floor was hot.

When she reached the edge of the pool, the old woman
grabbed the edge of the towel and yanked. Elizabeth jumped
into the water.

It was—

Incredible.

Crouching down so that her breasts were submerged, she
spread her arms out to retain her balance. The water caressed
every inch of her skin, her breasts, her hips, her thighs. Elizabeth
had never felt so—*liberated.*

"Are you all right?"

Elizabeth swirled around. "This is . . . quite remarkable."

The countess smiled; blond strands of hair stuck to her face.
"I am so glad you enjoy it. Were this a true Turkish bath, there
would be three pools; a hot bath, a lukewarm bath, and a cold
one. I find the heated one best suits the English climate."

Tendrils of hair slithered free of Elizabeth's bun. They clung to her wet neck and back. "Lord Safyre . . . does he have a Turkish bath?"

"Yes. Ramiel has retained many Arab customs."

Elizabeth wanted to ask the countess to enumerate, but thought better of it. Perhaps he kept an entire harem locked away in his house.

But why would he come home in the early hours of morning drenched in a woman's perfume if he had his own harem?

A cold chill raced down her back. "My carriage—it is outside. I never planned—that is, I meant only to have a short visit—" *To defy my husband.*

"Joseffa!" The countess's voice gently carried over the water. The old Arab woman came to the edge of the pool. "Joseffa—" The countess turned toward Elizabeth. "Would you like the carriage to return for you or would you rather go home in one of mine?"

"I—return, please."

"Joseffa. Tell Anthony to inform Mrs. Petre's coachman that he should return for her in three hours."

Three hours!

Joseffa was gone before Elizabeth could countermand the countess's orders.

The countess smiled at Elizabeth. "There. Now we shall have time for a nice, long chat."

Elizabeth tentatively waded out into deeper water. She imagined beautiful concubines gathered about the edges of the pool, talking, laughing, happy in the Bastard Sheikh's home.

"What are harem women like?" she asked compulsively. "Are they . . . beautiful?"

"Oh, yes." The countess gently rotated her arms in the water, creating small whirlpools. "Otherwise they would not be bought."

Elizabeth felt a pang of envy—not to be sold into slavery, of course, but it would be nice to be wanted by a man so much that he would pay sterling coin.

"Lord Safyre said they are more concerned about pleasing a man than they are pleasuring themselves."

"Ah . . ." The countess stopped her idle motions. "Of course it is true, for the most part, but I have never asked . . . Arab men are very secretive when it comes to talking about women."

"*Siba,*" Elizabeth murmured dryly.

The countess laughed delightedly. "It is such a pleasure talking to another woman who knows of these things."

Elizabeth walked deeper into the water, until it came up to her chin. "I wish I knew how to swim."

"Ramiel is an excellent swimmer. He had his first lesson here, in this pool."

Elizabeth tried to contain her curiosity, but failed. She had imagined Ramiel experiencing many kinds of love; the love between a mother and her son was not one of them. "How old was he?"

"Three. He wriggled out of Joseffa's arms and leapt into the water, right there." The countess pointed toward the very end of the pool, where it was five feet deep. "When I fished him out, he spat a mouthful of water into the air and laughed."

A reminiscent smile curved Elizabeth's mouth. "When Phillip was three he discovered that the banister made a wonderful slide. I caught him just as he sailed off the end. He laughed and threw his arms around my neck and asked if I would carry him back upstairs so that he could do it again."

The countess laughed. "How old is he now?"

"Eleven—soon to be twelve. He entered Eton last fall. Richard, my elder, will be taking exams for Oxford in six months." A mother's pride rang in Elizabeth's voice. "He's only fifteen."

"They sound like lovely boys."

"Oh, they are." Emotion roughed Elizabeth's voice. "I would not know what to do without them."

She would not let Edward take them away from her.

Water swirled and foamed; the resulting current buoyed Elizabeth's breasts. Her scathing remark about a woman's full breasts serving as buoys was more apt then not, she thought wryly.

The Bastard Sheikh's instruction promptly came to mind.
*He can position his manhood between her breasts and press
them together . . . as if they were a vulva.*

Hurriedly turning away from her thoughts, Elizabeth saw
that the countess floated on her back.

Her eyes widened in shock. The countess had no pubic hair.
In fact, she had no body hair whatsoever.

Pivoting, she used her arms to propel herself more quickly
through the water to the edge of the pool. She leaned her
forehead on the tile and closed her eyes against the forbidden
images that flooded her imagination.

Ramiel. Naked. A hard column of veined manhood jutting
out from a hairless pubis.

The water churned behind her. Elizabeth could feel the countess, solid rather than liquid. Her question came unbidden. "Did
you bring your son to England so that he would not be taken
away from you?"

The gentle slap of water lapped the tiles. Elizabeth did not
think the countess was going to respond. And then—

"No. I brought my son to England because I could not stand
to leave him behind."

"Do you regret . . . leaving?"

A gentle hand reached out, anchored a strand of hair to
Elizabeth's damp bun.

Elizabeth stiffened. The gesture was maternal, something
she would do to one of her sons. She could not recall her own
mother ever touching her in such a manner.

"Yes. But if I had to do it over again, I would do so."

"Do you not think that you owed it to your son to stay with
his father?"

The question was out before Elizabeth could stop it. She
waited for the answer, shoulders tense, eyes staring fixedly at
the wooden floor blanketed with steam.

"Yes. No. That is not an easy question to answer. I think
Ramiel would have been happy had we stayed in Arabia. *I*
would not have been happy, though, and I think my unhappiness
would have affected him far more than my bringing him to

England did. He was happy here, surrounded by friends and loved ones. When he turned twelve, however, I could no longer protect him from those who would slander him because of his birth. Arabia views a son borne out of wedlock differently than do the English. So I sent him to his father. And I cried. And I worried. And I trusted in the love that I gave him, that it was strong enough to carry him through manhood.''

A hot, wet trail of steam slithered down Elizabeth's cneek.

Other words, masculine words, reverberated inside her ears. *Your two sons will shortly be men. Who will you have then,* taalibba?

Elizabeth wondered what the countess would say if she told her that she had asked Edward for a divorce. She wondered what the countess's son would say if Elizabeth told him that Edward had retaliated by threatening to take away her sons.

Taking a shaky breath, Elizabeth faced the countess. ''Thank you for sharing your bath with me. It is an experience that I shall treasure.''

Elizabeth flinched away from the pale, slender hand that flicked moisture off her cheek.

The countess viewed her handiwork, reached out and swiped Elizabeth's other cheek. ''You may come and bathe here anytime you wish. I will leave instructions with my servants that you are to have complete access to my home. My only request is that you do not bathe alone. Joseffa must always accompany you; should anything happen while you are in the water, she will save you.''

Joseffa was probably eighty years old and weighed half of what Elizabeth did. ''And who will save Joseffa?'' she asked tartly.

Warm laughter riffled the steam. ''Do not judge people by size. The small are often strong. And now we must quit the water or we will both become wrinkled. Joseffa!''

Joseffa magically appeared holding two towels. Elizabeth started; she had not heard her return from the errand the countess had sent her on.

"I will show you another popular pastime in the harem. And then we will take coffee."

Short steps led up out of the pool. Elizabeth averted her eyes while the countess uninhibitedly dried off. She chose the shelter of the lacquered screen.

Her clothes were gone! In their place was a green silk robe.

Elizabeth hurriedly dried and shrugged into it. It was four inches too long and snug through the chest.

The countess, wearing a dark blue silk robe with a towel turbaned around her head, correctly interpreted Elizabeth's expression when she marched out from behind the screen. "It is very damp down here. Joseffa took your clothes upstairs and spread them out by the fire so they will dry."

Having no choice, Elizabeth hiked up the robe and padded barefoot after the countess up the stairs, past the second landing, up to the third. Hoping that no servants were peeking—the silk clung to her body like wet skin—she stepped into a hallway covered with pale rose carpeting.

The countess's sitting room was decorated in pale rose and leaf green with an Oriental wool carpet woven in various shades of matching rose and green. English with a distinct Arabic touch. A feminine version of Ramiel's home.

"Come, sit." The countess patted the sofa beside her. Reaching over, she plucked an odd, carafe-shaped object off a teak side-table. A long, thin hose curled away from its slender brass neck; it was tipped with a brass bit.

Taking the bit between her lips, the countess lit a match and placed it against the bowl atop the exotic object. A thin stream of smoke plumed up, as if from a pipe. A matching plume of smoke curled out of the countess's mouth.

The countess offered Elizabeth the hose. "There is nothing like a good smoke after bathing."

The Bastard Sheikh had offered her a smoke. She had rejected it because it was another act that a respectable woman did not indulge in. Had he thought she was rejecting his culture?

"What is this called . . . in Arabic?"

"It's called a hookah. There is water inside it; the smoke is drawn through it to purify it."

As if it were a snake that could strike her at any moment, Elizabeth accepted the hose and brought the brass bit up to her lips. "What do I do?"

The countess leaned forward; her gray eyes were bright with camaraderie. Elizabeth suddenly felt like the young girl she had never been, playing truant with a school friend. "Suck on it . . . gently . . . take the smoke into your mouth but not your—"

Raw fire erupted inside Elizabeth's lungs. She choked, she coughed, and suddenly she was laughing with the countess while she tried to draw the tobacco smoke into her mouth instead of her lungs.

"*Ummee,* you do not make a very good tutor."

Elizabeth sucked in more smoke, a little fire instead of a blazing conflagration. The countess gently patted her on the back while turquoise eyes blazed at her from across the expanse of the sitting room.

Abruptly, agonizingly aware of the damp silk robe clinging to her naked body and the wreath of smoke capping her head, she thrust the rubber hose at the countess. "I have to go—"

Lightning motion: The Bastard Sheikh stepped forward as if he would prevent her from rising from the sofa. At the same time, the countess held up an authoritative hand. "If my son's presence disturbs you that greatly, Elizabeth, then he will leave."

Those beautiful turquoise eyes—they were stark with pain.

Elizabeth sucked in a breath of smoke-filled air—held it inside her lungs until they ached.

If she rejected him here, now, in front of his mother, she would never see him again. She would not dance with him again. She would never hear the intimate drawl of his voice when he called her *taalibba.*

Her breath escaped in a sigh. "There is no need for that."

Between one blink and another Joseffa was there before her, bearing a large brass tray. A wrinkled lid drooped in a wink.

Elizabeth stared.

Ramiel relieved the old Arab woman of the heavy coffee tray and set it down on the table beside the countess. Joseffa spat out a volley of Arabic. Turquoise gaze settling on Elizabeth's breasts, he responded in her native language.

"English, please," the countess reprimanded. "Ramiel, you may sit."

Ramiel sat on the carpet near their feet, legs bonelessly crossed—a sheikh in brown wool trousers and tweed jacket. Elizabeth adjusted her robe, almost slipped off the sofa onto his lap. Silk on silk was more slippery than a two-year-old child.

Joseffa took away the hookah while the countess poured coffee. The aroma of the strong, sugary beverage mingled with the acrid incense of tobacco.

Elizabeth blurted out the question that had puzzled her since she had first met the countess. "Do you have your father's eyes?"

An identical smile blossomed on the two disparate faces, the one so dark, the other so pale. The twin smiles rumbled into shared laughter. The timbre in their laughter was identical, one softened by femininity, the other roughened by masculinity.

Elizabeth stiffened. She did not enjoy being the butt of a joke, no matter how delightful the sound of a person's laughter.

"Please forgive my curiosity—"

"Please forgive *our* rudeness." The countess held out a delicate gold-rimmed demitasse cup and saucer to Elizabeth. "We still have not been able to figure out which side of the family contributed to Ramiel's eyes. It certainly did not come from mine, but on the other hand, there is no one on his father's side who possesses that particular eye color either. They are Ramiel's eyes and no others."

Yes, Elizabeth had thought that when first she had seen him.

Ramiel extended a plate of sticky-looking pastries to Elizabeth. "It is baklava, a confection of pastry and nuts soaked in honey. Joseffa makes the best in the East or the West."

"It is Ramiel's favorite," the countess added softly.

Had the countess sent for her son while they were bathing? And did the thought anger Elizabeth . . . or did it please her?

She remembered her mother's disapproval. The memory was replaced by the countess's honesty.

I cannot cast stones, Elizabeth, because I would not trade one single moment I spent with my sheikh for a lifetime of English virtue.

Elizabeth solemnly chose a golden, bite-sized pastry sprinkled with almonds.

Ramiel next extended the plate to the countess. She, too, solemnly chose a piece of the baklava. Lastly, he himself took one. As if synchronized, they bit into the delicate pastries.

Elizabeth felt as if they exchanged vows. As if, inexplicably, they had become a family.

Edward was an orphan. She had never had a mother-in-law. *She had never had a husband.*

She swallowed. "These are delicious. What other foods do the Arabs enjoy?"

"Lamb." The countess delicately licked her fingers clean of honey. "Rice pilaff."

Ramiel held Elizabeth's gaze. "The heart of a dove prepared in wine and spices."

"The Arab people must have a plentiful supply of doves," Elizabeth countered briskly. "Or very small appetites."

Ramiel's eyes glinted turquoise fire. He stared at her as if he were a hungry man, and she were a very savory woman. "The Arabs are renowned for their appetites. As well as for their meritoriousness."

Elizabeth could not help it—she laughed. And realized that she would never think of him as the Bastard Sheikh again. He was, simply, a man.

Chapter Seventeen

Elizabeth felt drugged on tobacco, coffee and the affectionate love between a disreputable countess and her outcast bastard son. She gave Beadles one of her rare smiles, free of artifice and pretense. "Please send Emma up to my room."

"Mr. Petre is in his study, Mrs. Petre." Beadles stared over her head. "He requested that you join him the moment you came home."

Cold reality replaced the lingering warmth of the hot swimming bath. Elizabeth allowed Beadles to take her cloak, her bonnet, her gloves. They smelled of steam.

It was ridiculous, of course, but she was suddenly, terribly afraid. She gripped her reticule between her fingers. "I am not a coward," she said softly, bracingly.

"I beg your pardon?"

"Thank you, Beadles. Tell Emma I will be dressing for dinner shortly. I need her to press my burgundy satin ball gown for tonight."

"Very good, ma'am."

Johnny stood by the study doors. His easygoing face was

expressionless. It made him look older . . . and less like a
footman than ever before. Bowing, he opened the door for her.

The gesture should gratify her: Obviously, his footman skills
were improving. But all she felt was that cold, unreasonable
fear.

She stepped into the study—and froze with shocked surprise.
Her father sat at the long walnut table Edward used when other
Members of Parliament dropped by to talk. Her husband and
her mother sat on either side of him. The expression on the
three faces was identical.

The door closed behind her softly, irrevocably.

A dark cloud seemed to envelop the study. Perhaps it was
the approaching dusk that was unrelieved by artificial light;
perhaps it was the walnut paneling that absorbed the sun's
dying rays. All Elizabeth knew was that it required every ounce
of her willpower not to turn and run.

"Sit down, Elizabeth," Andrew Walters curtly ordered.

Mentally bracing herself, Elizabeth crossed the dark crimson
carpet and sat down opposite her father. "Hello, Father.
Edward. Mother."

A rose-patterned china cup neatly ensconced in a matching
saucer sat before each of them. Elizabeth automatically
searched the study for the tea tray. Silver glinted in the fading
light.

Of course. Her mother would be given the honor of pouring,
so the tea cart would naturally be by her.

Rebecca did not offer Elizabeth tea.

"You are speaking tonight, Father. Is there anything
wrong?" she asked, knowing what was wrong, dread knotting
her stomach. *Please don't let this meeting be about what she
knew it would be.*

Andrew's eyes bulged in fury.

Elizabeth had seen displeasure on his face; she had seen
condescension. She had never seen his face contorted with rage.

"You have twice danced with a man who is a disgrace to
society. You have entertained the bastard's whore of a mother
in your home and now you flaunt your husband's orders and

spend the day with the most bloody bitch in England. Have you no respect for your husband?''

''Edward did not forbid me to visit Countess Devington,'' Elizabeth returned calmly. Underneath the cover of the table she gripped the reticule so tightly a fingernail pierced the lined silk. *Her father had never sworn at her.* ''All he said was that I was not to receive her here, in his home.''

''You will not dance with the bastard or talk to the whore ever again.'' Andrew's voice bounced off the dark walnut panels. ''Is that specific enough?''

Elizabeth studied her father's hazel eyes, so like hers, yet she could not see anything of herself in him. ''I am thirty-three years old, Father. I will not be treated like I am seventeen. I have done nothing wrong.''

She focused on her husband's brown eyes, and could not see anything there of the last sixteen years that they had spent together. ''You have a mistress, Edward. How many nights a week—a month—do you sleep with her? Why do you not tell my father about that? How dare you sit there when you behave with far more impropriety than I ever have!''

''I have told you I do not have a mistress.''

Elizabeth's gaze, contemptuous in its own right, swept over the three of them, her father, her mother, her husband. ''And I am telling you that I have done nothing wrong. But that is not what this meeting is about, is it, Father?''

''Elizabeth!'' Rebecca warned sharply.

Elizabeth ignored the mother who for so long had ignored her. ''Mother told you that I want a divorce. *That* is what this is about. Isn't it, Father?''

Andrew sat as if turned to a pale, silvery-auburn-haired statue. Only his eyes were alive. They burned with murky amber fire. ''A man's reputation lies in his family. If he cannot keep his family together, no man will trust him to keep his country together.''

Reckless anger outweighed common sense. ''Does that mean you will not use your influence as prime minister to intercede on my behalf?''

Andrew leaned toward Elizabeth, his jaws knotted with the force of his emotion. "Are you deaf, girl?" Each word was carefully, perfectly enunciated, all the more terrible now that he was not shouting. "Edward is going to be England's next prime minister. If he cannot control you, everything we have worked for will be lost. Edward will be banned from Parliament. My career will go up in smoke. I will see you dead before I allow you to destroy our lives."

Hookah smoke, Elizabeth thought incongruously, *not political careers.* She pictured the countess, comfortably sitting with a towel wrapped about her head while Ramiel offered her a baklava, and now here was Elizabeth's family—

I will see you dead echoed hollowly inside her head.

Elizabeth's heart skipped a beat. Blinding, breathtaking pain engulfed her.

Surely he had not said that. *Surely a father would not threaten to kill his daughter.*

Andrew leaned back in his chair, once again the affable, dignified man who sponsored charities to assist widows and war-orphaned children. "Does that answer your question, daughter?"

Ramiel knew the moment Elizabeth entered the ballroom. His entire body charged with electricity. He pivoted, eyes searching, seeking—

There she was, a mere ten feet away, standing just inside the doorway, dressed in a burgundy satin ball gown. Beside her, Edward Petre nodded his head at an acquaintance, half bowed in the direction of another.

Senses prickling, his gaze locked onto Petre's arm. Elizabeth's small, gloved hand was pressed through the crook of his elbow. Petre's fingers were snugly clasped over hers. As if in loving affection . . . or to physically restrain her.

Ramiel's gaze snapped up to her face. Her skin was chalk white.

He had seen her only hours after her husband had rejected

her sexual advances. She had been pale then, but now—*she looked frozen.* The ice bitch he had originally mistaken her for.

Ramiel remembered her laughter in the countess's sitting room. Her cheeks had been flushed and her eyes full of life as she sampled the hookah and then the baklava. The woman he stared at now was dead.

What had the bastard done to her?

Common sense told him to wait until Petre left her side— no good would come out of a face-to-face confrontation in an overcrowded ballroom. Male possessiveness told him otherwise—Elizabeth was his woman; he would not tolerate another man touching her, *hurting her.*

He closed the distance separating them, planted himself squarely in front of them. "Mrs. Petre."

Elizabeth's face did not register any emotion—no welcome, no surprise, as if he were nothing. Her voice, when she spoke, was cold and polite. Lifeless. "Lord Safyre."

Petre's fingers convulsively squeezed her hand that he still held captive, as if in warning. *He knew* that Ramiel wanted her . . . just as Ramiel knew that Petre did not.

Ramiel was an inch shorter and four years Petre's junior. He coldly appraised the older man, knowing his weaknesses, weighing his strengths. "I have not had the pleasure of being introduced to your husband."

Petre returned his perusal, lip curled. "We do not associate with the likes of you, sirrah. Henceforth, you will stay away from my wife."

For one timeless second Ramiel seemed to be hurled outside his body. He could see the three of them standing together as if in intimate dialogue, Elizabeth with her auburn hair and white skin, Edward with his black hair and drooping mustache, and himself, golden-haired and brown-skinned. Farther inside the ballroom, couples swirled in a tangle of black evening jackets and jewel-colored gowns, while around them men and women promenaded or clustered to chat. A titter rose over the whine of the violins, was swallowed by a bark of laughter on the opposite side of the ballroom. Suddenly, he was yanked back into his body and he knew exactly what he had to do.

The line had been drawn, the positions taken. There was no going back.

"That is for Mrs. Petre to decide, surely," he murmured silkily, provocatively.

"I am her husband; she will do as I say," Petre retorted grimly, triumphantly.

Ramiel's heartbeat quickened; anticipation pumped through his veins. He felt a moment's regret, that Elizabeth was trapped in the cross fire. And then all he felt was the need to take Edward Petre out of her life.

"Really." A feral smile curved his mouth. "I believe you belong to a fellowship who call themselves Uranians, do you not, Petre? I wonder. Does your wife know of your interest in poetry?"

Stunned disbelief shone in Petre's brown eyes; it was followed by pure rage. Both confirmed his guilt.

"Let her go," Ramiel said softly.

Deliberately misunderstanding, Petre released Elizabeth's hand. A sneer twisted his face. "Tell Safyre you do not wish his company, Elizabeth."

Ramiel's gaze snapped back to Elizabeth.

Her clear hazel eyes were cold, blank. *They did not belong to the woman who had swum in a Turkish bath and smoked a hookah. They did not belong to the woman who had held an artificial phallus in her hands and told him that she had tried to look underneath a stone leaf covering a male statue because she was seventeen and pregnant and she wanted to see what had made her that way.*

Sharp pain sliced through Ramiel's chest, stealing his breath. The countess had offered to send him away today and she had *wanted* him to stay. They had shared baklava. And now she was going to deny *everything*.

Her pale, bloodless lips quivered, tightened. "Please accept my apologies for my husband's rudeness, Lord Safyre."

"Elizabeth!" Petre spat out.

"Enough, Edward. I will not be dictated to in this manner." She stared at Ramiel's white bow tie. "I will talk to and dance with whomever I please."

Jubilation burned through Ramiel's body like warmed cognac. *She had chosen.* Whether she realized it or not, she had finally made her choice.

He held out his hand, so close his breath fanned her hair. "Dance with me."

Show me that you aren't afraid to take a Bastard Sheikh.

"You will regret it if you do, Elizabeth."

Icy fingers swept down Ramiel's spine. The threat in Petre's voice was implicit.

"How will she regret it, Petre?" Slowly, he lowered his hand and turned his head away from Elizabeth. Turquoise eyes locked with brown eyes. "Will she regret it as much as you will? Will she regret it as much as your lover?"

Now Ramiel would see what Edward Petre was made of. Would he challenge Ramiel? Would he pretend that he didn't know what Ramiel was talking about?

Would he sacrifice Elizabeth—to save his career?

"What will it be, Petre?" Ramiel drawled dangerously, his message clear. *I will keep your secrets if you give me your wife.*

Edward walked away.

Ramiel smiled mirthlessly.

"Why did you do that?" Elizabeth's face was even more pale than it had been when she stepped into the ballroom.

"Will you regret dancing with me, Elizabeth?"

"Yes."

"But you will do it." Satisfaction tinged his voice.

"Only if you tell me what Joseffa said when you took the tray from her."

Ramiel's lashes veiled his eyes. "She said you have magnificent breasts. Breasts that are worthy to suckle sons . . . and a husband."

Bright pink colored her cheeks. "My husband has never suckled my breasts."

"There is a difference between begetting children and being a husband, *taalibba,*" he informed her gently.

"Is that in *The Perfumed Garden?*"

"Yes."

She held up her gloved hand. "Shall we dance?"

Emotion squeezed his chest; relief, regret, triumph. He offered her his arm, a belated concession to propriety, wanting to make amends for the rumors that were already springing up from the confrontation between the Chancellor of the Exchequer and the Bastard Sheikh. He could feel the stares, hear the whispers.

If Petre were a good politician, he would have graciously acceded and saved himself and his wife public embarrassment. Instead, he had abandoned her to the unmerciful *ton.*

Perhaps it was best that she learn to accept notoriety now. No matter what Ramiel did or did not do, society would talk. About his bastardy, about his Arab heritage, about his renowned sexual appetites.

About his woman.

At the edge of the dance floor he took Elizabeth's right hand and clasped her waist, corseted but not as tightly as it had been the night of the charity ball. She reached up and rested her left hand on his shoulders. Mentally counting "one, two, *three,*" he twirled her into the waltz.

He looked down her dress at the white skin straining for freedom. And remembered the soft, full curves and long, hard nipples the damp silk robe had so lovingly cupped when she sat in the countess's sitting room. "You do have magnificent breasts."

The quiver of her lips belied her aloofness. "What is a Uranian, Lord Safyre, and why did it upset my husband when you mentioned it?"

Ramiel could tell her . . . and she would be free. Conversely, he did not want to tell her for fear that she would come to him because a bastard was more acceptable than a man like Edward Petre.

"It is as I said, a fellowship of minor poets."

"Minor . . . as in . . . youthful?"

Ela'na, damn, she was sharp. But it was not young girls that Edward liked.

"Minor also means of little importance."

She lowered her head so that he stared at auburn hair instead of hazel eyes. Jagged shadows darkened her cheeks. "Your mother sent you away when you were twelve."

He leaned closer to hear her; his cheek brushed her hair, a silky warm caress. "Yes."

"Did you miss . . . England?"

Ramiel realized she was imagining sending her own sons off to a faraway land. She did not realize that her pain would be greater than theirs. "For a month or so," he said laconically.

Her eyelids sprang open. She stared up at him in blatant disbelief. "Only a month or so?"

"You have two sons. You know what boys are. When my father gave me a horse, I realized that sun and sand can be rather pleasant."

"I shudder to think what you realized when he gave you your own harem," she said acidly, her motherly sensitivities offended at a child's fickle love.

Ramiel laughed softly, pulled her close so that when he whirled her around he stepped between her legs. Her stomach rubbed against his groin, smooth satin on hard silk. "I would be happy to show you what I realized."

"Do irises grow in Arabia?"

His fingers tightened around her small, slender hand. He could feel her delicate bones underneath silk and flesh. "Pink irises," he murmured huskily, breathing in the clean, unperfumed scent of her hair and body. "With silky soft petals that grow hot and moist."

She abruptly stopped dancing, hazel eyes wide, avid, wanting everything Ramiel wanted to give her, everything he wanted a woman to give to him.

"Come home with me, *taalibba.* Let me show you the ways to love."

All forty.

Her hand resting on his shoulder clenched convulsively. Temptation glimmered in her eyes, evaporated.

He had said too much, too soon.

Snatching her hand from his shoulder, she stepped back, curtsied. "The dance is over, Lord Safyre. Thank you." And turned her back on him. Again.

Ramiel leaned against the wall and moodily watched her mingle with the *ton*. Gossip had already spread. Men filled her dance card. Chaperones protectively hovered over their charges when she came near them.

Sometime after midnight a braying laugh erupted from the dance floor. Ramiel straightened. He knew that laugh and he *would* not stand by and see Elizabeth preyed upon by men like Lord Hindvalle.

Another mark against Edward Petre.

He had the right and privilege of protecting her and he did not; Ramiel's protection would further damn Elizabeth in the eyes of society.

Just when Ramiel came abreast of Elizabeth, he saw Hindvalle's face turn purple. The seventy-year-old roué abruptly turned and walked away, spine erect as it had not been in many years.

Elizabeth stared up into Ramiel's dark, brooding face. "I asked him if he was a member of the Uranian fellowship."

Healing laughter spewed up out of his chest and drowned out the surrounding drone of men and women gossiping, flirting, maligning, and complaining.

"Take me home."

He stared down into her hazel eyes, laughter forgotten.

"To my home, Lord Safyre. Edward has not returned to the ball. I have no carriage."

A pulse throbbed in his right temple. An identical throb swelled and pounded in his groin.

"Here, in this ballroom, Elizabeth, I am not your tutor. I will not be your tutor in the carriage."

She lifted her chin. "You would touch me against my will?"

It would not be against her will. They both knew that.

Ramiel rapidly calculated how to leave together yet attract a minimum of attention. Now that he knew she would soon be his, he felt strangely protective of her reputation.

"I'll have my carriage drawn up. A servant will come get you. We do not need to be seen leaving together."

Gratitude softened her face. "Thank you."

The footman accepted Ramiel's generous tip with a blank face. "You will summon Mrs. Petre when I tell you to. Then you will escort her to my coach. If you say one word to another living soul, I will personally castrate you and send you to Arabia, where eunuchs are sold like whores."

The footman had a large Adam's apple; it bobbed up and down. "Yes, my lord."

Ramiel paid his servants well; in return, they performed their jobs well. The coach was in front of the marquis's palatial house inside of ten minutes. "Now," he told the footman.

Damp, insidious fog blanketed the night and seeped inside the coach. Ramiel leaned his head against the leather upholstery and closed his eyes, trying to control his body, his wants, his needs. He did not move when the door opened. Nor did he move when the coach tilted and he was surrounded by the essence of Elizabeth, her smell, the heat of her body. She had no sooner settled across from him with a swish of satin and a squeak of leather than the door slammed closed and the coach lurched forward.

"Last Thursday night I ran into a lamppost."

He opened his eyes and stared at the dark outline of her cloak and bonnet. She had touched him but had not confided in him. "You were hurt . . . and you didn't tell me."

"My pride was hurt more than my head." Her voice, so proximate in the close quarters, was remote. A dim glow of light from a passing lamppost briefly illuminated her face. "But I was frightened that night, because there were only me and the coachman and neither of us could see in the fog. We could have fallen into the Thames and all I thought about was that I would die and I would never know what it is like to love. May I kiss you?"

A bolt of heat shot up his body. *May I kiss you?* reverberated over the grind of the carriage wheels. "Take off your bonnet."

The sleek silhouette of her head replaced the bulky shape of the bonnet. Springs creaked; she perched on the edge of the seat, knees rubbing his through the layers of their individual clothing.

He leaned forward, tensed when gloved hands cupped his head.

She jerked away.

"Elizabeth—"

Instantly, her hands were back without the gloves, warm skin cupping his ears, sliding forward to the hard planes of his jaws. He closed his eyes on a wave of pleasure pain. *It had been so long . . .*

"Your skin feels different from mine. Harder. Rougher."

He choked back a laugh, eyes opening, wishing he had lit the lamps inside the coach so he could see her face as she indulged her passion. "You are a woman; I am a man."

Ramiel held his breath, waiting, *waiting,* and then she was leaning closer, her breath fanning his lips—

The carriage bounced; her lips skidded across his chin.

"I'm sorry—"

"No. Don't stop." If she pulled back, he would put his hands on her and he would take her. "Here." He reached out his arms, braced himself between the carriage windows. "Now. Again."

Tentatively, she leaned forward, breath caressing, lips touching . . .

Sizzling electricity galvanized Ramiel. Blindly, hungrily, he angled his head downward and opened his mouth over hers, sucking at her lips, swaying with the coach, moving with her as she explored the moist friction of a kiss, *ferame,* her first kiss by a man.

Not enough.

Easing back slightly, her lips soft and wet against his, he whispered shakily, "Open your mouth. Take my tongue inside of you."

She sucked in air, his breath, and then he was inside her. A low groan worked its way up from his chest. She gripped his head as it she wanted to pull him into her mouth, but her tongue nervously danced away from the prod of his.

Ramiel would not let her retreat. He circled, he probed, he licked until she imitated his motions, circling him, tasting him. *Ela'na,* she was hot. *He wanted her. . . .*

Ramiel licked the roof of her mouth, listened to the accelerating cadence of her breathing. Exultation so sharp that it was painful peaked inside of him. *She wanted him too,* and that was almost as potent as his own needs.

"Dear God . . . I did not know."

The words vibrated inside his mouth. He nipped her bottom lip, asked, "Did not know what?" and heard her swallow his breath.

"I did not know that a man's lips were so soft." Her lips moved against his, a soft abrasion, warm breath feathering his skin while her fingers dug into his scalp. "I did not know that a kiss was so . . . *personal.* So intimate. Is it not better if a man holds a woman when he kisses her?"

"I will not touch you against your will." He was surprised the palms of his hands pressing against the two windows did not shatter the glass. Purposefully, he teased her lips with his tongue, imitating the moist glide of a man's verge against a woman's wet vulva, thrust only to withdraw. "It you want me to touch you, Elizabeth, you are going to have to tell me to."

Her fingers knotted in his hair. "You do not consider a kiss . . . touching?"

"Lips kiss; teeth nibble; a tongue licks and tastes. Only hands touch. They cup a woman's breasts, warm and heavy with the weight of her need; they guide a woman's hips, soft and round beneath a man's hardness; they squeeze a woman's buttocks, to soothe and urge her closer; they hold open a woman's thighs, stretching her wide for pleasure; they caress a woman's vulva until she's slick with her passion. A tongue can taste that passion, but only through touch can a man's fingers slide inside her body where she's hot and wet and aches

with desire. Touch prepares a woman for deeper penetration.
When you tell me to touch you, Elizabeth, I will touch the very
depths of your body.''

Lips slanting, hardening, he took her mouth, unleashed the
full strength of his need, and sucked her tongue inside him.
She stiffened; he refused to let her go, sucking and sucking
her lips, her tongue, until she groaned into his mouth and
clutched his hair in both hands, pulling him closer, *closer*.
When he released her mouth, she gasped for breath.

He leaned his forehead against hers, skin bumping and grinding hers as the coach bumped and ground along the cobbled
street. His voice was raw with need. ''Ask me to touch you,
taalibba.''

Her voice was equally raw. ''What would you do if I did?''

''I would unfasten your gown and take out your breasts and
suckle your nipples until you scream for release. Then I would
suckle them until you gain it.''

Her breath audibly caught in her throat. ''A woman does
not obtain release through her breasts.''

A pained smile twisted his lips, remembering her earlier
confession. ''And how do you know that?''

''I have two sons,'' she whispered breathlessly. ''My nipples
have been suckled.''

''Not by a man, *taalibba*.''

''I cannot!'' she suddenly cried.

''You can!'' he returned, feeling her pain, feeling his own
pain from her fingers that clenched in his hair. ''You came to
me wanting to learn how to give a man pleasure. I want to be
that man. I want you to want me so badly, you will do anything
to learn how to give *me* pleasure. *Tell me to touch you,* Elizabeth.''

Suddenly, he was free, and it took every ounce of control
that he possessed not to plunge after her. He had tasted her
mouth; he wanted far, far more. He wanted to taste her pleasure,
her cry of release.

''You do not know what you are asking.''

Yes, he did.

Lowering his arms he closed his eyes and took a shuddering breath. "A kiss, Elizabeth. If you will not let me touch you, let me kiss your breasts. Let me take your nipples inside my mouth and suckle them like I suckled your tongue. Give me that, *taalibba*."

A rustle overrode the grind of the carriage wheels.

Ramiel's eyes snapped open.

Elizabeth slipped her cloak off her shoulders. "Just a kiss." Her voice shook with need.

He licked his lips and stared at the white skin that shone above the neckline of her dress that was black in the dark, then burgundy in a flash of streetlight. "Just a kiss," he agreed hoarsely. And prayed he could stop when the time came.

If he took her before she was ready, she would never forgive him . . . or herself.

"I cannot reach the buttons—"

"Turn around."

More rustling. She sat on the edge of the seat and presented him her back.

Hands trembling—the bouncing of the carriage did not aid him—he found the tiny buttons and one by one worked them free. His fingers tingled, aching to touch more than cloth. "I have to unlace your corset."

"Yes." He heard her ragged whisper over the drumming of his heart.

Laces . . . He thanked both Allah and God for the nine years he had spent in England, learning Englishwomen's undergarments. Quickly, efficiently, he freed her.

She turned, clutching the dress to her chest.

"Give me your breasts, *taalibba*."

"I can't."

"*Ela'na*, Elizabeth—"

"My chemise . . ."

Reaching out, he gently pulled the straps of her dress over her shoulders, trapping her arms at her sides. Peeling the corset down, he exposed the chemise, a white square of cloth cut low across the pale curve of her breasts.

Breath rasping in his throat, he slowly, carefully, slid his fingers underneath the cotton. Soft heat seared his fingers as he delicately lifted her left breast free of the restraining chemise. Unable to resist, he brushed the hard, exposed bud of her nipple.

She gasped. "Ramiel—"

He stilled. She had never called him by his given name, never called him a bastard, an animal, a dirty Arab. *She had apologized for her husband's rudeness.* So many firsts, for her, for him.

"It's all right," he crooned, lifting free her right breast, contact minimal, more than he had promised, but he would not abuse her trust any further.

"It's all right," he murmured again, slipping down onto the carriage floor, down onto his knees, digging his fingers into the leather seat on either side of her to prevent himself from taking more than she wanted.

"It's all right," he repeated, leaning forward into the warmth of her body, lips grazing soft, smooth skin. Her fingers threaded through his hair, cupped his head, caressed the tips of his ears. He breathed in the heat of her; it washed over him in a scalding wave. Suddenly his entire world consisted of this moment, this woman, and he wanted her to share that wonder.

He wanted to give her the gift of sex.

Nuzzling, he found her, a hard, tight bud of pure passion, and sucked her deep into his mouth. Elizabeth cried out; an answering cry ground out of his chest as he tongued her and suckled her and lost himself utterly in her wants and her needs.

She drew him closer, leaned into his face, body arching with her need, bouncing with the coach. "Oh, my God. *Stop.* Ramiel. What are you doing? I feel . . . please. Stop. *Oh, my God!*"

Halfway there, taalibba.

He rooted for her left breast, spared a moment to nuzzle her, to lick a hard, straining nipple in quick welcome, and then he took her into his mouth, became a part of her, heart pounding in time to her heartbeat, lungs expanding and contracting with the labored cadence of her breathing. He tongued the tiny indentation that had once spurted milk into the mouths of her sons, imagined her giving him a son and letting him drink from her after she had fed their child. Imagined drinking and drinking until she could give no more and there was no need to worry that it wasn't enough.

"Ramiel, *please,* you have to help me, I cannot—I don't—" Elizabeth's sob strangled in her throat.

Ramiel gently sank his teeth around the base of her nipple, giving her the extra sensation that she needed while he continued licking and suckling, licking and suckling. He could feel the arch of her body, hear the rush of air whooshing inside her lungs, could see her orgasm growing behind his eyelids, expanding, *erupting—*

He jerked free of her nipple and took her cry of release inside his mouth, plunging his tongue inside the hot wetness of her, taking her pleasure and making it his own.

She abruptly tore her mouth away from his, gulping oxygen. Her cheek was wet.

Ramiel opened his eyes—harsh gaslight penetrated the coach window. His throat tightened. "Don't cry, *taalibba.* It was only a kiss." He licked away the trail of salt. "Just a kiss."

"The coach has stopped."

He buried his face into her neck, knowing what she was going to do, hoping he had the strength to let her do it. Sighing, then, he moved away from her, sat across from her as if she had not shared her first orgasm with him.

She wriggled, freeing her arms from the vise of her dress, tucking her breasts back inside the chemise, pulling up the corset, the dress, wrapping the cloak about her.

"Divorce Edward Petre."

"I cannot."

Ramiel steeled himself against the finality in her voice. "I can give you love, Elizabeth. What can he give you?"

"He can give me my sons."

"You have your sons."

Elizabeth reached for the door. "I have to go."

He could not let her go, not with the taste of her still coating his tongue. "I want you, Elizabeth."

"And my husband does not," she rejoined flatly. "But you know that, do you not?"

Yes, he knew.

"Do you think I want to live the rest of my life with a man who does not want me?" Her low cry echoed inside the coach. "You just gave me a memory I will always cherish. And now I have to go. Please do not ever ask me to dance again, because *I cannot.*"

Wrenching open the door, she tumbled out of the carriage. Ramiel jumped to help her.

Elizabeth leapt to her feet, clutched her cloak about her. Golden light from the gas lamp by the town house door danced in her hair. "I asked for a divorce. It is not advantageous to either my husband's or my father's career. *Ma'a e-salemma,* Lord Safyre."

She slammed the carriage door in his face, leaving him with only her bonnet and her gloves and the lingering taste and smell of her body.

It occurred to Ramiel that he had underestimated Elizabeth. And that he had quite possibly jeopardized more than her reputation.

Chapter Eighteen

Johnny sat on a chair inside the foyer, fast asleep. Either Edward had not come home yet or he had posted the footman as sentry to clock the time she returned from the ball.

Elizabeth dashed away the salty stains on her cheeks. Underneath her cloak, her dress had slid off one shoulder; the loosened tapes of her corset tickled her back. Her lips tingled, her breasts ached, and she should feel tawdry and used, allowing a man who was not her husband such familiarities. She did not. She felt—alive. Empowered yet humbled. Like she had received far, far more than just a kiss.

Stealthily, she closed the front door to the town house and tiptoed by the footman, up the stairs, foot landing on the telltale creaking board. *She could not go on with her marriage, having sampled the intimacy that a man and a woman could share.*

She could not—*but she must.*

Elizabeth eased open her bedroom door—and stopped dead in her tracks. A black-haired man dressed in evening clothes sat at her desk. He was reading—what?

"What are you doing, Edward?"

The distant bong of Big Ben sounded over London's rooftops;

it was followed by a more proximate chime—the Westminster clock downstairs. It was two o'clock.

Edward continued perusing whatever it was that he was reading. "I am amassing the evidence of your adultery, Elizabeth."

Elizabeth's heartbeat pounded against her loosened corset. "You are a Uranian, Edward. Exactly what does a Uranian do?"

She had the satisfaction of seeing his back stiffen. Edward swung around in his chair. "Your lover did not tell you?"

Elizabeth shut the door and leaned against it. "Ramiel is not my lover," she retorted, too late realizing she had called him by his given name.

Contemptuous eyes raked her body. Elizabeth was acutely conscious of her state of disarray, of the swollen heat of her lips and her nipples and the dull throb inside her womb.

"You were given an ultimatum this evening, Elizabeth."

She had expected to regret her dance with Ramiel. But now that it was time, she could not. All that she felt was gratitude, that he had shown her the ecstasy of a man's kiss. She regretted only that she had not told him to touch her until he plumbed the very depths of her body so that she would never again feel dirtied by her husband.

"Are you going to threaten to kill me too, Edward?"

Shadow deepened his dark brown eyes. "I know how much you love your sons. I do not have to threaten your life."

Sick horror rose in her throat. "Are you threatening to harm your own children?"

"I do not have to."

"But you would."

She could see it in his eyes. For the first time, Elizabeth was glad that Richard and Phillip were away at school, out of harm's way.

"I will do whatever it takes to become prime minister."

Desperately, she tried to call his bluff. Edward had backed down when Ramiel threatened to expose his membership in the fellowship of Uranians. *She would not let him threaten her sons.* "Is your mistress a Uranian too, Edward?"

"As a matter of fact, my lover is a fellow Uranian."

Elizabeth sucked in air. The hair on the back of her neck stood up. "You said you did not have a mistress."

"I don't."

"Is there a difference between a lover and a mistress?"

Edward rolled up a sheath of earmarked papers. "I will strike a bargain with you, Elizabeth."

Elizabeth stared at the roll of papers in his hand, suddenly realizing what he had been reading and what he now held. *Her notes from* The Perfumed Garden. She had not been able to throw them away. "What deal is that?"

"I will tell you the difference between a lover and a mistress if you will tell me why you thought you could get away with sneaking out to meet your bastard."

Betrayal raced through her veins—which one of the servants had given her away? It was chased by fear.

How could he know she met Ramiel—unless he had engaged someone to follow her?

The watching eyes at the Women's Auxiliary.

Edward had summoned the constable, claiming he was worried because she was late, even though the fog would delay anyone. Had he hired someone to follow her? And had that someone intended to frighten her . . . or had he intended to kill her?

Damn him, *he would not make her afraid.*

"I will not ask for a divorce again, Edward. That is what you wanted, is it not?"

"Elizabeth, I want you to be the perfect wife. A mother and a hostess with an impeccable reputation so that you will be an asset rather than a hindrance. *Fucking* the Bastard Sheikh is not acceptable behavior in the wife of a future prime minister."

Elizabeth had heard that particular word, of course. It was commonplace on the streets, like the word *dolly*. Never had she imagined hearing it from her husband.

"Perhaps, Edward, you are jealous because you cannot."

Her mouth snapped shut, wishing the words back as soon as she uttered them.

Edward laughed loudly.

It was the first time Elizabeth had heard him laugh other than the polite guffaw. There was no boyish charm or warmth in it as there was in Ramiel's laughter.

"Elizabeth, you have absolutely nothing for me to be jealous of."

It should not be possible for a man who called her breasts udders to inflict further pain. It was.

"You did not used to be like this, Edward."

"Nor did you, Elizabeth." He stood up, completely at his ease. "You have some very interesting notes here. Quite immoral, in fact. Not at all what one would expect from a virtuous wife and mother."

Elizabeth pushed away from the door, more angry than afraid now. *She would not let him spoil the memories of the lessons she and Ramiel had shared.* "They are mine. Give them back to me."

"Everything you have is mine, Elizabeth, including your body." Edward smiled, enjoying her powerlessness. *How could she have lived with him all these years without knowing what kind of a monster he was?* "I will keep this as evidence of your illness."

She twisted her cloak more tightly around her throat. "What illness is that?" she asked, already knowing the answer.

"Why, nymphomania, of course." He opened the door connecting their bedrooms, paused. "I will have your maid bring you some hot milk. Distraught women need their sleep."

Elizabeth fought down nausea.

Death. Confinement. Separation from her children.

All because she wanted to be loved.

She did not have to ask who it was when a soft knock issued from her outer door. It was Emma, come to calm her distraught nerves. She carried a small silver tray. Hot steam rose from its solitary occupant, a mug.

The abigail was fully dressed, as if she had waited up for

Elizabeth. But Elizabeth did not demand that her maid wait up for her. If Elizabeth could not undress herself, she rang and Emma came to her dressed in nightgown and robe.

Ramiel had said she would know who Edward's mistress was when the time was right. *Was it Emma?*

"Is there laudanum in the milk, Emma?"

"Yes, ma'am."

An unconscious wife would be much more easily conveyed to an asylum than one who kicked and fought and screamed.

"You may put it down on the nightstand."

"Mr. Petre said that I should wait until you drank it."

Feeling strangely numb inside, while outside her body still tingled and burned from Ramiel's lips and tongue and teeth, Elizabeth took the mug, set it down on a side table beside the window, hoisted up the window, and poured the steaming milk out onto the withered rosebushes below. She returned the cup to the maid. "You may tell him that I did not leave a single drop."

Emma stared for long seconds at the mug before taking it out of Elizabeth's hand. "Very well, ma'am," she said, not meeting her mistress's eyes.

"Then you may go to bed. I do not require your services tonight."

Emma's mouth opened to object—to remind her that the satin ball gown buttoned down the back, that she would not be able to unfasten the buttons by herself. She swallowed the objection. "Very well, ma'am."

Elizabeth listened carefully, hearing the soft knock on Edward's door, muffled voices, then absolute quiet. At any moment she expected her husband to barge through the connecting door; he did not. Either he did not care whether she was unconscious tomorrow morning—or Emma had not snitched.

A black wave of exhaustion washed over her. Shadows flickered on the walls, a skeletal hand here, a scythe there, death and deception everywhere. She turned the flame down on the gas lamp before taking off the cloak, the satin gown, the loosened corset. The top of the chemise was damp from her sweat.

Unerringly, her fingers skimmed over the soft cotton, felt the silky flesh swelling above it, the hard nub of her nipples underneath it.

She had never dreamed that a woman's breasts were so sensitive. Or that a man could give her a climax by suckling them.

Ramiel had said that marriage was more than words spoken in a church. Now she believed him.

What was she going to do?

She would not endure Edward's threats on the lives of her two sons. Nor would she sit back and allow him to commit her to an insane asylum.

A woman's choices . . .

But she had only one choice. And that was to leave Edward's house, now, *tonight,* while she was still free to do so.

She had money. She had jewelry.

She was not a coward.

Elizabeth yanked out a velvet skirt and bodice from her wardrobe, struggled into them. Sitting in the armchair in front of the fireplace, she waited for the light beneath the connecting bedroom door to go out.

The banked coals emitted seductive warmth. It reminded her how hot Ramiel's mouth had been. How soft the tips of his ears.

Memory rolled over her, drowning her in sensation, the sharp contraction of her womb when he had stroked the roof of her mouth, the pleasure-pain bite of his teeth sinking into her nipple, and the hot, wet suckling of his lips, his tongue, the surge of moisture between her legs when she had blindly arched into his mouth, holding him closer and closer until her body clenched in a flash of white light. A quiet peace had followed, then Ramiel buried his head into the crook of her neck, *so like Richard . . .*

I want you.

Elizabeth slipped into sleep. It was not her son who pursued her.

"Elizabeth . . ."

A feminine whisper invaded her dreams.

She didn't want to hear it, to respond to it. She wanted Ramiel, the rasp of his voice, the stroke of his tongue, the vibration of his groan filling her mouth. Edward stared at the two of them from across the ballroom as they danced with her breasts spilling out of her satin ball gown; beside him stood the parliamentary member who had claimed him at the Whitfield ball and the golden-haired young man from the charity ball.

My lover is a fellow Uranian.

You said you did not have a mistress.

I don't.

Ignoring the staring, condemning eyes, she threaded her fingers through Ramiel's hair, soft as spun gold.

When you are ready for the truth, you will see for yourself who your husband's lover is.

"Elizabeth . . ."

Sunlight stabbed her eyes. She rolled her head on the back of the armchair to escape it. A *whoosh* sounded between one heartbeat and the next, as if someone sighed or blew out a candle, and then Elizabeth was aware of nothing but Ramiel and the intimate bonding of a man suckling at her breasts.

"Mrs. Petre! Mrs. Petre! You must wake up! Please, Mrs. Petre!"

The bed shook underneath Elizabeth. No, not the bed. Her shoulders. Someone was shaking her back and forth, back and forth. She flapped a limp wrist in protest.

"Mrs. Petre! Please! Wake up!"

Elizabeth groggily opened an eye . . . and stared at Emma. Her hair straggled about her face.

Elizabeth had never seen Emma untidy.

"Tired," she whispered. "Come back. Drink. Chocolate. Later."

The idea of chocolate made Elizabeth's stomach roil.

"Don't let her go back to sleep. I'll get her a glass of water. Is there a bucket in the WC?"

The darkness pulled Elizabeth down and down. It smelled faintly rancid, like . . . It dawned on her that Emma had two voices, one female and one male.

"Mrs. Petre. Drink. Mrs. Petre, open your eyes and drink."

Emma's male voice was very commanding. Something hard and cold pressed against her lips, clicked on her teeth.

"Drink, Mrs. Petre."

Water. Icy cold.

Elizabeth suddenly realized what the darkness that weighted her eyelids smelled like. *Gas.* The water tasted just like the gas smelled.

Everything Elizabeth had eaten and drank the evening before rushed up into her throat. She doubled over and heaved.

"That's good, Mrs. Petre. Get it all up. Emma, hold that bucket for her."

The masculine voice sounded vaguely familiar. Just when Elizabeth was on the verge of identifying it, every muscle in her body seemed to convulse. She heaved until she felt as if she were regurgitating her stomach instead of its contents. Every time she thought she was finished, she would get another whiff of gas or taste it again on her tongue and the sickness would start all over again.

She knew where the gas odor came from. It came from the bedside lamp—which had been burning when she fell asleep.

She recalled a woman's voice and the *whoosh* of a sigh . . . and knew that someone had blown out the flame in the lamp while she slept.

More exhausted than she would have thought it humanly possible to be, Elizabeth sat up in the armchair. The banked coals had long died. She was cold and her neck was cramped from sleeping sitting up. Her buttocks were numb, which was no doubt better than the pain she would otherwise have been experiencing, perched on a bustle for heaven knew how long. She wiped her mouth with unsteady fingers.

Emma knelt on the floor beside the chair. Her round brown eyes were guarded. Johnny the footman knelt beside the maid.

Elizabeth closed her eyes. "You blew out the lamp," she

thickly accused Emma, remembering everything, Edward stealing her notes, then ordering the milk dosed with laudanum that the maid had brought her.

"No, Mrs. Petre. I would not do that."

Elizabeth forced her eyelids open. There was truth in Emma's eyes. Truth . . . and knowledge.

She was too sick to be frightened, but she knew that neither condition would last long. "You know who did it."

Emma did not answer. Elizabeth had not expected her to. Edward paid Emma's salary, for all that she was Elizabeth's maid. Just as he paid the salary of Mrs. Sheffield, the cook, and Mrs. Bannock, the housekeeper. Both women had been hired at the same time as had the abigail.

She shivered and hugged her body. Icy sunlight and February air poured in the open window. No wonder she was so cold. "Where is Mr. Petre?"

"Mr. and Mrs. Walters and he had breakfast together. They all left afterward. Mrs. Walters wanted to wake you, but Mr. Petre said to let you sleep."

Her husband. Her father. It really did not matter which one plotted to kill her or what servant had carried out the order.

"Thank you, Emma. You may leave me now."

"Shall I ring up the doctor?"

So that Edward could accuse her of being suicidal?

Perhaps he had not intended to kill her with gas. A woman who was both a nymphomaniac and suicidal would be an ideal candidate for bedlam.

"No, no doctor."

"Shall I run you a bath?"

Elizabeth envisioned the countess's Turkish bath. She had said Ramiel had one too.

"No. Nothing."

She wanting *nothing* from this house. Not clothes, not jewels.

Emma rose with a creak of her knees. Johnny stayed where he was. "You cannot stay here, Mrs. Petre."

A loyal servant.

"Yes, I know."

She closed her eyes and clamped her mouth tightly shut, holding back a dry heave.

"Do you have somewhere to go?"

A hotel. Countess Devington.

Come home with me, taalibba.

"Yes."

"Do you want Emma to pack a bag for you?"

He was on a first-name basis with her abigail. Perhaps Johnny was not as loyal as she had thought.

"No." She did not want to take anything with her that had been purchased with Edward Petre's money. "I just want to get up . . ."

Her legs were so shaky, she had to grab the footman to keep from collapsing back onto her bustle. Righting herself, she slowly walked down the hall to the water closet. Inside, she brushed her teeth and rinsed out her mouth, then leaned heavily against the sink, forehead pressed to the cold mirror above it.

Someone had tried to kill her . . . *and had very nearly succeeded.*

What would she tell her sons? That either their father or their grandfather was a potential murderer?

When she opened the door, Johnny waited outside with her cloak. Swaying slightly, she stood as still as she could while he tossed it around her. He was far too familiar for a servant; he buttoned the wool snugly about her neck.

"Who did it, Johnny?"

He concentrated on adjusting a black bonnet on top of her head. His skin was dark but without the golden tint Ramiel's skin possessed. He tied the ribbons of the bonnet beneath her chin as if she were a child.

"I don't know, ma'am." He stepped back and produced her reticule from inside his black coat. "All I know is that it wasn't Emma."

"How do you know that?"

"She said you told her you wouldn't mind her marrying. A servant don't kill a good mistress."

Elizabeth remembered relaying that piece of information to

Emma. It had been later in the day after her first lesson, Tuesday. She also remembered the expression on Emma's face when she offered to redress Elizabeth's hair that should have hung down her back in a braid but that Elizabeth had carelessly left in a bun after visiting Ramiel, and then again when she retrieved her cloak that was still damp from early morning London fog.

Emma may not have tried to kill her, but she would lay odds she had been the one to alert Edward about her early morning jaunts.

"How is it that the two of you arrived in such a timely manner?"

Elizabeth watched with detached interest the dull red that spread over the footman's dark face. "Emma's room be above yours, ma'am. We were . . . together . . . and I smelled the gas."

Together. No wonder Emma's hair had been mussed.

The numbness of near-death burst in a *pop* of pain. Emma had found love . . . and betrayed Elizabeth because she sought it.

She would almost prefer Emma to be Edward's lover.

"I have no doubt that Mr. Petre will provide Emma with a glowing recommendation." She peered inside her reticule, spotted her change purse. "You will forgive me, but I am feeling less generous. Good-bye, Johnny, and I wish you the best of luck."

"Where are you going, ma'am?"

Elizabeth stiffened her spine. "I appreciate your concern, but it really is none of your business."

"Shall I have a carriage brought around for you?"

Either Tommie the groom or Will the coachman had told Edward of her visit with the countess. She did not want anyone in this household knowing of her whereabouts. "That is not necessary."

The front door was left unsecured, as if the servants were deliberately occupied elsewhere so that she might escape unnoticed. The sun was bright, only faintly obscured by coal smoke.

After walking six blocks, she spied a hack. It sped on by. Two more hacks passed her by before one stopped.

"Where to, ma'am?"

Straightening her shoulders, she looked up at the cabbie's prematurely aged face and told him in measured, precise words exactly where she wanted to go. And prayed that she would not regret it.

Elizabeth fumbled inside her reticule; her fingers closed around two shillings. She rode the distance clutching the coins. The sickening smell of impending death followed her.

Her life would never be the same again, a voice inside her head warned. *She* would never be the same.

But she did not need her conscience to tell her that.

The hack jerked to a halt. Pushing open the door, she stepped out onto the cobbled street, stiffened her legs to prevent them from giving out underneath her.

She stared about her, the London landscape almost unrecognizable in the full light of day. The house was of Georgian design, the lines pure, speaking of an age less cluttered by minutiae than was the age of Queen Victoria.

Her heart lurched; the hack was leaving. Too late. She had made her choice; there would be no going back. She raised her hand and grabbed the lion-headed brass knocker. That, at least, looked the same.

The Arab butler who was no Arab but a European man dressed in a turban and flowing white robe opened the door. At sight of Elizabeth his head reared back.

"*El Ibn* is not here."

Elizabeth felt like she had come full circle.

"Then I will wait for him."

Chapter Nineteen

Ramiel awoke abruptly, every sense in his body alert.

Muhamed stood in the doorway of his bedroom. His face was shrouded in shadow.

"What is it?" Ramiel asked tautly.

"The woman is here."

Air rushed into Ramiel's lungs.

Elizabeth . . . *here.* She would not come to him in broad daylight unless she meant to stay. Especially after she had asked Edward Petre for a divorce.

He closed his eyes, savoring the feel of her presence in his home, anticipation rising, heat building—Ramiel threw the bedcovers back.

"*El Ibn*—"

The glint in Ramiel's eyes halted the Cornishman's warning. He cinched a turquoise silk robe about his waist. "Is she in the library?"

"Yes."

Ramiel descended the stairs two at a time, barefoot, naked underneath the robe. He would shock her, perhaps, but it was a sight she would soon get used to.

Silently, he opened the library door, closed it behind him. He leaned back against the mahogany wood and watched her.

Elizabeth stood looking out of the bay windows. He had a curious feeling of déjà vu. She had stood thus when first she had braved his home, dressed head to foot in shapeless black wool, surrounded on either side by twin columns of yellow silk drapes and ribbons of gray fog. Now her hair glinted red fire in the sunlight and a gray velvet dress snugly hugged a proud back and curvaceous waist before bulging out in a curiously flattened bustle.

Electric awareness shimmered in the air like dust motes in sunshine. Between one breath and the next she turned, facing him.

He stared at the rhythmical rise and fall of her full breasts underneath the gray velvet bodice. Blood pumped into his groin at the memory of the taste and texture of her. Last night he had felt her heartbeat and had listened to the quickening rush of air inside her lungs as he had suckled her and brought her a woman's pleasure.

He closed his eyes, suddenly overcome with a vulnerability that he had not felt since he was thirteen years old. Would she find him meritorious? Or would she be repulsed by the length of him, the thickness of him, the blunt reality of a man?

"My husband tried to kill me."

Ramiel's eyelids shot open. Behind her a sparrow fluttered against a windowpane, seeking impossible entry. "What did you say?"

"Or my father." Elizabeth's voice was tight, like stretched wire. "He could have arranged it. Two days ago I told my mother that I wanted a divorce and asked if she would petition my father to intercede on my behalf. Yesterday, when I got back from visiting with the countess—and you—he said he would rather see me dead than have me ruin his and Edward's political careers."

Ramiel pushed away from the door, stalked her. Reaching out, he grabbed her shoulders, swung her around so that both of them were profiled by the warm rays of the sun.

Elizabeth's face was ghastly white; her shoulders underneath his fingers trembled. She smelled of gas—her clothes, her hair, her skin.

Many Londoners perished of gas asphyxiation. There would have been no questions had she died, just condolences for the bereaved husband and father.

And with a single word she could have prevented it.

As he could have.

The fear and anger and guilt increased rather than replaced the heat that hammered through his body. ''Why didn't you tell me this last night?''

She looked up at him, pupils dilated, eyes black instead of hazel. ''Edward was waiting in my bedroom. He had the notes that I took when I read *The Perfumed Garden.* He said he knew about our lessons. I thought he was going to commit me to an insane asylum. For nymphomania, he said. He had my maid bring me a cup of hot milk. It was laced with laudanum, and I poured it out of the window. I knew then that I would have to leave him. I changed clothes and sat down in an armchair to wait until he turned his light out—we have a connecting bedroom door, you see—but then I fell asleep and I heard someone whisper my name. I was dreaming about you and I did not want to wake up, so I turned my head away and then I heard a sound as if someone blew out a candle. The next thing I knew, someone was shaking me and everything smelled and tasted of gas. *I did not think my father meant it when he said he would rather see me dead.*''

Elizabeth's lips trembled; tears shone in her eyes, hazel again instead of shocked black.

Ramiel had known that the potential for danger existed when Elizabeth told him some hours earlier that she had asked for a divorce. He had not expected any action this quickly. Especially since he had made it clear in no uncertain terms that he was aware of Petre's secret life and would not hesitate to reveal it to the public.

''I smell of—gas. The countess said that you have a Turkish bath. May I bathe in it, please? Then I would like to kiss you and take you in my hands and pump and squeeze your manhood until you are erect. I want to kiss and suckle you there like you did my breasts.''

Ramiel sucked in air. *The third lesson.* She remembered verbatim how he liked to be held.

His fingers tightened about her shoulders before he released her and stepped back, heart pounding as if he had raced his stallion across the desert sands into the sunrise. ''You do not have to do this, Elizabeth. If all you want is a bath, then I will bathe you and that will be an end to it. You came to me for help. You may stay here as long as you wish. I do not require that you sacrifice your virtue for payment.''

''I am not sacrificing my virtue. I am trying to make sense out of what is happening. Last night in your coach I experienced something that was—quite wonderful. I have driven one man to murder. *I need to give you pleasure.* I need to know that I can bring wonder to someone too.''

I need to give you pleasure reverberated in the semicircular bay of windows. It was silently chased by Ramiel's thoughts. *But not enough to come to me freely without the threat of death.*

He closed his eyes against her raw desperation and fought down the encroaching bitterness. The sun burned the right side of his face; the left side of him was ice cold.

Elizabeth offered him more than any other woman had ever offered. The past nine years had taught him to take what he could get.

Opening his eyes, he lowered his head and stared at her lips. ''Do you know what you are asking, Elizabeth?''

Her lips tightened, as they had the first morning he had asked it. ''Yes.''

And she lied to herself again.

He held out his hand. ''Then, come.''

She took his hand, her fingers cold and uncertain.

He padded down the mahogany-paneled hallway inlaid with mother-of-pearl, impervious to the scratchy wool of the cold Oriental runner beneath his bare feet, aware only of her hand in his, the heat of her skin, the swish of her skirts, and the blood pulsing in his manhood.

With each step the anger built. At Edward Petre. For hurting Elizabeth. At Andrew Walters. For threatening his own daughter's life. At himself. For wanting Elizabeth to flaunt society and come to him for no other reason than because she wanted *him*.

He came to a door, opened it. Relinquishing her hand, he reached for a switch, found it. Harsh light flooded the stairwell.

"You have electricity." Her voice was a hollow echo.

"A recent acquisition. Someday soon I plan on replacing all of the gas fixtures. Electricity is less hazardous."

"Yes."

Ramiel winced. She would not have been near gassed if Petre had invested in electricity. He would make certain that the rest of his house was wired within the month.

He gestured for her to descend the spiral staircase. At the bottom she did not wait for him to open the door. She turned the knob herself and stepped into the cavernous pit that was the bathing room.

Ramiel followed behind her, guided by the heat of her body and the icy tiles underneath his bare feet. He searched the wall for—

Blinding light clicked into being. Ramiel had installed electricity because of the added convenience and privacy of not having to rely upon servants to light gas fixtures whenever he wanted to swim. He stepped up behind her and tried to see the room as she might see it—the large swimming bath wreathed in a thin haze of steam, the floor that was a mosaic masterpiece of intertwining fauna, the empty black marble fireplace in the far right-hand corner, a small porcelain tub painted in delicate yellow, blue, and red against the outside wall.

It belonged to her now. Everything he possessed was hers.

He would not let her go again.

"It's—colder here than it was at your mother's."

Ramiel nudged her toward the porcelain tub. "My mother is lazy. She prefers to relax in her swimming bath, whereas I prefer to swim. I keep the water warm but not as hot as a regular bath. I wash here.'' He reached down and put a stopper into the porcelain tub before twisting twin gold faucets; hot and cold water gushed from the dolphin-shaped spout. ''And then I swim.''

Straightening, he untied the silk belt holding together his robe.

Elizabeth stared fixedly at the water cascading into the tub. A pale pink flush infused her cheeks.

Ramiel shrugged out of the robe, let it slide off his body until it puddled around his feet.

The flush in her cheeks darkened. ''I have never done this before.''

Steam coiled around the two of them. ''You swam at the countess's.''

''Yes, but I undressed behind a screen.''

''I don't have a screen.''

''Would you turn your back, please?''

''No,'' he said baldly.

He would not allow her to genteelly hide behind a screen or false modesty. He wanted what she offered too badly to accept anything but naked honesty.

She stiffened her spine and studied the array of brushes and soaps on top of the mosaic-tiled shelf above the tub. ''I have had two children.''

''So you have said.''

''My body is not . . . what it used to be.''

''Elizabeth, I want the woman you are now, not the girl you once were. If you want to please me, then undress for me.''

''If you do not like what you see, you must tell me.'' He strained to hear her over the muted roar of the cascading water. ''I would not force myself upon you.''

As she had her husband. Someday, perhaps, she would tell him what Petre had done and said when she tried to seduce him.

Elizabeth clumsily took off her bodice. She wore the same

chemise she had worn the night before, the square neckline cut low over the curve of her breasts.

Ramiel's breathing quickened.

Averting her face from that place on his body that amply showed what a fully erect man looked like, she glanced about for a place to hang the velvet bodice. Ramiel calmly took it from her. He tossed it toward the fireplace and waited, the roar of the water filling the tub loud in the silence.

Head bowing, she unhooked the waist of her skirt and let it fall around her feet. Untying the flattened horsehair-stuffed bustle, she let that drop too, the thud muffled by the velvet covering the ceramic tiles.

Ramiel's body tightened, in anticipation, in apprehension. She had almost been murdered; no doubt she was still in shock. He should stop her from taking this step until she was recovered, because once she gave herself to him there would be no going back. She had said she would regret dancing with him last night. He would not stop at a quick waltz around the swimming bath. He would not stop until they had fully explored all forty positions of love plus all the other variations that Ramiel had learned in the past twenty-five years.

One by one she untied the two petticoats and he still did not stop her. White cotton mounded over her feet.

Without thinking, he reached over and bunched the shapeless chemise in his hands. His knuckles rested on her ribs; her skin was taut underneath the flimsy cotton. "Lift your arms over your head."

He pulled the chemise over her head and froze, her arms still in the air, the chemise holding them captive.

Magnificent, Joseffa had said. Ramiel had never seen anything more beautiful in his life.

Her breasts were creamy white with puckered rosebud nipples, swollen and tender from his kisses the night before. She had a slender waist that flared to generous hips, concealed only by clinging cotton drawers.

Sexual heat flushed his face; it traveled all the way down to his feet—

"Ela'na!" He jerked the chemise over her arms and tossed it he knew not where. Bending down, he twisted the gold faucets to the off position.

The tub had overflowed. Elizabeth stood as if she did not know what to do with her hands while the clothing at her feet soaked up hot water.

Ramiel knew what she could do with her hands. She could pump him, stroke him, *suckle him*. . . . All the things she said she wanted to do to him but which she had planned to do for her husband.

He straightened. "Turn around and look at me."

Tensed, body hard as the stone leaf she had once tried to remove from a statue, Ramiel waited for approbation.

He could hear her intake of breath, could see the widening of her eyes. "You—have pubic hair."

The observation momentarily took him by surprise . . . until he remembered that she had bathed with his mother. Apparently, the countess was more Arabic than what she led others to believe. "My English half. I am not inspired by the Muslim faith. It is a risky business when a man removes hair from certain body parts."

Her gaze was rapt. "You—are longer than the artificial phallus."

"Yes."

"And thicker."

"Yes," he gritted, impossibly lengthening and thickening even more.

"It has a reddish-purple head, like a plum, only larger. Are you certain I will be able to take all of you?"

Ramiel's body involuntarily flexed. He drew a shaky breath. "There is a special place inside your body behind the mouth of your womb. It allows a man to fit more deeply inside a woman who might otherwise be unable to accept all of him." He willed her to raise her head, snared her gaze. "I could show you this place."

There was neither revulsion nor fear in her eyes, just a

woman's curiosity and a yearning to experience the closeness of sexual union. "How?"

"Take off the rest of your clothes."

Her hands trembled as she fumbled with the two buttons at the waist of her cotton drawers. He wondered if she was aware of the commitment she would make by giving herself to him. And then he did not wonder at anything, because she stood naked save for flesh-colored stockings and shoes that were buried underneath the pile of damp clothing.

Her fleece was dark auburn, like the hair on top of her head. Her thighs were voluptuous. Dimpled knees tapered down to slender ankles.

He imagined himself cushioned between those soft white thighs, imagined her slender ankles locked around his waist, taking all of him, every single inch.

"Put your right foot onto the edge of the tub," he ordered hoarsely.

Modesty and titillation warred inside her. "Should I not . . . take off my shoes and stockings?"

Later, he thought. But then, perhaps not. With the stockings circling her thighs she was every man's sexual fantasy.

"Not now. Now I want to show you that special place inside your body."

Her breasts quivered with the force of her breathing. "Is there not a more dignified position I can assume for you to show me this place?"

Her response was so quintessentially Elizabeth that he bit back a smile. "Elizabeth—"

"Ramiel . . . I am embarrassed." She tilted her chin, daring him to mock her. "I have never been naked . . . like this."

"You said you wanted to give me pleasure," he challenged her rawly. "That you wanted to bring wonder to someone."

Her chin lifted higher. "I did. I do."

"Then, let me be that someone. Tell me to touch you, *taalibba*. Raise your leg and open your body so that I can reach inside of you *and tell me to touch you*."

Her pulse raced in her throat; steam trickled down between

her breasts. She stood poised for an endless heartbeat before awkwardly freeing her right foot from the trappings of her drawers, sodden petticoats, and velvet skirt. Lifting her leg, she perched a square-heeled slipper onto the edge of the water-rimmed tub.

His body clenched at the sight of the black patent-leather shoe, lingered on the black silk bow fastening across the top of her narrow foot, slowly traversed the length of the flesh-colored stocking to the V of her thighs and the delicate inner lips peeping out from auburn curls, rose-tinted like her nipples. A drop of pearly moisture glistened on the inside of her thigh.

Sharp need stabbed through his groin. That pearl of moisture did not result from shock.

"Please touch me, Ramiel." Her voice shook. With nervousness. With desire at this unfamiliar game between a man and a woman. "Reach into my body and show me how to take all of you inside me."

Heart slamming against his ribs, he stepped closer, closer yet, until he felt the heat of her exposed body. Curving his left hand about her right hip to steady her, he feathered her auburn bush with his right hand, tested the plumpness of her lips and the slickness of her feminine moisture.

She grabbed his shoulders, forging a primordial link, man touching woman, woman touching man.

There was passion in her eyes and there was him, two miniature blond heads, two sets of bastard turquoise eyes. He combed through her damp fringe of pubic hair, lightly sawed a finger back and forth until her lips parted and furled about him like a hothouse flower.

"Did he touch you like this?" he asked in a low, choked voice, hating himself for asking but unable to stop the question. *If Petre or her father had not tried to kill her she would still be with her husband.*

The desire dimmed in her eyes. She wedged her hands between their bodies—she was going to push him away.

He touched her hot, wet portal, fingertip circling the place that she had offered *him* after Ramiel had aroused her. "Did he touch you here?"

Elizabeth stilled, sensing the danger of his mood. "Edward has not touched me—ever. He came into my bed and shoved himself into me, then it was over and he was gone. And he has not even done that in twelve and a half years. All he wanted to do was to make me pregnant. No one has ever touched me, Ramiel. No one but you."

Ramiel closed his eyes, blocking out her pain, his pain, his fingertip swirling and swirling against the hot wetness of her, teaching her to accept his touch, preparing her for the moment when something far larger would seek entrance. "But you would have taken him inside you last Saturday. You used the things I had taught you that aroused me to seduce another man."

"No." She twined her fingers into the mat of dark blond hair that covered his chest. "No, I could not do that."

He opened his eyes, fighting the anger, the hurt, needing to lose himself inside her body, needing her to lose herself inside his body. "Then relax down here." He pressed his finger against her only to have her muscles tightly clench, blocking entrance. "Take me inside you."

She slid her hands up his chest and grasped his shoulders, breasts rising, offering themselves to his mouth. "I am trying, Ramiel. I want to take you inside me."

Forbidden memories, unwanted memories flickered to life.

Sliding his left hand over the soft roundness of her hip, Ramiel reached back and grasped her heart-shaped buttocks to hold her still. "Let me help you take me, *taalibba.*" *Let me help you make me forget.* "When I touch you here"—he slid his finger back up through the moist folds of her flesh and found the hard little bud whose sole purpose is to give a woman pleasure, caressed it for long seconds—"hold yourself open. And when I slide down here"—he matched his actions with his words, teasing her portal that was tensely closed—"push your hips forward to press your clitoris against the palm of my hand.

"Now. My finger is on your clitoris." She strained against his hand. It would not take much to make her orgasm, but he did not want that for her yet. "And now I am sliding down."

She instinctively thrust her hips upward to retain contact, portal relaxed, unguarded. His finger sank home deep inside her, stretching her where she had not been stretched in over twelve years.

Elizabeth convulsed around his finger. "Ramiel, take it out. I am not pre—"

He took her cry into his mouth, thrusting his tongue inside her to counteract the small invasion between her other lips. If she had fought him, if she had shown in any way that she truly was not ready for penetration, he would have eased out of her. But she did not.

He could feel her entire body trembling, not entirely with passion. She was not prepared for the reality of a man or the intensity of his desire. But she soon would be.

Gently, he licked the roof of her mouth while he eased his finger more deeply inside her until his progress was stopped by an inner hardness, the mouth of her womb. Ramiel raised his head and looked at her swollen lips, at her breasts that quivered with each breath, at the white skin of her stomach, her auburn fleece, and the dark line of his wrist disappearing between her legs.

"Does this hurt?" He delicately prodded the hard dimple of her cervix.

She fought for composure. "It burns. And there is . . . pressure. This is not what I came for. I want to give *you* pleasure."

He prodded again. "*Shhh.* Not yet. Let me show you how to take me. . . . This is the opening to your womb. Here is where a woman takes a man's seed and later opens up to give him his child. I'm going to insert another finger inside you."

Her silky tissue pulsed around him. Her nails sank into his shoulder. "Please . . ."

Please don't hurt her. Please give her pleasure.

Please don't reject me.

He lowered his head in a whisper of a kiss. "Always so

polite. I am not your husband, *taalibba*. I don't want your politeness. I want you to moan and groan and beg me to take you.''

Her nails sank into his shoulders. "Intimacy is not very dignified.''

"No, sex is not very dignified," he agreed. And gave her a second finger. He took her cry, a high, keening sound of unbearable pleasure and unbearable pressure.

She was so tight. Ramiel did not remember ever having a virgin who was this tight.

He probed her mouth while he probed her body; her tongue tentatively stroked his while his fingertips firmly stroked the mouth of her womb. Pressing gently, inexorably, he explored the back of her vagina, searching, pushing higher, deeper . . . forcing his way until suddenly her body yawned open and his fingers were clamped inside the special pocket behind the cervix that affords a large man an extra couple of inches.

Hot air filled his mouth, Elizabeth's breath. Her inner flesh nipped his fingertips in a painfully tight vise. "This is the special place, *taalibba*.'' He gently thrust his two fingers back and forth, careful not to withdraw from the tight pocket. "When I come inside you and the pressure or the pain becomes too great because I am entering you too deeply, remember to tilt your hips so that I will slide past your cervix and enter here.''

She squeezed her eyelids shut. Steam misted her face, dripped from the tip of her nose. "I did not know a man could enter a woman this deeply.''

He kissed the drop of steam off her nose. "This is just two fingers, *taalibba*. There is more. Much, much more.''

Slowly, gently, he withdrew, feeling her body clutch him as if to keep him in her special place, *their* special place now, no one had ever penetrated her as deeply as he had, as deeply as he was going to enter her. He eased out of her vagina, slid upward, and found her swollen little bud. It pulsed frenetically underneath his wet fingertips.

"Tell me to touch you, *taalibba*,'' he whispered thickly into her mouth.

"Touch me, Ramiel," she whispered back, breath searing his lips.

"Where? Tell me where to touch you."

She clutched his shoulders, straining closer toward his caressing fingers. "There. Please. *There.*"

"You don't want me to touch you inside?"

She panted softly into his mouth, body bearing down against his circling fingertips. "Yes. Please touch me inside—oh there, *yes,* please don't stop!"

"Tilt your hips."

He deliberately strummed the turgid little shaft of her clitoris through the soft, moist lips of her labia while he lightly licked the seam of her mouth. She tilted her hips forward, arching into the palm of his hand to gain the pressure she needed.

"Now tell me to stick three fingers inside of your special place."

"*Three*—" Ramiel could hear her unspoken words, too much, she could not accept a third finger, she had barely taken two.

"Tell me, *taalibba.*"

She licked her lips, encounte. ˙ i his. "Please stick three fingers inside of my special place, only please, *please*—"

Savage pleasure surged through Ramiel. Slanting his mouth over hers, he sucked her tongue inside his mouth . . . and thrust three fingers inside her body, open for him in that unguarded moment, anticipating a caress instead of invasion.

She grabbed his hair and pulled, sharing her pain as he butted up against the dimpled cervix.

"Tilt your hips, Elizabeth. Take me, *taalibba.* If you can't take three fingers now, you'll never be able to take all of me later."

A little sob filled his mouth, and then she tilted her hips forward and he found the special place inside her body. She clamped down on his fingertips so tightly that he could not withdraw even if he wanted to.

He buried his face into the crook of her neck; steam and sweat dripped off his forehead. She smelled faintly of gas;

overriding it was the scent of her, of hot, moist skin and even hotter desire.

"Why didn't you come home with me last night?" The tight inner core of her pulsed in time to his heartbeat. Slick feminine desire leaked from her body, pooled in the palm of his hand. He tightened his fingers around a deliciously soft, plump cheek—*How could she think that she forced herself upon him when all he wanted was for her to come to him, for him, with him?*—and pulled her closer, needing the reality of her sex, the assurance of her body. "Why did you risk death rather than come to me?"

Moisture trailed down his shoulder, steam, sweat, *tears.* She rubbed her cheek against him, skin slick again skin, outside, inside. "My sons. Edward threatened to take my sons away from me."

Salt burned his eyes. "Would you have come to me last night . . . if it had been only you?"

"Yes." He felt the word all through his body, the movement of her lips against his shoulder, the dark heat of her breath, the soft sigh of sound.

"Just for this?" He wiggled his fingertips deep inside her.

"No, for something more."

"You would bond with a bastard?"

"I would bond with *you.*"

Ramiel buried his face more deeply into her neck, melting, his fingers, the last nine years of his life, the anger, the jealousy borne of fear. *He was a man.* For her he was a man, and that was more than enough.

"I will not let him take your sons away from you, *taalibba.* As long as we are together, you will be safe. You must trust me."

"I have three of your fingers inside me, sir." The tart primness of her voice was spoiled by an inner trembling. "I *must* trust you, or I would not be here."

He would protect that trust. No matter what the cost. He had the knowledge. Petre had given him the means.

"Let me bathe you."

Let me remove the last remnants of Edward Petre from your skin.

"*Now?*"

Her body had relaxed around his fingers; she was almost ready.

"*Now.*"

"Ramiel, I hardly think—"

"Trust me, *taalibba.*"

"But I need to remove my stockings and shoes—"

"When it is time I will remove them."

"Ramiel, I am afraid."

"Not of this, Elizabeth. Don't be afraid of this."

Her hazel eyes flickered with uncertainty. "Do you tremble with passion, Lord Safyre?"

The memories of their lessons were there, a part of her as surely as his fingers were now a part of her.

"I tremble with passion, *taalibba.* For you."

"You will bathe me . . . how?"

"With my tongue. While my fingers hold you open for me."

Her muscles reflexively tightened. "A woman trembles in her passion too."

A pained smile twisted his lips. "I know."

"What if I fall?"

For answer he knelt down on the wet bundle of her clothing and breathed in the scent of her, savored the sight of her, embracing him. The dark skin of his fingers disappeared inside a rose-tinted ring of flesh. Glistening drops of feminine desire dripped down his palm.

A flash of flesh-colored stocking folding inward caught his eyes. At the same time, her muscles clenched around the base of his fingers.

His left hand shot out, grabbed her thigh. "Keep your foot on the tub, *taalibba.*"

"You can see me."

"And smell you." He leaned closer. "And taste you." He nuzzled her damp auburn fleece with his nose, flicked her with his tongue. "And kiss you."

She tangled her fingers into his hair. "I will fall."

He raised his head and met her stare. Fear. Recognition. A need that was as much pain as pleasure. It was all there in her hazel eyes.

"I won't let you fall, *taalibba.*" Leaning forward, he sucked the swollen bud of her clitoris between his lips, bathed the petal-soft folds of her flesh with his tongue, explored the hardness of his hand and the hot, wet opening stretched paper-thin to take his three fingers. He licked her, licked her off his hand, licked her until he knew every nuance, every fold, every texture of her. Spreading his fingers, he licked through the spaces and tasted the very essence of her. Ramiel licked and licked until all that held her up was the pillar of his fingers between her thighs and his hand gripping her buttocks.

Elizabeth suddenly yanked so hard on his hair that his head tilted back. "I need you, Ramiel. Now. Please. Come inside me. *You.* Not your fingers. Please don't let me be alone now."

Her hoarse voice matched his need.

"I don't have anything down here to protect you."

Comprehension dawned on her flushed face. The thought of pregnancy had never crossed her mind.

She released his hair, soothed the small pain away. "*The Perfumed Garden* . . . did it not include preventive measures?"

He leaned his head into the softness of her gently rounded abdomen and imagined it big with his child. And damned himself for the thought that if he impregnated her, she would give him the same devotion that she had given Edward Petre. "They are not infallible."

"And what you have upstairs is?"

"No."

Forcing himself to look up, he watched her swollen, reddened lips. They were compressed.

This was the reality of bonding with a bastard. Disgrace. Social ruin. *Bearing the child of a bastard sheikh.*

"I can give you this, Elizabeth." He agitated his fingers inside of her; more moisture spilled down his hand. "But I cannot give you respectability. Not even if I wanted to."

"What would you do if I ... if we ... if I did become pregnant?"

"I would watch you suckle our child. And then I would drink the milk our son or our daughter did not drink."

Her lips quivered, relaxed. Her vagina tightened, pulsed. "I want you, Ramiel. Now. I am tired of sleeping alone. I want to feel your body inside mine. I want to know what it is like to give and take pleasure."

Now she was ready.

"Then you shall have what you want."

Chapter Twenty

One second Elizabeth was impossibly stretched with three fingers inside her while she gazed down into eyes so intensely turquoise, it was painful to look into them; the next second she was impossibly empty and her entire world turned topsy-turvy.

She clutched Ramiel's shoulders, taut and corded from the strain of lifting her, half afraid he would drop her, half wishing he would. Was it not enough that he had seen every flaw, every stretch mark? Must he also know her weight? *Must he continue to tease and taunt her?* "I am quite capable of walking on my own," she protested stiffly.

"You won't be," he murmured, brushing her lips with his. His mouth was hot and moist from her essence.

Searing heat shot through her body at the image of him watching her nurse . . . then drinking milk from her breasts.

"What . . . what type of preventive measures are you going to use?"

Ramiel tilted his head to one side, eyes lighting with familiar mockery. She was acutely conscious of his arm underneath her bare bottom. And the moisture that dripped from her breached body.

"Champagne, I think."

"Champagne?" She stared at his chin; it was covered with golden brown stubble, the same shade as had been the hair around his manhood. "The Arabs drank champagne . . . three hundred years ago?"

"Probably." His lips were shiny wet . . . *from her.*

He had seen her. Smelled her. *Tasted her.*

"I hardly think getting inebriated is going to prevent pregnancy."

He smiled, flashing white teeth. "I was thinking of a champagne douche. Followed by a champagne lunch."

She tried to squeeze the memory out of her head, failed. "At my wedding breakfast I was allowed one glass of champagne."

"Then today you shall have an entire bottle."

The special place that he had found inside her body burned and throbbed at the erotic image his words conjured. *Surely he did not mean . . .*

Her gaze leapt up to his, only a heartbeat away. Carnal knowledge glittered in their depths. Of her. Of her needs.

"You are not doing this out of pity, are you?"

His eyes darkened. "Elizabeth, a man does not taste a woman's body because he pities her."

"But you could do it out of kindness, I think."

"I am half Arab. Arabs are not kind."

"You are half English," she insisted.

"And they are not kind either," he replied dryly.

"You surely have known kindness from the countess."

"Do not confuse kindness with love." His breath was hot but a coldness settled behind his eyes. "I have known love; but there comes a time when it matters little if you are Arab or English. We cannot always be kind, especially to those we love."

Elizabeth had known neither kindness nor love with her husband. She would not allow fear to destroy the opportunity of experiencing one if not the other.

"The champagne will not be chilled, I hope."

The coldness in his eyes vanished. Laughter rumbled out of

his chest; it shook her entire body. "It will be an experience, *taalibba,* for the both of us."

A pulse throbbed at the base of his neck. "You have never before . . . administered a champagne douche?"

"There has been no need. If you prefer, we will go upstairs to my bedroom. I have condoms there."

Elizabeth took a steadying breath. "I do not want you to use a condom. I want to feel your flesh inside of my flesh. I want to feel you ejaculate inside of me." *Out of pleasure instead of duty.* "And then I want you to fill me with champagne and drink from me."

His mouth took her breath away. She squeezed her eyelids together and opened her mouth for him. There was hard masculine intent in his kiss, but there was tenderness too. His tongue was an uncompromising invasion; it imitated the motions his fingers had established earlier.

She wrapped her arms around his neck and pulled him closer, wanting the thrust of his tongue, the thrust of his fingers, the thrust of his manhood. *No man had ever wanted her.* Virtue seemed cold compensation. Death colder yet.

An icy hardness impacted her naked buttocks. She instinctively released the warm column of a neck for the support of— a ceramic iris. He had set her down by the edge of the swimming bath.

A splash exploded in the silence; warm drops of water sprayed her breasts.

Elizabeth's gaze darted up—Ramiel stood in the swimming bath. Dark blond hair arrowed down his abdomen and curled around the base of a large, thick penis. The bulbous purple crown of it skimmed the rippling water.

She was about to do the unforgivable. She was going to have sex with a man who was not her husband. A man society called the Bastard Sheikh. A bastard who could give her a bastard.

Elizabeth studied the solid length of him. He could hurt her. He could reject her. He would prove once and for all that there was more to the joining of a man and a woman than empty, lonely frustration.

As if aware of her thoughts, he waded toward her and grabbed her ankles. She followed his gaze, peered at the black-patent slippers and the flesh-colored stockings that bit into her thighs. There was indeed something rather lascivious in a woman thus dressed.

The hard heat banding her ankles tugged her across the cold ceramic tiles that separated them. ''Scoot forward, bend your knees, and plant your feet wide apart on the edge of the bath.''

Her head snapped up. He had seen her when she had one leg raised onto the tub, but this—''I will be—indecent.''

''You will be wide open and totally accessible. *Lebeuss el djoureb, taalibba.* Only I will be standing instead of sitting. With you spread out before me . . . so that I can rub my verge against your vulva . . . and knock at the door of your vagina . . . until you are so wet . . . and so open . . . that you will swallow me whole.''

The note.

He remembered.

She had her own memories. He wanted a warm, wet, wanton woman who was not afraid of her sexuality or ashamed of satisfying her needs.

''Is this a part of bonding?''

Ramiel did not pretend to misunderstand her. ''Lust is a part of bonding, *taalibba.* But lust is easily satisfied. It does not require that a woman open herself so completely to a man that she is vulnerable to his every touch, his every desire.''

As he wanted her to be open for him.

Watching his darkly intent face, she scooted forward, bent her knees, and spread them wide for his delectation.

The moist heat rising from the water was a warm caress. She felt as if he could see inside her body, as if her flesh pouted open where he had penetrated her with his fingers. He firmly positioned her feet on the edge of the tiles; she supported herself on the heels of her palms.

''No regrets, Elizabeth.''

Her breasts shimmied with the force of her pounding heart; she sucked in warm, misty air.

"No regrets, Ramiel. I did not regret dancing with you last night. I regretted only that we did not do this."

His fingers tightened around her ankles; he stretched them even farther apart. "Lean back on your hands."

She would not look away from his desire . . . or hers. "I want to watch. I want to know—*everything.*"

Every little touch that she had been denied the last sixteen years.

He reached down and lifted his erect manhood for her perusal. The purple head was far larger than had been the artificial phallus.

Slowly, deliberately, he guided himself to her splayed body. "Then watch."

Scalding heat notched her vagina.

She gasped. He gasped.

Electricity had singed her fingertip when she had touched his lip. This—this was like being rent apart by lightning.

Her gaze shot up from where their bodies touched.

His gaze was waiting for hers.

"You—it's hot." Almost as hot as his turquoise eyes.

"So are you, *taalibba.*" Scalding heat spread up from her vagina, nudged apart the lips of her labia, rubbed back and forth until she was totally open and her passion mingled with his. "Like molten silk."

She struggled to regulate her breathing, failed. "I can feel you pulsing against me, like a tiny heartbeat. Will it be like that when you are inside me?"

His eyelids drooped; she followed his gaze. Her glistening pink lips were spread wide by the engorged purple crown. Even as she watched, it slipped lower. The bulbous knob of him notched the slick heat of her, a kiss of sex, pressing but not entering, making her feel the muscles in his body straining to thrust while he felt the muscles of her body straining to adjust.

"Do you feel me pulsing now?"

"Yes." *Oh, God. Yes.*

His pulse. Her pulse. She could feel it all. *See it all.*

He rocked gently against her, her wetness lapping at the

crown of him while the water lapped around his thighs. As if drawn by her delicate folds and creases, he again sandwiched himself between the lips of her labia. Reaching out with his left hand, he spread them wider, revealed the little hard bud of her clitoris. He twirled the bulbous knob of his manhood around and around it, the most sensitive part of him against the most sensitive part of her.

Liquid heat surged inside her. *She was melting.* Or he was. They were both wet and hard there.

"Tilt your hips."

Elizabeth automatically obeyed, watching the miracle of a man and a woman, her auburn curls pressed flat by his dusky brown hand while his other hand guided the purple knob of his verge, bigger than a plum, harder, hotter . . . It slid down the wet slide he had created, and then there was pressure that was more than pressure followed by an internal popping sensation and the thick bulb of him was fully encased inside her.

Her flesh frantically tightened around him, too late. It burned. It stung. He felt as big as a fist and *she was not prepared for this melding.*

Ramiel glanced up from where he pierced her and captured her gaze. Purposefully, he eased another inch inside her while her body strained to accommodate him.

"Can you still feel me pulsing?"

"Yes." It matched the beat of her heart. She gritted her teeth. "I do not think we are going to fit, Ramiel."

"We will fit, *taalibba.*"

Still holding her gaze, he slowly pulled out of her; *she was so wet,* she heard as well as felt him when he exited her, *the tinkler,* and he was right—the English language did not do justice to the Arabic reality. She burned and throbbed where he had penetrated her. He made her burn and throb even more, rubbing and rubbing the hot, pulsing heat of him against the hard little bud that she had never seen before, only felt, holding it exposed as her portal was exposed.

Elizabeth could feel herself sinking, sinking into a world

where there was only a man and a woman who were named Ramiel and Elizabeth. *How could this be wrong?*

"Tilt your hips."

She involuntarily raised her hips to increase contact with her clitoris, *there;* she had never imagined a man could be so soft yet so hard. At the same time, Ramiel glided through the glistening pink lips of her labia and thrust, one man's duty another man's desire.

Why would anyone kill . . . to stop this?

"Wait . . . talk to me." She panted as if he plugged her very lungs. "I feel like . . . I am falling."

"That's good," he crooned. "That's the way I want you to feel."

She did not want to be the only one experiencing this incredible beauty. *This was not what she had came for, to indulge her own selfish needs.* "But what about you? *I want you to feel what I feel.*"

"Then take more of me, *taalibba.*"

"Oh . . ." Elizabeth braced herself against the tiles, body stretching, burning, taking him deeper, deeper. She desperately cast about in her thoughts for support. "What does *El Ibn* mean?"

"The son." Slowly, slowly, he drew out of her—*she could feel her flesh collapsing behind him.* He returned to the swollen lips and her throbbing clitoris, *she could see it pulsing, could feel the same pulse in him.* "Tell me what you dreamed about."

"What? . . ."

"This morning, you said you dreamed about me. Tilt your hips."

He tunneled more deeply inside her.

She threw her head back in agonized pleasure and stared at the twenty-foot-high ceiling, at the turquoise ripples of water reflected off the white enamel paint.

"I dreamed that you suckled my breasts. And that I cradled your head against me while I nursed you."

"Did you give me milk?"

"No." The sound that escaped her mouth was more of a groan than a word.

"Would you like to?" She barely recognized his voice; it was strained and hoarse.

"Yes." Even her voice matched his, she realized dimly. *It was not enough.*

"Tell me."

He held himself still. "Tell you what?"

"Tell me . . . how meritorious you are."

The flesh pulsing inside her flexed. "Two of my handbreadths."

Ten inches.

"Tell me how much of you is inside me. I want to know everything. I want to remember every detail of this."

And maybe, just maybe she would be able to forget the long, lonely nights she had lain in a bed purchased by a man who had never wanted her. All of it made possible by a father who would kill her because she wanted more.

"A handbreadth, *taalibba.*"

Five inches.

"I want more. I want all of you."

He gave her more.

"How much was that?" she gasped.

"An inch. Now take another."

One more heart-stopping inch. And then—

"Oh, my God!" She scrambled for more purchase, for a firmer hold on reality.

"Look. Look at us."

With difficulty Elizabeth brought her head back down and stared where they were joined. The hand holding her lips apart moved down and under her hip to provide her with an unobstructed view. Slippery moisture oozed from her body around the thick stalk that penetrated it. Their pubic hair, his dark blond, hers auburn, met but did not mingle. *Two more inches to go.*

"Do you feel the pulse, Elizabeth?"

"I feel it, Ramiel." It throbbed against her cervix, a hot, blunt pressure.

Air rushed out of her lungs. He was drawing out of her, taking the pulse. She felt as if she were being cleaved in two, as if he were taking half her soul.

"Please come back."

"In a moment." He teased her with the plum-shaped purple knob that glistened with her slick desire, swirling around and around her clitoris, nudging her vagina, swirling, nudging, swirling. "Did you think of this when you rotated your hips on the mattress?"

Elizabeth had thought of many things that night. "Did I think of what?"

"Did you think that you would lie with me?"

She bore down on a spasm of pleasure. "No."

Her voice was that of a woman enduring unbearable pain. Or pleasure. Elizabeth could no longer tell the difference.

"But you wanted to."

"Yes . . . oh, my God!"

"Tilt your hips," he hoarsely ordered, and then he was sinking inside her and her body opened up and swallowed him until her auburn pubic hair meshed with his dark blond hair and she was falling and there was nothing to catch her.

She had taken all of him and nothing in her life had prepared her for this melding, this *bonding*. He was a part of her, there was no room to catch her breath. " '. . . Big as a virgin's arm . . . with a round head . . . Measuring in length a span and a half,' " she quoted, half crying, half laughing.

Warm breath gusted the top of her head. " 'And, oh! I felt as though I had put it in a brazier,' " Ramiel finished the verse. *She felt like the brazier had been put into her.*

"The sheikh knew even then. . . . A man and a woman *were* made for each other, to be like this . . . together."

Ramiel had known too.

"There's more, *taalibba*. Take down your hair."

Elizabeth tore her gaze away from the indescribably erotic

sight of their intimate embrace. She didn't think she could
survive anymore.

"Hold still." He grasped her just below her breasts. "Let
me hold you. Now . . . you can use both hands. Reach up. Take
down your hair for me."

More conscious of his body pulsing inside of her than she
was of her own heartbeat, she slowly raised her arms. Elizabeth
had never known there was pleasure that surpassed agony, but
she knew it now. With each hairpin she removed, her vagina
rippled around him; with each impact of a hairpin against a
ceramic tile he pulsed against the back of her womb.

Her breath rasped in her throat; or perhaps it was his breath
she heard. *She did not know where one ended and the other
began.*

"Now shake your hair out."

A warm net of flaming red silk spilled over her shoulders,
her breasts, his hands. Her flesh undulated around his while
the water gently slapped his thighs. And suddenly, she could
no longer hold it back; she grabbed his shoulders and cried out
as her entire body convulsed with pleasure. And then she really
was falling.

A heavy weight pressed down on her, stealing what little
breath remained in her lungs. Ramiel leaned over her, joining
their bodies inside and out, crotch to chest.

Sweat glistened on his dark skin; a matching film covered
her body. She could feel his heartbeat—it pounded against her
breast, throbbed in the special place behind her womb. His hips
spread her already splayed legs even farther apart while her
inner flesh fluttered around him in the aftermath of her orgasm.

She closed her eyes against the overwhelming intensity in
his.

Moisture. Breath. There was nothing that they did not share
in their current position.

*Why would anyone want to kill in order to prevent this
intimate bonding between a man and a woman?*

Warm, moist lips nuzzled her hair, her cheek, her eyes, her
right ear. "Don't cry, *taalibba*."

It was ridiculous, crying over the most wonderful experience of her life. She had not been able to stop the tears last night when he had suckled her breasts either.

Elizabeth turned her face into his, into the silkiness of her own hair trapped between them and the prickly bristle of his unshaven cheek. "I never knew that a man could so fully occupy a woman. I never knew how *beautiful* . . . but what Edward did is so ugly. I couldn't cry this morning, I couldn't feel. It was just so . . . *ugly.*"

Ramiel shifted; she could feel the slight movement throughout her entire being. Hard, hot fingers soothed hair off her forehead, her cheeks.

"It's all right, *taalibba.* Trust me. He will never hurt you again. I promise. Don't cry. I will never let anyone hurt you or your sons. Don't cry, *taalibba.*"

His hand trembled against her skin. With passion. For her.

He deserved more than tears from her.

She opened her eyes—and stared into his, mere inches away from her own. His gaze was dark, stark, more black than turquoise.

"When I exercised against the mattress, it was you I thought about, Ramiel," she whispered.

He stilled.

She had yet to experience the full strength of his desire. *And she wanted to.*

Elizabeth threaded her fingers through his glorious mane of hair; it was far softer than the crinkly body hair that teased her nipples and abraded her stomach. "Perhaps I am a nymphomaniac. I can feel you pulsing against my womb and all I want to do is to take you more deeply inside me. Would you suckle my breasts, please?"

His body seemed to swell even larger inside hers. Between one breath and another he straightened, bringing her up with him.

She slapped her hands against the tile, but he held her securely, arms arching her back so that her chest jutted forward.

"Lift your breast. Feed it to me."

There was no mistaking the blaze of fire in his eyes. She was about to receive everything—and more—that she had ever wanted from a man.

Hand trembling—*it was all right for a woman to tremble with passion*—she lifted a solid, heavy breast.

An udder.

No! Ramiel had said they were magnificent.

He bent over her, silky golden hair brushing her cheek, her shoulder, hot breath trailing down, down—he latched on to her nipple. Her hips jerked forward as electricity seemed to arc straight from her breast to her womb. A muffled sound erupted from his throat as if he felt it too, and then he was suckling her and grinding his pelvis into hers. *Dok,* the motion that made a man a pestle.

She gave him the female equivalent, *hez,* swinging her hips in lascivious accompaniment. It was impossible but the combined motions drove him deeper inside her body and it *still was not enough.*

Her right hand reached out, clawed at his hip, for his buttocks—she needed the pounding as well as the grinding.

Ramiel gave it to her, first drawing out and making short jabs that grew into long stabs and he was right, *there was more,* a hitherto unexplored world of sound as well as sensation, the slap of flesh, the ragged gasps of labored breathing, the churning of the water, the wet suction of her body that was opening like a flower in sunshine. The pop of his mouth when he released her nipple.

"Lie back," he ordered harshly, straightening.

"Wait—"

But he did not wait. He hooked her knees over his arms and she fell with no support, nothing to hang on to but the hard, breath-*whooshing* drive of his thrusts slamming into her. A sharp thud echoed off the rippling ceiling; it was followed by another—she had lost her shoes. Her stockinged feet, thrust up into the air, jerked and kicked with each slap of his body against hers.

Elizabeth had never felt so open, had never known a woman's

body could withstand so much punishment and ache for more, too much, *not enough,* too hard, *not hard enough,* too deep, *not deep enough.* She could not breathe. There had to be an end—*a woman could not survive such protracted pleasure.*

When it ended, she did not think she would survive the culmination.

She cried out; every muscle in her body cried out with her, convulsing, contracting. Dimly, she heard a hoarse, answering cry. "Allah! God!"

Body slick with sweat and steam, Elizabeth held perfectly still, eyes closed, heart pounding, and felt a burst of scalding liquid deep inside the very core of her, the gift of Ramiel's pleasure.

Home.

For seventeen years she had lived in the house of her parents; for sixteen years she had lived in Edward's house. And she had never, ever once experienced this rush of homecoming.

She opened her eyes and stared up into his turquoise gaze. "Thank you."

Sweat clung like raindrops to the stubble of his beard. Expression unreadable, he scooped her up, bodies still joined, and wrapped her stocking-clad legs around his waist. Turning, he waded into the swimming bath until warm water swelled her stockings and lapped her breasts. It rippled about them while her vagina rippled about his spent manhood.

"I can feel your seed. It's hot."

He gently twirled her around in the water, not answering, just staring into her eyes.

"What are we going to do?" she whispered, suddenly shy, remembering the echoes of her cries as she found release.

Perhaps she had disappointed him. Perhaps she had misread his invitation the night before. Perhaps she should have gone to a hotel.

His expression remained enigmatic. "What would you like to do?"

She would like to stay here with him, *like this,* until the insanity went away.

Elizabeth concentrated on the lapping waves of water instead of his impenetrable stare. "My maid is sleeping with the new footman and yet I am certain that it is she who alerted Edward to the fact that I was sneaking out of the house to meet with you. It is ironic, is it not? She found happiness, yet she would not allow me the same privilege. I think Edward hired someone to frighten me when I spoke for the Women's Auxiliary. I *am* frightened. *And I do not like being frightened.*"

He continued to lazily circle around and around, the water caressing her on the outside, his manhood caressing her on the inside. "You are safe with me, *taalibba*. When did you speak for the Women's Auxiliary?"

"Last Thursday night. I told you about running into the lamppost in the fog. But before that, after the meeting, the custodian mistook me for a prostitute and threatened to kill me. When I got home, Edward was waiting with the constable, as if he expected me to have been in an accident."

Ramiel lowered his head; at the same time he hoisted her up higher in his arms. Flesh bridged flesh—his forehead annexing her forehead; the crown of his manhood butting her cervix. "What did the constable say?"

Elizabeth's arms reflexively tightened around his neck. It was becoming increasingly hard to be frightened. "He said Edward was right to be worried over a wife who risks her life by not taking a companion with her and who then proceeds to get trapped in the fog."

He kneaded her buttocks; the rhythmical motion alternately pushed and pulled at other, more vulnerable parts of her body. Water leaked into her stretched vagina.

"What did Petre say?"

"He—" She convulsively tightened her muscles, trying to cut off the flow of water. Ramiel's manhood abruptly thickened, effectively stopping the leak. "He wanted me to dress for a dinner party. What are you doing?"

A smile crooked his lips. "I am plugging up the dike."

She sucked in his breath, smelling his sweat, her sweat, the moist heat of the swimming bath. "Having plugged up the dike, what are you going to do next?"

His verge lengthened until it had nowhere to go; he tilted her hips and deftly thrust into the tight pocket behind her cervix.

"I am going to ring for champagne."

Her breath caught in her throat. "And then?"

"I am going to give you a douche. Then I am going to lick you out and engage in the twenty-first manner, *rekeud el aïr,* riding the stallion. And *you* are going to straddle my hips and work your body up and down my *kamera* until you scream your release again and again."

Chapter Twenty-one

Elizabeth awoke slowly, reluctantly. Muscles ached that had not ached since she gave birth to Phillip almost twelve years ago, yet she had never felt more relaxed in her life. A bubbly effervescence fizzled inside her body.

The sheets were warm, soft as silk. She took a deep breath, smelling musk, sweat, and—

Her eyelids snapped open. The sheets were soft as silk because they *were* silk. Her flesh fizzled because it had been a goblet for two bottles of champagne. Ramiel had filled her with sparkling wine and then he had teased her with the bottle until she had begged him to give her his tongue, his fingers, or his *kamera* and not necessarily one at a time.

A cold chill swept over Elizabeth's body, bringing with it the memory of gas, its smell, its taste.

Her husband had tried to kill her.

The bed beside her was empty. It smelled of her, of him, of their unique scents commingled. Edward had never left his scent on her sheets.

Muted sunlight filtered through crimson silk drapes. Slowly, carefully, she sat up—it felt as if she had indeed been pierced by a "virgin's" arm. Vanilla silk sheets and a crimson satin comforter puddled around her waist.

Her hair hung down her back in tangled disarray. Ramiel had wrapped it about his hands and pulled her face down to his when she straddled his hips and rode him like a stallion. She glanced down at her breasts. Her nipples were dark and swollen, from his suckling, from the abrasion of his fingers and from the prickly hair matting his chest.

A hot rush of remembered pleasure flooded her body.

"You are awake." Stepping out from the shadows between a mahogany armoire and a plush red-velvet-upholstered armchair, Muhamed threw the drapes open.

Gasping, blinking at the abrupt change of darkness to light, Elizabeth jerked the covers over her breasts. "What do you want?"

"From you, Mrs. Petre? Nothing. I am a eunuch; I cannot harm a woman. Nor can I be harmed by one."

Elizabeth studied the man who she had once thought was an Arab. He was older than Ramiel, but while she knew that he and the countess had been sold in Arabia together, he did not look the fifty plus years of age that he must be. His skin was olive like Johnny's rather than the dusky tan that Ramiel had inherited from his Arab father.

The countess had alluded to the fact that Muhamed's abuse in Arabia had made him hostile toward women. Elizabeth could not even begin to imagine the pain he experienced, either when he had been made into a eunuch as a youth or the emotional trauma that came of being a man now but unable to love a woman. She could not hold his rudeness against him.

"Do not pity me, Mrs. Petre. I will not tolerate it," Muhamed barked. His black eyes glittered malevolently.

Elizabeth drew her shoulders back, belatedly realized that she wore nothing but a sheet and a comforter. Neither of which covered her bare shoulders. "I do not pity you, Muhamed." The man glaring at her incited fear, not pity. "Where is Lord Safyre?"

"I am to watch over you. *El Ibn* said you would need a bath.

It awaits you through that door.'' He briefly nodded in the direction of a door at the left end of the rectangular bedroom.

It was not the way she and Ramiel had come up from the Turkish bath last night.

''Thank you. I would like a bath, but I have been advised not to do so alone. Would you please send Lucy to accompany me?''

''It is an English bath that awaits you, Mrs. Petre. You do not need Lucy. I have been assigned to assist you.''

Fighting a tide of crimson heat, Elizabeth stiffened her spine. ''I assure you I am used to bathing alone, so there is no need to assist me.''

''It is *El Ibn's* instructions.''

Her eyes widened incredulously. *Surely not.* She clutched the covers more tightly over her breasts. ''To watch me bathe?''

''I am to watch over you,'' he repeated unemotionally.

''You are trying to intimidate me,'' Elizabeth determined shrewdly. ''You do not want me in this house.''

His black eyes glittered, the only sign of life in his otherwise blank face. ''I do not.''

The countess had said Muhamed had looked after Ramiel in Arabia like the son he would never have. Elizabeth would not take kindly to a woman who blackmailed one of her sons either. ''I will not hurt Lord Safyre, Muhamed. I would never have hurt him.''

''In Arabia you would be stoned to death. *El Ibn* deserves better than the likes of you.''

Embarrassment turned to bright anger. *She would not be judged.* Nor would she allow him to demean the beauty she had shared with Ramiel.

''This is not Arabia. My father threatened to kill me, my husband threatened to commit me, and yesterday one or the other tried to gas me, but they did not succeed and you are not going to succeed in intimidating me now. Furthermore, it is for Lord Safyre to decide what he deserves or does not deserve. If you wish to watch me bathe, then so be it.''

Elizabeth, still holding the covers clutched to her breasts, wriggled to the edge of the bed. She stuck her legs out from underneath the silk sheet and over the edge of the mattress. Her naked feet dangled above the Oriental carpet below.

Hazel eyes locked with black eyes.

It was Muhamed's choice now. Elizabeth only hoped he had as little desire to see her body as she did to show it to him, but whatever the outcome of this confrontation *she would not back down.*

Taking a deep breath, Elizabeth slid off the bed, dragging with her the silk sheet and satin comforter. Taking an even deeper breath, she released the covers.

Muhamed turned in a swirl of white cotton. "Do not leave the house without me unless you are accompanied by *El Ibn.* Those are his orders. Lucy will be here in exactly twenty minutes to take you to breakfast."

The door to the bedroom opened and closed with equal silence. Frigid air swirled about Elizabeth's naked body.

What if the servant had not backed down? What if, even now, he stood there and stared at her nakedness?

What was she becoming?

Knees trembling, she walked the distance to the door where an English bath awaited her. Hot, aromatic steam filled the mosaic-tiled room. The tub, a large porcelain one encased in mahogany, was filled with water and . . . orange blossoms.

A sharp pang filled her chest.

Ramiel had remembered that she could not wear perfume and had given her fragrant flowers instead. *To be crushed underneath her breasts and between her thighs.*

A washcloth was draped over the side of the tub. A variety of soaps and shampoos were laid out for her selection.

She stepped into the tub and gingerly sank down. The water was very hot. Whoever had filled it must have run scalding water in it and left it to cool naturally so that it would keep warm for a longer period of time. The ploy had succeeded. It took several seconds for Elizabeth to adjust to the heat.

Soaping a rag, she carefully ran it over her breasts. And remembered Ramiel's hands soaping her breasts after she had ridden him like a stallion. Then he had carried her upstairs to his bedroom and presented her with a condom-filled tin stamped with Queen Victoria's portrait. It had been strangely comforting to think that the queen inadvertently made respectable the very acts that Mrs. Josephine Butler of the Ladies National Association had decried: "If they really do enable men to sin without having to suffer for it, we shall only oppose them all the more."

The flesh between her legs was almost as hot as was the bathwater. Abandoning the washcloth, she rubbed flower petals into her skin, underneath her breasts, her arms. Daring the forbidden, wanting to know the changes Ramiel had made inside her body as well as outside, she stood up on her knees and touched the delicate flesh that he had stretched and fondled and kissed and licked and then stretched even more. She was tender, the opening pouted, and inside—

A soft knock reverberated inside the bathroom. "Mrs. Petre?"

Elizabeth jerked her hand away from her body, heart pounding. "Yes?"

"I'm Lucy, ma'am, and I've brought you your clothes. Shall I come in and assist you?"

"Thank you, that is not necessary. I am just finishing. Lay the clothes out on the bed, please. I will be there directly."

"Very good, ma'am."

Elizabeth quickly sluiced off the flower petals and stood up in the water, face flaming hot. Reaching for a towel, she briskly dried off and wrapped it about her body. Wet hair clumped on her bare shoulders and down her back.

She needed to take care of her teeth. . . .

A toothbrush lay on the sink cabinet. Beside it sat a tin of tooth powder. She vigorously brushed her teeth and rinsed her mouth. Half afraid that the maid would come into the bathroom, either on the orders of *El Ibn* or Muhamed, she perched on the wooden toilet seat and hurriedly relieved herself. A roll of tissue on the wall beside the toilet left no doubt as to its purpose. Most English homes hid such paper in boxes.

She paused with her hand on the door. No doubt the entire

staff was aware that the Bastard Sheikh and Mrs. Petre, the wife of the Chancellor of the Exchequer, were lovers.

No regrets, Elizabeth.

Bracing herself, she opened the bathroom door. Lucy stood by the four-poster. She had straightened the covers. A royal blue silk and wool blend skirt with a matching bodice were spread across the crimson comforter along with an array of lingerie.

They did not belong to Elizabeth.

Lucy held up a pair of transparent silk drawers edged with blue satin ribbons and smiled, as if it were commonplace to assist a married woman in her master's bedchamber. *As no doubt it was.* ''Ain't these pretty?''

Indeed they were. Elizabeth had never seen anything quite like them. They would hide—absolutely nothing.

''They be for you, ma'am.''

Elizabeth should not feel hurt that Ramiel would outfit her in his former mistress's clothes. But she did.

''I would prefer my own clothes, Lucy.''

''M'lord said you was to wear these, ma'am. I don't rightly know where any other clothes are.''

Ramiel's bedroom did not contain a dressing screen. Acutely aware of her swollen breasts, Elizabeth took the drawers, a chemise that was just as transparent, and a pair of black silk stockings into the bathroom and firmly shut the door in Lucy's face. When she exited, covered if not concealed, she found Lucy holding up what looked like a ruffled apron.

''It be a bustle. Ain't never seen anything like it. Here's your petticoats, ma'am.''

Elizabeth stepped into two fine lawn petticoats and firmly secured them around her waist. Lucy did not seem surprised that there was no corset. Loath to give up the ruffled bustle, she tied it over the bands of the petticoats, then tossed the skirt over Elizabeth's head. When she finished dressing Elizabeth, she stood back and surveyed her handiwork. ''Royal blue be a good color for you, ma'am. It goes ever so nice with your red hair. I'm not a lady's maid, but I can brush it out and put it up on top of your head for you.''

Elizabeth forced a smile. ''Thank you, Lucy.''

Damp hair neatly pinned to her head—her pins, she did not want to know who had rescued them or the gossip it had instigated—she slipped into black patent slippers—hers, again—and followed Lucy down to breakfast.

Ramiel sat at a round oak table in an elegant glass-enclosed breakfast room filled with late-morning sunshine. His golden head was bent over a newspaper. He wore a morning frock coat, so very English, yet surely no Englishman would do the things he had done to her last night.

Every touch, every word spoken between them, flooded her memory. She turned first cold and then hot, afraid of drawing attention to herself lest she be ridiculed, even more afraid that their time together had meant nothing more to him than an easy conquest. And she had been easy. She had held *nothing* back from him.

Ramiel suddenly raised his head. He stared at her for a long while, as if he, too, remembered every touch, every word. A slow smile lit up his dark face. ''*Sabah el kheer, taalibba.*''

Sunshine flooded Elizabeth's body. ''*Sabah el kheer.*''

Laying down the paper, Ramiel gracefully stood and pulled out the open-armed yellow-silk-upholstered chair beside his. ''Actually, the correct response is *sabah e-noor.*''

''I beg your pardon. *Sabah e-noor,* Lord Safyre.''

He cocked his head, his turquoise eyes knowing. ''You are feeling shy.''

Heat pulsed in her body. ''Yes.''

''Are you sore?''

She tilted her chin. ''A little. I think, perhaps, I would be more so if not for the bubbles.''

Heat that owed nothing to sunshine shimmered in the air. ''I would not mind a champagne breakfast.''

''And I would rather have my own clothes back,'' she replied evenly. ''I do not relish the idea of wearing your mistress's castoffs.''

He stilled. "Those are your clothes, *taalibba,* designed by Madame Tusseau."

Madame Tusseau was the premier modiste in London. She dressed the richest of the aristocrats . . . and courtesans.

"Indeed. How did she know my measurements?" she asked.

"I took her the dress you wore yesterday."

"And she just happened to have ready-made clothing in my size," she said flatly.

"Let us say that she appropriated clothing from several of her clients, one whose chest approximated yours and another whose hips did."

"How is it that Madame Tusseau holds you in such high regard that she will open her establishment to you in the early hours of the morning?" Elizabeth inwardly cringed. *She sounded exactly like what she was,* a jealous, insecure woman who had long passed her prime but for this man wanted to regain it.

"My mother is her client," Ramiel said quietly. "Also I have given her clients in the past. I have never brought another woman into my home, Elizabeth. Do not cheapen our relationship by comparing yourself to my past mistresses."

"Others will."

"Yes."

She did not want to care what other people thought. But it was difficult. Especially when she did not understand why one man would want her while another would kill her.

"The lingerie is quite—clever. Did you pick it out?"

A smile displaced the hardness that had settled over his features. "Everything you have on I picked out. You are a beautiful, sensuous woman, Elizabeth; you deserve beautiful, sensuous clothes. Why don't you sit down here beside me and show me your lingerie?"

Her breath quickened. No one had ever called her beautiful. Even knowing it for the lie that it was, *he made her feel beautiful.* "The servants—"

"Will not disturb us. I have instructed them that we will serve ourselves." He held out his hand—long, tanned fingers that had penetrated her body and shown her a special place that she had never known existed. He had splayed those fingers inside her and licked her essence from between them. "Come to me, *taalibba.*"

She went to him . . . only to be seated while he remained standing.

"What would you have for breakfast? Eggs? Kidneys? Kippers? Toast? Ham? Mushrooms? Fruit?"

"A champagne breakfast, please," she said primly.

A low chuckle filled the sunlit room. "First you must eat something."

Elizabeth turned her head and stared at the jointure of his legs only inches away from her face. She had taken him into her mouth and suckled him. He had tasted—hot and salty.

She threw her head back and stared up at him. "I would like tongue, if you have it. And then I would like a fresh ripe plum."

His eyes gleamed with appreciation. Bending, he took her chin between his thumb and forefinger. He gave her his tongue and she gladly took it, breath catching in her throat at the simple intimacy that was a man's kiss. *She had known him for less than two weeks, yet they were closer than she was with the man she had been married to for sixteen years.* Delicately nibbling and licking and sucking as he had taught her, she took her time sampling the taste and texture of him—dark, rich coffee and slick heat. When he stood, the front of his gray wool trousers were tented.

"You will pay for that, *taalibba.*"

"How?" she asked breathlessly. "How will you make me pay?"

Her demand yesterday to know exactly how deeply he filled her echoed between them.

His eyes crinkled in silent laughter. "By not telling you what I specially plan to do to you. Pour us coffee while I serve Madame."

Caught up in the play—she could not remember ever teasing or being teased by another adult—she reached for the silver coffeepot in the middle of the table. And stared dumbfounded at the newspaper Ramiel had discarded.

WIFE OF THE CHANCELLOR OF THE EXCHEQUER NEAR DEATH boldly marched across the front page.

She grabbed it, feverishly perused the story. *A gas leak . . . one of hundreds . . . Parliament to look into ways of subsidizing electricity . . .*

A plate filled with scrambled eggs, ham, and grilled mushrooms slid in front of her. A small bowl of strawberries drenched with cream was placed beside it.

"It *was* Edward," she whispered. "Why did he contact the newspapers?"

"You are a highly visible woman." The voice above her was curiously dispassionate. "Your absence would be noted. He needed a way to explain your disappearance."

"And to counter a murder charge."

"Yes."

Even in this, Edward would garner public favor.

She grimly folded the newspaper. "I want to visit my sons. They are bound to hear something. They will be worried."

"We will go together."

"I do not think now is a good time for them to make your acquaintance."

Ramiel sat down beside her and plucked the newspaper from between her hands. "You are ashamed of being seen with me."

She flushed guiltily. "That is ridiculous."

"Then you are ashamed of sleeping with the Bastard Sheikh."

When his flesh was locked inside her flesh . . . no.

"I have to explain to Richard and Phillip that I have left their father, Ramiel. If you are with me, they will think that I have disgraced my family merely to be with you."

"And of course we both know that is not the case."

There was bitterness in Ramiel's voice; his turquoise eyes were bleak.

Elizabeth remembered Rebecca's statement that all men were selfish in general and that a man like Lord Safyre in particular would not allow sons—especially sons who were not his—to interfere with his pleasures.

"My sons must come first."

"I have no desire for you to abandon your sons, Elizabeth. All I want is that the time you spend with me not be marred with shame or regret."

Shame. Regret. She would use many words to describe what had transpired between them last night, but she would not use those.

"Three events will always stand out in my memory: the birth of Richard, the birth of Phillip, and what we shared yesterday. I have no regrets, nor do I feel shame. But now I must go to my sons and I hope you can understand that. Someday soon I hope you *will* meet them . . . and like them. But that day is not today."

"And when will that day be, Elizabeth?"

How would her sons react to a man who was neither Eastern nor Western? How would they feel upon learning that she had thrown their future away on a bastard who had no claims to respectability or desire to acquire it?

"I do not know."

"You wanted to bond with a bastard, *taalibba.* This is part of it. I accede, *today.* As long as you realize that I fully intend upon meeting them soon. I will not be kept apart from your life."

A frisson of apprehension raced down her spine. It suddenly dawned on her that she knew very little about this man who was suddenly making demands on her life.

"Richard and Phillip are used to me bringing them treats. Do you mind if I have your cook prepare a basket to take with me?" she asked impulsively, needing to escape her unease. *She did not want to be frightened—not of Ramiel, not of the man who had shown her the wonders of being a woman.*

His turquoise eyes were enigmatic. "My home is your home. You may have or do whatever you wish. As long as you remember that someone tried to kill you. You came to me for protection. I will not allow you to put yourself in danger. Are you going to eat?''

She looked down at the circle of grease that surrounded the ham on the white china; then she looked at the bright crimson strawberry juice bleeding into the cream. ''No.''

''Then let us go down to the kitchen and I will introduce you to my chef. He will enjoy cooking for your young men.''

The chef could have been Arabian with his dark hair and skin or he could have been French. Elizabeth could not tell by either his accent or his face. He wore European clothing, but so did Ramiel, unlike Muhamed, who was not Arabic by blood. Nothing was as it should be, either in Ramiel's house or Edward's.

''Étienne, you will obey Mrs. Petre's wishes as you would mine. She has two sons at Eton and is going to visit them today. She wants to take them a basket of food.''

''Madame.'' Étienne's dark eyes lit up with pleasure. ''It will be an honor to prepare a little treat for your two sons. Just yesterday I baked a *basboosa,* a cake made with semolina and soaked in syrup. I also have *baskaweet,* biscuits that melt in the mouth. Or if you will wait, I will bake you *baklava* and my *atif* and my *kunafa.* . . .''

Elizabeth smiled. Étienne was everything that Muhamed was not. ''Please do not trouble yourself. The cake and the biscuits are more than enough. Thank you. Richard and Phillip will love them.''

Étienne bowed ''It is an honor, Madame. Lord Safyre, he does not do justice to my pastries.''

''If I ate everything you baked, I would not be able to pass through my own doorways,'' Ramiel retorted easily.

''How else does one honor a man of my talents?'' Étienne asked with feigned indignation.

Elizabeth solemnly intervened. ''I assure you, sir, that my two sons will do justice to your art. They eat like horses.''

Étienne appraised Elizabeth's body underneath her royal blue bodice and skirt. ''Perhaps we will put a little more flesh on your bones, too, Madame.''

Ramiel's gaze followed his chef's.

Elizabeth flushed. "Let us hope not."

"We are not used to cooking for a lady of the house; perhaps if Madame would prepare our menus . . ."

Elizabeth met Ramiel's gaze.

What had he told his servants about her? He had said he could not give her respectability. Why, then, was he going out of his way to make her feel at home?

"I am not here to disrupt your kitchen, Étienne."

"But you do not disrupt, Madame. You add beauty to our humble bachelor abode."

A reluctant laugh was won from Elizabeth. "We will see. Right now I merely wish a basket of food for my sons."

"I will prepare you a masterpiece picnic. Your sons will think their young palates have died and attained paradise."

Ramiel held out a hand to Elizabeth. "Come, let us leave this scalawag to his kitchen."

Elizabeth climbed the narrow servants' stairs ahead of Ramiel, holding the hem of her skirt high so that she would not step on it. "You have an interesting staff. Wherever did you get Étienne?"

"I liberated him in Algeria."

She stared at her black-patent slippers and the intermittent flash of black silk stockings. *Hers . . . and his.* "It is not my intention to inconvenience you or your household."

Hot, implacable hands gripped her waist, pulled her back even as she stepped up. "Elizabeth, you do not inconvenience me. Nor do I object to you spending time with your sons. If I did, I would take you upstairs now and see just how sore you are."

Elizabeth leaned back against the solid heat of his chest. "I prefer champagne to rubber."

Hot breath seared the nape of her neck. *"Ela'na!"*

"You say that rather often. What does it mean?"

"It means 'damn.' "

"What are your special plans for me?"

His hands gripping her waist tightened. *"El kebachi."*

She sucked in air. "Like the beasts in the fields," she whispered, body clenching.

Something hot and wet flicked her neck—his tongue.

" 'After the fashion of the ram.' I will place you on your hands and knees and mount you from behind. In that position I can freely touch your breasts and your vulva."

"It is one of your favorite positions, then."

It was not a question.

Sharp teeth nipped her nape. "It is."

She would not be jealous of the women who had come before her. Or worry about those who might come after.

"I will look forward to it."

"Elizabeth." A breath of laughter tickled her ear. "Take your time with your sons. Because when you get home, I will take my time with you."

She voiced a fear she had not realized she possessed. "You will be waiting for me?"

Edward had never been there for her.

"I will be waiting for you, *taalibba*. And now I, too, have things to take care of. I will arrange a carriage to take you to the station. When everything is ready, Muhamed will come get you. He is to accompany you."

Elizabeth stiffened. If her sons would have difficulty accepting a man who was half Arab but did not look it, how would they react to a man who was not Arab but did look it?

"Muhamed will wait outside." Ramiel flicked her ear with his tongue. A shower of hot sparks shot down her back. "If you do not take him with you, he will follow you."

"This is not necessary."

"I assure you, it is."

She did not want to think about death.

Yesterday had surely been a once-in-a-lifetime event. Edward would not go out of his way to harm her. He did not have time. Nor did her father. Politics was a demanding mistress. Especially when one of the two divided what little free time he had with a flesh-and-blood mistress.

She hesitantly placed her hands over the back of Ramiel's. They were hard and rough—like his body.

He had been hurt at the breakfast table when she had refused to take him with her to visit her sons.

She offered him what solace she could. "Phillip would find Muhamed interesting, I think. He would enjoy your swimming bath."

"What about Richard?"

"I am not sure. Richard seemed—changed when last I saw him."

"In what way?"

"I cannot explain."

"Does he confide in you?"

"A much as a fifteen-year-old boy will. Why are you interested in my children?"

Ramiel's hand slid down her waist, pressed against her lower abdomen. "They are a part of you."

The heat of his hand infused her womb. Elizabeth felt a rush of gratitude.

Rebecca was wrong. Not all men were selfish. Especially a man like Ramiel.

She closed her eyes and leaned her head back. "Thank you for the bath."

"You're welcome. I thought you might like it."

The heat of his hands evaporated from her abdomen, her waist. A gentle nudge set her feet in motion.

At the top of the stairs he did not kiss her. He merely looked down at her with that disconcerting way he had of veiling his eyes. "I have to go. Explore my home while you wait for Étienne to create his masterpiece. It is your home now."

She bit her lip to keep from asking where he was going, and then it was too late; he was gone. And he had not said one thing about the smell of orange on her skin.

How could his home be hers? she thought irritably. She was married to another man.

The decor throughout the house was a blend of exotic East and austere West, like the owner. Elizabeth idly explored first one floor and then another. All the while she thought about the newspaper article proclaiming her near-death status, the husband who had attempted to kill her, and the father who had threatened to do so. She thought about her life as it had been twelve days earlier, what it was now, and what it would be in the future, a divorced woman living with a bastard sheikh.

It was a woman's duty to put her children's needs first.

A guest bedroom on the third floor was painted pale yellow with orange and green flowers stenciled around the ceiling and the doors. Upon closer inspection, one of the flowers looked very much like a vulva.

"Mrs. Petre."

Elizabeth whirled in a swish of silk and wool. Muhamed stood in the doorway.

"What is it?"

His turban was startlingly white in the shadows. The triumph, however, was plainly visible on his face. "Your husband is here to see you."

Chapter Twenty-two

Edward. *Here.* In Ramiel's home. How had he known where to find her?

The same way he had known about her lessons with Ramiel, she abruptly realized. Someone had followed her.

Icy fear coursed through her body.

Legally, Edward could do anything he wanted with her. He could drag her out of this house and force her into a carriage. He could take her back to his town house. Or he could take her to an asylum. *And no one could stop him.*

Muhamed's black eyes glittered.

How convenient that Edward called when Ramiel was not there to greet him. Had he posted spies to watch the Georgian house and report to him the moment Ramiel left? Or was one of Ramiel's servants the spy?

Clearly Muhamed did not approve of her liaison with *El Ibn.* He could be working with Edward—the servant to get her out of Ramiel's home, her husband to get her out of his life.

She reined in a surge of pure panic. Ramiel had said he would protect her. Muhamed would not harm her for fear of him. *She was safe.*

Elizabeth straightened her shoulders. "Tell Mr. Petre that I am not at home."

Muhamed's face settled into an expressionless mask; he bowed. "Very well. The carriage and the basket of food are ready. We will leave at your convenience."

Elizabeth stared after the sweep of his cotton robe in amazement. How simple it had been.

So why did her legs tremble underneath the weight of her clothes?

She retrieved her reticule from Ramiel's bedchamber, gaze skimming over the mahogany nightstand and the tin stamped with Queen Victoria's portrait, over the massive bed that had rocked and rolled underneath them. It settled on the stark white face reflected in the mirror above the dresser.

She still did not like being afraid.

At the top of the curved staircase she paused.

What if Edward refused to leave Ramiel's home without first seeing her? What if Muhamed had deliberately failed to relay the message that she was not there?

But no one waited for her at the foot of the stairs. She almost laughed aloud in relief.

A hamper sat on a table in the foyer. The left lid was open, as if awaiting her inspection.

Curious, she peeked inside . . . and was greeted with the mouthwatering aroma of honey. Various biscuits and pastries were neatly arranged in linen napkins. Étienne truly had created a masterpiece picnic. Unable to resist, Elizabeth plucked a small slice of cake out of the basket. *Basboosa,* he had called it.

Syrup clung to her fingers. Dark, finely ground-up nuts garnished the top.

Phillip and Richard would love it.

Smiling, she daintily bit off the end of the cake. It was overwhelmingly sweet.

She glanced at the remaining sliver of pastry in her hand and then at the neatly arranged wedges nestling in the square of linen. Her sons would not fancy finding a half-eaten piece of cake in their basket. Wrinkling her nose, she popped the rest of the pastry into her mouth.

Underneath the syrupy sweetness and crunchy nuts was pepper. The cake burned a trail all the way down her throat into her stomach.

Turning, she bumped headlong into a black wool robe; it had muscles underneath it. She stepped back. "I beg your pardon. I was just—is the carriage outside?"

Muhamed inclined his head. Her cloak was draped over his arm; he carried her hat and gloves in his right hand. "It is here, Mrs. Petre."

Elizabeth could sense his hostility, even though he did not reveal it by so much as a flicker of an eyelid. It was not her desire to create disharmony in Ramiel's household. Nor did she wish to create friction between the two men.

She swallowed her pride. "Thank you for sending my husband away, Muhamed."

"I am to obey your orders."

She swallowed harder. "I am sorry that I employed the means I did to gain entry into Lord Safyre's home. I placed you in an untenable situation. Please accept my apologies."

Emotion flickered in Muhamed's inscrutable black eyes and was instantly veiled. "It is the will of Allah."

Gingerly, she took the black silk bonnet from him, perched it on her head, and tied the black ribbons underneath her chin. "Nevertheless, I would have you know that I meant you no harm." She accepted the black leather gloves and resolutely stuffed her hands inside them. "Any more than I would harm Lord Safyre."

Muhamed stoically held up Elizabeth's cloak. She turned around and allowed him to place it about her shoulders.

The pepper had irritated her mouth—even though it flooded with saliva, she felt parched with thirst. She thought about asking for a glass of water, then reconsidered. The public facilities on the train left much to be desired.

"I am sorry that you have to accompany me, Muhamed. If you would rather not . . ."

Muhamed silently opened the door.

A carriage drawn by two perfectly matched grays stood in the sunshine. Hot steam rose from the horses' bodies.

Elizabeth stepped forward.

She was simultaneously aware of two things. Muhamed closed the hamper and picked it up by the wicker handles. At the same time, a red hot ball of fire exploded in her womb.

Elizabeth gasped, staggered at the force of a physical desire that had no origin.

"Are you all right, Mrs. Petre?"

Muhamed's voice was loud, as if he shouted in her ear. She straightened with effort, shamed and humiliated at what was happening to her body. It was filled with mindless, animal lust, gushing moist desire, muscles contracting, convulsing.

Nymphomania.

Ramiel had not denied it yesterday when he had been buried so deep inside of her that he could not possibly go any deeper yet she had wanted him to.

"I am fine, thank you, Muhamed."

Her voice was too loud, abrasive. The traffic ambling along the street rose to a roar in her ears. The vibrations of the churning wheels and pounding hooves raced along her nerves straight to the flesh between her thighs.

Determinedly, she descended a step. If she could only reach the coach and her two sons . . .

Her silk-clad thighs rubbed together. The sensation was electric.

She dropped her reticule.

Elizabeth could feel the coachman and Muhamed staring at her. And she knew that she was losing her mind, because a man's eyes did not generate heat, yet she was burning up underneath their stares.

A fragmented shout pierced the air. "Mrs. . . . watch . . . steps!"

Her legs collapsed underneath her. Strong arms wrapped around her just as she should have tumbled out into open space.

She endured the touch with effort, every nerve inside her body alive and aware. Of a man's hold . . . a man's scent. She recoiled in horror at the realization that she wanted more than a servant's arms wrapped about her waist, she wanted—

Elizabeth wrenched out of Muhamed's arms. "Don't touch me," she whispered, or perhaps she screamed it. Eyes were everywhere—Muhamed's, the coachman's, servants that suddenly crowded the small stoop.

Edward's spy. One of them could be Edward's spy and he would report this incident and her husband and her parents and her children would know the truth at last, that she was a *nymphomaniac*.

"Wot's t' matter wi' 'er?" "She's gone stark, staring bonkers." "Should we ring up the doctor, Mr. Muhamed?"

Muhamed's eyes snapped with black fire. Throwing open the hamper, he grabbed a wedge of cake—Étienne had said *basboosa* was made of semolina and soaked in syrup; he had not mentioned that it had nuts and pepper, so she really did not know what she had eaten, Elizabeth suddenly, feverishly thought. The Arab that was no Arab sniffed the cake. Like a dog. *El kebachi*. Animals. *They were all animals.*

And she was one of them.

A gob of spittle and cake hurtled past her—Muhamed must have tasted it. He didn't like it either.

"*Allah akbar!* Get the countess!"

Didn't like cake. Didn't like women who satisfied their desires with a man who was not their husband.

Elizabeth turned, fleeing, burning, falling—

I won't let you fall, taalibba.

She stared dully at the sidewalk, inches instead of feet away from her face, then she stared at the dark hands that reached for her.

"In the name of Allah! Hurry up, you fools! Help me!"

Elizabeth felt laughter welling up inside her body. Ramiel had shouted *Allah* when he had climaxed. Immediately, her laughter was swallowed by a great black wall of blazing desire.

How hot a man's seed was, shooting inside a woman's body. *She needed that heat.* She needed Ramiel.

She needed him so badly that she was going to die.

Ramiel stared at the two men who sat in the corner of the darkened pub. One kept his head down, craggy features shadowed by the brim of a dusty felt hat with a low crown and wide brim. A groundsman, the bartender had said. The other man wore a tired derby, his lined, disgruntled face evident for all to see: He was a man who had cleaned up after too many boys.

Ramiel tossed the bartender a florin. Scooping up two pints of ale, he approached the men in the corner. "I understand the two of you work at the school."

"We work at th' school." The man wearing the derby looked up and scowled. "What o' it?"

Ramiel sat down at the small wooden table. "I have a job for you."

"Now, see 'ere, I don't mind makin' an extra shillin', but I ain't gonna pimp fur no man."

A hardness settled inside Ramiel's chest. "I assure you, my tastes run otherwise." He scooted the two pints of ale across the rough, beer-stained table. "I merely wish you to keep an eye out for two young men. And to share any information you have about a certain fellowship."

"We be simple men—we don't know nothin' ye be wantin' t' know."

Ramiel smiled cynically as the man wearing the derby grabbed the ale. Ramiel reached inside his coat for a bag of coins, laid two half sovereigns onto the table before him. "Is either of you familiar with two students named Richard and Phillip Petre?"

"Aye." The groundsman wearing the wide-brimmed hat spoke up now. He raised his head; his rheumy eyes were shrewd.

"Master Richard, he be studyin' engineerin', he says. Helped me build a walkin' bridge, he did. He be a good boy, not like those others that pull up me flowers an' shrubs for a lark.''

Elizabeth had good reason to be proud of her elder son.

"Master Phillip, aye, I knows 'im,'' the man wearing the derby grunted. " 'E poured me bucket o' scrub water on th' dormitory floor t' 'elp me 'swab th' deck.' "

Ramiel bit back a grin. And she had aptly called her youngest son a rascal.

"I wouldn' want nothin' bad to happen to Master Richard,'' the groundsman warned in a low voice.

"Neither do I,'' Ramiel rejoined evenly. "I want you to keep an eye on the two boys. Each morning and each evening a man will meet you in front of the chapel. He will wear a bollinger hat with an orange band. You will report to him.''

"What's in it fer us?'' the cleaning man asked.

"A half sovereign now, for each of you, and a crown apiece at the end of each week.''

"Aye.'' The groundsman again. "But what should we be reportin'?''

Ramiel silently studied the two men, trying to determine how much they knew and how best to get them to talk. "The fellowship of Uranians,'' he said bluntly.

The groundsman lowered his head like a turtle pulling back in its shell.

Bitter satisfaction coursed through Ramiel.

So the fellowship still existed. And it still solicited young boys.

"Don't know what yur talkin' about.'' The man wearing the derby gulped warm ale, wiped his mouth with an unsteady hand.

"Obviously, you do, or there would have been no reason for you to say you would not pimp for a man.''

"Don't know nothin','' he repeated stubbornly.

Shrugging, Ramiel reached for the two coins.

"There be a don,'' the groundsman muttered.

Ramiel paused. "A don?"

The groundsman slowly raised his head to half mast. "A teacher. I seen respectable-lookin' gents, like you, meet the don in the gazebo some nights. The don takes 'em young boys. After that I see the gentlemen drivin' up in their fancy carriages an' takin' the boys drivin'."

Ramiel held the groundsman's gaze. "Have you ever seen Richard or Phillip Petre go to this gazebo with the don?"

"Aye." The answer grumbled reluctantly out of his throat. "Once. Saw Master Richard 'bout a month ago. He ain't come round t' help me since."

Ramiel had expected the groundsman's answer because of Elizabeth's description of Richard's recent "illness"; it did not make the truth any more palatable. "Did you see who the gent was that this don took Richard to meet?"

"Didn't see his face, no."

"Who is the don?"

"Teaches Greek. Master Winthrop, he is."

Ramiel stood.

"So what're we s'pposed t' say t' this 'ere man wi' th' or'nge band on 'is 'at?" the man wearing the derby asked, eager for more money.

"The names of 'the gents.' " Ramiel's voice sent a chill over the cleaning man.

"Ain't right, what's goin' on," the groundsman said.

"No." Ramiel wondered what this would do to Elizabeth should she ever find out. "No, it's not."

Outside the small pub, Ramiel gulped air free of London fog. Perhaps he would catch the "don" taking lunch as he had the two laborers.

But he didn't. The don, said the dean's stooped-over secretary, was away until next week.

Ramiel wanted to ask the secretary if Elizabeth Petre had yet called on her two sons but did not. He did not want her to find out about his visit. Indeed, by entering the main hall he risked bumping into her himself.

Pulling his hat low over his ears and his scarf high around

his chin, he exited the hall and entered the hack that waited outside.

Richard was only fifteen. Another mark against Edward Petre.

He fought the urge to go back to the school and take them all away, Elizabeth and her two sons. Instead, he boarded the train and closed his eyes and shut out the pain that he knew Richard must be going through.

Ugly, Elizabeth had said of Petre's attempt to kill her. He hoped that she never found out just exactly how ugly Edward Petre really was.

It was too late to protect her elder son, but perhaps, when the time came, he could help him accept the deed and get on with his life. Just then he had to concentrate on how best to stop Edward Petre.

The London station was smelly, loud, and hectic. He wondered what Elizabeth would think of the desert, of the clean white sand and the endless blue sky.

Madame Tusseau was not happy when he walked into her shop and charmed more clothing for Elizabeth out of her. Anticipation filled him, walking up to the door of his Georgian home with his arms full of boxes.

He wished he could have spent more time with her that morning. She had been decidedly miffed when he had not pursued the subject of her bath.

Ramiel imagined her skin, hot and sweaty with the smell of her passion commingling with the sweet aroma of orange blossoms.

Without warning, the front door of the Georgian house swung open.

An invisible fist slammed into Ramiel's chest. Muhamed was supposed to be with Elizabeth, visiting her sons at Eton, not here. He would be here only if—

"Where is Elizabeth?" he asked hoarsely.

The Cornishman's face was stoic. "The husband called."

Fear twisted in Ramiel's stomach. "You did not admit him."

"I did."

Ramiel took the two stoop steps in one leap. Several boxes tumbled to the concrete. *"Where is she?"*

Muhamed stared over Ramiel's shoulder. "She is with the countess. In your bedchamber."

Relief knifed through Ramiel. *She had not gone back to her husband.* He moved to step around the Cornishman.

Muhamed blocked his way. "The will of Allah will prevail, *El Ibn*. A life for a life. So it is written. I offer you my life for that of Mrs. Petre."

Elizabeth . . . *dead.*

The remaining boxes in Ramiel's arms went flying. His hand snaked out and grasped the neck of the Cornishman's robe. "Explain."

Muhamed did not struggle to free himself. "I imperiled Mrs. Petre's life; you may do as you will with mine."

"What are you talking about?"

Muhamed's black eyes unflinchingly met Ramiel's turquoise gaze. "She was poisoned."

Poisoned rolled over Ramiel in cold waves of horror. Shoving Muhamed back, he raced for the stairs, took them three at a time. When he reached his bedroom door, he flung it open. The door banged against the wall, almost slammed shut in his face. Only a lightning-quick boot stuck in the doorway prevented it.

The countess had pulled up the crimson velvet armchair to the side of the four-poster. Dim light penetrated the closed drapes; her blond hair was silvery in the artificial twilight. At his entrance, her spine jerked upright. Relief spread over her features at sight of Ramiel.

She raised a thin, elegant hand to her lips. *"Shhh."*

Ramiel ate up the distance between the door and his bed. His heart skipped a beat at the sight of Elizabeth. Her skin was whiter than the pillow; red and gold highlights flickered in her dark auburn hair, as if it had consumed the life that should animate her body. Dark shadows lined her closed eyes.

"Do not fret, *ibnee*. She will be fine now."

"How?" His return whisper was harsh; it grated in his chest.

Unwittingly, he reached out, smoothed a strand of damp hair off Elizabeth's forehead. Her skin was cold and clammy.

"Let us go where we will not disturb her."

"No." Anger and fear warred inside his chest. He had promised Elizabeth that she would be safe with him, and he had failed her. "I will not leave her again."

Perching on the edge of the bed, he reached for her hand.

"Don't touch her."

Ramiel froze. Slowly, without moving his body, he turned his head toward the countess.

"I gave her a sedative. Her skin is still too sensitive," the countess explained. "If you wake her, you will cause her pain."

Ramiel's hand stayed frozen in the air above Elizabeth's fingers that lay curled upward on the coverlet. "What do you mean, her skin is still too sensitive?"

"She was poisoned, Ramiel."

"What kind of poison makes touch painful?"

The countess did not retreat at the dangerous softness of his voice. "Have you been away from the harem so long that you have forgotten?"

Cantharidin, known popularly as Spanish fly, was a common aphrodisiac used in harems, though normally it was mixed with other ingredients so that it inflamed rather than killed.

"Impossible." he said flatly.

"I assure you it is not."

"How?"

"*Basboosa.* It was heavily sprinkled with cantharidin. Muhamed gave her an emetic to rid her stomach of it. If he had not acted so quickly, she would have died."

If Muhamed had not admitted Edward Petre into his home, she would not have been poisoned.

"Edward Petre would know nothing of cantharidin poisoning."

"Are you so certain that it was her husband?"

"Are you suggesting it was my chef, Étienne?" he rejoined sharply.

"Are you certain that the poison was meant for Elizabeth?" the countess calmly countered.

The basket of treats. *The cake had been for Elizabeth's sons.*

No one had known of her intention to visit her sons save for him and his staff. Ramiel had placed a spy in Petre's household; had Petre placed one in Ramiel's?

Muhamed. The Cornishman knew that once ingested, there was no antidote for Spanish fly. The only solution for an over-dose was to immediately administer an emetic. He also knew that often even that was not effective. Cantharidin killed as well as excited. The dosage that caused desire was not that different from the one that caused death.

"I do not believe any of my servants are guilty, but I assure you, if one is, I will soon know," he grimly promised.

Gently, so as not to rock the bed, he stood up.

"Where are you going?"

"To find a traitor."

"You said you would not leave Elizabeth."

He could not keep the bitterness out of his voice. "You protected her better than I did."

"I will not be able to help her when she awakens, Ramiel."

Ramiel paused.

The effects of Spanish fly lingered in the body. Although the worst of Elizabeth's ordeal would be over when she awak-ened, her need would still be great.

Against his will he felt his groin tighten. And despised him-self for his weakness. Yet when Elizabeth awakened, she would need his sexuality. *She would need him.*

He would not fail her again.

Catherine watched Ramiel as he looked down at Elizabeth. His features, so like his father's, were a blend of harshness and tenderness.

Bittersweet regret tightened her chest. For the love that she had known. For what could have been and for what would never be now.

"Ramiel."

The turquoise eyes that met hers were so bright her heart constricted.

"Be gentle." A whimsical smile curved her lips. "But not too gentle."

She softly closed the bedroom door behind her.

It seemed like only yesterday when Ramiel had worn shortcoats and had seduced every maid in sight with his turquoise eyes, blond hair, and dark skin. They had fought to feed him his bottle and change his nappies.

The pain in her chest sharpened.

Had she stayed in Arabia, Ramiel would have been the darling of the harem. And she would have been . . . the sheikh's favorite. Ramiel's mother. Her brain would have turned to desert sand surrounded by empty chatter and the daily fear that another woman would gain the sheikh's favor. A woman with dark hair instead of fair. A woman whose skin matched the dusky hue of an Arab born. A woman who could submit in a man's world and be content with barred windows and muslin veils.

A woman who would accept physical pleasure beyond her wildest dreams and not confuse love with sexual gratification.

"Madam."

Catherine's heart jumped inside her chest. A turbaned ghost stepped out of the shadows, a figment of the past that she had rejected.

Anger replaced regret. She had given up the beauty of Arabia rather than be swallowed up by it, whereas the Cornishman before her wallowed in the traditions that had been responsible for destroying his very life.

"Did you poison the *basboosa*, Connor?"

He remained stoic. "You know that I did not."

"I find that the older I get, the less certain I become about anything. You claimed that Elizabeth Petre was a scheming whore who intended to ruin my son. You asked me to interfere with the lives of two people who desperately need to find love."

The Cornishman flinched, as if she had delivered a physical blow. Suddenly, it all became clear to Catherine.

"You are jealous," she said softly.

"I am protecting him, as is my duty."

"My son does not need your protection, Connor. Nor is it any longer your duty to do so. You are a free man yet you remain with my son. Why is that?"

"The sheikh bade me guard *El Ibn*. I will not shirk my duty."

"Ramiel loves you but he also loves Elizabeth. Do not turn his love for you into hatred."

"He is *El Ibn;* only an infidel puts faith in the love of a woman."

Catherine frowned. "You do not believe that, Connor."

"I must believe it. I must do my duty." The Cornishman's voice throbbed with pain. "If I do not, there is no reason for a eunuch to live."

Forty years suddenly dissolved, and Connor was once again a thirteen-year-old boy whose tears soaked the sand that he was buried in so that he would not bleed to death after being castrated. Catherine had been seventeen years old. She had survived rape and bondage. When the sobbing youth had begged her to kill him, she had not understood what had been done to him. In her ignorance she had failed him, but now she did understand, and now, perhaps, she could make amends.

"You are a handsome man, Connor."

"I am a useless man."

"Whose face is still youthful and whose muscles are taut," she said sharply. "Were you truly a eunuch, you would now possess breasts and your stomach and hips would be mounds of flab. But they are not."

"They cut off my stones," he gritted with uncharacteristic crudeness. "They took away my ability to create life."

"And so Ramiel is more of a son than a charge."

The Cornishman remained silent.

"Have you ever been with a woman, Connor?"

A brief smile lit Catherine's face at the Cornishman's expression of shocked outrage.

"I am a eunuch."

"But you have your manhood." If the light were brighter, she would swear that he blushed.

"I do not need a straw to urinate with," he said stiffly.

"Eunuchs who have been shaved off as cleanly as a girl baby take wives."

"They laugh at them in the harems."

"But at least they gain a measure of happiness. You were a young man when they removed your testicles, Connor. If you had been a youth who had yet to grow body hair, I could understand this—this martyrdom. It affects children differently than it does young men. Women in the harem value eunuchs such as you because they can grow erect and give them pleasure without impregnating them. Have you never wanted a woman? Have you never, ever wanted to find love in a woman's body?"

"You should not discuss such things with me." The Cornishman's voice gritted with anger. "You are the sheikh's woman."

No, never again, no matter how much she might wish it.

"No, Connor, I am my own woman. And I will not stand by and watch you alienate my son and the woman of his choice."

"I would never harm *El Ibn*."

"Yet you possess knowledge of cantharidins."

"If I had wanted to kill Elizabeth Petre, I would not have poisoned the food in the hamper. That was for her children. I would not harm her children."

"Not even to save them from a fate worse than death?"

Connor's black eyes did not blink. "Not even for that."

"Did Edward Petre truly call today?"

"Yes."

"Was he alone?"

"No."

"Who was with him?"

"I do not know."

Catherine's delicately arched eyebrows snapped together. "Connor, please do not lie to me."

"I do not lie, madam. It was a woman. She was heavily veiled. She did not speak. I do not know who she was. I am not even certain if it was a female."

Chapter Twenty-three

Elizabeth woke up with a gasp. The very darkness surrounding her throbbed. For a second she did not understand the pure, uncontrollable need that played on the surface of her skin like St. Elmo's fire. And then she remembered. The pain that was more than pain. The heat that did not cease. Muhamed, pouring a syrup down her throat. The countess, pouring water down her throat.

She had vomited, she had urinated, and still she had burned. As she burned now.

The slice of cake she had devoured had not been sprinkled with ground-up nuts; it had been sprinkled with ground-up insect. A blistering beetle, the countess had said, the sale of which was prevalent in both the East and the West.

Dear God. *Someone had tried to poison her sons.* Instead, they had poisoned her.

The pulsing darkness pressed in on her; it was as black as the beetle she had eaten. Gagging, she threw back the covers and slid her legs off the mattress.

A hand tangled in the man's silk shirt she wore in lieu of a nightgown.

Elizabeth froze.

The hand flattened against her spine through the thin silk, slid underneath the heavy weight of her hair, lightly caressed the nape of her neck. "Stay."

She shuddered. Ramiel's voice grated along her nerves while the heat from his hand traveled to places that had nothing to do with her neck.

"I have to go . . ." She bit her lip. "I have to go to the water closet."

"Do you need help?"

She jerked away from the temptation of his hand. "No, thank you."

Silently, she padded to the bathroom and closed the door behind her. When she returned, Ramiel sat on the edge of the bed, holding a glass, unashamedly naked. He had lit the hurricane lamp on the nightstand.

She blinked.

Touch, smell, *sight* . . . all of her senses seemed to be focused on one place, and that place was between her legs.

It was humiliating. She would not give in to it, no matter how great was her need. *She was not an animal.*

The passionless years she had spent married to Edward suddenly seemed like a haven. Perhaps society was correct. Perhaps women were not meant to enjoy the pleasures of the flesh.

Ramiel held out the glass. "Drink this."

She stared at the glass instead of his muscular brown skin. "You know what happened."

"I know what happened, " he calmly agreed. "Take it. You need fluids."

"I am not thirsty."

"The more water you drink, the more quickly the cantharidin will be flushed out of your body."

She avoided his turquoise eyes, so solemn, so knowing. Obviously, he had experience with the poison she had ingested. That he should know the needs that it engendered made her experience all the more humiliating.

"I have drunk gallons of water and I still . . ." She swallowed. "Burn."

"Then let me ease the burning."

Elizabeth's heart did a somersault. "I want to leave."

Somewhere in the house a door banged shut. It was followed by the squeak of the four-poster.

Ramiel padded across the floor until he stood in front of her. "Drink the water, Elizabeth. We will talk in the morning."

Her gaze traveled from the glass in his hand to the thick mat of dark blond hair covering his chest; it arrowed down to his stomach. His body was hard; a drop of moisture glistened on the tip of his manhood, ripe purple, like a succulent plum kissed by dew. *The forbidden fruit.*

The heat rose in Elizabeth's body until she felt as if she would burst into flames. *She did not want water. She did not want to talk.* Lashing out, she knocked the glass out of his hand. "I said I am not thirsty!"

Crystal water arched through the air, then the glass tumbled to the floor and bounced on the Oriental carpet. A dark stain spread across the brightly dyed wool.

For one timeless second it was as if Elizabeth were not there, as if someone else had perpetrated the small, senseless act of violence and then shock, anger, and fear, all of the differing emotions aggravated by the need that burned and throbbed in her body, swelled over her.

Ramiel did not look shocked by her outburst. He looked regretful, as if confronted with an onerous task. Elizabeth was not being an obedient daughter or a dutiful wife or even a compliant mistress, that look said.

"You lied to me, " she said icily.

His turquoise eyes darkened. "Yes."

"You said I would be safe with you."

"Yes."

"Then there is no need to wait until morning. We have nothing to discuss. If waking your servants is too much trouble, I will find a hack."

"You knew when you came to me, Elizabeth, that I would not let you go."

The heat inside her exploded into a conflagration. "So you would kill my sons that they not interfere with your pleasures."

Between one blink and another, his hands whipped out. His fingers dug into her shoulders. "What did you say?"

"My mother warned me." Elizabeth should be afraid, but all she could think about was the heat of his fingers that penetrated the silk of the shirt and how they had felt lodged deep inside her body when he had found her special place. "She said that you would not accept another man's children. You tried to kill my sons!"

The breath *whooshed* out of her lungs at the force that he hauled her up against his chest. "You don't believe that," he grated.

His breath was hot; it fanned the fire already consuming her and it did not matter if she believed it or not. The day before, he had asked her if she would have come to him if it had not been for her sons. Earlier in the day he had said he would not be kept apart from her life when she insisted upon visiting her sons—alone. The poison was prevalent in the East. Ramiel had knowledge of it. He had known that the basket was intended for her sons—sons that interfered with his pleasure. *It could have been he,* she thought wildly.

Averting her face, she pushed against his chest, but the crinkly blond hair covering it scratched her fingers and the heat of his skin was blistering. A laugh was born and died inside of her chest. *All of this burning, aching need . . . from a bloody insect.*

Elizabeth snatched her hands away from his chest. "Let me go."

He hauled her closer, chest flattening her breasts, pulsing manhood jabbing her stomach, lips only a kiss away. "Tell me you don't believe that."

She would die if he did not release her, yet he would not let her go and *she could not bear his touch any longer.* "Let me go!" she screamed, wanting to hurt him as badly as she now hurt. "I do not want you to touch me ever again! You were not there when I needed you! I do not want to want you!"

There was no mistaking the look in his eyes. She had accomplished her goal. She had wounded the Bastard Sheikh.

Why would he not let her go?

"Tell me you know I would not hurt your sons," he gritted out, breath scorching her face.

If she acknowledged that, then she must acknowledge that her husband had attempted to kill her sons, *his sons.* Like her father had threatened to kill her. She was an adult. Perhaps her actions warranted some sort of reprieve, but her sons were only children. Surely no father would be so depraved as to hurt a child!

"Never!" Reflexively, she brought her knee up to add greater impact to her denial.

Ramiel's eyes widened. He abruptly let her go.

Elizabeth did not know what she had done to gain her release, but she did not stay to ponder it. Flying across the Oriental carpet, she opened the wardrobe that overflowed with masculine clothing save for the two lone articles of feminine dress, the royal blue skirt and matching jacket the countess had hung there when Elizabeth could only gulp air and try not to scream her need. Frenziedly, she shucked off the silk shirt that did not belong to her, *nothing belonged to her, not in Ramiel's house, not in Edward's house.*

Suddenly, she was bodily lifted up into the air. Crinkly hair abraded her back; hard, moist flesh prodded her buttocks. And underneath it all was the heat that would not die.

"Bahebbik." Ramiel's voice was a dark growl. The Arabic syllables sounded as if they had been dredged up from the very depths of his soul.

Elizabeth squeezed her eyelids together. His heartbeat hammered against her left shoulder blade; it matched hers in rhythm. *Please, God, do not let her lose the fragile control that was even now hanging by a fraying thread.* "What does that mean?"

"Stay and find out."

Tears spilled down her cheeks. "You were not shocked when

my husband tried to kill me. You are not shocked by this. *What does it take to make you feel?''*

"I feel, *taalibba.''* His voice throbbed in her ear, a bastard sheikh rejected first by society and now by her.

She did not want to feel his hurt. "I thought I would die without you."

"I am here now."

"I felt like an animal.'' Her pain and need erupted into agonized speech. "My body . . . I did not care. Don't you understand? *I could have lain with any man!''*

"But you did not."

She opened her eyes and stared at a row of waistcoats, frock coats, and dinner jackets. "I do not want to feel this . . . this *lust.* When you touch me, all I want to do is to take you inside me. How do I know I won't someday feel like that about every man I see?"

"I won't let you."

"Lust is not love."

"Perhaps not, *taalibba.* But I can certainly satisfy your lust until you are too tired to worry about the difference."

Hysterical laughter rose in her chest. Along with the heat of his body. It left no room for mirth.

"Please let me go. I am not . . . myself right now."

"Lust is a part of bonding, *taalibba.* Share it with me."

She did not want to bond. She wanted to copulate.

"My sons—"

"Are safe. You must trust me, Elizabeth."

She pried at the arms locked about her waist. "You said that before."

"Elizabeth, I went to Eton today. I hired people to look after your sons."

Elizabeth stilled. "Why did you not tell me this morning what you intended?"

"I did not want to alarm you."

"You thought my husband would harm his own children?"

"I thought it possible."

Oh, God, it was true. Edward had tried to kill his own sons.

"I know you hurt, Elizabeth. Let me make it better for you. Let me love you."

Love. All her life she had wanted to be loved.

But this wasn't love. This was lust.

And she wanted that too.

She leaned her head back so that it rested against his. "You will be disgusted by me." *She disgusted herself.*

He nipped her ear; the small pain stabbed through her nipples. "Perhaps before the night is over you will be disgusted by me."

"No." The things he had done to her and that she had done to him had never disgusted her.

Slowly, he backed up, his arms still around her, and turned. She looked at the rumpled bed.

"When I put you down, lift up on your hands and knees." *El kebachi.* Like the beasts in the fields.

She lied to herself if she said she did not want this. And she was suddenly, sickeningly, tired of lies.

Shivering, Elizabeth did as she was instructed. Cool air caressed her buttocks. She felt . . . exposed. And vulnerable. At her pose. At the knowledge that he knew how badly she needed him . . . and did not judge her.

But she had judged him. She *was* ashamed to take him to visit her sons. Ashamed because of *this*—how could she be a good mother *and* a wanton woman?

The mattress sank behind her. His hand rested on her buttocks, a stinging imprint of flesh. "Spread your legs . . ." She quivered at the nudge of a hard, hairy thigh. "There."

Scalding heat plastered her behind; it prodded between her legs. Then he was inside her and there was an internal popping sensation and he was lodged so deeply that she could not catch her breath. "Ramiel!"

"*Shhh.*" He lifted her up by the shoulders—*oh, God,* it felt like she had a log rammed inside her that suddenly sprang tall into a tree, and then she was kneeling upright and they were one body, one heartbeat. Her back rested against his chest, a living, breathing wall of prickly heat and corded muscle. Deep inside her, his verge throbbed. Or perhaps it was her womb throbbing around him.

"You know the sundry names given to a man's sexual organ." Hot, moist breath feathered her hair. A callused hand smoothed her shoulder; she could feel every rough abrasion as it trickled down her chest, a breast, lightly grazed a rock-hard nipple—she clenched around him, a lightning prelude to orgasm knifing through her body. And then he was cupping her stomach, shaping the flesh rooted deep inside her, a part of her. Nuzzling her ear, he brought his other hand down and tangled his fingers in the damp curls at the V of her legs, whispered, "Now it is time to learn about the names given to a woman's body," and with a single finger he flicked her swollen clitoris.

Elizabeth screamed her release. "I'm sorry. " She gripped his hands to hold them in place while her body milked his manhood and tears streamed down her face. "I am so sorry."

For not being the lady she was raised to be. For embroiling him in the sordid reality of her life. For taking more than she was giving.

"Never be sorry for experiencing pleasure, *taalibba*. Give me your hand. . . . No, don't fight me." His hand cupping her stomach anchored her to him while the hand that had brought her to climax gripped hers. "I fantasize about teaching you this way, having you naked, touching me, touching yourself. This is *abou khochime,* 'the one with a little nose.' " Fingers intertwined with hers, he directed the motion of her hand, dipped between her swollen lips into liquid heat, gathered up moisture to glide and slide across the throbbing heart of her clitoris. "It is also called *abou djebaha,* 'the one with a projection.' "

Heat mushroomed inside Elizabeth, but he would not release her and she could not fight both him and her body. Gasping for air, she slammed her head back against his shoulder as another climax ripped through her.

He buried his face into the crook of her neck, hand firmly pressing her lower stomach, mapping the contractions of her womb, the ripples of her vagina around the thickness of his manhood. "That's good. . . . That's good," he crooned. "There is also *abou tertour,* the crested one. That name is used when a woman's clitoris rises at the moment of her enjoyment."

As hers had done, twice now. *And it still was not enough.*

Elizabeth turned her face into his thick gold hair. It smelled of sunshine and heat and the faint remnants of soap. She clung to the sanity of his voice. "Do you really fantasize about me?" she panted. His fingers pulsed around hers while her swollen flesh pulsed against their joined fingertips. Inside her body her vagina spasmed about his manhood while her womb quivered against the palm of his hand.

"Oh, yes, I fantasize about you. I fantasize about your hair, your breasts, your little fleece here that is the same color as the hair on your head, your little bud that gets so deliciously engorged. . . ."

She had never dreamed that a man would fantasize about her. Before Ramiel, she had never thought that a man would want her satisfaction.

He lifted his head, found her cheek with his nose, adjusted his position until he found her mouth. His tongue was as hot and wet as the other part of him that penetrated her. She convulsed, crying out in his mouth, body independently clenching, contracting, while he circled their fingers around and around.

"Three orgasms," he murmured against her lips. "That should take the edge off so that we can finish the lesson."

Gasping for air, Elizabeth felt her fingers being drawn down, through soft, moist folds until suddenly she felt a hard shaft. He *was* a part of her. Deep inside her vagina he flexed; simultaneously, she felt the motion with her fingertips.

"*Keuss* is a common word for a woman's vagina." He pressed their fingertips against the ring of flesh that clung to his manhood like a second skin. "And then there is *el taleb,* the yearning one that burns for a man's member. Do you burn for me, *taalibba?*"

She rolled her head forward and stared at the dance of light and shadow on the pale green wall. Embers glowed in the white marble fireplace. "You must know that I do."

"But I need to hear you say so."

She had said far more explicit words than that to him. So why was it so hard to say? "I burn for you, Ramiel," she choked.

He kneaded her stomach. "For me . . . or for a man?"

She closed her eyes and could not escape the truth. "Both."

"You could have taken another man today. A footman. Étienne."

Her eyelids shot open. "I would never do that."

"But you do it with me."

"It is not the same."

"No, it is not. Do you know what my favorite word for this"—he pressed their fingertips harder against the flesh stretched around his shaft, as if seeking entry alongside of it— "is?"

She concentrated on the slick external heat of him instead of the heat melding her spine with his chest. "What?"

"*El hacene,* the beautiful. But it is *el ladid,* the delicious one, that is the most wondrous vagina of all. The pleasure that it gives is compared to that felt by beasts and birds of prey, a pleasure that they fight bloody battles to attain. The sheikh writes that a woman who possesses such a vulva will give a man a foretaste of the paradise that awaits him when he dies. Give me a sample of paradise, *taalibba.* There is nothing wrong with feeling like an animal. Bend over and let us share the same pleasure that a ewe and a ram enjoy."

Elizabeth bent over . . . and gripped the satin comforter in both hands to keep her balance when his body slammed into hers.

A woman should not be able to take a man this deeply, she dimly thought. Suddenly, prickly heat curved the length of her back, and his calloused hands that steadied her hips slid down, around, one to cup her stomach while the other slid between her legs and he was touching her and kneading her and she fought to take him deeper, harder, *please, give me more, please don't let go* . . . Her inner pleas echoed in the bedroom.

"Keep your hips tilted for me, *taalibba*." He pressed inside and outside, positioning her, directing her, molding her flesh around his. "Don't tighten up. Bear down. Take me, Elizabeth. Allah. Moan for me. Let me know you want me. *Take me.* There. Deeper. Yes. God. *Yesss.*"

Sharp teeth sank into her shoulder. She incongruously remembered him saying that the sheikh did not advocate cannibalism, and then she did not think anything, she became the animal that she had always feared she would become, moaning and groaning and begging, lost in her pleasure, his pleasure, *their* pleasure, the raw beauty they created together, flesh to flesh, breath to breath, heartbeat to heartbeat. When her orgasm ripped through her, she did not know who cried out, or even whose pleasure it was that exploded inside her body in pulsating waves of repletion. Elizabeth and Ramiel. Ramiel and Elizabeth.

She collapsed under the weight of his body and lay there for long seconds, savoring the boneless feel of him pressing her into the cool satin comforter. Their bodies pulsed in unison, inside, outside. A pool of hot sperm bathed them both.

"I want champagne," she whispered.

He grunted. It was such a purely male sound that she smiled.

The smile instantly turned into a rush of gratitude. *He had given her so much.* "I want to bathe you in it."

The softened flesh inside her jerked. His fingers convulsively tightened about her stomach and pubes.

"And then I want to lick you dry."

His flesh buried inside her was no longer soft.

"And then I want you to ejaculate inside my mouth so I can taste your pleasure."

Ramiel stared down at Elizabeth.

Her face was flushed with satiation and sleep. Her eyelashes were spiked from tears and sweat and champagne. Gently, reluctantly, he pulled the silk sheet over her naked breasts, up to her neck.

She sighed and turned into his hand.

Ramiel's chest tightened. He would not let Edward Petre hurt her again.

Quickly, silently, he dressed, careful not to disturb Elizabeth. Extinguishing the flame in the oil lamp, he could not resist swooping down and tasting her.

She unconsciously opened her lips for him.

He regretfully pulled back.

There was another name that he had not relayed to her during their lesson: *el tsequil,* the vulva belonging to a woman who never tires of her man.

Elizabeth would not tire of him; and both Allah and God knew, he would never grow tired of her.

The foggy night was cold after the warmth of Elizabeth's body. Big Ben echoed over the rooftops—it was one o'clock in the morning. Parliament sessions lasted until two.

Ramiel eased through the darkness, whistled sharply when a hack neared him. It stopped.

"Where to, guv'nor?"

"The Parliament building."

The hack smelled of gin and musk. Elizabeth had smelled of oranges and hot, womanly need. The day before she had come to him smelling of gas and fear.

The cabbie expertly drove through the foggy London streets. When the hack stopped, Ramiel jumped out and paid his fare.

"Thank 'e, sir." The cabbie pocketed the generous tip.

"There'll be more money if you drive over there outside the lamplight and stay. I am meeting someone."

"It'll cost ye, me waitin'."

Ramiel smiled grimly. "It will be worth it."

He waited outside the Parliament building, hat pulled low and wool scarf high. His back, thighs, and calves ached pleasantly, a reminder of more agreeable moments. Elizabeth had given him three orgasms; he had lost count of the number that he had given her. The taste of her lingered on his tongue, a combination of her sweetness, his saltiness, and bubbly champagne.

Idly, he watched carriages line up along the street—and wondered if he would ever taste champagne without getting immediately, painfully hard. The cabbie's nag, out of the gas-light, neighed softly. And then the doors to the Parliament building swung open, and men, some exchanging banter, some dressed in formal dinner attire, poured out.

Instantly alert, Ramiel searched the crowd—there. Edward Petre was talking and laughing with a group of Parliament members. Stiffening, preparing his body for action, Ramiel waited for the right moment.

The animated discussion broke up as each man sought a carriage, either alone or in pairs. Ramiel moved quickly. He grabbed Edward Petre's arm just as he placed a bowler hat on his head.

"Uranian, Petre." Ramiel's voice was muffled but clear through the scarf. "Come with me now or every man here will soon learn about your little diversions. And while I am aware that several of them share your proclivities, they will not support you when the knowledge comes to public notice."

Edward Petre's face turned pasty white in the light of the gas lamps. His breath, a gush of silvery steam, punctured the air. "Take your hand off me."

"Soon. There's a cab waiting for us. You and I are going to your house for a little chat. Or I can kill you and dump you in the Thames. Since the latter would certainly simplify matters for me, I suggest you shut up and come with me. Now."

"You would not dare. Someone is waiting for me."

"I dare. I was exiled from Arabia for killing my half brother. I assure you, Petre, I dare."

Stark fear filled the older man's brown eyes. "You would not. You are fucking my wife. Even she would not want a man who killed the father of her children."

A cynical smile twisted Ramiel's mouth. "Perhaps. She might surprise you. In either event, you will be dead. Free of earthly concerns. Shall we go?"

Petre did not further protest. Ramiel guided him toward the hack, fingers digging into the wool of his coat, and gave the cabbie the address to drive to. Dull yellow light penetrated the dirty cab windows. The suffocating scent of Petre's cologne and the macassar oil that Europeans universally wore overrode the smells of the hack.

"Elizabeth will tire of you." The Chancellor of the Exchequer's voice was admirably calm. "And then she will come back to me."

Ramiel fought down a burst of dangerous rage. *He wanted to kill him.* "Softly, Petre. We will talk when we are inside your house."

"Afraid of scandal, Safyre?" Petre sneered.

Ramiel looked out at the gleam of lights on the river. "No. The Thames is too close. I am afraid I will give in to temptation."

The remaining journey passed in taut silence. Petre was angry, but he was a clever man: He was afraid of what a bastard sheikh who confessed to killing his half brother would do to a man who kept him away from his woman. Rightfully so.

While Ramiel paid the cabbie, Petre fumbled with his house key. Hoping, no doubt, that he could rush inside and lock the Bastard Sheikh out.

Ramiel calmly took the key from Petre's gloved hand and inserted it into the door. He mockingly inclined his head. "After you."

The servants had left a gaslight burning. A dangerous courtesy, considering what had happened to Elizabeth.

There was no sign of Elizabeth and her incredible gift of passion in the town house. It was not cluttered with a table in every corner or knickknacks on every surface but it was still a typical Victorian home with its drab wallpaper and predictable furniture draped in clothes lest the sight of their legs excite a man.

Petre walked stiffly down the floral-papered hall, wrenched

open a door. Ramiel followed. The older man lit a gas lamp more efficiently than he had opened the front door. But then, he was intimately aware of the dangers of gas.

It was a masculine room that Ramiel stood in. Darkly conservative. A heavy walnut table occupied one side of the study, while a Carlton House desk stood prominently in the center of the room.

Ramiel softly closed the door. Petre turned, faced him. His tall black bowler curled over his ears; he clenched a gold-knobbed cane in his right hand.

Tossing his own soft wool hat onto a side chair, Ramiel unwrapped the scarf from around his neck.

Fear suddenly exceeded Petre's anger. Dropping the cane, he darted around the desk.

Ramiel leapt after him. He slammed the desk drawer on Petre's hand that scrambled to gain purchase on the gun within. "Why didn't you shoot Elizabeth?" he grated. "It would have been more efficient. Servants are apt to notice gas. Just as they are apt to recognize poisons."

"I don't know what you are talking about."

Ramiel pushed harder on the drawer. He had the satisfaction of watching what little facial color Elizabeth's husband possessed drain away.

"Tell me, Petre. Why would a politician think that murder is less damaging to his career than divorce is?"

Petre's mustache quivered. "I tell you, I don't know what you are talking about."

"You tried to kill Elizabeth with gas. And then you tried to kill her sons, *your* sons, with Spanish fly."

Petre knew what cantharidin was. The knowledge was clear in his brown eyes.

"I had nothing to do with her lamp going out. She tried to commit suicide."

"How convenient for you, especially considering the fact that she was leaving you."

"You are smashing my hand."

"Good. Perhaps next time you will think twice before you try to harm Elizabeth or her children. But you have intrigued me. Why would you try to kill your wife when you could far more easily have committed her? You must know I would not have let you get away with murder."

"For the love of God, I never tried to harm her." Petre's left hand wrapped around Ramiel's wrist and tried to pry it away from the drawer. Ramiel was far stronger. "Elizabeth didn't have the stomach to face me in your home. I have not been near Eton or the boys. Let me go!"

Ramiel grabbed Petre's left hand, used the combined weight of their bodies to press harder on the drawer. "How badly do you want me to let you go, Petre? As badly as Elizabeth wanted a divorce?"

Sweat rolled down the older man's bloodless face, beaded off his waxed eyebrows and mustache. "I will divorce the bitch. Just let me go!"

"Not good enough. I will not have her name smeared all over London. Furthermore, you will grant her custody of her two sons."

"She has committed adultery."

"And what have you done, Petre? You have pandered your own son. I assure you the courts will be more concerned about your behavior than they will be hers."

Petre stopped struggling. "You have no proof."

"I have been to Eton. I have all the proof I need."

"Let me go." Petre's voice was dull.

"Make it worth my while."

"I will give her a divorce. Privately. She may keep her two sons."

Ramiel slowly released the drawer, deftly removed the gun from Petre's limp fingers. Blood dripped down the back of his hand. The knuckles had already started swelling.

"Neither you nor Andrew Walters will go near Elizabeth or her sons again."

Petre nursed his hand. "If word happens to leak out about my . . . 'little diversions,' as you call them . . . I will make sure that Elizabeth does not gain custody of Richard and Phillip."

Another secret. Another compromise.

Petre had the power to take away Elizabeth's sons; Ramiel had the power to prevent him. But not through death . . .

For Elizabeth's sake, he would not murder the father of her children. And perhaps for his own sake as well. Because he would not be killing Edward Petre; he would be killing his half brother all over again.

Slipping the gun into his coat pocket, he turned away. From the ugliness of the past. From the ugliness of the present. He had a future to look forward to: He would not jeopardize it.

"You were right. You're a canny bastard. Committing Elizabeth was the perfect solution. I left the morning her lamp went out to procure a lunacy order. I had no need to gas her. Nor did I try to kill my two sons. I have not needed Spanish fly since I last bedded my wife, your whore."

Petre was not as smart as he should be. A man did not denigrate the woman of a bastard who was the son of a sheikh. He especially did not deliberately conjure up images of the bastard's woman lying underneath another man.

Ramiel came very close to forgetting his resolution of not killing Petre.

"Then you hired someone to do it. Like you hired someone to threaten her last Thursday night when she spoke at a meeting," Ramiel said tightly, fully aware that solution did not explain the cantharidin poisoning unless Petre had placed a spy in his home. But unlike the private detective who had met the Petres' footman outside the town house and paid him to quit his employment, there were no new servants in Ramiel's home.

"I am a public figure; I would not hire someone to murder or threaten my wife for fear they would talk." All of Petre's arrogance had returned. "It was foggy last Thursday night. Elizabeth was late. I brought in the constable in the event that if an accident did befall her, he could quote me as a concerned, loving husband.''

Ramiel reached for his hat on the side table by the door. He noted that his hand trembled. "Then it was Andrew Walters who arranged everything.''

"So she told you about Andrew's regrettable outburst. He would no more kill her than would I. Not as long as there existed a safer method of controlling her. Andrew was with me the morning I signed the lunacy order.''

Ramiel did not turn around. "Then who do you suggest tried to kill her?''

"Perhaps Elizabeth is not the woman you think her, Safyre. Perhaps she tried to commit suicide. And failing that, she tried to kill her sons rather than face them in a divorce court.''

"And perhaps you are lying, Petre, because you don't want to feed the fish in the Thames.''

"Perhaps,'' Petre agreed mockingly.

But he was not. Ramiel was suddenly quite certain that Edward Petre had not attempted to kill Elizabeth. A politician did not kill when less risky avenues existed. He would have committed Elizabeth to an asylum without blinking an eyelash, but murder would be investigated.

Ela'na. Who had *tried to kill her . . . if not her husband or father?*

Ramiel opened the door and quietly closed it behind him to prevent giving Petre the satisfaction of seeing that he had neatly wrested control from his hands. A tall, shadowed man waited for him in the dimly lit foyer. Ramiel groped for the gun in his pocket.

"It is I. Turnsley.''

The private detective Muhamed had hired. The one who, according to Elizabeth, was sleeping with her maid.

"What do you want?''

"To talk.''

Ramiel did not want to talk. He was in the grip of an uncontrollable need to get back to Elizabeth to ascertain that she was safe. *He would not lose her.*

"You reported to Muhamed yesterday," he said shortly. And the report had been . . . that the detective did not know who had blown the gas lamp out.

"I reported what I knew then," Turnsley responded evenly. "But there is someone who knows more than I. And she is willing to talk."

Chapter Twenty-four

Elizabeth studied Ramiel's sleeping face. The dusky stubble of a morning beard shadowed his jaw. Twin fans of almost feminine lashes softened the sculptured hardness of his features.

He had forced her to acknowledge the darker side of desire and shown her that she was not immoral, merely a woman. Their union had been primal; it had been physical; it had forever splintered her convictions about right and wrong.

Blistering heat reached out underneath the covers, wrapped about her thigh. Immediately, the slight frown on Ramiel's face eased. He sighed.

Elizabeth's throat tightened.

She would not live in fear for the rest of her life. Nor could she endure the cold, sterile life that had been hers as a "respectable" wife. If Edward would not grant her a divorce with custody of her two sons, then she must find a means to force him to bow to her will. The law, he had informed her, allowed a woman to sue her husband for a divorce if he had a mistress and if he physically mistreated her. Attempted murder must surely qualify for abuse, especially when the man in question also tried to kill his own children. All she needed to do now was produce his mistress, or lover, as Edward called the woman who was a member of the Uranian fellowship.

For a second she contemplated waking Ramiel. He knew who Edward's mistress was.

But he had protected her sons; she could not ask more of him. Perhaps he was right. Perhaps when she was ready she would see the truth for herself.

Slowly, carefully, she loosened the long, hard fingers that so perfectly fit her body, both inside and out. Ramiel groaned in sleepy protest.

A flood of remembered pleasure washed over her body.

He had cried out when she had taken him into her mouth and suckled him like he had suckled her breasts, suckling and suckling until his entire body tensed and he grabbed her head to hold her still while he spasmed with ecstasy. *Bahebbik,* he had repeated in an oddly hoarse voice when she swirled her tongue around his deflating crown in search of more of the fluid that had shot into the back of her throat.

Elizabeth licked her lips, tasting him, tasting her, tasting their combined essence. Overlying the salty, musky flavor was the fizzling effervescence of champagne.

Muscles she had not known she possessed rudely presented themselves at the impact of cold wool carpeting and hard wood flooring. She wondered if a man also ached and throbbed after a night of strenuous sex.

Her reticule lay on top of the nightstand by the tin stamped with Queen Victoria's portrait. Silently, determinedly, with reticule in hand, she padded across the Oriental carpet to the wardrobe. The twin doors were closed. Boxes were piled high between the red-velvet-upholstered armchair and the massive mahogany wardrobe. They had not been there last night. Had Muhamed come into Ramiel's bedroom while they slept?

Immediately, she berated herself for the hot blood that flooded her face. Muhamed had seen more than her sleeping body bundled under the covers. Furthermore, he had saved her life, the countess had said, by pouring an emetic down her throat. It was ridiculous to get embarrassed because he had seen her sleeping in bed with Ramiel, when yesterday he had held her head over a chamber pot.

Grabbing the royal blue skirt and bodice Ramiel had purchased for her—oh, no, there were no underclothes save for the frilled bustle—ah, there were her shoes—she tiptoed to the water closet. Some minutes later, after hurriedly brushing her teeth, washing, and dressing, she stealthily opened the door.

Ramiel was still asleep; his breathing was a soft rasp in the murky silence. Smiling anew, she wondered if he ever snored. Her smile turned into a frown. Did *she* snore?

Gently closing the bedroom door behind her, Elizabeth realized that she was ravenous. Other than a light repast that had been washed down with champagne that first night she had spent with Ramiel, she had not had anything to eat in over two days.

She gingerly descended the curved mahogany staircase with its bright Oriental runner. Dancing slippers were not meant to be worn without stockings. Nor was a bustle meant to lie next to bare skin. Any more than was a heavily lined bodice and skirt. The sensitive flesh between her legs throbbed in agreement.

Stepping onto the landing, she turned in the direction of the breakfast room. A swirl of white robes stepped out from behind a man-sized vase.

Curtailing a scream, she focused on enigmatic black eyes. "*Sabah el kheer,* Muhamed. I would like breakfast, please."

The servant stood his ground. "Where is *El Ibn*?"

"Asleep." Elizabeth mutinously lifted her chin. "I do not wish him to be disturbed. He had a tiring night."

She closed her eyes as the full import of her words registered inside her brain. *El Ibn* had had a tiring night because he had brought her to orgasm over a dozen times to ease the burning of the poison. A side effect that Muhamed must know about.

"Come." Muhamed's voice was as emotionless as it had been yesterday. "I will serve you."

Elizabeth opened her eyes and stared at the folds of the white robe about his unlined neck. "I also seem to be without undergarments. Perhaps they have been laundered. If you would be so good as to . . . check upon them.''

"Very well. Follow me to the breakfast room.''

She did not have the courage to look up and see if Muhamed was as discomfited as she was. The breakfast room shone with sunlight, sparkling glass, and polished wood. Bacon, eggs, kippers, roast beef, grilled mushrooms, fried tomatoes, sliced fruit, and freshly baked rolls scented the air. Elizabeth allowed Muhamed to seat her at the round table so that she looked out the windows onto a garden green with exotically shaped shrubbery.

"What would you have, Mrs. Petre?''

She resigned herself to the fact that her appetite now, as it had been the previous night, was one of pure gluttony. "Everything, please.''

Avidly listening to the clang of dishes and utensils behind her, she poured herself a cup of coffee. No sooner did she raise it to her lips than two heaping plates of food were deposited in front of her.

"I trust that will keep you occupied while I see to your undergarments.''

Elizabeth fought back a fresh wave of crimson embarrassment. "Yes, thank you.''

He swirled to go, creating a brisk breeze.

"Muhamed.''

"Yes?''

The coffee was pitch black. A coffee ground floated on the surface. Like ground-up beetle. She set the cup down. "Thank you for saving my life yesterday.''

"Some would claim that it was I who administered the poison.''

A chill swept down her spine.

Yes, she had suspected that he might be spying for Edward. Nor did she doubt now that he had the knowledge and/or the opportunity to have administered the cantharidin. Yet—

"If you had poisoned the picnic, I do not think you would

have saved me. Nor do I think you would harm innocent children.''

But she spoke to empty air.

By the time the Arab that was no Arab returned, she had finished one plate of food and started on the other.

"You do not drink the coffee.''

"No.'' She put down her fork and knife. "It is . . . black.''

Nausea rose in her throat. *The ground-up beetles had been crunchy, like nuts.*

The rustle of robes behind her alerted her of the servant's proximity. Suddenly, a dark hand appeared in front of her face. Muhamed poured cream into the coffee.

"Drink. You need fluids.''

Like master, like servant, she thought resentfully. Ramiel had sounded just like Muhamed when he told her to drink the glass of water last night.

Remembering the outcome of her rebellion, she drank.

Muhamed refilled her cup with coffee and cream. "Your underclothes are in the library. You may finish dressing there when you complete your breakfast.''

"Thank you.'' Elizabeth toyed with the handle of the cup. It was azure blue edged in silver. "Please order a carriage to be brought around within the hour.''

"You will not leave the house until *El Ibn* rises.''

The butler's response was not unexpected.

"Very well,'' she lied. Pushing back the second plate of food, she tossed her linen napkin onto the table. "I cannot eat any more. Thank you for serving me. Breakfast was quite delicious.''

Elizabeth allowed Muhamed to pull back her chair and escort her to the library. Silk and fine lawn underclothing were neatly draped over the large mahogany desk where Ramiel had conducted the five lessons. *But not the sixth.*

She cupped her stomach through the heavy skirt, remembering . . . *everything.* He had felt her womb contract, both inside and outside.

Gold glinted from the wall of books; everywhere she looked

there was the beauty of Arabia. The credenza inlaid with mother-of-pearl. The silk screens on the walls. The floor-to-ceiling bay windows with the yellow silk drapes and the curved brass curtain rod.

Edward's den where her father had threatened to kill her was dark and ascetic. It possessed no beauty or memories of pleasure.

Quickly, efficiently, Elizabeth pulled on the transparent drawers and lawn petticoats. She was not about to undress to slide into a chemise; she crumpled up the thin silk shift and shoved it into a bottom desk drawer.

An odd surge of tenderness overcame her at sight of a leather ledger. It reminded her that Ramiel, for all of his exotic looks and background, was no different from any other Englishman. He ate. He slept. He was responsible for the normal day-to-day tasks involved in overseeing a household and managing his finances.

His chair was all wood with a back that tilted and coasters that sprang into action when she sat down—she grabbed the edge of the desk to prevent herself from shooting into the wall. Hurriedly, she pulled on black silk stockings.

Muhamed waited for her outside the library door.

Her plan was not going to work if the servant dogged her every move.

"This is a large house, Muhamed. I did not fully explore it yesterday."

Elizabeth swept by Muhamed. Muhamed followed.

She abruptly stopped, back turned to the servant. "Muhamed. I am not a child that you need fear will pilfer in drawers. There is no need to oversee my every move."

"I will not fail *El Ibn* again."

"You did not fail him yesterday. Rather than blame yourself for what happened, you should be grateful. If I had not ingested the poison, then my two sons would have. And they would not have had you to save them. Because of that incident, I know what to expect of my husband. I will not let him harm me or my children. Please accord me the courtesy of being private with my thoughts.''

''As you will.''

Elizabeth breathed a sigh of relief. Keeping a lookout for Muhamed, she idly explored the third floor of guest bedchambers. When she was certain that he no longer followed her, she sneaked down the servants' stairs.

He did not jump out from behind a vase. Nor, when she opened the coat closet by the foyer, did he jump out of that. Snatching up her cloak, bonnet, and gloves, she escaped the house. Apprehension gnawed at her stomach. She felt like she betrayed Ramiel by sneaking out of his home. Yet she felt compelled to protect herself and her sons.

She walked blocks and blocks. Dancing slippers were not meant to be so abused. They pinched her toes in retaliation. Her first instinct, when she spotted a hack, was to turn around and run back to Ramiel. He was no doubt still sleeping. She could slip into bed and snuggle up against the warmth of his body. When he woke up, they could engage in the seventh lesson.

She did not want to return to the place where one man had threatened to kill her and another man had attempted to carry out the threat.

Taking a deep breath, she straightened her shoulders. *She was not a coward.* Raising her hand, she stepped to the curb.

The hack pulled over. ''Where to, ma'am?''

Elizabeth gave the cabbie the address to Edward's town house.

The drive was far too short. By the time the hack jerked to a halt, her body was wreathed in sweat. Without a corset or even a chemise to absorb the moisture, it trickled down between her breasts.

Stepping out, she paid the cabbie the fare—and indulged in an attack of cravenness.

''Please wait. I will need transportation back. If for whatever reason I do not return within thirty minutes, I want you to go to Lord Safyre and tell him where I am.'' She gave him Ramiel's address and a florin. "Will you do that?''

The cabbie tipped his hat; he was old enough not to ask questions when it meant money. "Aye, ma'am.''

Hands shaking—her whole body shook—she walked up to the doorstep and rang the bell—a recent installment—a modern button to replace an archaic knocker.

No one answered her summons.

The servants had a half-day off on Friday, starting at noon. It was not noon. *Someone* should be about.

Elizabeth impulsively reached into her reticule. The key to the town house was there, as it always was. Her fingers, she noted grimly, trembled. It required both hands to fit the key into the lock.

Cracking open the door, she poked her head inside. "Beadles?''

Beadles echoed hollowly behind the door.

Taking a deep breath, she pushed the door all the way open and stepped inside. The foyer was ominously dark after the bright sunshine.

Every nerve in her body warned her to run. At the same time, common sense derided her cowardliness.

Beadles might spy on her, but he would not harm her. She needed to see Emma. The abigail knew who had blown out the gas lamp. Quite possibly she also knew the identity of Edward's mistress. Edward, if at home, need never know that she visited. She would take Emma driving or walking while they talked.

Shrill laughter trilled down the stairs.

A woman's laughter.

It did not belong to any of the female servants. Had Edward, now that he did not have a wife in residence, brought his mistress home?

Clutching the key in one hand and her reticule in the other, she gently closed the front door and traversed the steps, veering just in time to avoid the loose board. She pressed her ear to the door of her husband's bedroom—there was no sound inside, but she could feel—an energy, a presence—*something*.

Heartbeat drumming inside her ears, she eased open the door. There was her husband—he was dressed in trousers and a waistcoat. He stood facing his bed with his head twisted down and to the side in what looked like a kiss.

Feeling giddy with victory, Elizabeth pushed the door all the way open.

A woman dressed in a corset and drawers stood in profile; her hands were hooked around Edward's neck, holding his head down to hers in what was most definitely a kiss. She had mannishly short, graying auburn hair. Her legs, surprisingly muscular, were free of hair, as had been the countess's. Elizabeth stared at the woman's flat stomach below the corset for several moments before she comprehended what she was seeing.

A penis jutted out of the woman's drawers.

Elizabeth's gaze shot up to the face of the man who greedily kissed her husband.

The bedchamber suddenly tilted, righted itself. *It could not be.*

But it was.

"Oh, my God!"

Her husband and her father jumped apart. Andrew's hazel eyes that matched Elizabeth's widened in horror; Edward's brown eyes were round with surprise. A third man—no, he was only a boy, a nineteen-year-old golden-haired boy who had yet to grow hair on his chest—kneeled on the bed between them. He was naked. His lips were slack and his cornflower-blue eyes dazed.

Elizabeth had seen the boy at the charity ball, dressed in formal black and white evening wear. He had looked older with his clothes on.

Unable to stop herself, she stared at the swollen red penis that protruded from Edward's gaping black trousers. It was shiny wet. *From the boy's saliva.*

No wonder Edward had said she had udder breasts and flabby hips. It was hard to compete with a boy, she thought incongruously. *It was hard to compete with a* father.

Suddenly, the men's shocked immobility erupted into a flurry of activity. Andrew wrenched the comforter off the bed. Edward caught the golden-haired boy just as he catapulted to the floor and stood him upright. He was neither as tall as the Chancellor of the Exchequer nor as short as the prime minister. His penis was flaccid, unlike that of his mentors.

Clutching the comforter against his exposed body, Andrew's face contorted in the same rage-filled mask that he had worn when he threatened to kill her. "Get out of here, Elizabeth."

Elizabeth stared at the prim white corset peeping above the forest-green comforter. In her mind's eye she could still see his dark penis jutting out from between the seamless vent in the women's drawers.

This was the man who had stood up at the charity ball and boasted of his two grandsons—future prime ministers. He had proudly announced his political plans for his son-in-law. A son-in-law who was *his lover.*

Something flitted through her brain, something so obscure and so fantastic that she could not immediately bring it forward into consciousness. Edward's speech that night . . . Something about wives and sons . . . *And now I would like to thank the two women in my life. One gave me my wife and the other gave me two sons, whom I will train to follow in my footsteps as Andrew Walters has trained me to follow in his.*

Suddenly, all the clues that Ramiel had told her she would see when she was ready for the truth fell into place and the puzzle was complete, but *she was not ready for this.* Her gaze snapped up to Edward's eyes.

"Richard," she whispered.

"I am afraid that our son to date shows no talent for power, Elizabeth. Whereas Matt, here . . ." Brown eyes glittering with malice, Edward deliberately pulled the golden-haired boy against his side and wrapped a bandaged hand around his waist so that it rested on his flat stomach only inches away from a golden thatch of pubic hair. "Matt shows great aptitude. Perhaps Richard will fill a less important position in politics. There are other P.M.'s who are looking into his future career."

Edward had sounded like that when he had rejected her sexual overtures. Smug. Omnipotent. Heedless of anyone's life but his own.

All rationale splintered. She had lived with this man for sixteen years, a helpmate if not a wife. She had managed his household, campaigned for him, sacrificed her needs for his. *And he had done this to her son.*

"You despicable bastard!" she screamed, body hurtling forward, propelled by the maternal instinct to hurt him as he had hurt her son.

Hard, unyielding arms wrapped about her, held her immobile. The three men were in front of her, she thought irrationally; how could they be holding her from behind?

Raw heat, familiar heat, seeped through her cloak.

Oh, no, no, no. Not him, please, don't let it be him.

You know who his mistress is, don't you?

Siba, *Elizabeth . . .*

The pressure inside Ramiel's chest owed nothing to the press of Elizabeth's body. He had not wanted her to know. *Not like this.* Allah. God. Her father was dressed like a woman and her husband's prick hung out of his pants, while a boy not much older than her son stood naked between them.

"Let me go. You *are* a bastard. Let me go this instant!"

Ramiel ignored her struggles more successfully than he ignored her barbed words. *Yes, he was a bastard.* In every sense of the word. "The divorce, Petre. Quietly. Quickly. Or you will never be prime minister. That I guarantee you."

"The price is her silence, Safyre."

"So be it."

"Never!" Elizabeth's body strained to get away from him. "He abused my son!"

Ramiel lowered his head and nuzzled the scratchy wool of her bonnet aside to whisper against her cheek. "Think of Richard, Elizabeth. Come with me now and no one will ever hurt your son again. You cannot prove anything. If you fight them, Petre will have you committed and both of your sons will be his.''

Elizabeth did not struggle when he backed her out of the room, turned her around, and walked her down the hall, down the steps, and out into sunshine. Ramiel's carriage waited in front of the town house. Muhamed sat in the driver's box, looking neither left nor right.

"You knew." Elizabeth's voice was brittle. "All along when I asked you who my husband's mistress was, you knew."

Ramiel neither agreed nor disagreed. He had not known everything ''all along.'' But he had known about her husband and her father when she last asked him.

"You should have waited until I woke up," he said impassively.

"Would you have told me?"

"You will never know now, will you?"

Nor would Ramiel.

Would he have told her? Or would he have tried to cling to her innocence for a little while longer?

"Where is my hack?"

"A half sovereign is a bigger bribe than a florin."

She flinched at this final betrayal. Only it was not the final one, he thought bleakly.

He opened the carriage door.

Her bottom lip quivered. "I want my hack."

"You wanted the truth; you shall have it. All of it. Get in."

Elizabeth had no choice but to step inside the carriage. She sat in the far corner, as far away from him as she could get. Ramiel bowed his head to enter behind her. At the same time, he saw her reach for the door handle on the opposite side.

With lightning-quick reflexes—the same reflexes that had allowed him to slam the desk drawer on Petre's hand the night before—he threw himself forward and grabbed her wrist. "I told you I would not let you go."

Easing onto the seat beside her, he reached out, forcing her to lean with him away from escape, to slam shut the coach door that the two of them had entered through. The carriage lurched forward. Ramiel let go of her wrist. Her body beside him remained stiff and inflexible.

"Where are you taking me?"

To hell.

"Where it all started."

"You know where my husband and my father became lovers?" she asked bitterly.

He did not answer her right away. Instead, he studied the top of her bonnet. "This is the carriage in which I suckled your breasts until you orgasmed. I am the man who buried myself so deeply inside your body last night that you screamed. Then you took me into your mouth and made me cry out. Yet you still do not trust me."

"You allowed him to abuse my son." Her fear and shock metamorphosed into anger. She jerked her head toward him. *"Why did you not tell me?"*

He did not look away from the accusation in her gaze. "Would you have believed me?"

Yes. No. Ramiel could read the conflict in her eyes. Conflict . . . and suspicion.

"How is it, Lord Safyre, that you happened to be at Edward's house at that precise moment?"

"Muhamed woke me with the news that you had left the house unescorted. I knew that you left either to return to your husband"—*because I had frightened and disgusted you*—"or you left to confront him." *Because I was afraid to tell you the truth.* "Neither option was acceptable. So I came after you." *And did not catch you in time.*

She turned her head and stared out the window, presenting him with the top of her bonnet.

Muhamed and he had discussed more than Elizabeth's departure while they sat together on the driver's box and sped through the streets of London. She would soon learn about the results of their conversation. But it would not come from him.

He briefly toyed with the idea of telling her, and if not telling her, preparing her in some way.

But there was no way to prepare her for what would come.

The only thing he could offer her was the reaffirmation of their bonding. And hope that, in the end, it would be enough. As it was for him.

"Calling me by my title will not erase what happened last night, *taalibba*," he said softly. "Nor will it lessen the pain of what you have seen. I took you like the beasts in the fields and I would do so again. Do not confuse *el kebachi* with your father's and husband's performance. Animals do not engage in what you witnessed today."

She did not respond. As he had known she would not. *But he wanted her to.* He wanted her to turn to him and tell him that she would not send him away when the next hour was over.

Ramiel watched her watch the passing carriages and buildings. Surely she recognized key landmarks. Surely she realized that the truth had barely been scratched.

But perhaps not. He would spare her this too, but he knew she would not be safe until she experienced the final betrayal.

When the coach stopped, Elizabeth stared at him in surprise. "Why are we stopping here?"

Opening the door, he climbed out of the carriage and held his hand out for her.

She pressed her back into the leather cushion. "There is no need to tell my mother."

Ramiel ached for her ignorance. "You do not have to tell her. She has something to tell you."

"How do you know? My mother would not speak to the likes of you."

Dark red splotched her white cheeks. Elizabeth's politeness went deeper than superficial etiquette. She derived no pleasure in being rude.

"Come, Elizabeth." He lowered his eyelashes, ruthlessly playing on her softness. "Or are you ashamed of your Bastard Sheikh?"

She reluctantly scooted across the seat and allowed him to help her down. "You are not mine."

But he was. He had felt her womb contract against the palm of his hand and had known that she accepted him fully, bastard, Arab, animal, man.

Elizabeth stubbornly tilted her chin. She still retained enough innocence to defy him. "There is no need to accompany me."

"There is every need to accompany you."

"I want to be alone with my mother," she insisted coldly.

But Ramiel was already striding toward the Tudor mansion. The fan window over the double doors was like a great unwinking eye. Twin white marble pillars guarded the entrance.

He tried to imagine Elizabeth growing up there and could not. A child should have been sucked up into the coldness and the corruption, but she had not been. It defied imagination.

An aged, stooped man who should have been retired long before opened the door. He squinted up at Ramiel with milky eyes. "Good morning, sir."

"We are here to see Mrs. Walters."

"If you will be so kind as to give me your card, sir, I will see if she is—"

"It is all right, Wilson." Elizabeth stepped up beside Ramiel. "Is Mother home?"

The butler bowed. "Good morning, Miss Elizabeth. It is so good to see you up and about. Mrs. Walters did not tell me you had recovered from your ordeal. She is resting."

Elizabeth's lips tightened at the butler's reference to the propaganda that had been fed not only to the papers but also to the servants. "Thank you, Wilson. You may tell Mother I will await her in the drawing room."

"Very good, miss."

Ramiel silently stepped aside for Elizabeth to enter first; he followed close behind her. The foyer was a small, square room; a door identical to the front door complete with a fan window and twin white marble columns opened up to a hallway papered with rose-patterned silk. The drawing room Elizabeth led him to was dark despite the sunshine outside. All the tables were dressed to conceal their legs. Every space was crowded by family photographs framed in gold or silver. A small coal fire burned in a pillared white marble fireplace. On the mantel a gilded marble clock ticked away the seconds.

Clutching her reticule, Elizabeth sat on a horsehair-stuffed sofa. Ramiel restlessly roamed the parlor.

"Please do not tell her about . . ." He could feel her gaze following his paces. "There is no need. It would only hurt her."

Please.

How different the word sounded when a woman balanced on the edge of orgasm.

Ramiel walked toward the fireplace, behind the sofa where she sat, away from her eyes that stared at him as if he were a stranger. He picked up a silver-framed photograph of her sons, a recent one, he would guess. Phillip, the pirate, smiled into the camera; Richard, the engineer, studied it.

The doors to the sitting room abruptly swung open. Rebecca Walters was a beautiful, aging doll with her chestnut-brown hair only mildly streaked with silver and the faintest of lines fanning out from glittering emerald-green eyes. There was nothing of her in Elizabeth. Ramiel was devoutly glad.

At sight of Ramiel, Rebecca froze on the threshold. For one fleeting moment it was all there in her face. Shock, fear, icy frigid rage. *The game was over.* And she knew it.

She quickly recovered. "What is this man doing in my house? If you have no regard for your husband's reputation, Elizabeth, pray consider your father's."

Ramiel waited. The French clock did not. Time was running out.

Elizabeth was an intelligent woman. Her eyes were open now. It would not take her long to figure out the truth. He had helped her, a little, by telling her that she did not have to tell her mother about Petre and Walters.

"How long have you known, Mother?" Elizabeth's question was as dull as the rumble of the carriage driving past the Tudor home.

"I have no idea what you are talking about." Rebecca returned accusation with scorn. "I will not have you defile my

home by bringing this bastard into it. When you come to your
senses, you may visit; otherwise—''

''I wondered why you never mentioned the rumors about
Edward having a mistress. Now I know why. Because you
knew . . . that my father and my husband are lovers. Your
husband and your son-in-law. I saw them together today. Father
likes dressing in women's clothing. *How long have you known,
Mother?*''

Rebecca stared at her daughter as if she were an impertinent
dog that had nipped the hand that fed it. There was no remorse
in the woman's icy green eyes. No remnants of maternal
affection for the daughter she had borne.

''I have always known, Elizabeth. I knew about Edward
before Andrew brought him home to become your husband. It
is a trial that the women of this family must bear. My father
and my husband were lovers. My mother endured. I endured.
Why should you not endure?''

''You.'' Elizabeth's back stiffened with shock. Ramiel's fingers tightened around the silver frame. *He had not wanted her
to know.* And she would not, if only she had trusted him.
''Emma said you wanted to awaken me Thursday morning. It
was you who whispered my name. *You* blew out the lamp.''

Rebecca's unrepentant silence confirmed the question that
was no question.

''Why?'' Elizabeth's agonized whisper ricocheted down
Ramiel's spine.

''You have auburn hair.''

Ramiel stilled. That was not the answer he had expected.

Another factor he had not considered. Rebecca Walters was
insane.

And now Elizabeth would have that, too, to bear.

He walked around the couch, positioned himself to protect
her if need be.

Elizabeth visibly struggled to understand her mother's ratio-
nality, her face stark white underneath the brim of her black
bonnet. ''You would kill me because I have auburn hair?''

Rebecca's green eyes glittered. ''I would kill you for the

sins of your father, that they not be passed on through his bloodline," she said frigidly. "I would kill you because I have faithfully loved Andrew, whereas you would ruin his career and my good name," she added bitterly. "I would kill you because you would not endure what I and my mother endured. By seeking a divorce, you belittle the suffering of all Christian wives and mothers," she concluded venomously.

Rebecca's rigid posture did not invite pity. Nor would Ramiel grant it to her.

He held out the framed photograph. "Did you try to poison your grandsons . . . because of the sins of their grandfather . . . or because they would not endure either?"

Elizabeth sprang up from the sofa in a flurry of black wool. "Edward did that. This has gone far enough. It is time to leave."

Elizabeth was running, but it was too late to run.

Turquoise eyes locked with emerald-green eyes. "It was not Edward who tried to kill your sons, Elizabeth; it was your mother. She accompanied him that day. Heavily veiled. Perhaps she hoped Edward would be content to take the blame."

"No. Mother would not know of a poison that . . ." *Turned flesh into liquid desire.* "She would not know of . . ." *A need that killed.*

"Spanish fly, Elizabeth. It has a name. A name that you are familiar with, are you not, Mrs. Walters?"

Rebecca let her silence speak for itself.

Elizabeth stared at her mother in growing horror. *"Do you know how Spanish fly kills?"*

"Yes." Rebecca transferred her glittering green gaze to Elizabeth. A cold smile touched her lips. "Andrew took too much when he tried to get me pregnant with another child. He almost died. That is why I did not have any more children." The smile abruptly faded. "Whereas you, you had two sons. You should have been content. I had intended to give the drug to you in a cup of tea, but you hid in the Bastard Sheikh's bed. You always spoiled the boys; I knew that the basket in the foyer was intended for them."

"Did you never love me, Mother?" Ramiel winced at the raw pain of Elizabeth's plea. "Did you never love your grandsons?"

"No, I never loved you, Elizabeth. I always knew that whatever boy Andrew loved would one day be your husband and I would have to accept him in my home. That is the way of the Uranian fellowship. As for loving my grandsons . . . Phillip has auburn hair. And Richard refused to follow in my father's footsteps. Would you care for tea?"

Ramiel felt the impact of Rebecca's admission all through his body. Elizabeth's rage, that a woman would knowingly support the abuse of her grandchildren. Her pain, at all the years of lies.

Lies which Ramiel had perpetrated.

He had told her that the Uranians were a fellowship of minor poets. He had not told her that the so-called poets were a group of educated men who in the Greek fashion took boys underneath their protection for the purpose of guiding their lives, advancing their careers, and sodomizing their bodies.

"No, Mother, I do not want tea."

Elizabeth allowed Ramiel to take her arm. Rebecca stepped aside so that they could exit. She took the photograph of her grandchildren from his hand. Lowering her head, she ran her fingers over the glass front of the silver frame as if gathering strength from the photograph inside. "My father, being a literate man, allowed me to study classical Greek. Arabian philosophies, I believe, are also based on Greek traditions."

Ramiel stiffened.

Rebecca raised her head. Malevolence shone in the depths of her emerald-green eyes. She would do anything to destroy her daughter's chance of happiness. And she was about to do just that. *And there was nothing that Ramiel could do to stop it.*

"You are disgusted by what you have discovered today, Elizabeth. But pederasty is an ancient tradition. This bastard you rut with has lived in Arabia, where such things are looked upon differently than we do in England. Perhaps you should ask him about his preferences before you judge your father."

Ramiel had never hit a woman. It took all his strength now not to strike the smug righteousness off Rebecca's face.

He gripped Elizabeth's arm and forced her out of the drawing room, out of the house that had never been a home. Grimly, he lifted her inside the carriage and sat opposite her.

"Have you been with a man?"

Her question was so predictable that it brought tears to his eyes.

He had wanted more from her.

He had wanted her trust.

He had wanted her to accept him as he accepted her.

He had wanted her to accept what he had been unable to accept these past nine years.

"Yes."

Ramiel closed his eyes on a wave of remembered pain. He tried to cling to that. The pain was good; the pain was natural. But the memory of pleasure seeped through the crack of time as it always did. Along with self-doubt.

He had been asleep. *Hadn't he?*

He had not known who fondled him. *Had he?*

All he knew for certain is that he woke on a surge of pleasure that erupted into blinding, stabbing pain. Jamel rode Ramiel like he was a woman while eunuchs held him down for his brother's enjoyment. Afterward, Jamel had wiped himself onto Ramiel and jeered, "Not such a man now, are you, *brother*?"

When Ramiel had been thirteen, Jamel had taught him how to fight with a knife. Jamel had not lived long enough to brag about Ramiel's "deflowerment."

There was an Arabic word for what had been done to him, the rape of a man who has been rendered helpless by sleep or by drugs. Ramiel had not been able to tell his father that he had killed his heir because of *dabid*.

Elizabeth's voice snapped him back to the present.

". . . Then you are no better than my husband or my father."

Ramiel had thought he was, buried deep inside her body. Now he did not.

Ela'na. He would not be blackmailed by a woman into having sex. Nor would he be reduced to tears by one. He had control of that, at least.

"Will you come home with me?" The question was dragged from the very dregs of his soul—if he still possessed one. It was the closest he had ever come to begging anyone for anything.

He needed her. He needed her to make him whole.

"No."

Expectation did not cushion the pain of rejection.

"I will take you to the countess."

Elizabeth looked like a statue. No, she looked like her mother. A woman who had lost all vestiges of innocence and joy.

"Very well."

Lifting up, Ramiel held open the trapdoor in the roof of the carriage and shouted for Muhamed to drive to the countess's house.

The remainder of the journey passed in stony silence. When the carriage pulled up in front of the countess's white brick mansion, Elizabeth wrenched open the door on her side of the coach.

Rebecca Walters had succeeded in her purpose. Elizabeth would not even accept his touch in the simple courtesy of helping her out of the carriage.

Elizabeth stuck one foot out, turned her head, and met Ramiel's gaze with flat, lifeless eyes. "I wish I had never heard of you."

Awkwardly jumping down, she slammed the carriage door shut behind her. The coach immediately jerked into motion.

Ramiel leaned forward and ran his hand over the place where she had sat. The leather was still warm. As he was not.

Elizabeth was gone, but he could yet do one more thing for her. He could help her son accept as a boy what Ramiel had not been able to accept as a man.

Chapter Twenty-five

Any moment now the dean would return to take Richard and Phillip away from Elizabeth and *she could not let go of her babies.* Harrow. Eton. They were different words for duplicate institutions that held innocent boys hostage to the teachings of corrupt men.

She gripped the leather-covered arms of the lolling chair and stared at the dark paneling behind the large glass-topped desk that the dean had vacated. Richard and Phillip stood on either side and slightly behind her, the first patiently waiting, the second restlessly fidgeting.

"We do not have to do this." Elizabeth's voice echoed in the cavernous gloom. "I will hire a tutor. Richard, you can still take your exams in time to enter Oxford this fall. Phillip, I will buy you a little dinghy. We can float it in the park every day after studies."

Warm fingers enveloped Elizabeth's hand. They were man-sized but baby-soft still. Her little boy was irrevocably gone and she could not, *would not,* expose him to any more danger.

She blinked, stared into solemn brown eyes. Richard knelt

in front of her chair. His face was no longer gaunt and his black hair was glossy.

He reached up and wiped her cheek with his thumb. It slid wetly across her skin. "It's all right, Mother."

Elizabeth's voice was thick. "How can it be?"

How could anything ever be all right again?

Suddenly, there were two pairs of brown eyes staring into hers. "We're men now, Mum," Phillip declared with childish wisdom. His auburn hair glowed in the subdued light. "And men don't belong at home with their mums. Though the countess does have a banging fine house," he added wistfully.

Her sons, just as Elizabeth had prepared to leave for Eton the morning following Rebecca Walters's confession, had mysteriously arrived on the countess's doorstep. Lord Safyre had brought them down, they had merely said, because their mother needed them.

Elizabeth had cried the tears she had been unable to cry and endured the novel experience of having her two sons comfort her. Phillip had taken to the countess like fire to kindling. While she introduced Elizabeth's youngest son to the Turkish bath, Elizabeth had talked to Richard—about his father, about the Uranian fellowship, about her bitter regret that she had failed to protect him.

That had been two weeks earlier and now here she was, acting like a child again instead of a responsible parent. She sniffed, released the steadying anchor of the leather chair arms, and wiped her cheeks.

Richard produced a large white handkerchief and held it to her face. "You need to blow, Mother."

A choked laugh escaped the tightness of her throat. She took the handkerchief. "I can blow very well on my own, thank you.

"Don't worry, Mum. I didn't want a dinghy anyway." Phillip rested sharp elbows on her left knee. "I've decided I don't want to be a pirate. The countess gave us this jolly book called *The Arabian Nights*. I want to be a *jinni*. That way I can live in a magic bottle and make people's wishes come true. They usually wish bad things so that will be fun."

"Phillip, you are incorrigible." Elizabeth could not hold back a watery snort of laughter. "I don't suppose, you being a man now, that you would like a box of chocolates."

Phillip dove for her reticule. "Would I!"

"I wouldn't object to a box of toffees if you have one." Richard's voice cracked a little—not quite a man yet, no matter the circumstances.

"Excuse me, Mrs. Petre. If you would like a few more minutes . . ."

Phillip and Richard jumped up, both equally horrified to be caught in such an undignified position. "Men" did not kneel at their mother's feet. Phillip whipped the box of chocolates behind his back.

Elizabeth took a deep breath and squared her shoulders. *It was time to let go.*

"No, thank you, Dean Simmeyson." She stood up. "I must catch the train."

"Have a safe journey, Mrs. Petre." The dean, more bald than gray, bowed courteously. He did not mind associating with a woman, unlike Dean Whitaker at Eton. "Master Richard. Master Phillip. If you will grab your luggage, Masters Brandon and Lawrence will take you upstairs. You will have time to tour the premises before the noonday meal is served."

The two boys turned like young soldiers marching off to barracks. One day soon Richard's voice would no longer crack in that awkward stage between child and adult. Phillip, too, would grow up and would not need her to run interference for him.

But that day had not come yet.

"One moment, please," Elizabeth crisply ordered. "Your portmanteau is gaping open, Richard." Grabbing the box of toffees from her reticule, she leaned down and crammed it into his luggage.

When she straightened, Richard caught her up in a tight hug and buried his face into her neck. "It really is all right, Mother.

I talked to someone and he made me understand about . . . things. Please don't cry anymore. It's over. Phillip and I are glad you are divorcing Father. If you aren't happy, I will worry about you crying when I'm studying for exams and I shall never get into Oxford.''

''Well.'' Elizabeth held back more tears, concentrating instead on the familiar smell of Richard's hair and skin and the warm, moist gust of his breath. ''We cannot have that, can we?''

''No, we cannot.'' Richard rubbed his face against her neck, as he had when he wanted to wipe away tears; it had also made a handy handkerchief when he didn't want to blow. ''I love you, Mum. Please do not blame yourself for what happened. I don't.''

And then he was gone even though she clung to him and an innocence that no longer existed.

The train ride afforded her flashing glimpses of a borough of Greater London instead of southeast Buckinghamshire. The rhythmical click of the wheels and the swaying of the carriage lulled her exhausted body into reluctant relaxation. Without warning, the man whom she had desperately strove to forget these past two weeks exploded into her unguarded thoughts.

This is the carriage in which I suckled your breasts until you orgasmed. I am the man who buried myself so deeply inside your body . . . that you screamed. Then you took me into your mouth and made me cry out. Yet you still do not trust me.

Why didn't you tell me?

Would you have believed me?

Perhaps she would have believed him, she thought, eyes squeezing shut to block out the memories. *If he had given her the opportunity.*

He could have prevented her pain.

He could have told her and she would not have suffered the horror of witnessing her husband and her father in an intimate embrace.

He could have told her and there would have been no need

for her mother to try to kill her because there would have been no secrets to hide behind.

Once started, the memories would not stop.

This bastard you rut with has lived in Arabia, where such things are looked upon differently than we do in England. Perhaps you should ask his preferences before you judge your father.

Why did you leave Arabia, Lord Safyre?

Because I was a coward, Mrs. Petre.

Then you are no better than my husband or my father.

I am a man. . . . Whether I am called a bastard by an Englishman or an infidel by an Arab, I am still a man.

Why could Ramiel not have lied, like her father had lied, like her husband and her mother had lied? *She had not wanted the truth.*

No one had ever touched her. No one but Ramiel.

But you would have taken him inside you last Saturday. You used the things that I had taught you that aroused me to seduce another man.

No.

But she would have.

Why didn't you come home with me last night? Why did you risk death rather than come to me?

Her sons . . .

He had brought her sons home to her even though she had cited them as a reason not to commit herself to a Bastard Sheikh.

Whom do you have, Lord Safyre?

No one. That is why I know that sometime soon the pain will become too great for you to bear alone.

Elizabeth welcomed the noise and the smell of the train station. Soot and mist rained down on her bonnet when she hailed a cab, and she welcomed that too. She welcomed anything that turned her thoughts away from what was and what could have been but now would never be.

A carriage waited outside the countess's white brick house. Elizabeth froze with terror at sight of it.

Her husband could still commit her. Her mother could still kill her.

As long as we are together, you will be safe.

But she did not have Ramiel to turn to anymore. It was time that she learned how to take care of herself.

She resolutely stepped out of the hack and paid her fare. At the same time, a woman dressed in stark black stepped out of the waiting carriage.

Elizabeth could not control her fear: She darted for the house.

"Mrs. Petre! Mrs. Petre, please wait!"

The sound of Emma's voice did not reassure her. Perhaps Rebecca Walters had sent the maid to do her killing for her.

Elizabeth grabbed the brass door knocker.

"Mrs. Petre!" Harried steps flew up the stoop behind Elizabeth. "It wasn't me! I never told anyone about your meetings. It wasn't me, Mrs. Petre! We wouldn't have done that to you!"

More lies. Obviously *someone* had done that to her.

"It was Tommie, ma'am." The heat of the maid's body seeped into Elizabeth's back. "Mrs. Walters asked me that Tuesday morning when you . . . you slept in . . . if you often took laudanum." *Elizabeth had lied about taking the laudanum, as Emma had known.* "I told her no, you were merely having trouble sleeping of late, that Monday morning you had taken an early morning walk because you could not rest. Mrs. Walters told Mr. Petre and he had Tommie follow you. I did not mean you harm, ma'am. I did not know. . . ."

Tommie. The groom. He had supposedly gone home sick the night of the fog. Elizabeth remembered the custodian. The watching eyes. *The fear.*

She closed her eyes against the distorted white face staring at her in the brass plate. Gloved fingers suddenly numb, she let go of the knocker and turned to confront the round-faced maid. Only her face was no longer plump. It was haggard— as Richard's had been haggard two weeks before.

They were the same height, Elizabeth noted dispassionately. In the sixteen years they had been together, she had not even noticed that small reality.

"I have been coming here every day for over a week now. To explain," the abigail said doggedly, her breath a plume of gray vapor in the early March air. Mist beaded on her black bonnet. "But you wouldn't see me."

The countess's butler had announced merely that a woman requested to see Mrs. Petre. He had never mentioned a name. Elizabeth had thought it was her mother. She was not certain she would have wanted to see Emma any more than she wanted to see Rebecca Walters.

But yet . . .

If she had not gone to question the maid, she would not have discovered that her father and husband were lovers. And her sons would still be in danger.

Elizabeth tilted her chin. "You knew my mother blew out the gas lamp."

"I suspected it, ma'am."

"Then why did you not tell me?"

"Mrs. Walters hired me."

"I see," Elizabeth said. So much for Emma's claims about not tattling on her.

"Begging your pardon, ma'am, but I don't think you do. Mr. Beadles, myself, the cook, the housekeeper, the coachman—Mrs. Walters hired us outside a bridewell. Mr. Will, he drove Mr. Petre and he . . . saw . . . and heard . . . certain things. But if we had said anything, we would have been turned out without a character. These are bad times. Servants without a reference and with a criminal record would not have gained employment. And even if we had said anything, who would have believed us? But you, ma'am . . . We never intended that harm befall you. We quit our posts. It don't matter much to me—I have Johnny now, but the others—they don't deserve to suffer. Please, ma'am. Please give them references."

Bridewells were local houses of correction for persons convicted of minor crimes. In the outside world, however, servants who were convicted of minor crimes had no better chance of employment than those convicted of serious crimes. Rebecca Walters had planned very carefully to keep the sins of her husband and son-in-law from the voting populace. No wonder she had been so disturbed when Elizabeth upset her plans.

She did not want to feel any more pain. But it was there, waiting, like night waited for the day to end.

"You want references," Elizabeth said carefully, neutrally, "yet you all knew that Tommie was going to hurt me."

"No, ma'am. It was Mr. Petre who had Tommie follow you. It was Mrs. Walters who wanted him to frighten you. So you would stay at home."

And endure . . . what her mother and her grandmother had endured.

What crimes had Emma and the other servants committed that they would be put into a correctional institution?

Did it matter?

Elizabeth did not know who was at fault anymore. Herself, for refusing to see what should have been obvious. Her servants, for being ex-criminals afraid of losing their employment. The Bastard Sheikh, for not being what she had wanted him to be.

No one was what they seemed.

"Very well. Have them visit here on the morrow. I will give them references. You, too, if you wish."

Emma curtsied. "Thank you, ma'am."

Elizabeth suddenly felt as if a great burden had been lifted off her shoulders. The servants had not spied on her; at least, not the ones whom she had been on more intimate terms with. They had even, in the abigail's case, supported her lies.

"Emma," she said impulsively.

"Mrs. Petre?"

"I am glad that you found someone to care for."

Emma lowered her head. "Johnny . . . he isn't what you thought he was."

"No." Johnny had certainly not been a footman.

"He was hired to spy on Mr. Petre."

The sooty mist metamorphosed into full rain. Icy water stung Elizabeth's face. "By Lord Safyre," she said flatly.

Emma lifted her head, anxiously peered into Elizabeth's face. "He busted up Mr. Petre's hand, ma'am." Unbidden, an image of Edward's bandaged hand resting above a nest of golden blond pubic hair flashed through Elizabeth's mind. "When I told him who I thought had blown out your lamp . . . Well, he cares for you. You were a good mistress. You deserve happiness." Putting her hands up to shield her bonnet, Emma darted down the stoop. A masculine arm swung the carriage door wide for the maid to enter.

You were a good abigail, Elizabeth thought. And a brave woman to choose love with a stranger.

What does it take to make you feel?

I feel, taalibba.

Ramiel had hired a man to spy on her husband—a man who had ultimately saved her life. He had provided the same safety measures for her sons at Eton.

So many secrets.

I know you hurt, Elizabeth. Let me make it better for you. Let me love you.

Elizabeth turned her back on the past. The butler opened the rain-slashed door even before the muffled thud of brass impacting brass was swallowed by the steady downfall of dirty water.

She handed him her dripping cloak and bonnet, black as had been those of Emma. "Where is the countess, Anthony?"

"She is in the sitting room." The butler took Elizabeth's gloves. "You should have taken an umbrella, Mrs. Petre."

Elizabeth should have done many things. An umbrella was low on her list of priorities.

The countess sat near an Adam fireplace at an escritoire, writing. Her face, bathed by crackling heat, lit up when Elizabeth walked into the sitting room that was more Western than Eastern, more feminine than masculine.

The older woman had not once asked Elizabeth why she had left her husband. Or why Elizabeth did not go to her own mother.

"Would you help me seduce your son, Countess?"

A finely arched eyebrow rose. "Why?"

Because he had accepted Elizabeth for the woman she was instead of the girl that she had been.

"Because he does not deserve to be alone."

And neither did she.

Elizabeth blinked at the radiance of the countess's smile. Sometime later she faintly protested, "Are you quite certain that this will please him?"

Body glowing with Joseffa's ministrations, Elizabeth donned a satin-lined black velvet cloak with bell-shaped sleeves. It belonged to the countess and was four inches too long. She was naked underneath it.

Stepping up into the carriage that waited for her in the dreary darkness, she carefully tucked the cloak about her lest the groom see more than what he expected to see. When Lucy the maid allowed Elizabeth entrance into Ramiel's Georgian home and insisted upon taking her cloak, she almost ran back to the countess's carriage. A lady, no matter her intentions, did not visit a man dressed as she was. Especially a man whom she had rejected so summarily and who could very well have found a less cowardly lady to comfort him. But the groom had raced back to the coach when Lucy opened the door; seconds later a creak of leather and wood was accompanied by a "Get up, you nags!" and Elizabeth had nowhere to go but forward.

"That is quite all right, Lucy." Elizabeth held the cloak against her body with both hands. "Is Lord Safyre at home?"

"He's in the library, ma'am."

"Then I will announce myself."

"Very well, ma'am."

It was now or never.

"Lucy."

"Ma'am?"

"Please leave two bottles of champagne outside the library door."

Lucy fought to keep a knowing smile from spreading over her face, but failed. "Very good, ma'am."

Ramiel's servants were as knowledgeable as had been the Petre servants. Velvet cloak trailing behind her, Elizabeth walked down the hallway that was paneled with mahogany wood inlaid with mother-of-pearl. And knew that she had come home.

She knocked softly, heart pounding. With desire. With fear. Consciously, she may have refused to think about Ramiel, but her dreams had been full of him and the ecstasy they had shared. Her body had always accepted him. If only—

A muffled voice bade her enter.

Taking her future into her hands, she opened the door. Before he could order her out, she closed it behind her and leaned against the solid wood.

Ramiel sat at his desk; a book lay open before him. A fire flickered and flamed in the mahogany fireplace while rain steadily pattered against the bay windows. Light from the gas lamp on his desk touched his blond hair with gold, his dark face with shadow.

Turquoise eyes flicked over her cloak, her damp hair that was loosely caught up in a bun. There was no welcome in his gaze. Or desire.

"What are you doing here?"

The old doubts reared their ugly presence. *What was she doing here?* To appease her passions, because once having experienced sexual satisfaction, she could not forgo it, like an addict craving opium?

Stiffening her spine, she pushed away from the support of the door. "I came here to give you pleasure."

An ugly smile curled his lips. "Should you not first ask what my preferences are?"

Tears stung her eyes. She wanted to weep for the pain she had caused him, but now was not the time for tears.

"I cannot change the past."

He tilted his head back, as if the sight of her were more than he could bear. "I cannot change the past either."

But he wanted to.

A pulse throbbed at the base of his throat, or perhaps it was the flicker of gaslight.

"You never told me what *bahebbik* means."

Dark shadows slashed his cheeks—his eyelashes. "You didn't stay."

No. He had asked her to come home with him even after she had thrown unforgivably cruel accustations at him, and she had rejected him. Like Lord Inchcape. Like Rebecca Walters.

It was not supposed to be like this.

Hands trembling, she released the buttons on the cloak. Warm silk slithered down her back, her shoulders, her arms, leaving a trail of goose bumps in its wake. Velvet puddled around her feet. And still he would not look at her.

A spark of anger warmed her skin. "I cannot seduce you if you will not look at me."

Ramiel lowered his head and opened his eyes.

Elizabeth remembered the marble clock ticking on the mantel in Rebecca's house. It had been far less frightening facing her mother than it was now, standing naked in front of this man who had once trembled with passion for her but who now stared at her as if she were a stranger. Or a horse to be sold at auction.

Cold, relentless eyes weighed the heaviness of her breasts, judged the fullness of her hips, fastened onto her pubes, as hairless as the day she had been born—the manner, the countess had assured her, in which all Arab women greeted their men.

His turquoise eyes snapped upward. "What if I do not want to be seduced?"

Elizabeth faced the very real possibility of his rejection and knew that she would not turn back. She had the knowledge and she had the courage—she hoped.

Reaching up—his gaze flickered to her armpits, hairless as was her pubes—she released the pins that loosely secured her bun, dropped them to the Oriental carpet. Warm, heavy hair cascaded down her back, familiar as her role of seductress was not. "Then I will make you want to be seduced," she promised with a confidence she was far from feeling.

Acutely conscious of the sway of her breasts and the friction of her thighs pressing in on lips that were not meant to be so boldly exposed on an Englishwoman, she kicked off her slippers and closed the distance between them. Stepping around the massive mahogany desk, she knelt on the floor, hid a grimace. The carpet was cold and rough on bare knees.

Ramiel swiveled the chair around, legs slightly spread, eyes veiled. His hands rested on the arms of the chair, fingers curved to fit the wood instead of her body. One side of his face was in shadow, the other cast in flickering gaslight. "Are you not curious, Elizabeth? Do you not want to know the difference between a man and a woman?"

He was trying to drive her away—as she had driven him away two weeks before.

"Would you tell me if I did?"

Darkness glimmered in his turquoise eyes. "The Uranian fellowship is no longer a part of the Eton curriculum."

"You said you would keep the secret."

That ugly smile curled his lips again. "And so I did. Richard is much like you. He does not run from the truth. He told the dean of his experience."

"But he told you first." Things he had not told Elizabeth, any more than he had told her about informing the dean of the fellowship. Ramiel, she realized, was the "someone" who had made it "all right" for her son.

His lips tightened in harsh betrayal. "He was not supposed to tell you."

"He did not. You did."

"I don't want your gratitude," he grated.

"I know what you want, Ramiel." *He wanted what she wanted.* "And I am going to give it to you."

Ramiel could not hide the bulge in his black trousers. "What do you think I want, Elizabeth?"

What could a woman like her possibly know about the wants of a man like him? is what he really said.

Elizabeth took a deep breath, placed her hands on his thighs. His muscles underneath the broadcloth were rock hard—he was not as removed as he pretended to be. "I think . . . that you want me to unfasten your trousers and take your life into my hands."

The muscles underneath her hands jerked, recollection instantaneous. "The second lesson."

"The second lesson," she agreed. And wrestled with his buttons.

It was not at all a dignified struggle—undressing a man who sat as still as a statue was as difficult as dressing a squirming three-year-old boy—but the rewards . . . Dark blond hair filled the widening vent.

Breath bated, she reached inside his trousers and delicately pulled out the thick stalk of living, pulsing flesh. He was hard and hot and filled both her hands. She did not have to pump his manhood to coax the sensitive crown out from the hood of the foreskin.

Elizabeth studied him from underneath her eyelids. A drop of moisture pearled the tip of the engorged purple head.

"I think you want me to take you into my mouth and lick and suckle you like a nipple." She lifted her eyelids, snared his gaze. "Like you did my clitoris."

The fifth lesson.

Ramiel's intake of breath filled the silence. An ember popped in the fireplace. His manhood, lovingly cupped in her hands, flexed. Lowering her head, she inhaled his scent, musky with a hint of Eastern spices, tasted the essence of him with the tip of her tongue before sucking him deep inside her mouth.

The countess had said if she relaxed her muscles, she could take him more deeply.

It worked.

A low, guttural groan ripped out of his chest, pure, unadulterated music to her ears. This was a woman's power; this was the wonder of sex—*this was Ramiel.*

He arched into the wet heat of her mouth. The huge bulb of him pulsed deep inside her throat, a part of her. A matching pulse leapt to life between her thighs.

Elizabeth took as much of Ramiel as she could, swallowing him again and again, licking him like she would a—did Arabs have lollipops? she wondered. And then she did not wonder about anything, lost in the smell and taste and the silky smooth texture of him. There was no champagne to camouflage his flavor. He was, quite incredibly, the most delicious thing she had ever eaten.

When she could feel trembles rack his body, Elizabeth released him with an audible popping sound and was not at all concerned that it was not dignified. Ramiel's dark face was flushed with sexual arousal, his turquoise eyes bright. He gripped the wooden chair arms as if holding the reins on a runaway horse.

Keeping her eyes on his, she placed a soft kiss on the throbbing crown of his penis.

The skin over his knuckles whitened.

"I think," she whispered, deliberately bathing him with her hot breath, "that you want me to take off your shirt and nibble on your nipples."

The third lesson.

Seducing a man was strangely erotic. Elizabeth forgot that she had stretch marks on her hips or that Edward had said she had udders.

Standing up, she pulled his shirt out of the band of his trousers. Her breasts, heavy and swollen, swayed in his face— and it felt good to be naked and unashamed. She tugged at the slick white silk until he raised his arms, a reluctant participant in his own seduction.

His nipples were hard. As were hers.

She touched herself briefly, a hard nub of flesh, then she touched him, an even harder nub of flesh. His skin burned.

Suddenly, the shirt was wrenched out of her fingers. Ramiel jerked it over his head and tossed it aside. Male challenge and raw need glittered in his turquoise eyes. "Why are you doing this?"

She would not back down. With Edward, yes, but never with this man.

"I thought that was rather obvious. Do you not want me to nibble on your nipples, Ramiel?"

"I want you to tell me what you think you are doing."

"I am seducing my tutor."

"Why?"

She did not flinch away from his gaze. "Because I lied to you when I told you that I regretted coming to you."

"And when you told me I was no different from your husband and your father? Did you lie then?"

Ramiel was nothing at all like Edward.

"Yes."

"I cannot be what you want me to be, Elizabeth."

Kneeling again, Elizabeth rested her hands on his thighs; his heat warmed her fingers. "But you are. And now, if you do not mind, I find that I quite like seducing you."

Leaning forward, she delicately licked the hard bud of his left nipple before taking it between her teeth and gently worrying it. His heart pounded against her lips; his chest hair tickled her chin. Laving him with her tongue—wanting to please him, wanting to please herself, wanting to end the pain and the mistrust—she suckled him as if she could take nourishment from him.

She could. When she touched him, he became the focus of her entire world. *And it was all right.*

Heat cupped her head—his hands. Liquid warmth flowed through her body. His thighs that she blindly clenched opened; she leaned into the welcoming warmth of his veed legs until the moist crown of his manhood pulsed against her stomach and she drew and drew upon his nipple, drew until it was harder than a pebble and he tangled his hands into her hair and yanked her head back. He stared at her lips, swollen from suckling him. At her breasts, swollen from wanting him.

"What else do you think I want?" His voice was a dark rasp.

"I think you want me to sit on your lap, *dok el arz,* so that I can take you inside my body so deeply that our pubic hair meshes. So deeply that you cannot withdraw, not even an inch. I think you want me to grip you so tightly that your testicles ache for release, so tightly that the only thing you can thrust inside me is your tongue while you grind your pelvis against mine."

Ramiel's nostrils flared. "You don't have any pubic hair."

Elizabeth was abruptly, agonizingly aware of the fact that he wore trousers and she was naked—of both clothing and body hair. She had been so intent upon showing him that she could please him as well as a woman from the East that she had forgotten the one simple precept: In the fourth lesson he had specifically told her that he wanted a woman's pubic hair to blend with his.

She stiffened. What had ever made her think that a woman like her, a woman who was not in her prime, could seduce a man like Ramiel? "I'm sorry."

"Will you marry me?"

She had forgotten . . . so many things. "Muhamed would not approve."

Ramiel's fingers tightened in her hair, not causing pain exactly, but not exactly gentle. "Muhamed is gone."

She had not meant to come between the two men.

"Will he return?"

"Perhaps. He went back to Cornwall. To see his family." Loneliness reverberated inside Ramiel's voice; he had lost the last living remnant of a country that had exiled him. "Perhaps he will find some peace there. Will you marry me?"

Marry . . . the Bastard Sheikh.

"I would be honored."

A sharp creak of protesting wood cracked the air and suddenly Elizabeth was straddling his knees and the wet heat of her penetrated the broadcloth of his trousers. She grabbed for his shoulders.

"Lift your legs and put them over the arms of the chair."

Elizabeth squeezed her eyelids shut to block out the blazing light in his beautiful turquoise eyes. "It is not going to work, Ramiel."

Coldness. Elizabeth had never known that heat could turn into ice between one heartbeat and the next. Even though his arms continued to hold her securely, she could feel his withdrawal. "Why not, Elizabeth?"

She forced her eyes open and confronted the truth. "The

wooden arms of a chair simply are not designed to accommodate a woman's legs."

Laughter glinted in his eyes. Without warning, he grasped her right thigh and lifted it for her, hooking it over the wooden arm of the chair. She dug her fingernails into his shoulder.

A woman was not made to sit in this position. It was uncomfortable; the wood dug into her soft flesh. It forced open the lips of her denuded vulva so that no flaw was concealed. "Ramiel—"

His turquoise eyes waited, all laughter gone.

Elizabeth took a deep breath. And awkwardly lifted her left leg over the wooden obstruction. She was totally open, totally exposed for his perusal. The length of his manhood lay between them, purple tipped. It pointed toward her glistening pink vulva.

She dragged her gaze away from the evocative sight of a man and a woman's passion—and met his. "I want to make you knock at my door." Her voice shook with the force of her desire. "And when I put you inside me I want you to know that I accept you for who and what you are."

"Do you, Elizabeth?" The gas lamp flared, throwing the right side of his face into sharp relief.

"Yes, I do," she said firmly. "And you will demonstrate that you trust me implicitly by allowing me to put you inside me."

Moisture oozed out of her splayed body. He glanced down; she did not have to look to see what he saw: her flesh, her needs. Darkness suddenly seemed to envelop both sides of his face. "Then make me knock, *taalibba*."

Before she could discern his intent, he grasped her buttocks and lifted her up and inward until her breasts pressed into the scalding hot wall of his chest and his manhood lay directly underneath her. Cold air invaded flesh that was not meant to be invaded; it matched the chill that plied her dangling feet.

Biting her lip, she released his right shoulder and wormed her hand between them. Ramiel audibly gritted his teeth when her fingers fastened around the electrifying heat of him. Burying her face against the prickly haven of his neck, she guided the plum-shaped head of him to her vagina, so wet and vulnerable, his own flesh so hard and unyielding. She nudged and pushed and nudged and pushed until she ached, and she knew that he must ache too, holding her up. His arms were corded with strain; they trembled, or perhaps it was she who trembled, poised on the verge of a new life.

Raising her head, she looked into his turquoise eyes, only inches away from hers, and all resistance vanished from her body. She opened up and swallowed him in hot welcome *and yes,* it was a moment of bonding. Her breath *whooshed* from her lungs.

"Would you go to Arabia with me?"

Her muscles convulsed in protest, in greed. "To live?"

The countess had said that women were worth less than a horse.

"Perhaps."

"But my sons . . ."

"Can join us."

Fear. Uncertainty. His. Hers. *Theirs.*

"Yes. I would go to Arabia with you. Phillip said he wants to become a *jinni.*"

The heat that flared in his eyes almost blinded her. "You will be very sensitive with no hair to cushion you."

She gulped air. "Is that a hindrance?"

His smile was a sexual promise. "Not for me," he whispered. And slowly, inexorably, lowered her onto him, pushing deeper, deeper yet, until his pubic hair nestled her clitoris and a button burrowed into her buttocks.

She had forgotten how deeply a man could occupy a woman. Or how vulnerable was a woman's swollen flesh.

Elizabeth inhaled sharply, button forgotten, fingernails digging into his shoulder, body clenching to forestall further invasion, *but there was more.* He gave her his breath, then took hers when he hooked his arms underneath her outstretched thighs and pushed them higher, wider, grinding the last two inches inside her so that he could find their special place, *and she took him.*

"It was not my preference," he gasped.

She gasped with him when he ground up inside her, caught between pleasure and pain. "What?"

"My half brother. I did not realize how jealous he had always been of my relationship with the sheikh. When I . . . bought something that he wanted . . . he sneaked into my chambers while I slept . . . and he . . . toyed with me. When I woke up, his eunuchs held me down and he raped me. I killed him."

A month ago she would have been shocked. Horrified. Now she felt only compassion at the pain he had endured.

"You did not tell your father."

"No."

But he had told her. *Implicit trust.*

Self-loathing dulled the passion in his turquoise eyes. "In sleep, Elizabeth, the touch of a man is as pleasurable as that of a woman."

"But you felt no pleasure when you woke up."

"No." Events and emotions that she could not even begin to fathom reverberated inside the simple word.

Elizabeth leaned her forehead against his. "I enrolled Richard and Phillip in Harrow today. Just before I left, Richard said, 'I love you, Mum. Please don't blame yourself for what happened. I don't.'

"I love you, Ramiel. Please don't blame yourself for what happened in the past. I don't." Angling her head, she swiped his cheek with her tongue, tasted tears. "Let me make it better for you. Let me love you."

His head swooped down; he captured her breath into his mouth then gave her his when he ground his pelvis against hers, body grinding, tongue thrusting, *dok el arz,* belly to belly, mouth to mouth, her desires, his desires, they were one. He ground and ground into her, *dok,* until they were both slick with sex and sweat and her climax erupted inside her body while words erupted inside her mouth. "I love you."

She forced her head up and her eyes open. "What?"

"*Bahebbik.* I love you."

No. She would not cry. "How does a woman say it . . . in Arabic?"

"Bahebbak."

"Bahebbak, Ramiel." And then, before all reason was again lost in the churning, grinding motions, "Do the Arabs have a word for lollipop?"

AUTHOR'S NOTES

The first English translation of *The Perfumed Garden of the Cheikh Nefzaoui* was published in 1886 in a series of small volumes. They did not give credit to the translator, who is, of course, Sir Richard Burton. Neither did the second edition, which combined the series into a single book that was released later that same year.

It is this second edition that I refer to and, indeed, quote from in *The Lady's Tutor*. I took poetic license in the fact that my book opens up in February of 1886, with my hero presenting the second edition to my heroine as a textbook for learning how to give a man pleasure. In actuality, the second edition came out later that year. Also, in order to avoid confusion, I anglicized the spelling of 'Cheikh' to 'Sheikh.'

Please remember that all Arabic names for genitalia and or sexual intercourse in *The Lady's Tutor* are derived solely from *The Perfumed Garden*. As this Arabic treatise on erotic love is over four hundred years old, certain words or expressions may be obsolete. However, a really nifty Arabic dictionary that I consulted for nonsexual phrases is the *ARABIC Hippocrene Handy Dictionary*.

In England, the Contagious Disease Acts were repealed in 1886 and Mrs. Josephine Butler's zealous campaigning was responsible. As incomprehensible as it is to us a century later, one of her main premises for overriding the acts were that the mandatory (vaginal) examination of prostitutes to determine the presence of sexually transmitted diseases deprived women of their dignity.

There did indeed exist a fellowship of minor poets who called themselves 'Uranians;' they practiced pederasty in the Greek tradition. It is unknown as to whether this group of poets attended Eton.

Any inaccuracies in my portrayal of late Victorian times are, of course, my own. I assure you, I worked very hard to eliminate them.

I love hearing from my readers. You may write me at: P.O. Box 72725, Roselle IL 60172. Please include a SASE if you wish me to reply. Or you may visit my Web site at http://www.tlt.com/authors/rschone.